Not since her much-adored *Hummingbird* has LaVyrle Spencer told a story so warm and uplifting—a story of honesty and humor for anyone who has ever lived and loved . . .

The Gamble

Agatha was the picture of primness and propriety, but her green eyes could blaze with anger—or sparkle with humor . . .

Scott was the picture of lazy charm and happy indifference to what others thought was right and wrong . . .

They were enemies, then friends. Then the sweet innocence of a child opened their eyes and their hearts—and they were reborn in each other's arms by the soft, wondrous gift of love . . .

"LaVyrle Spencer is magic." —*Affaire de Coeur*

continued . . .

The Bestselling Novels of LaVyrle Spencer

THEN CAME HEAVEN
A triumphant story of faith and love . . .

"Touching." —*Chattanooga Times*

SMALL TOWN GIRL
A country music star rediscovers her heart . . .

"Warm and folksy." —*Kirkus Reviews*

THAT CAMDEN SUMMER
A shunned divorcee finds unexpected love . . .

"A modern fairy tale." —*People*

HOME SONG
A secret threatens to tear a family apart . . .

"Tug(s) at readers' heartstrings." —*Publishers Weekly*

FAMILY BLESSINGS
A widow is torn between her family and new love . . .

"A moving tale." —*Publishers Weekly*

NOVEMBER OF THE HEART
True love blooms for two hearts from different worlds . . .

"One of Spencer's best." —*Kirkus Reviews*

BYGONES
A moving story of a family at a crossroads . . .

"A page-turner." —*New York Daily News*

FORGIVING
A beautiful story of family ties renewed . . .

"A lively story!" —*New York Daily News*

BITTER SWEET
The poignant tale of high school sweethearts reunited . . .

"A journey of self-discovery and reawakening." —*Booklist*

THE ENDEARMENT
A woman's love is threatened by past secrets . . .

"A tender, sensual story."
—Lisa Gregory, author of *Before the Dawn*

MORNING GLORY
Two misfit hearts find tenderness . . .

"A superb book." —*New York Daily News*

SPRING FANCY
A bride-to-be falls in love—with another man . . .

"Incredible beauty." —*Affaire de Coeur*

THE HELLION
Sparks fly between a lady and a hell-raiser . . .

"Superb!" —*Chicago Sun-Times*

VOWS
Two willful lovers—one special promise . . .

"Magic!" —*Affaire de Coeur*

THE GAMBLE
Take a chance on love . . .

"Grand!" —*Good Housekeeping*

FORSAKING ALL OTHERS
True love endures—in bad times and good . . .

YEARS
Across the Western plains, only the strongest survived . . .

"Splendid." —*Publishers Weekly*

SEPARATE BEDS
First came the baby, then marriage . . . then love.

"A superb story." —*Los Angeles Times*

TWICE LOVED
A woman's missing husband returns—
after she's remarried . . .

"Emotional." —*Rocky Mountain News*

HUMMINGBIRD
LaVyrle Spencer's stunning first novel . . .

"Will leave you breathless." —*Affaire de Coeur*

LaVyrle Spencer

The Gamble

BERKLEY BOOKS, NEW YORK

A Berkley Book
Published by The Berkley Publishing Group
A division of Penguin Group (USA) Inc.
375 Hudson Street
New York, New York 10014

THE GAMBLE

This is a work of fiction. Names, characters, places, and incidents either are
the product of the author's imagination or are used fictitiously, and any
resemblance to actual persons, living or dead, business establishments, events,
or locales is entirely coincidental.

PRINTING HISTORY
Jove mass-market edition / March 1987
Berkley trade paperback edition / August 2003

ISBN: 0-425-19581-3

PRINTED IN THE UNITED STATES OF AMERICA

10 9 8 7 6 5 4 3 2 1

*With love
to
Marian Spencer,
from whom I learned
so much about love*

My sincere thanks to Mr. and Mrs. Robert Snow of Waverly Plantation West Point, Mississippi, for allowing me to borrow their beautiful antebellum mansion and its ghost in the creation of this book.

—L.S.

CHAPTER
1

1880

Agatha Downing looked out the window of her millinery shop and saw a life-sized oil painting of a naked woman crossing the street. She gasped and clenched her fists. *That man again!* What would he think of next? It wasn't enough that he'd set up business right next door selling spirits and encouraging honest men to squander their hard-earned money at gambling. Now it was pictures of naked women!

Aghast, she pressed a hand to her boned corsets and watched the jovial band of ne'er-do-wells coming her way. Shouting ribald accolades, they jostled their way toward the Gilded Cage Saloon, bearing the framed canvas on their shoulders. The street was wide and muddy; it took them some time to cross. Before they were halfway, all the men on the boardwalk had joined them, hooting, doffing their hats, paying lewd homage to the Rubenesque nude. The closer they got, the tighter Agatha pressed her corsets to herself.

The disgraceful figure stood a good six feet high with arms raised to heaven as if waiting to ascend—full front, voluptuous, and naked as a fresh-hatched jaybird.

Agatha dropped her glance from the disgusting spectacle.

Heaven, indeed! The entire lot of them were bound in the other direction. And, it appeared, they were aiming to take the children down with them!

Two young boys had spotted the revelers and came running down the middle of the muddy street to get a closer look.

Agatha flung her door open and limped onto the boardwalk.

"Perry! Clydell!" she shouted at the ten-year-olds. "Go home at once! Do you hear?"

The pair came up short. They looked up to see Miss Downing pointing a finger toward the end of the street.

"At once, I said, or I'll tell your mothers!"

Perry White turned to his friend Clydell Hottle with a sickly expression on his freckled face. "It's old lady Downing."

"Aw, shoot!"

"My ma buys hats from her."

"Yeah, mine, too," Clydell despaired. They gave a last inquisitive glance at the naked lady on the painting, turned reluctantly, and shuffled back toward home.

Mooney Straub, one of the town's drunks, raised his voice from the mob in the street and called after them, "Wait'll you're a little older, boys!" Coarse laughter followed and Agatha's outrage burned even hotter.

They were nothing but riff-raff. Though it was only ten o'clock in the morning, Mooney Straub could scarcely stand on his feet. And there was Charlie Yaeger, whose wife and six children lived in a hovel fit for pigs; and Cornelia Loretto's young son Dan, who'd been hired on next door as a keno dealer, shaming his poor mother terribly; and the fearsome-looking bartender with thick white hair growing over only the left half of his skull and a livid red scar covering most of his face; and the tall skinny Negro piano player whose eyes never seemed to miss a thing; and George Sowers, who years ago had struck it rich in the Colorado gold fields but had drunk and gambled away his entire fortune. And leading the troop, the one responsible for delivering this plague upon her doorstep: that man they all called Scotty.

Agatha stationed herself on the steps before the saloon and waited as the brigade of Satan's army splashed its way through the spring mud. When they reached the hitching rails, Agatha spread her arms wide.

"Mr. Gandy, I must protest!"

LeMaster Scott Gandy lifted a hand to halt his followers.

"Rein in there, boys. Seems we've got company." He turned slowly and raised his gaze to the woman standing above him like an avenging angel. She was dressed in dull gray. Her Austrian-draped tie-back skirt was cinched tightly, front to back. Her bustle jutted high like the spine of a spitting cat. Her hair was drawn back into so severe a knot it looked as if it gave her a perennial headache. The only spots of color she possessed were the twin blotches of pink on her stiff white cheeks.

Letting a grin lift one corner of his lips, Gandy lazily doffed his low-crowned black Stetson.

"Mornin', Miz Downin'," he drawled in an accent fairly oozing dogwood and magnolia blossoms.

Her fists clenched at her hips. "This is an outrage, Mr. Gandy!"

He continued holding the hat aloft, grinning lopsidedly. "I said, Mornin', Miz Downin'."

A fly buzzed past her nose but she didn't bat an eye. "It is *not* a good morning, sir, and I won't pretend it is."

He settled the flat-crowned Stetson on his coal-black hair, pulled one boot out of the mud, gave it a shake, and settled it on the lowest step. "Well, now," he drawled, reaching into his waistcoat pocket and extracting a cheroot. He squinted at the blue Kansas sky. He squinted at her. "Sun's out. Rain's stopped. Cattle're bound t' be comin' through soon." He bit the end off the cheroot and spit it into the mud. "I'd call that a middlin' good day, ma'am. How 'bout you?"

"You can't mean to place that . . ."—she pointed indignantly at the picture—". . . that sister of Sodom on the walls of your establishment for any and all to see!"

He laughed, the sun glinting off his straight, white teeth. "Sister of Sodom?" He reached inside his close-fitting black sack coat, patted his vest pockets, and came up with a wooden match. "If y'all find it offensive, no need t' worry.

Once I get it inside, y' won't have t' see it again."

"Those innocent children have already seen it. Their poor mothers will be horrified. And what's more, anyone, young or old, can peek beneath those ridiculous swinging doors any time." She shook a finger at his nose. "And you know perfectly well the children will!"

"Shall I post a guard, Miz Downin'?" His drawl was so pronounced, *guard* sounded like *god*. "Would that satisfy y'all?" He struck the match on the hitching post, lit the cheroot, tossed the match over his shoulder, and grinned up at her through the smoke.

The slow, nonchalant drawl aggravated her as badly as his cavalier attitude and the stench of his cigar.

"What would satisfy me is to see you send that sinful painting back where it came from. Or, better yet, use it for firewood."

He glanced over his shoulder and appreciatively scanned the naked image from head to foot. "She's here . . ."—he turned back to Agatha—". . . and she stays."

"But you simply can't hang such a picture!"

"Oh, but I can," he replied coolly, "and I will."

"I cannot allow it."

He smiled rakishly, took a deep drag of the cheroot, and said invitingly, "Then stop me." With the cigar he gestured over his shoulder. "Come on, boys, let's take the li'l lady inside."

A roar rose behind him and his henchmen lunged forward. Gandy took one step up only to find that Miss Downing had taken one step down. His knee came against her stiff gray skirt, sending her bustle higher up in back. His grin remained fixed, but he raised one eyebrow. "If y'all will excuse us, Miz Downin'."

"I'll do nothing of the sort." It took great fortitude for Agatha to hold her ground with his knee-high boot touching her skirt. But she stared him down. "If the respectable businessmen of this town are too timid to speak up against these dens of vice and corruption you and your ilk have brought upon us, the women are not!"

Gandy pressed both palms to his knee and leaned forward till his hat brim nearly touched her nose. He spoke quietly, the drawl more pronounced, but with an unmistakable note of menace. "I wouldn't like t' manhandle a woman in front of the townsfolk, ma'am, but if y'all don't step aside you'll leave me no choice."

Her nostrils narrowed. She drew herself up more erect. "Those who step aside to allow indecencies of this sort are as guilty as if they'd committed them themselves."

Their eyes clashed and held: his piercing black, hers defiant green. Behind Gandy the men waited in ankle-deep mud, their snickers having subsided into expectant silence. Down the street Perry White and Clydell Hottle shaded their eyes with their hands, waiting to see who won. On the opposite side of the street, a saloonkeeper and his bartender stepped to their own swinging doors, observing the confrontation with great amusement on their faces.

Gandy stared into Agatha Downing's determined eyes, realizing his steadiest customers and best friends waited to see if he'd back down to a female. To do so would make him the laughingstock of Proffitt, Kansas. He wasn't raised to be disrespectful to the weaker sex, but she left him no choice.

"As y' wish, ma'am," Gandy drawled, then nonchalantly anchored the cigar between his teeth, clamped his hands around Agatha's arms, whisked her off the step, and planted her eight inches deep in the mud. The men roared with approval. Agatha yelped, flailed her arms, and tried to pull her shoes out of the quagmire. But the mud only sucked her in deeper, and with an ignominious splat, she landed on her bustle in the ooze.

"Attaway, Gandy!"

"Don't take no guff offa no skirts!"

While Agatha glared at Gandy, his henchmen carried the naked lady up the wooden steps through the swinging doors of the Gilded Cage Saloon. When they'd disap-peared, he tipped his hat and offered a dazzling smile. "G'day, Miz Downin'. It's been a pleasure." He made his way up the steps, cleaned his boots on the boot scraper outside the door, then followed the rowdy rabble inside, leaving the half doors swinging behind him.

*   *   *

From the opposite boardwalk the entire confrontation had been observed by a woman dressed in unrelieved black. Drusilla Wilson paused with valise in hand. She had the build and rigidity of a railroad tie, a nose like a scythe blade, and eyes that looked as if they could drill through granite. Her thin mouth was downturned, the upper lip almost obscured by the lower. Her jaw was undershot, reminiscent of a grouper's. Beneath the undecorated brim of a stark black Quaker bonnet, a thin band of hair showed, and an inch of its center part. That hair—black, too, as if nature approved her bid to appear formidable—was drawn flat down over her temples and pinned her ears against her skull. She radiated the kind of sternness that caused people, when introduced to her, to step back instead of forward.

After witnessing the altercation across the street, Miss Wilson turned to a red-bearded man with a waxed handlebar moustache who stood just outside the swinging doors of the Hoof and Horn Saloon. He was clad in a red-and-white-striped shirt with elastic sleeve bands cinched around a pair of enormous arms. Those arms were crossed over a massive chest that bounced each time he chuckled. On his fiery hair sat a black felt bowler. The stub of a dead cigar protruded from the red brush surrounding his mouth.

"That woman's name—what is it, please?" Drusilla Wilson demanded officiously.

"Who? Her?" He nodded toward Agatha and chuckled again.

Drusilla nodded, unamused.

"That's Agatha Downing."

"And where does she live?"

"Right there." He removed the stogie and pointed with its sodden end. "Above her hat shop."

"She owns it?"

"Yup."

Drusilla glanced at the pitiful figure on the far side of the street and murmured, "Perfect." Lifting her valise in one hand, her skirts in the other, she started toward the stepping-stones that crossed the muddy thoroughfare. But she turned back toward the red-bearded man, who still smiled as he watched Agatha trying to extricate herself from the mud.

"And your name, sir?" she demanded.

He gave her his brown-toothed smile, then plugged his tiny mouth with the cigar once more. "Heustis Dyar."

She cocked one eyebrow at the scarlet lettering on the false-fronted building above his head. "And you own the Hoof and Horn?"

"That's right," he announced proudly, slipping his thumbs behind his suspenders, jutting out his chest. "Who wants t' know?"

She gave a smug half nod. "Drusilla Wilson."

"Drus——" He yanked the cigar from his mouth and took one step toward her. "Hey, wait a minute! What're you doin' here?" Scowling, he whirled toward his bartender, whose forearms rested on the tops of the swinging doors. "What's *she* doin' here?"

Tom Reese shrugged. "How should I know what she's doin' here? Startin' trouble, I reckon. Ain't that what she does everyplace she goes?"

Starting trouble was exactly what Drusilla Wilson was doing there, and as she turned toward her "sister" in the mud, she vowed that Heustis Dyar and the owner of the Gilded Cage would be the first to feel its impact.

Agatha was having great difficulty getting up. Her hip again. At the best of times it was unreliable; at the worst, unusable. Mired in the cold, sucking muck, it ached and refused to pull her weight up. She rocked forward but failed to gain her feet. Falling back, her hands buried to their wrists, she wished she were a cursing woman.

A black-gloved hand was extended her way.

"May I help you, Miss Downing?"

Agatha looked up into cold gray eyes that somehow managed to look sympathetic.

"Drusilla Wilson," the woman announced tersely, by way of introduction.

"Drus——?" Dumbstruck, Agatha stared up at the woman in awe.

"Come, let's get you up."

"But—"

"Take my hand."

"Oh . . . why . . . why, thank you."

Drusilla grasped Agatha's hand and hauled her to her feet. Agatha winced and pressed one hand to her left hip.

"Are you hurt?"

"Not really. Only my pride."

"But you're limping," Drusilla noted, helping her up the steps.

"It's nothing. Please, you'll soil your dress."

"I've been soiled by worse than mud, Miss Downing, believe me. I've had everything from beer to horse dung flung at me. A little of God's good clean mud will come as a welcome relief."

Together they passed the door of the Gilded Cage. Already the piano had started up inside and loud laughter billowed out into the otherwise peaceful April morning. The two women made their way to the adjacent shop, whose window announced in bright, gilded letters: AGATHA N. DOWNING, MILLINER.

Inside, Agatha forgot her soiled condition and said emotionally, "Miss Wilson, I'm so honored to meet you. I . . . why . . . I . . . I can't believe you're actually here in my humble shop."

"You know who I am, then?"

"Most certainly. Doesn't everybody?"

Miss Wilson allowed a dry chuckle. "Hardly everybody."

"Well, everyone across the state of Kansas, anyway— and I dare say across the United States—and most certainly everyone who's heard the word *temperance*." Agatha's heart beat fast in excitement.

"I should like to talk with you awhile. Might I wait while you change clothes?"

"Oh, most certainly!" Agatha gestured toward a pair of chairs at the front of the shop. "Please, make yourself comfortable while I'm gone. I live upstairs, so it won't be a minute. If you'll excuse me . . ."

Agatha moved through the workroom and out a rear door. Crude, wooden steps slanted along the back wall of the building to the apartments above. She took the stairs as she always did: two feet on each step, with a white-knuckled grip on the rail. Stairs were the worse. Standing and walking on a flat surface were tolerable, but hitching her left leg up each riser was awkward and painful. Her tie-back skirt made the going more difficult, severely restricting movement. Halfway up, she bent and reached beneath her hem to free the lowest set of ties. By the time she reached the landing at the top, she was slightly breathless. She paused, still gripping the rail. The common landing was shared by the residents of both apartments. She glanced at the door leading to Gandy's lodgings.

Another woman might have allowed herself tears in the aftermath of an ordeal such as he'd put her through. Not Agatha. Agatha only puffed out her chest with justifiable anger and knew an immense zeal to see the man brought to heel. As she turned toward her own door, she smiled at the thought that help had arrived at last.

It took her some time to remove her dress. It had twenty-eight buttons running up the front, eight tape ties caught up inside to form the rear bustle, and half that number lashing the apron-style skirt around her legs. As each tape was freed, the dress lost shape. By the time the last was untied, the bustle had given up all its bulges and grown as flat as the Kansas prairie. She held it aloft and her heart sank.

That man! That wretched, infuriating man! He had no idea what this would cost her in time and money and inconvenience. All her thousands of hand stitches, coated with mud. And no place to wash it. She glanced at the dry sink and the water pail beside it. The water wagon had come early this morning to fill the barrel, but it was on its wooden cradle beneath those long, long stairs. Besides, the dry sink wasn't large enough to accommodate a wash job like this. She should run it down to the Finn's laundry immediately, but considering who was waiting downstairs, that was out of the question.

Her ire increased when she removed her cotton bustle and petticoats. At least the dress was gray; these were white—or had been. She feared not even the Finn's homemade lye soap could remove mud stains as heavy as these.

Later. Worry about it later. Drusilla Wilson herself is waiting!

Downstairs, the visitor watched Miss Downing limp to the rear of the store and realized that limp had not been caused by her fall today. It appeared to be the sort of disability to which Agatha N. Downing had inured herself a long time ago.

As Agatha disappeared through a curtained doorway, Drusilla Wilson looked around. The shop was deep and narrow. Near the lace-curtained front window was a pair of oval-backed Victorian chairs tufted in pale orchid to match the curtains. The chairs flanked a tripod pie-crust table holding the latest issues of *Graham's, Godey's,* and *Peterson's* magazines. Wilson disregarded these in favor of a tour of the premises.

An assortment of hats in both felt and leghorn straw were displayed on *papier mâché* forms. Some were trimmed, some plain. The walls were lined with tidy cubbyholes holding ribbons, buttons, lace, and jets. An assortment of folded gauzes and jaconets lay fanned across a mahogany tabletop, representing the full prism of colors. In a wicker basket a selection of paste fruit looked nearly real enough to eat. Finely crafted artificial silk daisies and roses lay upon a flat basket. Upon another counter was displayed a selection of fur tippets and pheasant feather fans. Ostrich plumes hung on a cord near the rear wall. One glass cabinet appeared to contain an entire aviary of birds, nests, and eggs. Butterflies, dragonflies, and even cockchafers added to the collection. Set off by a pair of stuffed fox heads, the case looked as much like a scientific exhibit as a ladies' millinery display.

It took little more than two minutes for Drusilla Wilson to ascertain that Miss Downing ran a well-established business—*and,* she surmised, a line of communication with the women of Proffitt, Kansas.

She heard the shopkeeper's irregular footsteps and turned just as Agatha parted the lavender velvet curtains.

"Ah, a wonderful shop, wonderful."

"Thank you."

"How long have you been a milliner?"

"I learned the trade from my mother. When I was a girl I helped her do seamwork in our home. Then later, when she became a milliner and moved here to Proffitt, I came along with her. When she died, I stayed on."

Miss Wilson scanned Agatha's clean clothing. She found the periwinkle-blue a little too colorful for her taste and slightly too modern, with its fussy tie-ups at the rear and row upon row of tucks down the front. And she didn't hold with those tight apron skirts that showed the shape of a woman's hips all too clearly, nor with the form-fitting bodice that displayed the breadth of a woman's chest too specifically. Miss Downing didn't seem in the least concerned that she showed off both sets of contours with shocking clarity. But at least the tight, cleric collar was modest, though its lace edging was sinful, and the sleeves were wrist-length.

"So, Miss Downing, feeling better?"

"Much."

"One gets used to it when fighting for our cause. Whatever you do, don't discard the soiled dress. If the mud stains don't come out, you may want to wear it when standing up to the enemy in the next battle." Without warning, Miss Wilson briskly crossed the room and captured both of Agatha's hands. "My dear, I was so proud of you. So utterly proud." She squeezed Agatha's fingers very firmly. "I said to myself: *There* is a woman of stalwart mores. *There* is a woman who backs down at nothing. *There* is a woman I want fighting on my side!"

"Oh, nonsense. I only did what any woman would do in the same situation. Why, those two children—"

"But no other woman did it, did she? You were the only one who stood up for virtue." Again she gave Agatha's hands an emphatic squeeze, then released them and stepped back.

Agatha became flushed with pleasure at such high praise from a woman of Drusilla Wilson's renown. "Miss Wilson," she declared honestly, "I mean it when I say it's an honor to have you here. I've read so much about you in the newspapers. My goodness, they are calling you the most powerful scepter ever wielded for the temperance cause."

"What they say about me matters little. What matters most is that we're making headway."

"So I've been reading."

"Twenty-six locals of the national Women's Christian Temperance Union formed, statewide, in '78 alone. More last year. But we're not through yet!" She raised one fist, then dropped it as her lips formed a thin smile. "That's why I'm here, of course. News of your town has reached me. I'm told it's getting out of hand."

Agatha sighed, limped toward her rolltop desk set against the rear right wall, and sank to a chair before it. "You saw firsthand exactly how much. And you can hear for yourself what's going on next door." She nodded toward the common wall between her shop and the saloon. Through it came the muffled strains of "Fallen Angel, Fall into My Arms."

Miss Wilson pursed her lips and cracks appeared around them as upon a two-day-old pudding. "It must be trying."

Agatha touched her temples briefly. "To say the least." She shook her head woefully. "Ever since that man came a month ago, it's gotten worse and worse. I have a confession to make, Miss Wilson, I . . ."

"Please, call me Drusilla."

"Drusilla . . . yes. Well, as I began to say, my motives in confronting Mr. Gandy were not strictly altruistic. I fear you praised me a little too precipitously. You see, since that saloon opened next door, my business has begun to suffer. The ladies are reluctant to walk the boardwalk for fear of being accosted by some inebriate before they reach my door." Agatha's brow furrowed. "It's most distressing. There are horrible fights at all hours of the day and night, and since that man Gandy won't allow fisticuffs on the premises, his bartender throws the fighters out into the street."

"I'm not surprised, given the price of mirrors and glassware out here. But, go on."

"The fights aren't the only thing. The language. Oh, Miss Wilson, it's shocking. Absolutely shocking. And with those half doors the sound drifts out into the street so that there's no telling what my ladies might hear as they pass by. I . . .

I really can't say I blame them for hesitating to patronize my shop. Why, I might feel the same, were I in their place." Agatha knit her fingers and studied her lap. "And, of course, there's the most humiliating reason of all for them to avoid the general area." She looked up with genuine regret in her eyes. "There are those of my customers whose husbands frequent the saloon more than they do their own homes. Several of the women are so abashed at the idea of running into their husbands on the street—in *that* condition—that they shy away at the mere thought."

"Unfortunate, yet your shop looks prosperous."

"I make a fairly decent living, but—"

"No." Miss Wilson presented her gloved palms. "I didn't mean to inquire as to your financial status. I only meant it as an observation that you're well established here and undoubtedly have most of the women in town on your list of clientele."

"Well, I suppose that's true—or was, until a month ago."

"Tell me, Miss Downing, are there any other millinery shops in Proffitt?"

"Why, no. Mine is the only one. Mr. Halorhan, down at the Mercantile, and Mr. McDonnell, at the Longhorn Store, sell the ready-mades now. But," she added with a touch of superiority, "of course they're not trimmed to match."

"And if I may be so forward, might I inquire if you're a churchgoing woman?"

Agatha scarcely managed to keep from bristling. "Why, most certainly!"

"I thought as much. Methodist?"

"Presbyterian."

"Ah, Presbyterian." Miss Wilson cocked her head toward the saloon. "And Presbyterians do love their music, don't they?" Nothing could bring tears to a drunken man's eyes like a chorus of voices raised in heavenly praise.

Agatha gave the wall a malevolent glance. "*Most* music," she replied. The song had changed to "Buffalo Gals Won't You Come Out Tonight?"

"How many saloons are currently—shall we say—*prospering* in Proffitt?"

"Eleven."

"Eleven! Ach!" Drusilla threw back her head in vexation. She marched around with both hands on her hips. "They chased them out of Abilene years ago. But they just kept moving farther down the line, didn't they? Ellsworth, Wichita, Newton, Hays, and now Proffitt."

"This was such a peaceful little town before they came here."

Wilson whipped around, jabbed a finger into the air. "And it can be again." She strode to the desk, her face purposeful. "I'll come straight to the point, Agatha. I may call you Agatha, may I not?" She didn't wait for an answer. "When I saw you stand up to that man, I not only thought: There's a woman who'll stand up to a man. I also thought: There's a woman worthy of being a general in the army against the Devil's Brew."

Agatha touched her chest, surprised. "A general? Me?" She would have arisen from her chair, but Drusilla blocked the way. "I'm afraid you're wrong, Miss Wi——"

"I'm not wrong. You're perfect!" She braced herself against the desktop and leaned close. "You know every woman in this town. You're a practicing Christian. You have additional incentive to fight for temperance, since your business is being threatened. And, furthermore, you have the advantage of juxtaposition to one of the corrupted. Close him down and the others will follow, I assure you. It happened in Abilene; it can happen here. Now what do you say?"

Drusilla's nose was so close, Abigail pressed against the back of her chair. "Why, I . . . I . . ."

"On Sunday I intend to ask your minister for a few moments in the pulpit. Believe me, that's all it'll take, and you'll have a regular army at your command!"

Agatha wasn't sure she wanted an army, but Drusilla rushed on. "You'll not only have the backing of the national Women's Christian Temperance Union, but of Governor St. John himself."

Though Agatha was aware that John P. St. John had been elected on a strong prohibition platform two years ago, beyond that she knew nothing whatever of politics, and little more of organization on such a scale.

"Please, I . . ." She released a fluttery breath and inched herself up to her feet. Turning away, she clasped her hands tightly. "I wouldn't know the first thing about organizing such a group."

"I'll help. The national organization will help. *The Temperance Banner* will help." Wilson named the statewide newspaper inaugurated two years before to support temperance activities and prohibition legislation. "And I know what I'm talking about when I say the women of this town will help. I've traveled well over three thousand miles. I've crossed and recrossed this state and have even been to Washington. I've attended hundreds of public meetings in schoolhouses and churches all across Kansas. In every one I've seen a rousing group of supporters formed almost immediately for The Cause."

"Legislation?" The word scared the wits out of Agatha. "I'm ignorant of politics, Miss Wilson, nor do I wish to be involved in them. Running my business is quite enough for me to handle. I will, however, be happy to introduce you to the women from Christ Presbyterian if you wish to invite them to an organizational meeting."

"Very well. That's a start. And could we hold it here?"

"Here?" Agatha's eyes widened. "In my shop?"

"Yes." There was nothing timid about Drusilla Wilson.

"But I haven't enough chairs and . . ."

"We'll stand, as we often must at the doors of barrooms, for hours at a time."

It was easy to see how Wilson had managed to organize an entire network of W.C.T.U. locals. Her eyes pinned Agatha as successfully as a lepidopterist's pin holds a butterfly. Though Agatha was unsure of many things, she was certain of one. She wanted to get even with that man for what he'd done to her this morning. And she wanted to be rid of the noise and revelry reverberating through the wall. She wanted her business to thrive again. If she didn't take this first step, who would?

"My door will be open."

"Good." Drusilla clasped Agatha's hands and gave them one firm pump. "Good. That's all it will take, I'm confident. Once the women gather and see that they're not alone in their fight against alcohol, they'll surprise you with their staunchness and support." She stepped back and drew on her gloves. "Well." She picked up her valise. "I must find the hotel, then take a walk through town and pinpoint the objects of our crusade, all eleven of them. Then I must visit your minister, Reverend—?"

"Clarksdale," Agatha supplied. "Samuel Clarksdale. You'll find him in the small frame house just north of the church. You can't miss it."

"Thank you, Agatha. Until Sunday, then."

With a whisk and a flourish, she was gone.

Agatha stood rooted. It felt as though an August tornado had just blown through. But when she looked around, things remained magically unchanged. The piano tinkled on the other side of the wall. Outside a dog barked in the street. A horse and rider passed beyond the lace curtains. Agatha pressed a hand to her heart, released a deep breath, and dropped to her chair. A member, yes. But an organizer, no. She hadn't the time nor the vitality to be the head of the town's temperance organization. While she was still pondering the issue, Violet Parsons arrived for work.

"Agatha, I heard! *Tt-tt!*" Violet was a titterer. It was the only thing about her that Agatha disliked. A woman with hair as white as snow and a mouth with more wrinkles than a Spanish fan should have outgrown tittering long ago. But Violet tittered constantly, like an organ grinder's monkey. "*Tt-tt-tt.* I heard you came face to face with our proprietor right on the saloon steps. How ever did you get up the nerve to try to stop him?"

"What would you have done, Violet? Perry White and Clydell Hottle were already hurrying down the street, hoping for a better look at that heathen painting."

Violet placed four fingertips over her lips. "Is it really a painting of a . . . *tt-tt-tt* . . ."—the titter changed to a whisper—" . . . naked lady?"

"Lady? Why, Violet, if she's naked, how can she be a lady?"

Violet's eyes brightened mischievously. "Then she really is . . ."—again, the whisper—" . . . naked?"

"As a jaybird. Which is precisely why I interfered."

"And Mr. Gandy . . . *tt-tt-tt* . . . Did he really set you in the mud?" Violet couldn't help it; her eyes—the exact shade of Agatha's dress—sparkled as they always did when Gandy's name came up. Violet had never been married, but she'd never stopped wishing. From the first time she'd seen Gandy sauntering down the street with a flirtatious grin on his face, she'd started acting like an idiot. She still did, every time she caught a glimpse of him. The fact never failed to sour Agatha.

"News travels fast."

Violet blushed. "I stopped down at Halorhan's for a new thimble. I lost mine yesterday, you know."

Already the incident on the street was being discussed at Halorhan's Mercantile? How disquieting. Agatha produced the thimble and clapped it down on a glass countertop. "I found it. Underneath the leghorn straw you were working on. And what else did you learn at Halorhan's?"

"That Drusilla Wilson is in town and spent close to an hour in this very shop! Are you going to?"

"Am I going to what?" Agatha grew vexed at Violet's assumption that she knew everything being discussed at Halorhan's on any given morning. Violet thrived on gossip.

"Hold a temperance meeting here?"

Agatha's torso snapped erect. "Heavens! The woman walked out of here less than fifteen minutes ago, and already you heard that at Halorhan's?"

"Well, are you?"

"No, not exactly."

"But that's what they're saying."

"I agreed to let Miss Wilson hold one here, that's all."

Violet looked petrified. Her blue eyes grew round as two balls. "Gracious, that's enough."

Agatha moved to her desk and sat down, discomfited. "He won't do anything."

"But he's our new landlord. What if he evicts us?"

Agatha's chin rose defiantly. "He wouldn't dare."

But the thought had already occurred to LeMaster Scott Gandy.

He stood at the bar with one boot on the brass rail, listening to the men make ribald comments about the painting. Business was brisk already, considering the hour. Word traveled fast in a town this size. The place was crowded with curious males who'd come to get a look at the nude. When Jubilee and the girls arrived, business would thrive even more.

Unless that persimmon-mouthed milliner continued harassing him. Gandy frowned. That woman could develop into one bodacious, infernal nuisance if she put her mind to it. It took only one like her to rile up a whole townful of females and start them nagging at their husbands about the hours they spent at the saloon. If she was upset about the painting, she'd be incensed about the girls.

Gandy tipped the brim of his Stetson low over his eyes and rested both elbows on the bar behind him. He stared thoughtfully across the quiet street at Heustis Dyar's place, wondering when the first beefs would come. That's when the fun would really start. When those rowdy, thirsty cowpunchers hit town, that little do-gooder next door would more than likely pack up and light out for other parts and his worries would be over.

He smiled to himself, extracted a cheroot from the pocket of his vest, and struck a match on his boot heel. But before he applied it, the object of his thoughts—Goody Two-Shoes herself—materialized from next door and moved past the saloon. For no more than five seconds her head and feet were clearly visible above and below the swinging doors. But that's all it took for Gandy to realize she wasn't walking normally. The match burned his fingers. He cursed and dropped it, then hurried toward the swinging doors, standing in the shadows to one side. He watched her make her way along the boardwalk. He listened to the shuffling sound made by her shoes. He began to grow warm around the collar. Five doors down, she descended a set of steps, gripping the rail tightly. But instead of using the stepping-stones to cross the street as all the ladies did, she lifted her skirts and trudged laboriously through the mud to the other side.

"Dan?" Gandy called.

"Something wrong?" Loretto didn't look up. He fanned the deck of cards into a peacock's tail, then snapped it together. It was too early in the day for gamblers, but Gandy had taught him to keep his fingers nimble at all times.

"Come here."

Loretto squared the deck and rose from the chair with the same unjointed motion he so admired in the boss.

He came up behind Gandy at the swinging doors. "Yes, boss?"

"That woman." Agatha Downing had reached the far side of the street and was struggling up the steps to the boardwalk, clutching an armful of clothing that looked suspiciously much like the gray dress she'd been wearing earlier. Gandy scowled at her clean skirts—blue now. They churned unnaturally with each step. "Is she limping?"

"Yessir, she sure is."

"Good God! Did I do that t' her?" Gandy looked horrified.

"Not hardly. She's limped ever since I knew her."

Gandy's head snapped around. "Ever since you knew her?" This was getting worse.

"Yup. She's got a gimp leg."

Gandy felt himself blush for the first time in years.

"A gimp leg?"

"That's right."

"And I set her in the mud." He watched Agatha disappear with her dirty clothing into the Finn's laundry down the block. He felt like a heel.

"You didn't exactly set her in the mud, Scotty. She fell."

"She fell *after* I set her in the mud!"

"Whatever you say, boss."

"Well, why didn't somebody say somethin'? How in tarnation was I supposed t' know?"

"Just figured you did. You been doin' business next door to her for a month now. You collected rent from her. She walks down to Paulie's twice a day so regular you could set your clock by her. Breakfast and supper. Never fails."

But Gandy had never looked twice at the woman. She was the kind who blended into the weatherbeaten board-
A dull, gray moth upon a dull, gray rock. When

he'd gone next door to introduce himself as the new owner of the building, she'd been sitting at her rolltop desk and hadn't risen from her chair. Instead of bringing the rent over herself, she'd sent it with a timid, twittering old woman who looked as if she'd just swallowed a frog. The few times he'd eaten at Paulie's he didn't recall seeing her there.

Sweet Jesus! What would the women of Proffitt say? If it was true that there was an "organizer" in town, he'd have them all on his head. And they'd have plenty to say in that nuisance of a rag they printed. He could see the headline now: SALOON OWNER TOPPLES CRIPPLED TEMPERANCE WORKER IN THE MUD.

CHAPTER
2

At five-thirty that afternoon Scott Gandy left the rear of the saloon and walked up the same steps to the same landing Agatha had ascended earlier. He glanced at the two long windows, one on either side of her door, but as usual they were shrouded by thick lace. He tossed his cheroot over the railing and entered his own door. The saloon and its overhead apartments occupied three-fourths of the building, the millinery shop and corresponding apartment, one-fourth. Upstairs, his portion was bisected by a hall with the door at its west end and a window at its east. To the left were four rooms of equal size. To the right were Gandy's living quarters and his private office. He entered the office, a small, spare room with wainscoted walls, a single west window, and only the necessary furnishings: a desk, two chairs, coat-tree, safe, and a small cast-iron stove.

It was a cold room, the window curtainless, the wall above the waist-high wainscot painted a drab sage-green, the oak floor raw, bare. He moved to the safe, knelt, and spun the dial, locked away a packet of bills, then, with a sigh, stood and rubbed the back of his neck. Lord, it was quiet. Getting close to suppertime. Ivory had deserted the piano downstairs and Jack had gone to eat. Gandy glanced out the window, hooked his thumbs in his waistcoat pockets, and absently drummed a rhythm on the silk. The view outside offered little to buoy him. Unpainted frame buildings, muddy streets, and prairie. Nothing but prairie. No spreading water oak trees festooned with Spanish moss, no scent of magnolia drifting in on the spring breeze, no mockingbirds. He missed the mockingbirds.

This time of day at Waverley, the family used to gather on the wide back veranda and sip glasses of minted iced tea, and Delia would toss cracked corn to the mockingbirds, trying to entice them to eat from her hand. He could see her yet, squatting in a billow of hooped skirts, cupping the corn in her palm. Golden head with ringlets down to her shoulders. Skin as white as milk. Fiddle-waisted. And her eyes, as dark and arresting as the notches on a dogwood petal, forever alluring.

"Why don't you feed the peacocks?" his father would call to her.

But Delia would kneel patiently, cupped hand extended. "Because the peacocks are too audacious. And besides"— Delia would rest her chin on one shoulder and look back at her husband—"no fun tryin' to get a tame bird to eat from your hand, is there, Scotty?" she would say teasingly.

And his mother would glance his way and smile at the look she saw on her son's face. But he never cared who knew it. He was as smitten with Delia as he'd been the first time he'd kissed her when they were fourteen years old.

Then Leatrice would waddle to the door—good old Leatrice, with her skin as dark as sorghum syrup and breasts the size of watermelons. He wondered where she was now. "Suppuh, suh," she'd announce. "Pipin'."

And Dorian Gandy would take his wife's arm, and Scott himself would rise from his chair and slowly extend a hand to Delia. And she'd smile up at him with a promise for later and let herself be tugged to her feet. Then, hand in hand, they would follow his parents inside beneath the high, cool ceilings.

But those days were gone forever.

Gandy stared at the prairie. He blinked once, hard. His stomach rumbled, reminding him it was suppertime now. With a deep sigh, he turned from the window toward the desk and glanced at the calendar. Nearly four weeks he'd been here. Jubilee and the girls would arrive any day. They couldn't get here fast enough to suit him. Things were dull without Jube.

Leaving his office by a second door, he entered the adjoining sitting room of his private apartment. It was much cheerier, with burgundy draperies, a factory-made rug, and sturdy, masculine furniture. It held a leather settee with matching chairs, heavy mahogany tables, and two banquet lamps. To his left a door led directly to the hall; to his right a dresser held his humidor and hat block. On the wall above it hung a watercolor behind which was stuck a branch from a cotton plant, its three bolls grayed in their brown clawlike husks. The painting was that of a pillared mansion with a wide front veranda, flanked by lush greenery and sprawling lawns on which stood two poised peacocks.

Waverley.

His gaze lingered on the picture while he placed his hat on the block. Nostalgia hit him with the force of a blow. From the humidor he took a cheroot, as rich and brown as the soil from which that cotton boll had sprung, the rich Mississippi bottomlands of the great Tombigbee River. Lost in thought, he forgot to light his cigar, but absently stroked its length. He thought about Waverley for so long that he eventually laid the cheroot on the dresser, unused.

He wandered into the adjoining bedroom and tossed his jacket onto a double bed. He recalled the rosewood fourposter at Waverley where he'd brought his bride and bedded her for the first time. The gauzy netting hanging all around, circling them in a private haven of their own. The flickering gas lantern sending trellised shadows through the mesh against her skin.

Again he blinked. What was it that had triggered all these thoughts of Waverley? It wasn't good to pine for the old days. He stripped off his vest and shirt and tossed them across the hobnail bedspread. At the washstand he used the pitcher and bowl. Delia had taught him that. She liked her man clean, she'd always said. Since Delia he'd learned that a lot of women liked a clean man, and clean men were so rare they could get a woman to do almost anything for them. It was only one of the sad things he'd learned since he'd lost Delia.

Stop it, Gandy! There's no goin' back, so why do you punish yourself?

Toweling his face, he ambled to the front window. It overlooked main street, giving him a view of something that at last took his mind off Delia and Waverley: Miss Agatha Downing limping toward Paulie's Restaurant to have her supper. The towel stilled against his chin. Her limp was very real, very pronounced. How could he have missed it before? He frowned, recalling her plopping backward in the mud. Again, he almost blushed.

She entered Paulie's and disappeared. He lunged to the bed and pulled the watch from his vest pocket. Six o'clock exactly.

He glanced toward the street, flung the towel aside, yanked a clean shirt from the chifforobe, and threw it on. There was no logical reason for him to hurry, yet he did. Holding the vest in his teeth, he grabbed up his jacket and hat and hit the stairs at a run, still stuffing his shirttails in. By the time he reached Paulie's, everything was buttoned and tucked into place.

He saw her immediately upon entering. Her dress was the color of an evening sky and the top of her bustle poked through the back of her chair as Cyrus Paulie stood taking her order. Her shoulders were narrow, her neck long. She was small-ribbed and thin-armed and her dress fit with remarkable snugness. She wore a mountainous hat decorated with butterflies and bows beneath which little of her hair showed.

Gandy moved inside and took a seat behind her, heard her order chicken.

So why was he here, staring at the back of an old, lame woman? All those remembrances of home, he thought. Mississippi gentlemen were raised to have better manners than those he'd displayed today. If his mother were alive, she'd take him to task for his rudeness. And if Delia were alive—but if Delia were alive, he wouldn't be living out here in this godforsaken cowtown in the first place.

Cy delivered a plate of chicken dinner to Miss Downing, and Gandy ordered the same, studying her back while they both ate. When Cy came to deliver her apple cobbler and pick up her dirty plate, Scott signaled him over.

"How was the meal, Scotty?" Cyrus Paulie was a jovial fellow with a ready smile. Unfortunately, his teeth looked as if someone had opened his mouth and thrown them in without caring where or in which direction they landed. He piled Scott's dirty plate atop Agatha's and displayed his sorry collection of snags.

"Meal was fine, Cy."

"Get you some apple cobbler? Made fresh this afternoon."

"No, thanks, Cy. I'll just settle up." Scott drew a silver dollar from his waistcoat pocket and dropped it into Cy's palm. "And take out the price of Miz Downin's supper, too."

"Miss Downing?" Cy's eyebrows nearly touched his hairline. "You mean Agatha?"

"I do."

Cy glanced at the woman, then back at the saloon owner. No sense reminding Gandy he'd set the woman on her rump in the mud that very morning. A man didn't forget a thing like that.

"Sure thing, Scotty. Coffee?"

Gandy patted his flat belly. "No, thanks. Full up."

"Well, then . . ." Cy gestured with the dirty plate. "Stop in again soon."

At the same time, Agatha took the proper coins from her handbag and caught Cyrus Paulie as he passed her table.

"Well, how was everything, Miss Downin'?" he inquired as he stood beside her, resting the plates against the long white apron lashed around his middle.

"Delicious, as usual. Give Emma my compliments."

"Sure will, ma'am, sure will."

She extended her coins. He ignored them and picked up her cobbler bowl. "No need for that. Your meal's already paid for."

Agatha's eyes widened. Her head snapped up, her hat teetered. "Paid for? But—"

"By Mr. Gandy." Cyrus nodded to a table behind her.

She spun in her chair to find the bane of her morning seated at a nearby table watching every move she made.

Apparently, he'd been doing so for some time; there was a soiled napkin on his table and he was enjoying an after-dinner cigar. His dark eyes were riveted upon her. While they stared at each other, the only thing that moved was the smoke coiling about his black hair. Until he politely nodded his head.

The color leaped to her face. Her mouth tightened. "I can very well pay for my own, Mr. Paulie," she declared, loudly enough that Gandy could hear. "And even if I couldn't, I would not accept a meal from a lowlife like him. Tell Mr. Gandy I would cheerfully starve first."

She threw two coins on the table. One hit a sugar bowl and ricocheted to the floor, where it rolled for a full five seconds, then circled to a halt. In the silence it sounded like thunder.

Agatha rose from her chair with all the dignity she could muster, feeling the curious eyes of other diners watching as she shuffled past Gandy to the door. He watched her all the way, but she lifted her chin high and glared at the brass doorknob.

Outside, her eyes stung with humiliation. Some people got their satisfactions in cruel ways. She supposed he was chuckling.

At home she struggled up the stairs, wishing once—just once!—she could stomp up the steps with all the outrage she felt. Instead, she was forced to stump up like an old woman. Well, she wasn't an old woman. She wasn't! And to prove it, when she got to the top she slammed the door so hard a picture fell off her parlor wall.

She tore her hat off and paced the length of her apartment, rubbing her left hip. How humiliating! With a whole roomful of people looking on he chose to do a thing like that. But why? To taunt her? She'd put up with taunting since she was nine years old and had gone bouncing down a flight of stairs. Forever after, children had giggled, teased, and found disparaging names for "the gimp." And even adults couldn't resist a second glance. But this—this was debasing.

In time her anger subsided, leaving her empty and forlorn. She put her hat in a bandbox, stowed it on the chifforobe shelf, wandered to the front window, and looked down on the street. Dusk had fallen. Across the way the lights from the Hoof and Horn splashed onto the boardwalk from behind the swinging doors. Below, they most likely did the same, though she could see no more than the railed roof of the boardwalk, just outside her floor-length window. The piano had started up. Its faraway tinkling, coupled with the sound of laughter, made her sad. She turned, studying the apartment: the perimeter of her world. One long, stuffy shotgun room filled with her old maid's furnishings. Her prized Hepplewhite bed and matching chest with its inlay of white holly, the maroon horsehair settee with ivory crocheted antimacassars, the gateleg table, the lowboy, corner curio cabinet, the six-plate stove, the banjo clock, the sampler she'd knocked off the wall.

With a sigh she went to pick it up. Hanging it on the nail, she read the familiar lines:

Needle, thread, embroidery hoop;
Satin stitch, French knot, and loop;
Patience, care, and fortitude;
Practice makes my stitching good.

As she gazed at the sampler, a sad expression covered her face. How old had she been when her mother taught her to stitch? Seven? Eight? Before the accident, most certainly, because one of her earliest recollections was of standing beside her mother's chair in the shabby house in Sedalia, Colorado, where her father had staked his claim in the gold fields, certain that *this time* he'd strike it rich. She remembered the house clearly, out of all the rest they'd lived in, because it was the one where *it* had happened. The one with the steep steps and the dark, narrow stairwell. Her mother had gotten an ivy plant from somewhere and had hung it in the kitchen window. The ivy had been the only cheerful note in the otherwise pitiful place. There was a worn wooden rocking chair below the plant. It was beside this chair Agatha had been standing, watching her mother demonstrate a perfect petal stitch, when she had piped up in her childish voice, "When I grow up I'm going to have little girls and I'll do embroidery on all their fancy dresses."

Regina Downing had laid down her handiwork, drawn Agatha against the arm of the rocker, and kissed her cheek. "Then you be sure to get you a man who doesn't drink up all the money for those pretty little dresses. Promise me that, will you, Gussie?"

"I promise, Mommy."

"Good. Then sit down here on the stool and I'll teach you the petal stitch. Got to know that one for making daisies."

The memory had lost none of its clarity over the years. Not the warm autumn sun cascading through the window. Not the sound of steam hissing from a kettle on the cookstove. Not the smell of barley soup and onions stewing for their supper. Why it had remained so clear, Agatha didn't know. Perhaps it was the promise she'd made her mother, the only one she ever recalled her mother asking of her. Perhaps it was the first time she'd voiced her wishes about having little girls of her own. Perhaps it was nothing more complex than the fact that she had learned the petal stitch that day, and she'd been stitching ever since.

For whatever reason, the memory persevered. In it she was a hale and healthy little girl, leaning her belly against the arm of her mother's rocker, standing on two sturdy legs. Her only other memory of that house was the night she made that fateful trip down the stairs, pushed by her own drunken father, ending forever the possibility of acquiring daughters or a husband to give them to her. For what man wanted a cripple?

In the gloom of her lonely apartment, Agatha turned from the sampler and prepared for bed. She locked her door, hung up her clothing, including the cotton pad she wore over her left hip to make it match the right. She donned her nightdress and gave the weights of the banjo clock their nightly pull. Then she lay in the dark and listened to it.

Tick. Tock. Tick. Tock.

Lord, she hated the sound. Night after lonely night she went to bed and heard it marking off the days of her life. There were things she wanted, so many things. A real house, with a yard where she could plant flowers and vegetables, and where she could hang a swing in a tall cottonwood tree. A kitchen where she could cook suppers, a kitchen with a big oak table set for four, or six, or even eight. A clothesline where she could hang washing: snow-white socks from short to long, the longest hanging beside a man's oversized chambray shirt. Someone who'd toiled all day and came home hungry and shared the supper table, laughing with his children. Those children, scrubbed shiny, wearing the beautiful hand-stitched nightdresses she would make herself, tucked into beds down the hall at this time of day. And someone there beside her at bedtime. Another human being telling her how his day had been, asking about hers, then holding her hand as he sighed off to sleep. Another's even breathing in the same room with hers. He need not be handsome, or rich, or doting. Only sober, and honest, and kind.

But none of it would happen. She was thirty-five already; her child-bearing years were nearly gone. And she worked at a business whose customers were only women.

Tick. Tock.

Foolishness, Agatha. Nothing but an old maid's muse. Even if by some miracle you met a man, a widower, perhaps, who needed someone to look after his children, he'd take one look at you and realize you wouldn't last long kneeling in gardens, or standing at washboards, or chasing nimble-footed children. And, besides, men don't want women who have to pad their bodies to be symmetrical. They want the uncrooked ones.

Tick. Tock.

She thought of all the thousands of women who had men such as she imagined, yet complained about having to weed the garden, toil over a hot stove, scrub socks, and listen to children quarrel. They didn't appreciate what they had.

I would be such a good mother, she thought. It was a conviction she'd had for as long as she could remember. If her legs were strong enough to birth a baby, the rest would be easy. *And I'd be a good wife, too. For if I were ever blessed with the opportunity, I would never take it for granted. I would protect what I had by giving my best.*

From below came the tinkle of the piano, and instead of a man's steady breathing at her side, the last thing she heard was a gambler shouting, "Keno!"

When Violet Parsons came in for work at eleven the next morning, she burst into the workroom babbling.

"Is it true? Did Mr. Gandy really-take you out for supper last night?"

Agatha sat at the worktable near the window, stitching a raspberry-silk lining into a Dolly Varden hat. Her needle kept moving, but she glanced up irritatedly.

"Who told you that?" Violet lived in Mrs. Gill's boardinghouse with six other old ladies. They carried news faster than Western Union, though it was a mystery how.

"Did he?" Violet's eyes grew as bright as periwinkles.

Agatha felt her neck grow warm. "When you left here yesterday, you went straight to Mrs. Gill's for supper. This morning you walked a mere four blocks to get here. How in heaven's name could you have heard such a thing so fast?"

"He did! I can tell he did!" Violet covered her lips. "*Tt-tt.* I'd give my mother's pearl brooch if a man like that would take *me* out to supper. *Tt-tt.*"

"Violet, shame on you!" Agatha formed a knot, snipped a thread, and began to rethread the needle. "Your mother would be horrified if she could hear you say such a thing, may she rest in peace."

"No, she wouldn't. My mother liked handsome men. Did I ever show you the daguerreotype of my father? Come to think of it, Mr. Gandy looks rather like Papa, but Mr. Gandy is even handsomer. His hair is darker and his eyes are . . ."

"Violet, I've heard quite enough! I swear people will begin to snicker if you don't stop rhapsodizing over that man."

"They say he bought you a roast-chicken dinner last night at Cyrus and Emma's."

"Well, they're wrong. After what he did to me yesterday morning, do you think I'd accept dinner from him? Why, the food would stick in my throat."

"Then, what *did* happen?"

Agatha sighed and gave up. If she didn't answer, she'd get no work out of Violet all day. "He offered to pay for my meal, but I told him in no uncertain terms I'd starve first. I paid for my own."

"He offered . . ." Violet's eyes glittered like sapphires. "Oh, wait till I tell the girls." She pressed a hand to her heart and closed her wrinkled eyelids. They twitched while she sighed.

Senile, thought Agatha. *I love you dearly, Violet, but you're going senile living with all those old women.* Not one of "the girls" would ever see sixty again.

"Aren't you a little old to be getting spoony over a forty-year-old man?"

"He's not forty. He's only thirty-eight."

Agatha was abashed that Violet knew, precisely. "And you're sixty-three."

"Not yet I'm not."

"Well, you will be next month."

Violet ignored the fact. "Five different times I've passed him on the boardwalk, and every time he's smiled and doffed his hat and called me ma'am."

"Then gone down the street and hired one of the soiled doves, no doubt."

"Well, at least he doesn't have any of them working in his place—you have to say that for him."

"Not yet he hasn't. But the punchers haven't arrived yet either."

Violet's eyes grew troubled. "Oh, Agatha, do you think he will?"

Agatha lifted one eyebrow. Her needle poised eloquently. "After what he carried in there yesterday, I wouldn't put anything past him."

"The girls said Mr. Gandy was a . . ." Violet's words halted as the shop door opened in the front room. "Just a minute. I'll see who it is."

Agatha continued stitching. Violet parted the lavender curtains and stepped through. "Oh!" Agatha heard. Breathless and girlish.

"Mornin', Miz Parsons. Fine mornin', isn't it?" drawled a deep baritone voice.

Agatha's spine stiffened. She gaped at the swaying curtains.

"Why, Mr. Gandy, what a surprise." Violet sounded as if she'd just run full tilt against a fence post and knocked herself stupid.

Scott Gandy doffed his hat and bestowed his most charming smile. "I dare say it is. I reckon y'all don't get a lot o' gentlemen customers comin' round."

"None at all."

"And I suspect I'm not any too welcome after what happened out front yesterday mornin'."

Loving Savior, he has dimples! thought Violet. And he's carrying Agatha's dress! The gray frock and a white petticoat were folded neatly over his arm. It reminded Violet that she must not excuse his rudeness too readily. She bent closer and whispered, "Agatha was very upset, I'll grant you that."

He bent, too, and whispered back, "I'm sure she was."

"She still is."

"It was a most ungentlemanly thing for me to do. Most ungentlemanly." Their noses were so close Violet could see herself reflected in his black irises. She caught a whiff of fine tobacco and bay rum, scents she rarely smelled working in a millinery shop and living with the girls. Still, she couldn't let the scoundrel get off without a scolding.

"See to it that it doesn't happen again, Mr. Gandy," she chided, still in an undertone.

"It's a promise." He looked properly contrite, the smile gone, the dimples erased. Violet's heart melted. Suddenly, she realized they were still nose to nose, and she straightened with a snap, blushing.

"Can I help you, Mr. Gandy?" she inquired in a normal tone of voice.

"I was hopin' Miz Downin' would be in. Is she here, Miz Parsons?"

In the back room Agatha clasped the edge of the worktable, wishing she were nimble enough to leap to her feet and streak out the back door.

"She's in the back. Just follow me."

Don't you dare, Violet! thought Agatha. But it was too late. The curtains parted and Violet led the way into the workroom, followed by their landlord.

"Mr. Gandy is here to see you, Agatha." Violet stood aside and let Gandy pass into the room. He moved with the unhurried pace of those accustomed to surviving in the humidity and heat of the Deep South, crossing slowly to the woman at the worktable beside the west windows. She sat stiff-backed, tight-mouthed, pouring her attention solely on the stitches she was furiously applying to the lining of a felt hat. Her face was as bright as the silk on which she sewed.

Gandy stopped beside her chair and removed his hat.

"Mornin', Miz Downin'," he said quietly.

She refused to answer or look up.

"Can't say I blame you for not wantin' t' talk t' me."

"If there's something you need from the shop, Miss Parsons can help you."

"I've come t' see you, not Miz Parsons."

"I've already had my breakfast. And paid for it myself." She jabbed the needle through the felt as if it were his hide.

"Yes, ma'am. I saw you goin' down t' Paulie's this mornin'." Her head snapped up and their gazes collided. For the first time she saw that he held her gray dress and white petticoat over one arm. Her face turned a shade brighter. "Thought about tryin' t' talk t' you there, but decided it'd be best t' do so in private."

The needle seemed to grow slick in her fingers. What possible reason could he have for observing her comings and goings?

"Last night at Paulie's, I wanted t' say that—" He cleared his throat nervously.

She gave up all pretense of sewing and glared up at him. "Last night at Paulie's you should have had the good grace to leave when you saw I was there. Was it amusing, Mr. Gandy? Did you enjoy humiliating me in front of people I know? Did your . . ." She paused disdainfully. "Did your *friends* in the saloon get a good laugh when you told them how you offered to buy supper for that old-maid milliner with the game leg?" She threw down her work. "And what, pray tell, are you doing with my personal belongings?"

Scott Gandy had the grace to blush effusively.

"Is that what you all think? That I offered t' buy your supper to make fun of you?" His black eyebrows curled. A wedge of creases appeared between them.

She picked up the hat and stabbed it again, too upset to meet his eyes. "Isn't it?"

"Not at all, ma'am, I assure you. I'm from Miz'sippi, Miz Downin'. My mama taught me early t' respect womenfolk. Whatever it might look like, I had no intention of setting you in the mud yesterday or of embarrassing you last night in the eatin' saloon. I wanted to pay for your supper by way of apology, that's all."

Agatha didn't know whether to believe him or not. She was making hash of her stitches, but she kept pushing the needle because she didn't know what else to do, and she was too embarrassed to look up at him.

"I truly am sorry, Miz Downin'."

His voice sounded contrite. She looked up to see if his eyes were the same. They were; and his mouth was somber. Rarely in her life had she seen a face more handsome. It was easy to see why featherheads like Violet became unhinged over him. But she was not Violet, nor was she a featherhead.

"You think a mere apology excuses such gross behavior?"

"Not at all. It was inexcusable. However, I didn't know at the time you had difficulty walking. Later I saw you goin' on down to the Finn's with your dirty clothes and I thought I'd injured you when I knocked you down. Dan Loretto set me straight. However, when he did, I felt even worse."

Agatha dropped her chin, squirming under his direct gaze.

"I know I can't do anythin' about the embarrassment I caused, but I figured the least 1 could do was take care o' the laundry bill." He laid her dress and petticoat carefully across the worktable. "So, here. All clean and paid for. If anythin's damaged beyond repair, ya'll be sure t' let me know and I'll make it right."

No man had ever touched Agatha's petticoats. To have a man like him do so was rattling. His hands were very dark against the white cotton. She glanced aside, distraught. Her eyes fell on the hand that held his black hat against his thigh. On his little finger glittered a pea-sized diamond ring set in gold. The hat was a good one—if there was one thing she knew, it was hats. This one was a Stetson, by the look of it, a "wide-awake" beaver felt with low crown and wide brim, the newest profile for men. He had money enough for diamonds and new Stetsons and sheet-sized oil paintings— let him pay her laundry bill. She deserved it.

She braved meeting his eyes directly, her own cold and accusing. "I suspect, Mr. Gandy, that you've gotten wind of the battle about to be waged in this town over the sale of spirits, and you're here seeking to protect your interests by placating me with a few hollow apologies. Some women . . ."—it was all Agatha could do to keep from glaring at Violet—" . . . might have their heads turned by your smooth talk. I, however, know when I'm being hogwashed by a stream of self-interested ooze. And if you think I'll back down on the issue of the lewd painting, you're mistaken. Violet is afraid you'll evict us if I cross you; however, *I'm* not."

In her zealousness, Agatha did something she rarely did before strangers—she got to her feet. Though Gandy still topped her by a good ten inches, she felt seven feet tall. "I intend not only to cross you, but to find others who'll do the same."

Near the curtain Violet was waving like a windmill in a gale, trying to shut her up. Agatha went on, all the more aroused. "I may as well tell you—you'll find out soon if you haven't already—I've given approval for Proffitt's first temperance meeting to be held here in my millinery shop this Sunday evening." She paused, folded her hands over her stomach, and retreated with one dragging step. "Now, if you feel within your rights to evict us, go ahead. Right is right and wrong is wrong, and selling spirits is wrong, Mr. Gandy; so is hanging filth like that on a public wall."

"I have no intention of evicting you, Miz Downin', and bringin' every temperance worker and that newspaper o'

yours down on my head. Neither do I intend t' quit sellin'
liquor. Furthermore, the picture is hung, and that's where
it'll stay."

"We'll see about that."

Gandy paused, thought, and then his face took on the
expression of a poacher watching a doe approach a snare.
He absently reached into his vest pocket for a cigar.

"Oh, you will?"

The cigar had scarcely touched his lips before she exploded. "Put that thing away! You may smoke your devil's weed
in your own filthy brothel, but not in my millinery shop!"

As if suddenly realizing what he held, he looked down
and stuck it back in his pocket. But he did so grinning,
dimpling only one cheek.

"Yes, ma'am," he drawled. He glanced over his shoulder,
turned slowly, and confronted Violet. "And what are your
views on all this, Miz Parsons?"

Violet acted like a perfect ninny, touching her lips and
blushing like a scalded pig. Disgusted, Agatha watched
Gandy work his wiles on her. "Men've been drinkin' and
gamblin' and likin' their ladies for as long as this country's
been here. Let the men have a little fun, we thought. No
harm in that now, is there?"

Violet answered, *"Tt-tt."*

"It's indecent!" Agatha reproved, incensed.

Gandy turned back to her. "It's free enterprise. I try to
make an honest livin', ma'am, and to do that I have to keep
one step ahead o' those other enterprisin' chaps along the
street."

"Honest? You call it honest, taking men's hard-earned
money at gambling tables and a brass rail?"

"I don't force 'em to come to the Gilded Cage, Miz
Downin'. They come o' their own free will."

"But it's ruining my business, Mr. Gandy. All that drinking and revelry—the ladies don't want to come anywhere
near the place."

"I'm sorry about that, truly I am, but that's free enterprise, too."

Agatha became outraged at his blithe claim of irrespon-
sibility. Her voice grew sharper. "I'll say it once more.

Evict us if you will, but I intend to do everything in my power to shut you down."

To her utter consternation, he grinned. Matched dimples appeared this time in his swarthy cheeks and a twinkle came into his onyx eyes.

"Is that a challenge, Miz Downin'?"

"It's a fact!" she spat. Agatha found she detested his Southern drawl. She detested even more the cocky way he settled the Stetson on his head and fixed his lazy grinning eyes on her, taking his sweet time about leaving.

Gandy had come into the shop contrite. He was now amused. He studied the bridling female in the subdued blue dress with its high, tight collar and its stern, tied-back skirts. He'd taken her for an old woman when he'd first seen her. Upon closer scrutiny, he discovered she wasn't really old at all. Younger than himself, probably. Slim, well shaped, and with a spark of conviction he grudgingly admired. Her hair held a surprising glint of red, with the window light behind it. She had a magnificent jawline. Clear, clear skin. Unyielding green eyes as pale as sea spray. A damned pretty set of lips. And a lot of old-lady ways.

But she certainly wasn't old. Put a feather in her hair, paint a little crimson on those lips, loosen up a few springy ringlets in that hair, teach her to sing a bawdy drinking song, and she'd look as good in the saloon as Jube or Pearl or Ruby. He withheld a silent chuckle, imagining how aghast she'd be if she knew how he was picturing her.

"I'll take it as a challenge. Y'all do everythin' in your power t' shut me down. March, make banners, sing— whatever it is you temperance workers take it into your heads t' do. And I'll do whatever is necessary to attract customers to the Gilded Cage."

"You think it's a game, don't you? Well, it's not. Miss Wilson doesn't play games. She's here on a mission."

"I know, I know." He held up both palms and acknowledged blithely, "She's aimin' t' clean me out, too."

"She most certainly is."

"Well, then, I'd best get back to work and prepare for the war, hadn't I, ladies?" He touched the brim of his hat and bowed. "G'day, Miz Downin'." He turned and approached

Violet, who'd remained by the curtained doorway, looking as if he'd just complimented her on her underwear. "Miz Parsons," he said softly, taking one of her blue-veined hands and raising it slowly to his lips. "It's been a pleasure."

Violet's eyeballs threatened to roll in their sockets. Looking on, Agatha's did.

"Violet, see the landlord out, will you!" she snapped. "Then leave the front door propped open. The place suddenly reeks of stale cigar smoke."

Gandy turned, grinned, nodded, and left.

When Violet reappeared, she flopped into her work chair, fanning her face with a handkerchief. "Did you see that, Agatha? He kissed my hand!"

"Perhaps you'd best check it for twin punctures."

Violet's euphoria would not be dampened. "He actually kissed my hand!" she repeated breathily.

"Oh, Violet, will you act your age!"

"I am. I have a weak heart, and I'm having terrible palpitations."

Agatha seethed. Oh, that Gandy was a shrewd manipulator. He knew a besotted old hen when he saw one, and he didn't pass up any advantage.

Violet half lay against the edge of the worktable, exaggerating his Southern accent. " '*Y'all do everuhthin' in yoah powuh tuh shut me down . . . .* Have you ever heard anything so wonderful in your life? When Mr. Gandy talks, I swear I can smell magnolia blossoms right here in Proffitt, Kansas."

"All I smelled was stale tobacco."

Violet popped up. "Oh, Agatha, you have no romanticism in you. He smelled like bay rum, too. I remember my papa used to wear bay rum."

"Your papa didn't operate a saloon, nor was he kicked off the riverboats for having cards up his sleeve."

"Nobody knows that for sure about Mr. Gandy."

"Oh?" Agatha inquired with asperity. "You mean there's something *the girls* haven't been able to verify?"

Suddenly, Violet spied Agatha's dress and petticoat on the worktable. She laid her hand on them almost reverently.

"He paid to have these washed. Imagine that."

Agatha sniffed.

"And he offered to buy you supper."

Agatha sniffed louder.

"And he came in here especially to apologize for everything."

Had she sniffed any harder, Agatha might have sucked in some stray threads and choked herself. So she preached instead. "Oh, he's an oily-tongued dandy, all right. But with the help of Drusilla Wilson and the women of Proffitt, Kansas"—Agatha raised one hand and pointed toward heaven—"I'll wipe that insufferable grin off his brown hide!"

On the other side of the wall, LeMaster Scott Gandy stalked into the saloon, sending the doors flapping wildly behind him. "Jack, make up a sign!" he bellowed. He bit the end off a cigar, spit it into the cuspidor with deadly accuracy, and blew the first smoke ring with equally deadly accuracy; it appeared to wreath a florid nipple on the nude behind the bar. He narrowed one eye on the nipple and the ring, as if taking a bead down the bore of a Winchester. "We're goin' t' have a picture-namin' contest. The man who tags our rosy-breasted li'l lady here gets the first dance with Jubilee when she arrives!"

And so the battle lines were drawn.

CHAPTER
3

On Sunday, Reverend Samuel Clarksdale of Christ Presbyterian Church was upstaged in the pulpit by Drusilla Wilson whose message was concise and inspiring: Those who stood by and watched a loved one chained to the evils of alcohol without helping when they could were equally as guilty as if they themselves had placed the bottle in the loved one's hands.

When Sunday services ended, Miss Wilson was greeted effusively by the women in the congregation. Many squeezed her hand heartily, some with tears in their eyes. Many did the same to Agatha Downing, thanking her in advance for providing them with a gathering place.

Agatha outfitted herself for the meeting in a stiff-necked dress of somber brown, her bustles lashed firmly behind her, skirts tied back so tightly her steps were considerably shortened. She was ready well before seven, so she went downstairs and dusted the countertops and lit the lanterns. Dusk had not quite fallen when she opened the shop door to greet Drusilla Wilson. As usual, the woman was ready with a firm handclasp.

"Agatha, how nice to see you again."

"Come in, Miss Wilson."

But before stepping inside, Drusilla glanced toward the door of the saloon. "You've seen what we're up against, I imagine?"

Agatha appeared puzzled, then stepped onto the boardwalk herself.

The swinging doors were thrown back. The painting

behind the bar could be viewed from an oblique angle along the left wall. On the boardwalk out front stood that wretched Southerner, dressed to the nines, with a smoking cheroot in his mouth and one elbow draped on a double-sided billboard announcing:

NEW LADIES IN TOWN

NAME THE PAINTING BEHIND THE BAR
AND WIN THE FIRST DANCE WITH

MISS JUBILEE BRIGHT

THE BRIGHTEST GEM OF THE PRAIRIE
SOON TO APPEAR AT THE GILDED CAGE
WITH HER JEWELS
PEARL AND RUBY

He thoughtfully allowed Agatha time to read it before tipping his hat and grinning slowly. "Evenin', Miz Downin'."

Oh, he had gall. Standing there smirking and drawling. She'd like to knock that sign out from under him and send him sprawling!

"Y'all expectin' a pretty good turnout, are ya?"

"Most certainly."

"Not as good as mine, I'll wager."

"Have you no decency? It's the Lord's day!"

"None whatsoever, ma'am. Got t' have the welcome mat out when that first herd hits town. Could be any minute now, for all we know."

She lifted one eyebrow toward the sign. "Jubilee, Pearl, and Ruby? Polished gems, I'm sure." She could see them already—lice-carrying, diseased whores with singed hair and fake moles.

"Genuine, all three."

She snorted softly.

He puffed on his cigar.

At that moment a tall lanky mulatto with deepset eyes and kinky black hair rolled the piano near the door. He was so thin he looked as if a gust of wind would blow him over. "Time to make some music, Ivory?"

"Yessuh."

"Ivory, I don't believe you've met Miz Downin', our next-door neighbor. Miz Downin', my piano man, Ivory Culhane."

"Miz Downin'." He removed a black bowler, centering it on his chest as he bowed. Replacing the hat at a rakish angle, he inquired, "What can I play for ya, ma'am?"

How dare these two act as if this was nothing more than an afternoon ice-cream social! Agatha had no wish whatever to exchange pleasantries with the pimp saloon owner, nor with the man whose infernal plunking kept her awake night after night. She gave the latter a sour look and replied tartly, "How about 'A Mighty Fortress Is Our God'?"

His teeth flashed white in a tea-brown face as he smiled widely. "'Fraid I don't know that one. But how 'bout this?" With one fluid motion Ivory seated himself on a clawfooted stool, revolved it to face the keys, and struck up the opening chords of "Little Brown Jug," a song recently composed by the "wets" to rile the "drys." Agatha drew herself up and swung away.

When the ladies began arriving the two were still there, Ivory's songs filling the street with his musical invitation, Gandy with his nonchalance and grin intact, excreting Southern charm like so much musk from a muskrat. He greeted each lady who came along.

"Evenin', ma'am," he said time after time, touching his hat brim. "Y'all enjoy your meetin', now." His grin was especially dashing for Violet and the delegation from Mrs. Gill's boardinghouse. "Evenin', Miz Parsons. Nice t' see y'all again, and your friends, too. Evenin', ladies."

Violet tittered, blushed, and led the way next door. She was followed by Evelyn Sowers, Susan White, Bessie Hottle, and Florence Loretto, all of whom had a personal stake in the goings-on at the Gilded Cage Saloon. There were others, too. Annie MacIntosh, sporting a bruise on her left cheek. Minnie Butler, whose husband had a yen for the gaming tables. Jennie Yoast, whose husband made the rounds of all the saloons every Saturday night and sometimes was found sleeping on the boardwalk on Sunday mornings. Anna Brewster, Addie Anderson, Carolyn Hawes, and many others whose men were known to have exceedingly limber elbows.

Attending the meeting were thirty-six women, most of them eager to stamp out the evils of the ardent spirits; a few were merely curious about what "those fanatics" did when they got together.

Drusilla Wilson personally greeted each arrival at the door with her hostess at her side. The meeting began with a prayer, followed by Miss Wilson's opening statement.

"There are four thousand rum holes spreading death and disease through all ranks of American society, vile dens that respectable people abhor from a distance. Your own fair city has become blemished by eleven such chancres. Many of your husbands are wooed away from home night after night, robbing your families of their protectors and providers. The human wreckage caused by alcohol can come only to tragic ends—in hospitals, where victims die of delirium tremens, or in reformatories such as Ward Island, or even asylums such as that on Blackwell Island. I've visited these institutions myself. I've seen the creeping death that preys upon those who've begun with a single innocent drink, then another and another, until the victim is abysmally lost. And who is left to suffer the effects of intemperance? The women and children—that's who! From half a million American women a wail of anguish is sounded over an otherwise happy land. Over the graves of forty thousand drunkards goes up the mourning cry of widow and orphan. The chief evils of spirits have fallen on women. It is eminently fitting that women should inaugurate the work for its destruction!"

As Wilson spoke, the faces in the audience grew rapt. She was earnest, spellbinding. Even those who'd come only out of curiosity were becoming mesmerized.

"And the saloons themselves are breeding places for the vermin of this earth—gamblers, confidence men, and *nymphs du prairie*. Let us not forget that Wichita, at its most decadent, sported houses of ill repute with no less than three hundred painted cats! Three hundred in a single city! But we cleaned up Wichita, and we'll clean up Proffitt! Together!"

When her speech ended, the crowd voiced a single question: How?

The answer was concise: by educating, and advocating prayer and willpower. "The W.C.T.U. is not militant. What we achieve, we shall achieve by peaceful means. Yet, let us not shirk our duty when it comes to making that destroyer of men's souls—the barkeeper—aware of his guilt. We shall not destroy the vile compound he sells. Instead, we will give his clientele something more powerful to lean on— faith in his God, his family, and hope for his future."

Miss Wilson knew when to evangelize and when to cease. She had them aroused now. To bag them for the cause, all she needed were three or four gut-wrenching stories from their own lips.

"You've all been at home growing impatient for this day. Now is the time. Bare your hearts to your sisters who understand. They've suffered what you've suffered. Who would like to rid themselves of their grief first?"

The women exchanged furtive glances, but none came forward.

Wilson pressed on. "Remember, we, your sisters, are not here to judge, but to support."

Through the saloon wall came the cry of "Keno!" And from the piano, "Over the Waves." Thirty-six self-conscious women all waited for someone else to start.

Agatha's teeth and hands clenched. Her own agonizing memories came back from her past. She considered telling her story at last, but she had held it inside for so long she was unable to bring it forth. Already an object of a certain amount of pity, she had no desire to be pitied further, so she held her silence.

The first to speak was Florence Loretto. "My son . . ." she began. Every eye settled on her. All was silent. "My son, Dan. He was always a good boy when he was young. But when my husband was alive, he used to send the boy down to the saloon to fetch his whiskey. Claimed he had a touch of the rheumatism and hot toddies took the pain out of his joints. That's how it started. But by the time he died, he was liquored up more than he was sober. He was a grown man, but Dan . . . Dan was young, and he'd found out he liked the atmosphere at the saloon. Now he's dealing cards right next door, and I ... I ..." Florence covered her face with one hand. "I'm so ashamed, I can't face my friends."

Addie Anderson rubbed Florence's shoulder and offered, quietly, "It's all right, Florence. We all understand. You did what you thought best when you were bringing him up." She faced Miss Wilson as she went on forthrightly. "My husband, Floyd, he used to be sober as a judge, except for maybe when somebody got married or on the Fourth of July. But he got sickly a couple years back and had to take on somebody to look after the shop while he was down. Jenks, his name was, fine-lookin' young man from St. Louis, with letters to recommend him. But they was all phony. Jenks got his fingers in the books and rigged 'em so's he could swindle us without Floyd ever knowin' what he was up to. By the time Floyd discovered it, it was too late. Jenks was gone, and so was the nice nest egg we'd saved up. That's when Floyd started takin' to drink. I try to tell him, 'Floyd,' I says, 'what good does it do to spend what little money we got gettin' drunk every night?' But he don't listen to nothin' I say. We lost the store and Floyd went to clerk for Halorhan, but it's a big come-down to him, clerkin', after he was his own boss all those years. The money Halorhan pays him goes nearly all for whiskey, and we're behind six months on our account at the store. Halorhan's been good, but lately he's been warnin' Floyd, if he don't pay some on what we been chargin', he's gonna have to let him go. Then ..." Suddenly Addie broke into tears. "Ohh ..." she wailed.

It made Florence Loretto's plight seem less drastic, and she, in turn, comforted Addie.

After that the women opened up, one by one. Their plights were all similar, though some stories were more pitiful than others. Agatha waited for Annie MacIntosh to admit where she got the bruise on her cheek. But Annie, like Agatha, remained silent.

When a lull fell, Drusilla Wilson took the meeting in hand once again. "Sisters, you have our love and support. But to be effective, we must organize. And organization means becoming a recognized local of the national Women's Christian Temperance Union. To do so you must elect officers. I'll work together with them to draft a constitution. Once that is accomplished, committees will be formed to draw up temperance pledges." She displayed several varieties, all of which could be pinned on a reformed man's sleeve. "One of your first goals will be to get as many pledge signatures as possible, and also to solicit new members for your local."

Within a quarter hour, Agatha found herself—over her own protests—voted the first president of the Women's Christian Temperance Union of Proffitt, Kansas. Florence Loretto became vice-president, over her own protests. Annie MacIntosh surprised everyone by speaking for the first time that evening, volunteering to be secretary. Agatha nominated Violet for treasurer, observing that it would be easy for the two of them to work together, since they saw each other every day anyway. Violet also objected, to no avail.

Dues were set at twenty-five cents—the price of one shot of whiskey—per week. A pledge committee of four was formed for the purpose of hand-lettering pledges until some could be professionally printed. A committee of three was delegated to query Joseph Zeller, editor of the *Proffitt Gazette,* on the cost of printing pamphlets and advertisements and pledges. A rally was scheduled for the following night for the purpose of soliciting signatures on temperance pledges, starting in the closest saloon.

The meeting closed with Miss Wilson teaching the ladies their first temperance song:

> Cold water is king
> Cold water is lord
> And a thousand bright faces
> Now smile at his board.

They sang it several times, in rousing harmony, until their voices drowned out the sound of "Camptown Races" coming from the other side of the wall.

As the meeting closed, everyone agreed it had been an exhilarating evening. As Drusilla Wilson left, she assured Agatha that help and directives would come from the national organization as well as through *The Temperance Banner*. And Miss Wilson herself would remain in town until the organizational wrinkles had been ironed out.

Agatha closed the door behind the last woman, leaned back against it, and sighed. What had she gotten into? More than she'd bargained for, most certainly. Not only organizer, but president. Why ever had she agreed to hold the meeting here in the first place?

With another sigh she pushed away from the door and turned out the lanterns. In the darkness she left the work-room by the back door. The rear of the building gave on to a path leading to a storage shed and the smaller building she genteelly referred to as "the necessary." After visiting it, she made her way upstairs, head down, as usual, watching her feet. She was two steps from the top when a voice brought her head snapping up.

"So how did the meetin' go?"

She couldn't see him, only the glow of his cigar in the dark on his half of the landing.

"What are you doing here?"

"Inquirin' about the meetin', Miz Downin'. No need t' jump so."

"I did not jump!" But she had. How awkward to think he'd been sitting up here watching her walk out to "the nec-essary" and back, equally awkward to realize he'd observed her struggling up the stairs in her shuffling, one-two fash-ion.

"Pretty good turnout y' had there."

"Thirty-four. Thirty-six, counting Miss Wilson and myself."

"Ahh, commendable."

"And I've been elected president." It was the first time she'd taken any joy in the fact.

"President. Well, well . . ."

Her pupils had dilated enough to see that he was sitting on a chair tipped back against the wall with his boots crossed on the railing. The acrid scent of his cigar smoke reached her as the tip glowed orange once more.

"We had such a rousing meeting that none of us even minded the sound of Mr. Culhane's piano coming through the wall. As a matter of fact, we sang so loud, we drowned it out."

"Sounds inspirin'."

She could hear the grin in his voice.

"I dare say it was."

"And what did y' all sing?"

"You'll know, soon enough. We'll come in and do it for your patrons. How would that be?"

He laughed, the cigar still clamped in his teeth.

"T' tell the truth, we won't be needin' you. Jubilee and the girls'll be here any day, and we'll have all the singin' we'll need."

"Ohhh, yes. Jubilee and the girls—from the billboard? My, they sound wonderful," she intoned sarcastically.

"They are. You'll have t' come over and take in a show."

His cigar smoke irritated her. She coughed and struggled up the last two steps.

"How can you smoke those disgusting things?"

"Habit I learned on the riverboats. Kept my hands filled when I wasn't playin' cards."

"So you *were* thrown off the riverboats!"

He laughed and his chair clunked down on all fours. "The ladies o' your club been speculatin' 'bout me, have they?" He rose and his boot heels resounded with calculated laziness across the narrow landing until he stood before her at the top of the stairs.

"Hardly. We have bigger fish to fry."

"Supposin' I was, though. Supposin' I was a big, bad gambler who knew every trick in the book. Man like that'd know how t' handle a few old squawkin' hens who set out t' shut down his saloon, don't ya think?"

Fear quickened her blood. He stood ominously close, backing her up to the stairs. She had a dizzying sense of déjà vu, certain that in an instant she'd go tumbling down as she had long ago. Her muscles tensed as she anticipated the sharp blows, the scraped skin, the sickening disorientation of somersaulting from tread to tread. With one trembling hand she grasped the railing, knowing it would do little good should he decide to give her a shove. His eyes became red sparks as he drew on the cigar once more. The smell grew sickening, and her palms began to sweat.

"Please," she choked in a whisper, "don't."

Immediately, he stepped back and took the cigar from his mouth. "Now wait a minute, Miz Downin', you do me an injustice if you think I was entertainin' thoughts of pushin' you down those stairs. Why, I . . ."

"You pushed me down once before."

"In the mud? I told you, *that* was an accident!"

"So would this be, I'm sure. Anybody who's seen me climb stairs knows I'm not too steady on them. But if you think threats will stop me, you're dead wrong, Mr. Gandy. They only serve to refresh my zeal. Now, if you will kindly let me pass, sir, I'll say good-night."

She sensed his reluctance to let her go thinking ill of him. Yet his belligerence radiated palpably. They stood nose to chest for ten crackling seconds. Then he stepped back. The sound of her solid step followed by the dragging one alternated across the landing. All the way to her door she kept expecting to be lifted by the scruff of her neck and thrown bodily down the stairs. When it didn't happen she was surprised. She reached her door, slithered inside, closed and locked it. The shakes started immediately. She pressed her palms and forehead against the cool wood, wondering what she'd gotten into by allowing herself to be buffaloed into the presidency of an organization setting out to close down not only Scott Gandy, but ten others like him.

Jubilee and her Gems arrived the following morning on the eleven-oh-five train. Three women with their looks couldn't step off a coach without causing a stir.

The one known as Pearl appeared to have been named for her skin. It was as pale and luminous as a perfect ocean pearl. Against it, her brown eyes appeared to take up a good quarter of her face. They were darkened with kohl, adding to their size. Her lips were tinted scarlet and flashed like a wine spill on white linen. But her delicate features were shown off to best advantage by the stand-up collar of her fuchsia traveling costume, which bared a goodly amount of her throat and fit like a banana skin. Her hair was the glossy brown of caramelized sugar, piled into a nosegay of curls high on her head, pitching her shepherdess hat provocatively forward.

"Hiya, fellas!" she called from the train steps, and old Wilton Spivey set sparks off the trackside ballast churning to reach her first. He dropped the tongue of the baggage dray and leaped over two tracks, beat out Joe Jessup, who'd started from the opposite direction, and reached the foot of the train steps, panting. Wilton was toothless as a frog and balder than a brass doorknob, but Pearl didn't care. She smiled down, cocked one wrist, and extended a hand.

"Just what I was needin'. A big handsome man with lots of muscles. My name's Pearl. What's yours?"

"Wiwton Thpivey, at your thervith, ma'am." Wilt didn't talk so good with those bare gums, but his eyes sparkled with lecherous delight.

"Well, Wiwton, come on, honey. Don't be shy."

Wilton lifted her down, revealing Ruby, behind her.

Ruby was a shapely young Negress with skin the color of creamed coffee. Her hair was straighter than any black woman's hair Wilton Spivey had ever seen. It swept back from her left ear, straight up from her right, sleek as fast water on a black rock, ending in a curl like an inverted ocean breaker looping the edge of her high canary-yellow hat. She had magnificent upsweeping eyebrows, heavy-lidded black eyes, and lips as puffy as a pair of bee stings, painted a violent magenta. She rested eight knuckles on her cocked hips, gave a little jiggle that shimmied her tight yellow dress, and announced in a deep, rich contralto, "And I'm Ruby."

Joe Jessup gulped and uttered, "Holy smokes, if you ain't!"

When Ruby laughed it sounded like thunder building on a mountainside—deep, chesty, voluptuous.

"What I s'posed t' call you, honey?"

"J . . . Joe J . . . Jessup."

"Well, J . . . Joe J . . . Jessup." Ruby sidled down one step, leaned over till her breasts hovered only inches before his face. With one unearthly long nail she left a pale white

line all the way from Joe's ear to the center of his chin.
"How 'bout I call you J.J.?"

"F . . . fine. R . . . ride to wherever you're goin', Miss
Ruby?"

" 'Preciate it, J.J. That'd be the Gilded Cage Saloon.
Y'all know where that is?"

"Sure do. Right th . . . this way."

By this time there were four others in queue, waiting
their turns at the foot of the train steps.

Above them, like an angel straight from the pearly gates,
appeared Miss Jubilee Bright—as promised, the brightest
gem of the prairie. If the others seemed suited to their
names, Miss Jubilee seemed born to hers. She was—incredibly—white all over! Her hair was white, not the blue-
white of Violet Parsons's, but the blinding white of spun
glass. It frothed high upon her head like a tempting ten-egg
meringue. She was dressed, too, in unadulterated white,
from the tip of her tall velvet hat with its trimming of
egret feathers to the toes of her ankle-high kid boots. Her
dress, like that of Pearl's and Ruby's, sported no bustle
out back, but clung to her generous curves from shoulder
to knee before flaring into walking pleats. It sported a
diamond-shaped neckline revealing a tempting glimpse of
cleavage, with a fake black mole placed low enough to draw
any man's eyes in its direction. Another mole dotted the left
cheek of a face lovely enough to need no beauty marks.
The startling almond eyes, the pouting lips, the pretty little
nose could hold their own in any company. It truly was an
angel's face.

She raised both arms and called, "Just call me Jube,
boys!" And she leaned out with her arms still extended,
allowing two cavaliers to grasp them and lower her to the
ground. When she got there she left her arms around their
shoulders, rubbing their muscles approvingly.

"My, my, I do love my men strong . . . and polite," she
purred in a naturally kittenish voice. "I can tell we're goin'
to get along ju-u-ust fine." Simultaneously, she gave them
each a clap. "So, who'm I hangin' on to here?"

"Mort Pokenny," answered the man on her left.

"Virgil Murray," answered the man on her right.

"Well, Mort, Virgil, I want you to meet our friend, Marcus Delahunt. Marcus plays the banjo for us. Meanest picker this side of N'awleans."

The last man off the train carried a banjo case and wore a straw panama with a wide black band. His boyish face wore a happy smile revealing one crooked tooth, which only added to his appeal. His blue eyes were set wide in a fair face framed by collie-blond hair. Not a particularly manly face, with its pink complexion and sparse blond whiskers, but one forgot that when viewing his open expression of apparent pleasure with the world. Standing with one long-fingered hand on the rail, the other gripping the banjo case, he smiled and nodded silently.

"Marcus here can't say a word, but he can hear better than a sleeping dog, and he's smarter than the rest of us all put together, so don't ever let me catch you treating him like a dummy."

The men offered hellos, but immediately returned their interest to the women. "So what do you boys do for excitement around here?" asked Ruby.

"Not much, ma'am. Been a little dull lately."

She laughed throatily. "Well, we're gonna fix that, aren't we, girls?"

Jubilee scanned the train platform and inquired of Mort and Virgil, "You seen that rascal Gandy around these parts?"

"Yes, ma'am, he's—"

"Enough of that ma'aming now, Virgil. Just call me Jubilee."

"Yes, ma'am, Miss Jubilee. Scotty, he's over't the Gilded Cage."

She flapped one hand, affected a winning pout. "Isn't that the way with a man—never there when you need him! Well, we're going to need some strong arms. Got a little something that needs hauling over to Gandy's saloon. You boys willing to give us a hand with it?"

Six males tripped all over themselves, shouldering forward.

"Where's that wagon of yours, Mr. Jessup?"

"Comin' right up!"

Jubilee gave a "come on" with one shoulder and led the troop toward the freight cars at the rear of the train. Already the doors were being rolled back. The freight master stood beside one, looking in, scratching his head.

"Durnedest thing I ever seen," he remarked. "What in tarnation they gonna do with a hunk of junk like that?"

"Yoo-hoo!" Jubilee called, waving.

The freight master glanced up and saw the crowd advancing.

"Did it make it all right?"

"It did," he called back. "But what in tarnation you gonna do with it?"

Jubilee, Pearl, Ruby, and all their eager escorts reached the open freight car. Jessup arrived with his wagon. Jube rested her hands on her hips and winked at the aging freight master. "Come on over to the Gilded Cage some night and find out, honey!" She turned to the others. "Gentlemen, let's load this thing and get it over to Gandy's!"

Violet was minding the front of the store several minutes later when she looked out the window and shrieked. "Agatha! Agatha, come here!"

Agatha lifted her head and called, "What is it, Violet?"

"Come here!"

Even before reaching the front room, Agatha heard banjo music from outside. It was a warm spring day; the shop door was propped open with a brick. "Look!" Violet gaped and pointed to the street beyond. Agatha came up quietly into the shadows behind her.

Another delivery for the saloon next door. One glimpse told Agatha she should order Violet to close the door, but there was too much that appealed to her in the scene outside.

Joe Jessup's buckboard came up the street piled with a crowd of exuberant men, three gaudy ladies, and the most enormous birdcage Agatha had ever seen. Six feet high it stood, made of bright, shining gold that caught the noon sun and sent it shimmering. Suspended from its onion-shaped roof was a golden swing, and upon it perched a fancy lady dressed in pure white. Another, wearing heliotrope pink, sat on the tail of the wagon between Wilton Spivey and Virgil Murray, the three of them swinging their legs and swaying to the music. The third woman, looking like a bumblebee in her black skin and yellow clothes, sat on Joe Jessup's lap as he drove the wagon. The banjo player stood just behind them, nodding from side to side in rhythm with the song. The wagon was packed with people crowded around the birdcage, and, like the Pied Piper of Hamelin, the wagon had attracted a trail of children and bright-eyed young fellows who'd left their desks and clerking stations to be part of the music and to ogle the women in the startling costumes. As they came down the street, the entire troupe was singing lustily.

> Buffalo gals, won't you come out tonight,
> Come out tonight, come out tonight,
> Buffalo gals, won't you come out tonight
> And dance by the light of the moon.

Agatha tried very hard to be critical. But she couldn't. She was gripped instead by envy. Oh, to be young and attractive and unfettered by self-consciousness. To be able to ride down the street on a wagon at high noon, singing one's heart out to the sky and laughing. Shouldn't there be, in everyone's life, at least one such reckless memory? But there was none in Agatha's.

This was as close as she'd ever come: tapping her hand against her thigh in rhythm with the music. When she realized what she was doing, she stopped.

As the wagon drew abreast of her store, she got a closer look at the woman in white. She was the prettiest thing Agatha had ever seen. Delicate face with slanting eyes and cupid's own smile. And she knew how to choose a good hat. She wore one of fashion's current entries in the war between the high- and flat-crowned hats, the kind called "three stories and a basement." It was exquisite: towering, but well balanced, and trimmed with expensive egret feathers. Even when the woman swang on her perch, the hat sat securely.

"Look at that white hat," she whispered.

"Look at all of them," replied Violet.

"Good hats."

"The best."

"Their dresses, too."

"But look—no bustles, Agatha."

"No." Agatha envied them for not having to hang fifteen pounds of metal on their rumps every morning.

"But so much chest. *Tt-tt.*"

"They're fancy ladies, I'm sure." The thought saddened Agatha. All that bright promise would grow to nothing. All their young beauty would grow faded before its time.

The wagon came to a stop before the saloon. Mort Pokenny opened the cage door and the woman in white stepped out. She stood with hands akimbo and shouted at the swinging doors. "Hey, Gandy, didn't you send for three dancing girls from Natchez?"

Gandy himself materialized, surrounded by his employees, all calling out greetings, reaching for the ladies, shaking hands over the side of the wagon with the banjo player. But Agatha watched only the woman in white, high on the wagon, and the man in black, below her. He hooked one boot on a wheel spoke and tilted his hat to the back of his head. In the middle of the melee they had eyes only for each other.

" 'Bout time you were gettin' here, Jube."

"Got here as fast as I could. Took 'em a month to build the damned cage, though."

"That all it's been?" His dimples formed as he grinned.

"You wouldn't't've missed old Jube, now, would y'?"

Gandy threw back his head and laughed.

"Never. Been too busy gettin' the place set up."

Jubilee scanned the boardwalk. "Where's that town full o' cowboys you promised I could pick from?"

"They're comin', Jube, they're comin'."

Her gaze returned to Gandy and her eyes glittered with teasing and impatience. "You gonna stand there flappin' all day, or help a lady dismount?" Without warning she launched herself over the side, flying through the air with feet and arms up, never doubting for a moment that a pair of strong arms would be there to catch her. They were. No sooner had Gandy caught her than they were kissing boldly, mindless of the hoots and whistles around them. She twined her arms around his shoulders and returned his kiss with total unconcern for the spectacle they were making. The kiss ended when his hat started slipping off. She snatched it off his head and they laughed into each other's faces. She plopped the hat on his thick black hair and tilted it well forward.

"Now put me down, you rebel dandy. I got others to greet, you know."

Looking on, Agatha felt a curious flutter within her stomach as Gandy's black eyes lingered on the woman's beautiful kohled ones and he held her a moment longer. Watching them, one could almost guess what fun they had alone together. Pleasant mischief radiated between them. Even their vocal exchange had been filled with it. How did women learn to act that way around men? In her whole life Agatha had never been in the same room with a man without feeling ill at ease. Nor had she carried on a conversation with one without groping for a topic. And, of course, to leap off the side of a wagon would be, for her, nothing short of a miracle.

Gandy set Jubilee down and greeted the others.

"Ruby, sweetheart, y' knock my eyes out." He gave her a kiss on the cheek. "And Pearl, you're bound t' break a few hearts in Proffitt, Kansas, before the season's over." She, too, got a kiss on the cheek. Next he clamped both hands on the banjo player's shoulders and looked him square in the face. "Hello, Marcus. Good t' see you again." The man smiled. He made a strumming motion across his banjo and raised his eyebrows. "That's right," Gandy answered, "good for business. Y'all got the town stirred up already. They'll be mashin' the door down tonight."

Gandy turned back toward Jubilee, shrugging out of his jacket. "Here. Hang on to this for a minute." He gave her a wink and Agatha watched the woman clasp the jacket to her breast and bury her nose in its collar. It seemed so intimate a motion that Agatha felt guilty witnessing it. She wondered how any woman could look so entranced by the smell of cigar smoke.

"Let's get it inside, boys." Gandy leaped onto the wagon and with five others hefted the cage. She watched his black satin waistcoat pull taut across his shoulder blades, his fore-arms knot as he lifted the contraption. He wasn't overly brawny, yet neither was he flimsy. But he had muscles in all the places a man was supposed to; enough to deal with an impulsive woman who came flying through the air into his arms, or a nettlesome one who organized a local temperance union. She recalled last night at the top of the stairs—had he thought about pushing her or not? Now in broad daylight, watching him work in the sun, he hardly seemed capable of malevolence. Perhaps it had been her imagination after all.

The work gang inched the heavy cage off the wagon, up the boardwalk steps, and inside the saloon. The ladies and the loiterers followed, leaving the street to the children. Violet and Agatha retreated into the shop but could still hear the sound of happy chatter and occasional laughter.

"So that was Jubilee and the Gems."

"Such lovely names . . . Jubilee. Ruby. Pearl."

Agatha thought all three names sounded concocted, but she reserved her opinion. "So, he's brought in calico queens after all."

"We don't know that for sure."

"Violet, they were wearing kohl on their eyes, and car-mine on their lips, and their chests were showing."

"Yes," Violet uttered disappointedly, "I suppose you're right." Suddenly, she brightened. "But, oh, my!" She sighed, a rapt expression on her face. "Wasn't that something the way Mr. Gandy kissed the one named Jubilee?"

"Doesn't it seem a bit shameless to you, right out there on the street?"

"Well, perhaps a bit. But I'm still jealous."

Agatha laughed and experienced a shaft of appreciation for Violet. The woman was so forthright. And earthy in her own way. How was it she'd never found a young swain to kiss her in the middle of a street in springtime? "Come." Agatha held out an arm in invitation. "Let's get to work. That'll take our minds off it."

But within five minutes the sound of hammering and sawing became so distracting they found themselves gazing time and again at the wall.

"Now what do you suppose they're doing that's making all that racket?"

"I don't know." Violet's eyes sparkled. "Would you like me to go take a peek?"

"Certainly not!"

"But aren't you curious?"

"Maybe I am, but you know what curiosity got the cat."

Violet drooped in resignation. "Honestly, Agatha, sometimes you're no fun at all."

Their thimbles pushed in unison.

Push, pull. Push, pull.

It was as bad as the clock at bedtime, Agatha thought.

Push, pull. Two old maids, stitching their lives away. No! One old maid and one not-so-old maid!

The sound of footsteps in the front room interrupted her musings.

"Hullo?" It was Gandy again.

Violet dropped her thimble, pressed a hand to her heart, and went pink as a baby shoat. "Oh, my sakes!" she whispered.

"Go see what he wants this time."

But before Violet could move, Gandy stepped through the lavender curtains, hatless, jacketless, and slightly breathless, with his sleeves rolled up to the elbows. He stood before them with feet widespread, his hands on his waist. "Got a rush job for you, Miz Downin'."

Agatha raised one eyebrow and let her gaze drop from his black tumbled hair to the toes of his polished boots.

"Something in a rose bengaline, perhaps? Should go well with your dark hair."

He laughed and ran eight fingers through his hair, leaving it standing in attractive rills. "We'll save that for Jube. What I need is much simpler. A big drawstring sack— doesn't matter what color or what material. Somethin' big enough to cover up a six-foot birdcage. But I need it by tonight."

Agatha lay aside her work with strained patience. "I'm a milliner, Mr. Gandy, not a dressmaker."

"But you have all those bolts o' cloth out there." He thumbed toward the front. "They're for sale, aren't they?"

"Not for birdcage covers."

"Why not?"

"And not to saloon owners."

"My money's good. And I pay well."

"I'm sorry, Mr. Gandy. Try Mr. Halorhan. He handles yard goods."

"The cloth won't do me any good without someone t' sew it."

"Even if I were willing, it could never be done by evening."

"Why not? It's a simple enough job."

"It would be if I had a sewing machine, but, as you see, I don't."

She glanced to the advertisement for a Singer hanging on the wall. His eyes followed.

"How many hands would it take to have it done in . . ."— he withdrew a gold stem-winder from his vest pocket— "five hours?"

"I told you, I don't do work for saloon owners."

He put the watch away and frowned at her. "You're one stubborn wench, Miz Downin'."

Wench? The word brought a swift flag of color to her cheeks and she supposed she, too, now looked like a shoat. Never in her life had she been called a wench. It was disconcerting to find that it made her feel giddy. But she quickly picked up her work again. He studied her for a full ten seconds, scowled a while, then pivoted and shouldered through the velvet curtains, leaving them swaying.

Agatha and Violet gaped at the doorway, then at each other.

"*Tt-tt.*"

"Violet, you must stop tittering every time you see that man. And you're blushing, for heaven's sake."

"So are you."

"I am not!"

"You are, too! Why, Agatha, he called you a wench! *Tt-tt.*"

"I've never been so humiliated. The man has no manners at all."

"I think he's adorable."

Agatha sniffed. But inside, she was beginning to agree with Violet.

Violet fanned her warm face. "My, my, my." She studied the curtains that had brushed his shapely shoulders. "A cover for that birdcage?"

"Saloon people are crazy. Don't try to figure them out."

"But why would he want such a thing?"

"I'm sure I have no idea."

They hadn't time for speculation before they were surprised by the reappearance of Gandy, this time bursting in through the back door, towing Miss Jubilee by a wrist. She was followed by Ruby and Pearl.

Again both milliners blushed highly. And Agatha became so incensed, she got to her feet. How dare he bring those painted women in here!

"Girls, I want y'all t' meet Miz Downin' and Miz Parsons, our closest neighbors. Ladies, these three delightful creatures are Jubilee, Pearl, and Ruby, the gems of the prairie."

Jubilee dipped her knees. "Charmed."

"Pleased to meetcha," said Pearl.

"Miz Downin', Miz Parsons," Ruby greeted.

Agatha and Violet stared. Gandy stalked out to the showroom and returned immediately with a bolt of red satin. He flopped it onto the worktable and clinked down a stack of gold coins beside it.

"Ten of 'em. Count 'em. They're yours if you can have a drawstring cover made for that birdcage by seven o'clock tonight. Jube, Pearl, and Ruby'll help you stitch it."

"Aw, Scotty, come on . . ."

"Now, Jube, honey, you're a female, aren't you? All females know how t' sew."

"Not this one!"

Agatha's gaze flashed between the two brightest things in the room: Miss Jubilee and the stack of gold coins. One hundred dollars. Her mouth watered. Her eyes flickered to the drawing of Mr. Singer's masterpiece with the price printed in bold numbers beside the flywheel. Forty-nine dollars. When would she ever again see enough money to cover the price of the only thing in the world she coveted?

Her lips opened but no sound came out. What would Miss Wilson say? What would her fellow union members say? The president of the local W.C.T.U. sewing accoutrements for the Gilded Cage Saloon. But, oh, all that money!

Pearl was complaining. "I never sewed anything in my life!"

"I did. And plenty," put in Ruby. "Nothin' to it."

"But, Ruby—"

"Quit your frettin', Pearl. If the boss say stitch, we stitch."

"I'm with Pearl," Jubilee said. "I'm no seamstress."

Agatha found her voice at last. "Neither am I. I'm a milliner. And at seven o'clock tonight I will be in the Gilded Cage soliciting signatures on temperance pledges from the customers at the bar. What would my coworkers think if they knew I'd made the red cover for your birdcage?"

"Nobody has t' know," Gandy interjected, stepping closer to Agatha. "That's why I brought the girls in the back door, so nobody'd see them." He stood so near she smelled tobacco smoke on his clothing again. She dropped her gaze to the floor. Her chin snapped up again when he lightly grasped her upper arms.

"Please, Miz Downin'?"

How disconcerting to be taken so by a man. "It would be a conflict of interests, don't you see?"

"Then perhaps a little added incentive . . ." He turned and she thought he was going to add another coin to the stack. Instead, he took one away and slipped it into his waistcoat pocket.

"We've wasted five minutes already. In another minute the price goes down ten dollars. The sooner you say yes, the better."

"But you . . . I . . ." Agatha clasped her hands and glanced helplessly from Gandy to his ladies to the stack of coins.

"Agatha," Violet warned, "don't be foolish."

"Violet, shush!" She would not be coerced this way, especially by a woman without enough sense to see they were being bribed.

"Your money undoubtedly came from the poor unfortunate souls of this town who frequent your estab—"

"Eighty," he interrupted calmly, removing another coin and dropping it in his pocket.

"Mr. Gandy, you're despicable."

He glanced in a circle. "Don't see an overabundance o' customers in here today."

He directed his next question to Violet. "How's business been lately, Miz Parsons?"

"Not too—"

"Violet, I'll thank you to take a lock!"

"Well, he can see it's true, Agatha. All he has to do is look around. And weren't you just saying the other day—"

"Violet!"

Violet ignored her boss and leaned confidentially close to Gandy. "Things aren't going so well in the hat business. Seems with all this talk about women's suffrage the hat is becoming the symbol of emancipation. Tsk, tsk." She shook her head sadly. "Some women are actually giving up wearing them altogether. It's bound to get worse, too, now that we've started our own temperance union."

Gandy's dimples appeared. He stretched out a hand and plucked up another coin. Then he grinned askance at Agatha.

"Seventy."

Agatha's throat went dry. She stared at the remaining coins, wishing she could gag Violet.

"I haven't the foggiest notion of what it is you want in the first place," she said, less forcefully. "All I know is hats."

"Something t' cover the birdcage. Use your imagination. Tied at the top, loose at the bottom, split up the side so the door can open. Jube can show you."

"I sure can, Miss Downing."

Agatha looked into the stunningly beautiful slanted eyes of Miss Jubilee and recalled her sitting perched like a snow-white dove on the swing as the wagon rolled down the street.

"Sixty," Gandy said in the softest tone yet.

Agatha's head snapped around. Her glance dropped to the dwindling stack of coins, then lifted to the picture of the sewing machine. Greed buoyed her heart. Despair weighted it. Two more coins and the sewing machine would be beyond her means. Gandy's hand moved again.

"Stop!" she called.

He hung the hand by one thumb from his waist and waited.

She dropped her head guiltily. "I'll do it," she agreed quietly.

"Good. Jube, Pearl, Ruby, y'all do whatever she says. Just be ready t' greet the customers at seven o'clock sharp." His hand moved to the coins again. *King-k-k-king!* The four rescinded gold pieces joined the others. "A deal's a deal," he said, then stepped close to Agatha, extending his hand. "By seven, then, Miz Downin'?"

She stared at his hand. Long, dark fingers peppered with wispy black hair. Clean nails. Thin wrist. The conspicuous diamond glittering from his little finger. She removed her thimble and placed her palm in his very warm one. He squeezed firmly and shook hands with the solidity he'd afford any man. Somehow, she felt flattered. Against her will, she looked up. His dimples were deep. His eyes were unduly attractive. He had disarmingly perfect lips. Why did it seem that only the scoundrels were so blessed?

"By seven," she agreed.

But it felt as if she'd made a pact with the devil.

CHAPTER
4

Agatha sent Pearl over to measure the height and circumference of the cage. Then the five women set about making the cover. It was a simple enough design, like a flat window curtain with a drawstring at the top. She lit a fire in the stove and warmed the irons to press a one-inch hem around the perimeter. She handled the irons herself, while Violet and Ruby worked just ahead of her, marking the width with chalk, and Pearl kept the silk flowing wrinkle-free from the pressing board. Jubilee, meanwhile, took the cool irons to the stove and brought the hot ones back. Then the women sat in a rough circle and began stitching the hems into place.

It was immediately evident that Jubilee and Pearl had told the truth; they were hopeless with a needle. Ruby, on the other hand, was nimble-fingered and careful to make her stitches uniform and invisible. It wasn't long before Jubilee jabbed her finger. "Ouch!" She stuck it in her mouth and sucked. "Damn and double damn anyway! I can't sew! I'm making a regular mess of it, and now I'll get blood on the silk."

"Why don't you just sit back?" Agatha suggested. "Actually, with Ruby being as adept as she is, we'll finish with time to spare."

"Can I quit, too?" Pearl pleaded. "I'm no better at this than Jube is."

Agatha glanced at Pearl's pitiful handiwork. "You, too. If you'll just hold the satin on your lap and help guide it

64

around to keep it from wrinkling, that will be sufficient."

Three thimbles clicked against three needles and the shimmering cloth shifted slowly across their laps.

"Would you look at Ruby!" Jubilee exclaimed after some time. "Where did you learn to stitch like that, Ruby?"

"Where you think? Waverley, o' course. My mama work in the big house for Miz Gandy and she teach my mama t' do fine stitches, and my mama teach me."

"You mean the young Mrs. Gandy or the old Mrs. Gandy?"

"Old one. Young one too flighty for stitchin'." The black woman gave the white one a meaningful grin. "She jus' like you, Jube."

The three laughed good-naturedly.

Violet missed a stitch at the mention of the young Mrs. Gandy. "Waverley?" she probed.

"Waverley Plantation, down in Columbus, Miz'sippi, where Mr. Gandy grew up."

"You mean our landlord grew up on a plantation?" Violet's romantic visions became evident in her eyes.

Ruby's husky voice reminisced. "Prettiest one you ever seen. Big white columns out front and back, big wide verandas. And cotton fields all around, reachin' farther than a fox can run on a cool mornin'. And the Tombigbee River shuggin' through the middle of 'em. It a glory sight, that place."

Agatha's interest had been aroused, but she let Violet ask the questions.

"You mean he owned it?"

"His daddy did. That was the old Mr. Gandy. He dead now and so's his missus. But they was as fine a white folks as you'll find. My mama and daddy was slaves for old Mr. Gandy. Me, too, before the war come. Me and Ivory and the boss, we all born on Waverley. Runned barefoot together and shucked pecans and swum in the river in our nothin'-ons. Whoo-ee, that was a time! 'Course, that was before the war."

Agatha tried to picture Gandy as a young boy running barefoot with a pair of black children but the picture wouldn't gel. She saw him instead with a cigar in his mouth and a glass of whiskey in his hand.

Violet was so curious she sat on the edge of her chair. "What happened to Waverley?" she prompted.

"Still there. War missed Columbus. They fight in a big circle all around it, but not there. All the big houses still standin'."

"Waverley," Violet repeated dreamily. "What a romantic name."

"Yes, ma'am."

Try though she might, Agatha could not keep her curiosity at bay. "Who owns it?"

"He does, the boss. Only went back once since the war, though. Found too many ghosts, I reckon."

"Ghosts?" Violet's eyes rounded.

"The young Miz Gandy—she and the little girl."

Agatha's needle stilled. She looked across the red satin at Ruby. "He had a wife . . . and a daughter?"

Ruby nodded, never taking her eyes off her stitching. "Dead. Both of 'em, and after the war ended, too. But he never made it home in time t' see 'em again."

It flashed through Agatha's mind that other men had turned dissolute for far less reason. Still, it was a shame. He was young, after all.

Violet had become so engrossed in the story she had to be reminded to keep sewing. Still, she asked more questions.

"How did they die?"

Ruby's glance lifted briefly, but her fingers kept moving. "If he know, he might go back, but nobody know for sure. Found 'em on the road, halfway to town, layin' upside the wagon, and the mule standin' there between the hitches, waitin' to be drove on. Young Mr. Gandy, he gits back and they's already buried inside the black iron fence 'cross the road beside his mama and daddy."

"Oh, my, that poor man," sympathized Violet.

Ruby nodded. "Lef' to fight them Yankees an' come back to nothin' but a few niggers tryin' to scratch some collard greens outta them used-up cotton fields." She shook her head sadly. "Second time he lef' he never go back."

"And he took you with him?"

"Me?" Ruby looked up, surprised. She laughed in her

throaty contralto. "No, not me. I one uppity nigger. When they tell me I free, I go off to the city. Natchez. Figure to live fancy an' have me easy days till I see my chariot comin'." She chuckled again, ruefully. "Ended up on my back on the rivuh-boats, pleasurin' the gennulmen. No chariot comin' for me no more," she finished realistically.

To Agatha's surprise, Jubilee leaned and pressed her white cheek to Ruby's black one. "Now, Ruby, that's not true. You're a good woman. The best. Why, look what you did for me. And for Pearl, too. Right, Pearl?"

Pearl said, "You listen to Jube, Ruby."

Ruby kept stitching, her winged brows lifted as if with superior knowledge. "Wasn't me did it. It was him."

"Him?" Violet's eyes glittered with interest. "Who?"

"Young Mr. Gandy, that who." While she continued her story, Ruby stitched steadily, her eyes on her work. "Took to gamblin' on the riverboats, an' he git wind Ivory an' me workin' the *Delta Star* outta Natchez. I was doin' what I was doin', and Ivory, he was a roustabout—roosters, they called 'em. 'Hey, rooster, we got to double trip this load,' they'd call, and them poor deckhands has to unload a hunnerd tons o' cargo to lighten the load when the river she's low, then load it all again when the captain come back after leavin' off the first half upstream. They got to cut firewood an' dive under when we hit snags—don't mattuh how many snakes in that watuh! Cap'n say dive, roosters they dive. Poor Ivory, he never been whupped before, not while he work for old mastuh Gandy. And me, I nevuh know how good Waverley is till I go 'way on my own.

"So after the war is over, young boss he find Ivory workin' deckhand, bein' whupped by dat bastuhd mate, Gilroy, whenever he took a mind to whup 'im. An' me and the girls here, workin' that floatin' crib, hatin' every minute of it. Hogg, too—Gandy's bartender?—he a fire-man, workin' in that stinkin' engine room, standin' in river water to his knees. An' Marcus, playin' banjo but gittin' laughed at 'cause his tongue ain't right an' he can't mutter nuthin'. We all on board one day when the cap'n send down the order t' tie down the valve—ice jam ahead. Jack Hogg, he says, 'Can't do it, suh. She ready to blow now, suh.'

Cap'n holluh, 'Tie de son-bitch down and stroke 'er good, fireman. I got apples and lemons'll be worth half as much, that suckuh Rasmussen beat me to Omaha!'

"So Jack Hogg, he ties 'er down. Next thing you know, Jack Hogg an' most the res' o' us flyin' th'ough the air like we on our way to glory land. But we all live. Marcus, he up front plink-a-plinkin' in the gamblin' saloon, where Mistuh Gandy sit gamblin' and jus' win hisself a pot o' money, so them two all right. Me an' the girls, we strollin' the decks, lookin' for our nex' lay, so we fly straight into the water. Ivory, he lucky, too. He up by d' woodpile, gittin' set to load some down. But Jack, he down by the boiler. He scarred bad.

"Young Mr. Gandy, he take care of us all, though. 'Riverboat days endin',' he says. 'Got to git out while there's someplace else to git to.' He say he got friends— us. 'Nuff poke to start a saloon. Got Marcus to play the banjo. Ivory—shoot, Ivory ain't cut out to be no rooster nohow. Ivory, he a piano man, an' the boss know it. And Jack Hogg, he never want to be near no boiler again, but he tend bar; soon as he heal. An' Pearl an' Jube an' me— no more entuhtainin' the gennulmen, huh, girls? We young. We pretty. We gonna be dancin' girls, the boss say. And what we think 'bout that?

"We say, whatever you say, boss.

"He say only one place t' make money quick. Head o' the Chisholm Trail, where the railroads is. So we come, an' the cowboys come. An' things is better than they been since before the war. We ain't fam'ly, but we 'bout as close as can be without bein' kin blood. That why when Mr. Gandy say sew, we sew, right, girls?"

The girls agreed.

Agatha sat through Ruby's recital with growing surprise. Gandy was their benefactor? He had taken these three women *away* from a life of iniquity? "You mean, you don't . . ." Her glance took in Ruby, Pearl, and Jubilee. "You're not . . ."

Jubilee laughed. Unlike Ruby's laugh, hers was light and lilting and seemed to match her wonderful uptilted eyes. "Prostitutes? Not anymore. Like Ruby said, just dancers now. And it's a welcome change. No more whiskey tongues choking us. No more greasy hands pawing us. No more . . . oh!" Jubilee noted Agatha's dropped gaze, her florid cheeks. "I'm sorry, Miss Downing. Never learned my manners proper."

"Like Jube says," added Pearl, "it's a sight better, just dancin'. And we're good dancers, too, aren't we, girls? And pretty fair singers, though Jube outshines Ruby and me in that department. Wait'll you hear her, Miss Downing, you won't believe it. Scotty says she's got a voice that'd shame a mockingbird."

"Oh, Pearl, you're always saying that." Jubilee turned bright eyes on the pair of milliners. "But wait till you see Pearl's high kick. Why, when Pearl starts kicking, you'd better hang your lantern someplace else, or she'll put it out! Isn't that right, Ruby?"

Ruby laughed her throaty rumble. "Tha's right. Pearl got a li'l specialty she perfec'ed. She can kick the hat off any man 'thout rearrangin' one hair on his head, can't ya, honey?"

Now it was Pearl's turn to laugh. "But it was Ruby's idea. Ruby's always the one with the best ideas. Tell 'em about your disappearing trick, Ruby."

"Aw, go on." Ruby flapped a pink palm.

"Well, the men sure love it."

"The men—humph!—what them men know anyhow?"

"Tell 'em, Ruby," they both cajoled.

"Tell us, *tt-tt*."

"Tell 'em yourself, if you think it's anythin' two ladies like them'd wanna hear."

Pearl told it. "Scotty's gone straight now, but that doesn't mean he couldn't palm a card if he wanted to. Well, back on the riverboat, he showed Ruby a little sleight of hand and Ruby put it to work in our act. She can get any man's watch and chain without him knowin' what she's up to. And by the time he finds out it's missing—where do you suppose it turns up?"

Against her will, Agatha was captivated. "Where?" she asked.

"Yes, where?" Violet repeated eagerly.

Pearl cupped a hand around her mouth and answered in a stage whisper, "Between her bosoms, that's where!"

Violet covered her mouth. *"Tt-tt."*

Agatha pinkened. "Oh . . . oh my!" Yet she was less horrified than she'd have been a week ago. There was something infectious about this trio. Perhaps it was their great camaraderie or their unselfish pride in one another. It seemed unusual that three women in their line of work could harbor so little jealousy among themselves.

"It's surprising," Pearl went on. "A man'll do near anything when you're alone with him behind a locked door, but put him in public and he'll blush like a fool at the least teasing. Now, when Ruby lets a man's watch chain dangle out of her bodice—and he has to pull it all the way out if he wants it back—why, you've never seen a funnier sight. Especially if the watch is made of gold. Gold warms up faster than silver, just bein' against your skin. And when they feel that warm gold . . ."

"Now, Pearl," interrupted Jubilee, "you're forgetting these are ladies we're visiting with. You can't talk to them like we talk to one another."

"Oh! Oh, you're right." Pearl colored becomingly. "Didn't mean to make you uneasy, Miss Downing, or you either, Miss Parsons. Sometimes my tongue runs away with me."

"It's quite all right. You see, Violet and I had the mistaken impression that you were going to do much more than dance at the Gilded Cage. Since you aren't, we're quite relieved. Well!" Agatha snipped a thread and tended to business because she didn't quite know how to respond to the subject under discussion. "All we have to do is string the cord through the top and we're finished."

"How're we going to do that?" Jubilee asked, staring at the casing.

Agatha got up and limped toward the supply cabinet. "It's quite simp—"

"Why, Miss Downing, you're limping!" Jubilee exclaimed.

Agatha felt a rush of blood, a moment of awkwardness as she wondered how to respond to such a blatant observation.

Thank heavens she was reaching into the honeycombed case for a hank of cord and a thick darning needle. By the time she faced the group again, she'd regained her poise. "It's nothing."

"Nothing? But—"

"I've had it for years. I'm used to it by now." But Jubilee's beautiful almond eyes were wide with concern.

"You mean you weren't born that way?"

Oh, dear, how dreadfully acute she is, thought Agatha. *Isn't she bright enough to know she's being tactless?* Rattled, Agatha nevertheless answered truthfully, "No."

"Then how did it happen?"

"I fell down some stairs when I was a young girl."

Agatha could tell Violet was curious, too. Oddly enough, in the years they'd known each other Violet had never ventured to ask these questions.

Jubilee looked smack down at Agatha's skirts. "Oh, gosh, you poor girl. How awful!" Several thoughts struck Agatha at once: it had been years since anyone had called her a girl; Jubilee was not being nosy, but, in her naïve way, compassionate; because of this, Agatha could no longer be annoyed.

Jubilee followed her first impulse. "Here, let me help you with that." She approached Agatha, closed the door of the cabinet for her, and took the items from her hands. Chattering, she carried them back to their chairs. "And here we are talking about high kicks. We should have known better, but how could we? Still, it doesn't seem fair, does it?"

Agatha found it disconcerting to have her recurring thoughts spoken by a woman who was supposed to be "wicked." She couldn't help warming to the impetuous Jubilee.

"I'm not an invalid, Miss Jubilee," she advised her with a wry smile. "I can carry my own needle and cord."

"Oh!" Jubilee glanced at the things in her hands and gave a fluttery laugh. "Oh, of course you're not! What's the matter with me?" She stuffed the cording back into Agatha's hand and passed her the needle.

How could anyone help but be charmed by Jubilee Bright?

Nobody ever confronted Agatha's lameness head-on. Now that she'd adjusted to the direct questioning, it became a welcome change from the sidelong glances of curiosity she usually received. And Jubilee did it with such refreshing lack of embarrassment Agatha felt her own tongue loosening.

"I do quite well, actually. Stairs are the worst, and I live upstairs." She pointed up.

"Upstairs? You mean above the store?" Jubilee peered at the stamped-tin ceiling.

"Yes."

"Then we're going to be neighbors!" When Jubilee smiled she was a breathtaking sight, all sparkle and animation. The tilt of her wide eyes matched that of her open lips, giving her a look of youthful eagerness. She must have been greedily sought after in her former profession, Agatha thought. "We're going to be living upstairs, too, so listen, if there's ever anything we can do to help you— haul things up and down, or run and fetch—you be sure to call on us." Jubilee turned to her friends. "Isn't that right, girls?"

"Sure thing," Pearl agreed. "We sleep late in the mornings, but we always have afternoons free."

"Me, I'm strong as a horse, and I was born takin' orders," claimed Ruby. "Any way I can he'p, just beller."

How was Agatha supposed to dislike these three? Whatever their pasts, Ruby, Pearl, and Jubilee appeared to have intrinsic generosity that ran deeper than that in some of the Presbyterians she knew.

"Thank you all, but for now, just stretch the top of the curtain flat so I can get the cord through the casing."

"How you going to do that?" Jubilee inquired.

"Easily. Tie the cord through the eye of the needle and run it through backward." Jubilee's eyes grew bigger and bigger as she held the edge of the red satin and watched Agatha work. "Balls o' fire, would you look at that!"

A spurt of laughter escaped Agatha. "You girls certainly have colorful language."

"Sorry, ma'am. It's where we've worked. But that's amazing."

"What?" Agatha busied herself pursing the fabric on the cord.

"That! What you're doing! How'd you learn such tricks?"

"My mother taught me."

"Why, I never would've thought of a thing like that. I'm lucky I can tie my own boot strings."

Agatha had known how to thread a casing for so long she took it for granted. She looked up at Jubilee's entranced almond eyes and felt a flicker of pride in her work.

"I've been doing it so long it's second nature to me."

"You sure are lucky, knowing a trade like you do."

"Lucky?" When was the last time Agatha had thought of herself as lucky?

"And having a mother to teach you. I didn't have a mother. I mean, she died when I was born, they tell me. Lived in St. Luke's Orphanage when I was little." Suddenly she flashed a mischievous smile. "Wonder what those nuns would say if they could see me now?" There wasn't the faintest note of self-pity in Jubilee's revelation. With a quicksilver shift of expression, she became engrossed in Agatha's occupation again. "Your mother, did she teach you lots of sewing tricks? I mean, like how to make dresses and petticoats and other things besides hats?"

"Well, actually, yes, I make all my own clothing."

"All your own! You mean you made that?" She took Agatha by an elbow and inspected the intricate shaping of her bodice—welts, gussets, flutes, and tucks. She turned to her and exclaimed, "Would you look at this, girls!" The three of them examined the details of Agatha's Austrian draped tie-back, and her even more elaborate cascading bustle. "That's some fancy work!"

They oohed and ahhed, even Ruby, who was handy with a needle herself.

"Petticoats, too?" Before Agatha could object, they lifted her rear hem to inspect the cagelike bustle, which fell from waist to heels in a set of horizontal ribs securely set in white cotton. Agatha was so surprised, she forgot to object.

"She could do it, couldn't she?" Jubilee asked Ruby.

"Do what?" Agatha demanded.

"Do what?" repeated Violet.

The girls ignored them. Jube was waiting for an answer. "Couldn't she?"

Ruby closely studied the construction of Agatha's clothing. "I b'lieve she could."

"Do what?" Violet insisted.

"Make those new skirts we been wanting for that French dance."

"New skirts?"

"French dance?"

"The cancan," Pearl informed them. "No offense, Miss Agatha, but I've been practicing my high kick especially for it. But I can't do the cancan without one of those ruffled skirts."

"Ruffles run clear around in layers," Ruby added, gesturing. "Like the old crinolines, only *inside* the skirt."

"You could do it!" Jubilee said enthusiastically. "I know you could, and I'll talk to Gandy about paying—"

"Please, ladies, please!" Agatha held up both palms. "I'm sorry. I can't."

They all talked at once.

"What you mean . . ."

"Oh, please say you will . . ."

"But where else are we going to . . ."

Agatha chuckled, beleaguered but flattered by their enthusiasm. "I can't. How would it look if the president of the local W.C.T.U. sewed costumes for the saloon dancers? The cover of the cage was bad enough, but if I do any more somebody is sure to find out. And furthermore, I have no sewing machine."

Three dejected dancers looked around to find it was true.

"Oh, damn," Pearl said, plopping down on a chair, "that's right."

"Pearl, you mustn't use such words," Agatha reprimanded gently, touching her shoulder.

With her chin in her palm, Pearl sulked. "I suppose not. But I'm disappointed."

"You know . . ." Agatha struggled a moment. Finally, she admitted, "So am I. I could have used the business, but I guess you can see it is neither possible nor advisable."

Violet began, "But, Agatha, couldn't we—"

"No, Violet, it's out of the question. Girls, you saw how long it took five of us to hem this. Ruffles require yards and yards of hemming. And to do it by hand . . . well, I doubt Mr. Gandy would be willing to pay for my time."

"You let us handle Mr. Gandy."

"I'm sorry, Jubilee, really I must say no."

The girls continued looking glum. Finally Jubilee sighed. "I guess we might as well go, then. Should we take this with us now?" She lifted the red silk between two fingers.

"You may as well. It'll save me taking it over, and Mr. Gandy's already paid me for it."

"Well, thanks for the rush job, Miss Downing. You, too, Miss Parsons. If you change your minds, let us know."

As Pearl opened the back door, Agatha suggested, "Perhaps you can order the dresses from St. Louis or . . . or . . ." It suddenly struck Agatha how absurd her suggestion was. Cancan dresses weren't exactly advertised in the ready-made catalogues.

"Sure," Jubilee said. Then they filed out despondently.

When they were gone, Violet gazed at the door. "Well, my stars," she said breathily, touching her temples.

"My sentiments exactly," Agatha rejoined, dropping into her chair. "That's the most zest this old shop has seen since it opened."

"They're wonderful!" Violet exclaimed.

Yes, thought Agatha sadly, *they are.* "But we cannot befriend them, Violet, you know that. Not when we've just been voted officers of the temperance union."

"Oh, bosh! They don't sell spirits. And they're not ladies of the evening anymore. They just dance. Didn't you hear them?"

"But their dancing promotes the sale of spirits. It's all the same."

Violet's mouth pursed. For the second time in several hours she declared in a piqued voice, "Sometimes, Agatha, you're no fun at all!" Then, leading with her chin, she left the shop for the day.

Alone, Agatha pondered the strange afternoon. She'd felt more alive than she had in years. She'd laughed and for a time completely forgotten that the young women were unsuitable clientele for her millinery shop. She had simply enjoyed them instead. But most amazing of all was that she'd actually told them about her accident. It had felt wonderful. And the girls had been amusing. But now that the hubbub had died down, she felt depressed. She wondered what it felt like to be part of a sorority such as that shared by Jubilee, Pearl, and Ruby, to be true friends as they were. Violet was her friend, but not in the sense that the three young dancers were friends. They radiated a real understanding and acceptance of one another, a pride in their limited accomplishments, and an amazing lack of competition. Also, they had the group they called their "family"—not a real family, but better, perhaps, because they were related by choice, not by blood. And that "family" was headed by a riverboat gambler they followed as if he were the Messiah. Curious. Enviable.

Enviable? The notion jolted Agatha. Women who'd pleasured men for money, who'd learned how to lift pocket watches from unsuspecting dandies, who danced in saloons with pictures of naked women on the wall and kicked hats from men's heads. How was it possible she could believe for an instant she envied them?

But if she didn't, why was she suddenly so sad?

It was getting late. Soon it would be time to get ready for the seven o'clock gathering.

Agatha rose from her chair and saw the gold coins winking at her from the worktable, right where Gandy had left them. She wondered how long it would take to get a sewing machine shipped in from Boston.

Agatha, don't be silly!

But the girls are so lively, so much fun to be around.

Agatha, you're getting as senile as Violet!

And imagine what you could earn, making three cancan outfits.

It would be tainted money.

But so much of it. And he pays so well.

Agatha, don't even think it!

Well, he does. A hundred dollars for less than three hours' work. And three helping hands thrown in!

It was a bribe and you know it.

Bribery money buys sewing machines the same as other money.

Listen to yourself. Soon you'll be stitching cancans!

I've a mind to try it, with or without a sewing machine.

Since when did you become mercenary?

Oh, all right, so he paid me too much!

And what do you intend to do about it?

She picked up the ten gold coins and feathered them onto her palm. They were so heavy! She'd never known before how heavy ten ten-dollar gold pieces were. And they warmed fast, as the girls had said. She peeled off six and set them aside, then layered the remaining four like dominoes along her palm. Forty dollars was a lot of money. Warm, heavy money.

In the end she listened to her conscience, resolutely clamped her palm shut, and headed for the back door. Even as she did she wished she were as uninhibited as Pearl so she could curse at herself for what she was about to do.

The back door of the Gilded Cage opened on to a short corridor between a pair of storage rooms. Standing in the shadows, Agatha went unnoticed at first. There was neither piano nor banjo music, only the sound of happy chatter. A gay band of saloon regulars, and all the establishment's employees, clustered around the gilded cage as Gandy and the girls settled the cover over it and arranged its folds. Momentarily, Agatha envied them again. The camaraderie. The way they laughed and teased one another.

She saw immediately what all the hammering had been about. A rope led from the tip of the cage to a pulley mounted in the ceiling, where a trapdoor had been installed. They were bantering about it, pointing, looking up. Jubilee said something and they all laughed. Then Gandy looped an arm around her shoulders. They looked into one another's faces and shared a private chuckle. Then his hand swept down the hollow of her back and lingeringly squeezed her buttock.

Agatha's mouth went dry. Her neck felt hot.

She had no idea people did things like that out of their bedrooms.

She gathered her equilibrium and moved down the hall

toward them. The scar-faced bartender saw her and left the group to greet her.

"Evenin', Miss Downing." He tipped his bowler.

She was surprised that he knew her name. But he treated her politely, which demanded politeness in return. "Good evening, Mr. Hogg."

Immediately, she could tell he was surprised that she knew his name as well. The unscarred half of Jack Hogg's face smiled. It was grotesque but she forced herself not to look away, as people sometimes looked away from her.

"Cover looks wonderful, ma'am. Just what Scotty wanted." When he spoke, the right corner of his mouth drew down; the left corner didn't move at all.

It struck Agatha how ironic it was that she was standing in the saloon with the picture of the naked woman on the wall, receiving compliments on the red cover she'd sewn. Heaven help her if anyone should walk past the door and glance inside.

"I didn't come to chitchat. May I speak with Mr. Gandy, please?"

"Sure thing, ma'am." He raised his voice. "Hey, Scotty! Lady here to see ya."

Gandy turned from the talkative group near the cage. When he saw Agatha, his dimples appeared and he dropped his arm from Jubilee. He flicked down his shirtsleeves, reached automatically for his jacket from the back of a chair, and shrugged it on while crossing to her.

"Miz Downin'," he greeted her simply, coming to a halt before her. He thrust his head forward, still adjusting his lapels, a simple enough motion, yet masculine. She was unaccustomed to witnessing men don their clothes. It did something restive to her stomach.

"Mr. Gandy," she returned civilly, fixing her gaze on his chest.

"Y'all did a fine job. 'Preciate your hurryin' like y' did."

"You overpaid me." She held out the four gold pieces. "I cannot in good conscience accept all this money."

Still holding his lapels, he glanced at the coins. "Deal's a deal."

"Exactly. Sixty, I believe it was. I'll accept that much, even though it's still more than equitable."

He remained silent for so long that she glanced up. He was considering her with his head tilted to one side. His hair touched his white collar. His necktie hung loose. His dimples were gone.

"You're an amazin' woman, y' know that, Miz Downin'?"

Her gaze dropped beneath his disconcerting perusal.

"Please, just take the money."

"You're plannin' t' come back here in . . ." He pulled his watch out and she concentrated on his dark thumb as it released the catch. The cover flipped open. It was made of bright, shiny gold. She wondered if he'd ever extracted it—warm—from between Ruby's breasts. Or was it only Jubilee he touched intimately?

She returned from her woolgathering to hear him asking, "Why?"

"I . . . I'm sorry. What were you saying?"

One of his eyebrows curled like a question mark fallen sideways. "In less than an hour you're plannin' t' come back here and begin the ruination of my business. Yet you come in here with forty dollars sayin' I overpaid you for a sewin' job you didn't wanna do in the first place. Why?"

She glanced up again. More quickly down. He was too ungodly handsome. "I told you, my conscience would bother me if I kept it all."

She'd never met a man so adept at insouciance. His voice became so soft it alone triggered her blush. "It'll take some money t' shut me down. Why don't y'all add it t' your temperance fund?"

Her head snapped up. He was grinning like a stroked cat, laughing at her.

"Take it!" she demanded, grabbing his wrist and slapping the coins into his palm.

His dimples deepened and she turned to leave. He grabbed her arm to stop her. She pierced his hand with a malevolent look and he immediately released her. "Sorry."

"Was there something else, Mr. Gandy?" she inquired sharply.

"The girls tell me they asked you t' make some costumes for them but you refused."

"That's right. I'm all through doing business with you. From here on out I fight you."

"Ah, commendable." He raised one long index finger. "But don't forget free enterprise. You know now that I really do pay well."

"I explained to the girls that I have no sewing machine. It would take an impossible length of time and it wouldn't look good to the ladies of the temperance union. Besides, I'm a milliner, not a seamstress."

"That's not what they said after watchin' you put together that cover."

"The answer is no, Mr. Gandy."

"Very well," he conceded with a half bow. "Thank you for returnin' my money. Maybe I can buy a nude for the other wall."

She realized as she stood there sparring with him that her heart was beating a little too earnestly. Her face, however, remained stern.

"Until seven o'clock, then," she said, repeating his earlier words, offering the faintest bow.

He raised his chin and laughed. "We'll be expectin' y'all. And the doors'll be open."

As she left, he withdrew a cigar from his pocket and studied the rear of her skirts—poufs and froufrous. And enough cloth to make a revival tent! He wondered how in tarnation the woman put together such a rig. Nimble-fingered little thing, he thought. And living on a shoestring, if his guess was right. He'd be willing to bet that ten-dollar gold pieces weren't the only things that spoke louder than words . . . in her case, so did sewing machines.

He was a gambler. He'd put money on it.

CHAPTER
5

The ladies of the Proffitt Women's Christian Temperance Union met on the boardwalk shortly before seven P.M., bringing their temperance pledges with them. At the top was the organization's name and motto, coined by Frances Willard, the founder and president of the national W.C.T.U.: For God and Home and Native Land. The pledge contained the promise that he who signed, "with God being his helper, would never touch, taste, or handle, for beverage purposes, any intoxicating liquor, including wine, beer, and cider," and that he would "use all honorable means to encourage others to abstain." Below were blanks for name and date.

When the ladies arrived, Gandy, wearing a convivial smile, came out to the boardwalk to greet them. From the shadows Agatha studied him. The saloon lanterns threw a cone of light through the open doors as he stood pressing them open. The orange glow highlighted only parts of his face. It appeared freshly shaven for the occasion. From the low crown of his black hat to the tips of his shiny black boots, he was indecently attractive. Freshly brushed black suit, ice-blue waistcoat, immaculate white collar, and black string tie. Even the malodorous cheroot was absent from his fingers.

He took his time, letting his glance pass from one female face to the next until he'd met each pair of eyes. Only then did he leisurely tip his black Stetson.

"Evenin', ladies."

Some shifted nervously under his indolent perusal. Sev-

eral nodded silently. Others glanced uncertainly at Drusilla
Wilson. Agatha stood stiffly, watching. How confident he
was of his charm, of his effect on those of the opposite
sex. His very pose seemed calculated to enhance his striking appearance—weight on one hip, jacket gaping open,
hands draped lazily over the tops of the swinging doors,
the diamond ring winking even in the twilight.

Gandy's dark, amused eyes picked out Agatha.

"Miz Downin'," he drawled, "you're lookin' exception-
ally fine this evenin'."

Agatha wished she could slip between the cracks in the
boardwalk. Momentarily, she feared he would mention the
job she'd done for him—she wouldn't put it past him to
thank her drolly. To her relief his attention moved on.

"Miz Parsons. My, my." His dimples proved more effective than flowery words. Violet tittered.

Stepping farther onto the boardwalk, Gandy turned to
Drusilla.

"Miz Wilson, I don't b'lieve I've had the pleasure."

She glanced at his extended hand, clasping her own
together. "Mr. Gandy, I presume."

He nodded.

"I'll shake your hand when it has put your signature
on this." She thrust forward the pledge and a pen. Gandy
scanned them coolly, then threw back his head and laughed.

"Not today, Miz Wilson. With three dancin' girls and
that white-limbed beauty on the wall in there, I b'lieve I
have the winnin' hand." He pressed both swinging doors
back against the wall. "But y'all do what y' can t' reverse
the odds."

With a half bow he turned and left them.

It became obvious with the arrival of the saloon's first
patrons that its attractions far outweighed those of any
temperance pledge. The swinging doors remained folded
back. From inside came the welcoming sound of the piano
and banjo. The oil painting beckoned from the wall. The
green baize of the gambling tables welcomed like oases in a
desert. Gandy himself greeted his customers. And everyone
awaited the appearance of Jubilee and the Gems.

Outside, the ladies took up a chorus of "Cold Water Is

King," singing at the top of their lungs, only to inspire Gandy to send Marcus Delahunt onto the boardwalk to play his banjo and muddle their song. When Mooney Straub, Wilton Spivey, and Joe Jessup approached, the music grew louder from both factions.

Drusilla Wilson herself approached the trio, shouting to be heard above the din.

"Friends, before you set foot inside to support this ally of Satan, consider how you might better work toward your final salvation. Beyond these doors is the twisting road to ruin, while on this paper is the . . ."

Their laughter covered the remainder of her plea.

"Lady, you gotta have a wheel loose if ya think I'm signin' that thing. Ain't ya heard? There's dancin' women here!"

"And that pitcher o' the naked lady," added Mooney.

"And we aim to name 'er!"

Guffawing, they jostled three abreast through the open door. The place began to fill fast. Things were much the same with Drusilla's next three attempts to waylay Gandy's customers. They laughed in her face and hurried inside, already reaching for their coins.

Then came a ne'er-do-well named Alvis Collinson who'd lost his wife to pneumonia two years earlier. A surly man with a nose like a mushroom, Collinson was known around town for his hair-trigger temper. He worked at the stockyards when he worked. When he didn't, he spent most of his time drinking, gambling, and starting fights. Countless knuckles had rearranged his face. The left eyelid drooped. The nose bulged hideously. The cheeks, with their broken capillaries, had the appearance of a red cauliflower. His filthy clothing appeared oily from body excretions. When he passed Agatha the air turned sour in his wake.

Evelyn Sowers surprised everyone by stepping forward and accosting him.

"Mr. Collinson, where is your son?"

Collinson stopped. His head jutted and his fists clenched.

"What business is it o' yours, Evelyn Sowers?"

"Have you left him home alone while you sit here night after night pickling your innards?"

"What the hell ya doin' here anyway, all you old bid-
dies?" Alvis cast a hateful glare across the entire group.

"Trying to save your soul, Alvis Collinson, and give your
son back his father."

He swung back to Evelyn. "Leave my boy outta this!"

Evelyn stepped directly in front of him. "Who's taken
care of him since your wife died, Alvis? Has he had his
supper? Who'll tuck him into bed tonight? A five-year-old
boy—"

"Get outta my way, hag!" He gave her a push that sent
her stumbling backward. Her head struck a post and several
ladies gasped. Their song faded into silence. But Evelyn
bounced off and grabbed Collinson's arm.

"That boy needs a father, Alvis Collinson. Ask the Lord
where he'll get one!" she shouted.

He shook her off. "Haul your bustles back to your kitchens if ya know what's good for ya!" he roared, stamping
inside.

By now Marcus Delahunt's fingers had stopped moving
on the banjo strings. In the sudden silence Agatha's heart
hammered with fear. She glanced inside to find a frowning
Gandy observing the altercation. With a jerk of his head he
motioned Delahunt inside, calling, "Close the doors."

The musician went in, leaving the doors flapping.

"Ladies, let us sing," Drusilla interjected. "A new song."

While they sang "Lips That Touch Whiskey Shall Never
Touch Mine," the saloon filled to capacity and not a man
had signed a pledge. As the last verse began outside, a
roar went up inside. Over the tops of the swinging doors
Agatha saw Elias Potts being clapped on the shoulder and
congratulated for winning the picture-naming contest. The
portly druggist was hoisted to a tabletop and seated in a
spindle-backed chair. Then they lifted their drinks in a
toast to the nude, shouting, "To Dierdre and her garden
of delights!"

Overhead, the new trapdoor opened and the red-shrouded
cage began descending on a thick red satin rope. The men
roared, and clapped, and whistled. The background music of
the banjo and piano was scarcely audible above the uproar.
Potts, scarlet to the fringe of his near-bald head, grinned

and dried the corners of his mouth as the cage hovered before him.

The piano player struck one fortissimo chord.

A long leg jutted out from between the folds of red.

The banjo and piano hit and sustained another chord.

The high-heeled white boot rotated on a shapely ankle.

A glissando rolled.

The leg shot out and the toe of the boot braced on Elias Potts's left knee.

The music stilled.

"Gentlemen, I give you the jewel of the prairie, *Miss Jubilee Bright!*"

The music swelled and the red drapes swooshed to the ceiling! The men went crazy. There stood Jubilee, dazzling in unrelieved white.

The words about whiskey faded from Agatha's lips as she stared. Jubilee leaned from the cage in a dress slit from hem to hip, its strapless bodice covered in glittering white sequins. In her incredible white hair bobbed an even whiter curved feather whose tips, too, flashed with sequins. She braced her toe on Potts's knee and leaned forward to stroke his jaw with a fluffy white boa. Her voice was sultry, the words slow and ripe with innuendo.

"It's not because I wouldn't . . ."

Never had Agatha seen a more beautiful leg than the one braced on Potts's knee, never a more enviable face than the one leaning close to his. She could not tear her eyes away.

"And it's not because I shouldn't . . ."

Jubilee sidled in a full circle around Potts's chair, letting her shoulder blades graze him.

"Lord knows it's not because I couldn't . . ."

She flipped the boa around Potts's neck and sat on his lap with the heel of one white boot crossing her opposite knee. She slid the boa back and forth in time to the music.

"It's simply because I'm the laziest girl in town."

The men whooped and hollered while Potts grew ripe as an August watermelon. Ivory Culhane raised his voice. "Gentlemen, the gems of the prairie, Miss Pearl DeVine and Miss Ruby Waters!"

From above, two vampish bodies slithered down the red satin rope. It twined around and between their legs—black fishnet stockings, high-heeled black boots—and along their skimpy costumes—black satin and sequins and scarcely enough material to make a corset. Hand below hand, Pearl and Ruby came down the rope while whistles and wolf calls drowned out their song. The nearest hands plucked them from the roof of the cage and deposited them on the edge of the green-topped table where they sat, leaning back against Potts's legs, peering up at him provocatively. Behind him, Jubilee cradled the back of his head against her bosom and tickled his nose with the boa.

"It's not because we wouldn't.
It's not because we shouldn't.
Lord knows it's not because we couldn't.
It's simply because we're the laziest girls in town."

Watching, listening, Agatha was both repelled and mesmerized. So much skin! But so healthy and beautiful.

"We'll accomplish no more here tonight," Drusilla Wilson announced, bringing Agatha to her senses. "We'll move on to the next saloon."

Resisting the urge to look back over her shoulder, Agatha followed the others. At the Branding Iron Saloon they marched directly inside and signed up their first reformer, Jed Hull, who became frightened by the newspaper drawing of the Blackwell Island Asylum for Inebriates that Drusilla Wilson passed around.

Angus Reed, the Scot who owned the Branding Iron, couldn't believe his eyes when he saw Hull being shepherded out the door. He leaped over the bar and shouted, "Where the hell you going, Hull? Haven't you got enough guts to stand up to a bunch of female do-gooders who belong at home breeding babies?" But he was too late. With a violent curse he swatted the bar with a wet towel.

Inspired by their first success, the reformers marched on to the Cattlemen's Crossing, where the price of drinks had been cut to twenty cents and had lured several hard-core imbibers away from the show being staged down at the Gilded Cage. The owner, an irascible former cowpuncher who went by the name of Dingo, suffered inflammatory rheumatism from drinking too much gyp water in his trail days. Though his stiff joints kept him from leaping over the bar as Reed had, they lent him a perpetual orneriness. He hobbled from behind his kegs and kicked Bessie Hottle smack in her bustle. "Git your ass outta my saloon and don't come back!"

Red to the ears, Bessie led the quick retreat.

Next they invaded the Alamo, where Jennie Yoast and Addie Anderson encountered their husbands and more wrath from the owner, a half-breed Mexican named Jesus Garcia who cursed a string of Spanish epithets when he saw two of his best customers shamed in public and chased home by their wives.

The next three saloon owners were too amused to object when the band of women descended upon them, singing "Lips That Touch Whiskey." Slim Tucker laughed his guts out. Jim Starr offered each of the ladies a drink on the house. And Jeff Diddier swigged down a double shot of bourbon, backhanded his mouth dry, and joined in singing the last chorus of their song.

At The Sugar Loaf Saloon, the owner, Mustard Smith, pulled a shotgun from behind the bar and gave them thirty seconds to clear out. It was rumored that Smith wore his full black beard to cover a scar that ran from ear to ear. The ladies didn't stop to inquire if it were true. Everyone knew he'd ridden with B. B. Harlin's gang, and three of them had been hanged from a railroad trestle. When Mustard ordered, "Clear out," they cleared.

At the Hoof and Horn they had little luck. The place

was empty, having lost its few customers to the lively show across the street. The ladies said a simple prayer for the salvation of Heustis Dyar's soul, then left peaceably. Behind them, Dyar stood with hands akimbo, eyes burning, chewing his cigar stub as if it were a piece of raw meat.

At Ernst Bostmeier's Saloon they signed up their second reformer of the night, one of the customers who frequented Ernst's place because he served a free pickled egg with each glass of beer. As the ladies walked out the door with their saved soul in tow, the grumpy old German proprietor threw a pickled egg that missed Josephine Gill's shoulder by a mere inch. "Dere's more vere dat come from!" he bellowed in his thick German accent, shaking his fist. "Ent I only miss ven I vant to!"

The remainder of the saloon visits proved uneventful. In each, the owners, bartenders, and clientele were merely amused by what they considered a pack of distempered old maids and errant housewives with not enough dirty socks to keep them at their scrub boards.

It was well after eleven o'clock when Agatha climbed the stairs to her apartment. Downstairs the laughter and music still poured into the night. On the landing it was dark. Before she could unlock her door her fingertips brushed a paper hanging on it.

Her heart lurched and she spun about, backing up against the door.

Nobody was there.

Chills crept up the backs of her arms. She held her breath, listening. The only sound came from the continuing revelry in the Gilded Cage.

Quickly, she jerked the note free. A tack dropped to the landing floor and rolled away. She spared not even a moment to pick it up, but hurriedly unlocked the door and slipped inside.

Somehow she knew even before the lamp was lit what she'd find.

**STAY OUT OF THE SALOONS
IF YOU KNOW WHAT'S GOOD FOR YOU!**

It was printed in capital letters on a clean sheet of white paper. She hurried back to the door and locked it, tested the knob, then leaned against it with a sigh of relief. She scanned the narrow apartment—the bed and chifforobe were the only two places large enough to conceal a man. She stood stock-still, listening for breathing, rustling—any sound at all. The faraway chords from the piano and banjo covered any faint sounds the room might have held. She struggled to her knees, peered beneath the bed from across the room.

Black shadows.

Don't be silly, Gussie, your door was locked.

Nevertheless, her heart pounded. She inched closer until the lamplight revealed nothing but dust balls hiding under the bed. On her feet once more, she tiptoed to the chifforobe, paused with her fingers on the handle. Abruptly, she flung its doors wide, then wilted with relief.

Only clothing.

Who were you expecting, silly goose?

She pulled down her window shades, both front and back, but the creepy feeling persisted while she undressed and retired.

It could have been any of them. Angus Reed, who'd jumped over the bar and shouted angrily when they took away one of his customers. That rheumatic old cowboy, Dingo—people said his rheumatism made him ornery as a rabid skunk when it acted up. And how about Garcia? He was visibly upset to have two of his regulars carted home by their wives. Bostmeier, the German? Somehow she doubted it; in the dark she smiled at the memory of that pickled egg flying through the air. If Bostmeier wanted to threaten anyone, he'd do it in person. But what about Mustard Smith? Agatha shivered and pulled the covers tightly beneath her chin. She saw again the drooping batwing moustache, the full beard, the hooded eyes, and the crooked mouth. *The shotgun.* If it were true, if Smith *had* ridden with B. B. Harlin's gang, if they *had* all been hanged, if he *was* the only one to have lived through it, what kind of malevolence might lurk in such a man?

She considered all the others—Dyar, Tucker, Starr,

Diddier, and the rest. She didn't think any of them had
taken the W.C.T.U. seriously.

So what about Gandy? Lying on her back, she crossed
her arms tightly over her breasts.

Gandy?

Yes, Gandy.

Gandy, with his dimples and his "Evenin', ladies"?

Exactly.

But Gandy has no reason.

He owns a saloon.

The busiest one in town.

For the moment.

He's too cocksure to resort to threats.

What about at the top of the stairs last night?

You don't really think . . . he wasn't going to . . .

You thought so, didn't you?

*But tonight he was so charming to all of us, and I could
see he was upset when Alvis Collinson shoved Evelyn.*

A clever man.

What are you saying?

What are you saying?

No. I refuse to believe it of Gandy.

See, Agatha? See what ten gold pieces will do?

The Gilded Cage closed at midnight. Dan Loretto went
home. Marcus Delahunt polished the neck of his banjo, then
tucked it away in its velvet-lined case. Ivory Culhane closed
the key cover on the piano and Jack Hogg washed glasses.
Pearl stretched, Ruby yawned, and Jubilee watched Gandy
close and lock the full outer doors. When he turned, she
smiled.

Smiling, too, he weaved his way through the tables to
her. "So what's the smile for?"

She shrugged and walked toward the bar with him. "It's
good to be back, that's all. Hey, fellas, isn't it good to be
back together again?" Reaching Ivory, she gave him an
impulsive hug. "Gosh, I never thought I'd miss everybody
so much."

"Hey, how 'bout me?" Jack Hogg put in.

Jubilee leaned across the bar and hugged him, then gave

him a peck on his cheek. "You, too, Jack." She leaned both elbows on the varnished mahogany surface and propped up her chin. "So, how's business been around here?"

Gandy watched her and the others as they gathered around. Jack, Marcus, Ivory, Pearl, Ruby, and Jubilee—the only family he had. A bunch of loners who'd all been scarred in one way or another. Not all their scars showed, as Jack's did, but they were there just the same. When he'd gathered them together after the explosion on the riverboat two years ago, something magical had happened; he had felt a oneness of spirit, a bond of friendship that filled the voids in all their lives. Superficialities mattered not a whit—skin color, relative facial beauty, or lack of it. What mattered was what each brought to the group as a whole. They'd been split up for a month while he got the Gilded Cage set up and operable. It had seemed twice that long.

"I went down to New Orleans to visit the girls in a crib I used to work," Pearl was saying.

"As long as you weren't tempted to stay," Ivory remarked.

"Uh-uh! Never again." Everyone laughed. "You see the doc in Louisville, Jack?"

"Sure did." Jack removed his white apron and laid it across the bar. "Doc says it won't be long I'll be lookin' as pretty as Scotty here."

Again they laughed. Ruby turned and looped an arm through Scotty's. "What you want a face like that for? Look a little coluhless t' me."

Jack's scar grew brighter as he laughed again with the others.

"So, where'd you go, Ruby?"

"Went down t' Waverley. Visit my mama's grave."

Every glance shifted to Scotty. He revealed none of the emotions he felt. "How is it?"

"Looks seedy. A few o' the old ones still there, shiftin' for theirselves, growin' greens an' livin' in the cabins. Leatrice"—the strange name rhymed with mattress—"she still there, waitin' for Lord knows what."

At the news, Gandy felt a stab of nostalgia, but he only inquired, "You give her a kiss for me?"

"Mos' suttenly did not. Y'all wanna kiss Leatrice, ya'll go down an' do it yourself."

He pondered momentarily, then replied, "Someday, maybe."

Jubilee stood near Marcus, half leaning against him. "Marcus and I saw about getting the cage made and picked up a couple jobs here and there playing and singing before we met the girls in Natchez. We did one place called the Silver Slipper." She draped an elbow over Marcus's shoulder and looked smug. "They wanted us to stay awful bad, didn't they, Marcus? We drew crowds that filled the hat every night."

Marcus smiled, nodded, and made motions, as if counting out dollar bills. Everybody laughed.

"Is this a bribe, you two?" Scotty inquired. "I already pay you more than you're worth."

"What do you think, Marcus?" Jubilee lounged on Marcus's shoulder while looking teasingly at Scott. "Should we go across the street and offer our talents to one of the saloons over there?"

"Just try it," Scotty replied, taking aim with a forefinger as if it were a gun, pointing it straight at Jubilee's pretty pink nose.

"What about you, Ivory?" Pearl asked.

"I stuck with the boss. Had to get the piano hauled in here and tuned up, and plenty to do gettin' the whole place set up. Had to help him pick out the picture for the wall." Ivory raised one eyebrow and half turned toward the nude. "So what do you think of her?"

The men smiled appreciatively. The women looked away and arched their eyebrows with a superior air.

Pearl said, "With those thighs she doesn't look like she could kick a hat off a kitchen chair, much less a man's head, does she, Ruby?"

"Pro'bly couldn't sing a note, eithuh," Ruby added.

"Tsk-tsk," Jubilee added. "And the poor thing certainly is running to fat."

When they trooped upstairs they were all in good spirits. Ivory and Jack retired to the first room on the left. Marcus took the next. Pearl and Ruby shared the one just beyond the gilded cage, which now occupied the dead center of the hall, where the new trapdoor had been cut. That left Jubilee and Scotty.

She stepped into her room and lit a lamp, while he lounged against the doorframe.

"It's a nice room, Scotty. Thanks."

He only shrugged.

She flung her white boa over a pink oval-backed settee. "A window. A view of the street." She moved to the front of the room, leaned both palms on the sill, and looked down at the row of coal-oil lights. Then she glanced over her shoulder at the man in the doorway. "I like it."

He nodded. It was good just looking at her. She was a strikingly beautiful woman and he'd missed her.

"Whew!" She swung around, hands to the ceiling, flexing her shoulders. "What a long day." She plucked the feather from her hair, discarded it, and picked up a buttonhook. Dropping to the pink settee, she held it out to him. "Help me with my shoes, Scotty?" Her voice was quiet.

For several seconds he didn't move. Their eyes exchanged messages. Unhurriedly, he pulled his shoulder away from the doorframe and crossed the room to go down on one knee before her. He cradled her white boot against his groin and unhurriedly freed the buttons. Without looking up, he asked, "So how'd things go in Natchez? You meet anybody who struck your fancy?"

She studied his thick black hair. "No. Did you?"

"Uh-uh."

"No sweet young Kansas thing, fresh from her mama's arms?"

He pulled off one boot, dropped it, and looked up, grinning. "Nope."

He took her other boot against him and began applying the hook. She watched his familiar dark hands perform the personal task. In the lamplight the ring flashed brightly against his dusky skin.

"No pining Kansas widow who's been alone since the war?"

His dimples formed as he looked up into her familiar almond eyes and spoke lazily.

"Kansas widows don't cotton to Johnny-reb gamblin' men who open up saloons in their towns."

She threaded her fingers through the hair over his right ear. "Well, gosh-a-mighty, if we aren't two of a kind. Natchez mamas don't turn their sons loose to no soiled dove-turned-dancer, either."

He dropped the second boot, kissed her toes, and rubbed them with his thumb. "I missed you, Jube."

"I missed you, too, you no-count gamblin' man."

"Wanna come t' my room?"

"Just try to keep me away."

Rising, he held out a hand. He led her past a tapestried screen, snagging her turquoise dressing gown from over the top of it and flinging it over his shoulder. "Bring the lantern. You won't be needin' it in here tonight."

In the blackness at the other end of the hall a door remained slightly ajar. From his own dark room Marcus watched the lantern light splash the hall. Through the bars of the gilded cage he saw Scotty lead Jube by the hand to his doorway. Her hair shone so brightly it seemed as if it alone could have lit their way. Her white dress and bare arms appeared ethereal as she padded silently behind Scotty. What would it be like to take her hand? Walk her barefoot to bed? Remove the pins from that snow-bright hair and feel it spill into his hands?

Since the first time he'd seen her, Marcus had wondered. During the past month, while they'd traveled alone together, there were times when Jubilee had touched him. But she touched anyone and everyone without compunction. A touch didn't mean to Jube what it meant to Marcus. Tonight by the bar she'd draped her arm over his shoulder. But she never suspected what happened inside him when her hand took his elbow or she adjusted his lapel, or—most of all—when she kissed his cheek.

She kissed all their cheeks whenever the spirit moved her. She'd kissed Jack's only thirty minutes ago. They all knew it was Jube's way.

But nobody knew the hidden torment of Marcus Delahunt.

Often he had to touch her to get her attention, so he knew

what her skin felt like. Sometimes when she'd turn to watch him communicate some silent message, he'd have to remind himself to make the motions. To look into Jube's eyes, those stunning pale brown windows of her soul, was to lose his own. How often he'd longed to tell her how beautiful he thought she was. Locked in perpetual voicelessness, he could only think it. Often he played it to her on his banjo. But all she heard were musical notes.

Down the hall Scotty's door closed. Marcus pictured him taking the white dress from Jube's body, laying her across his bed, murmuring love words to her, telling her the thousand things Marcus himself wanted to say. He wondered if sound made a feeling when it rose from one's throat. He wondered what laughter felt like when it was more than the shaking of one's chest, and what it was like to whisper.

To love a woman, a man had to be able to do all those things. He pictured Scotty doing them now. Nobody else Marcus knew was good enough for her. Her pale beauty deserved Scotty's dark good looks. Her bright laughter deserved his teasing grin. Her perfect body deserved another equally as perfect.

What would a man say first?

You're beautiful.

Do first?

Touch—her cheek, her lips, her angel hair.

Feel like?

As if the world and all its glory were in his hand.

Jube . . . Jube . . .

"Jube, let me do that," Scotty was saying in the room across the hall. He did all the things Marcus Delahunt could only dream of doing. One by one he pulled the pins from Jube's fluffy, white hair. He felt it tumble into his hands and smoothed it over her milk-white shoulders. He unbuttoned her dress, then freed her corset stays and watched her long-legged body emerge as she kicked free of garters and stockings. When she turned and looped her arms around his neck, he placed his hands on the sides of her breasts and kissed the black mole between them, the one the rest of the world thought she glued to her skin each morning. He kissed her willing mouth, touched her in ways that temporarily held loneliness at bay. He laid her on the bed and murmured endearments and told her how he'd missed her and how glad he was to have her back. He linked their bodies with the most intimate of caresses and found within her a surcease for emptiness. He even cleansed her and himself when it was over. And wrapped her close in the big, soft bed and slept naked with her breast within his palm.

But between them the word *love* was never spoken.

CHAPTER
6

The first herd of Texas longhorns arrived the following day. Bawling and bullheaded they came, driven by men who'd been three months in the saddle on a dusty, dry trail. Both the cattle and the men were dirty, thirsty, hungry, and tired. Proffitt was ready to accommodate them all.

Its inordinately wide streets were designed first to handle the unlovable beasts with horns twice the width of their bodies; next, to assuage the frustrations of the weary Texas cowboys who drove them.

Agatha looked out the window of her millinery shop and watched two boys race across the street—their last chance to do so for some time. From the far end of town the rumble of hooves could already be felt. Resignedly, she said, "Here they come."

The herd passed through Proffitt from west to east, a shifting, drifting, sometimes unmanageable mass of beef flesh that created a stream of red, brown, white, and gray cowhide for as far as the eye could see. Beside them rode the hardscrabble cowpunchers as tough as the hundreds of miles of mesas they'd crossed. Saddle-weary and lonely, they wanted three things: a drink, a bath, and a woman, usually in that order.

The prostitutes had already returned to the cat houses on the far west edge of town after wintering in the bagnios of Memphis, St. Louis, and New Orleans. Garbed in dressing gowns and scanty corsets, they stood on the railed roofs and hung from the windows, waving and beckoning.

"Hiya, cowboy! Don't forget to ask for Crystal!"

"Tired of that saddle, cowboy? Li'l ole Delilah's got somethin' softer ya can ride."

"Up here, big boy! Hoo-ee! Would you look at that beard, Betsy?" Then cupping her hands to her mouth, she called, "Don't shave off that beard, honey. I *lo-o-ove* beards!"

The trail-worn cowboys stood in their saddles and waved their battered John B's, white teeth flashing in their grimy faces. "What's your name, honey?"

"Lucy! Just ask for Lucy!"

"Keep it hot, Lucy! Big Luke'll be back!"

The cattle flooded the street from hitching rail to hitching rail, sometimes even clattering onto the boardwalks themselves. Unruly and stupid, they often reverted to their wild, untamed nature, charging into the open doorways of saloons, breaking windows with their horns, rolling their eyes and charging anything that got in their way.

"Here goes the last of our peace for the summer," lamented Agatha as the lead bull led the herd past her door.

"I think it's exciting." Violet's eyes glittered.

"Exciting? All that dust and noise and smell?"

"It isn't dusty."

"It will be. As soon as this mud dries."

"Honestly, Agatha, sometimes I don't know what it is that tips your damper."

At that moment Scott Gandy and Jack Hogg stepped onto the boardwalk and stood watching the mass of moving beef. Hogg wore a starched white apron tied around his belly. Gandy wore his usual black trousers but had left his sack coat behind. Today his vest was coral. His sleeves were rolled up to the elbow. He braced one boot on the rail and leaned on his knee.

Violet poked her head outside and shouted above the sound of the herd, "Hello, Mr. Gandy!"

He swung around and dropped his foot. "Miz Parsons, how are you?"

"Better be careful. Sometimes those creatures take a mind to visit the saloons."

He grinned. "I will. Much obliged." The late morning sun lit his boots and trousers, but the shadow of the roof fell across his head and shoulders. His eyes moved to Agatha, hovering behind Violet. His voice cooled.

"Miz Downin'." He tipped his hat.

For a moment their eyes clashed. Was he the one? Certainly he lived closest, could easily have left the saloon and run upstairs to tack a note to her door anytime while she was gone last night. Was he capable of such duplicity? Standing in the morning sun with the dimples decorating his face and the reflection from his coral-colored vest lighting his chin from below, he certainly didn't look ominous. Still, her heart tripped with uncertainty. She nodded curtly.

"Close the door, Violet."

"But, Agatha—"

"Close it. All that noise gives me a headache. And the stench is unbearable."

When the door closed, Jack Hogg observed, "I don't think Miss Downing likes us."

"That's puttin' it mildly."

"You think she and that temperance union of hers can do us any harm?"

Gandy propped his foot on the handrail again and reached into his vest pocket for a cheroot. "Not with Jube and the girls here." His eyes followed a driver who rode higher than the herd, flapping his hat and cursing at the beasts. "We'll have those cowpokes fightin' for a place t' stand in the Gilded Cage."

Hogg's eyes lit with amusement. The unscarred corner of his mouth lifted. "Think Jube and the girls opened a few eyes last night, huh? Did you see that Downing woman gawk when Jube came out of the cage?"

Gandy lit his cigar and chuckled. "Can't say's I noticed."

"Like hell you didn't. You were enjoying it as much as I was."

"Seems t' me I do recall seein' her face over the top of the swingin' doors, lookin' a little interested."

"Shocked, you mean."

Gandy laughed.

"That's probably more skin than she ever saw on her own body."

Gandy drew deep and expelled a cloud of smoke. "Probably."

"A woman like that, heading up a group of females with reform on their minds, they get up a head of steam and they can cause plenty of grumbles."

Gandy's boot hit the worn floor of the boardwalk. He tugged his vest down, crooked the cheroot in one finger, and turned to Jack Hogg.

"Y'all just leave Miz Agatha Downin' t' me."

The cattle milled and mooed all that day—and the next and the next—bisecting Proffitt in an ever-shifting mass of hooves, hides, and horns. Tucked up beside the railroad tracks on the east edge of town, the stock pens stretched across the prairie like an endless crazy quilt. Trains clanged in empty and went out full, headed for the packing houses of Kansas City. The drumming of hooves on the loading ramps rolled steadily from sunup to sundown. Cowpunchers with long poles walked or straddled the wooden rails, earning their trade name by prodding and poking the cattle to keep them moving. Only when the last brand had been counted, and their tally books were folded away inside their vest pockets, did the "punchers" get paid by their foremen.

Sporting a hundred dollars' trail wages in their pockets, raring to spend every last cent, they took Proffitt by storm. They hit the saloons first, then the clothing stores. But the busiest place in town was the Cowboys' Rest, where for two bits they leaped into a tub of hot bathwater—some fully clothed. They shucked off and threw away their filthy, rawhide-patched britches, emerging from the bathhouse in stiff new Levi Strauss blue denims and crisp yoked shirts with pearl buttons running down their chests. At Stuben's Tonsorial Parlor they lay back in comfort and received their first haircuts and hot shaves in three months. They tied new silk bandannas around their throats and hit for the women and whiskey. Smelling of blue dye and hair pomade, some with new Stetsons that had cost them a third of their poke, or new boots that had cost them half, they visited the likes of Delilah, Crystal, and Lucy, whose yard signs warned: NO ADMITTANCE TO UNBATHED MEN.

As the town's population swelled from a modest two hundred to fifteen hundred, merchants' tills rang as incessantly as the hammer from Gottheim's Blacksmith Shop. Proffitt's three livery barns were busier than anthills. The Kansas Outfitters sold enough harness to reach across the entire state. At the Drover's Cottage—offering *real* mattresses and pillows—all one hundred rooms were filled. Halorhan's and the Longhorn Store sold enough Bull Durham tobacco to fill a hayloft. Union suits practically walked out on their own legs. But of all the establishments in town, eleven did better than the rest. Eleven proprietors of eleven saloons stood back and watched themselves get rich overnight selling Newton's whiskey at twenty-five cents a glass, keno cards at twenty-five cents a game, and Lazo Victoria cigars at a nickel a smoke.

Prosperity was a difficult thing to fight, the ladies of the W.C.T.U. found out. The night after the first herd arrived, they broke up into small groups and dispersed to all eleven saloons to solicit pledge signatures. Agatha's group took the Gilded Cage. Though they tried to get the cowboys' attention, it was impossible. Their interest in throwing whiskey down their throats was too intense. When the bar became so crowded that it could not accommodate all the drinkers at once, they formed a double flank. Someone cried, "Fire and fall back!" And every glass went bottoms-up. Then the second contingent took its turn bellying up to the bar. Once Jubilee and the girls appeared, the noise inside grew so horrendous, the clientele so unruly, that Agatha declared it was useless and sent the women home.

In her apartment she settled down to read the book Drusilla Wilson had given her, T. S. Arthur's *Ten Nights in a Barroom*. It told the story of Joe Morgan, a likable but weak-willed man who frequented a saloon run by the hardhearted, money-grubbing Simon Slade. Gradually, Joe became addicted to alcohol and lost whatever will he'd once possessed. Devoid of ambition, he became increasingly irresponsible and spent all his time in the bar, where his daughter Mary came to beg him to return home. One day poor Mary was struck in the head by a beer mug, thrown at her father by Slade. Poor Mary died. Within a few days, Joe had died as well, a victim of delirium tremens. Joe's wife was left a widow, childless and impoverished.

The story left Agatha depressed. Listening to the music and revelry from downstairs, she tried to think of Gandy as another Simon Slade. The picture wouldn't gel. When she was reading the book, Slade came across as a whiskered, crude oaf of rough-spoken ways and greedy bent. Gandy was none of these. He was mild-mannered, neat to a fault, and apparently generous. Though it would be difficult to fight such a charming man, fight him she must.

But not without proper ammunition. During the next few days temperance activities were suspended until Joseph Zeller could get their pamphlets printed. When he did, Agatha sent Violet, as the official W.C.T.U. treasurer, to the *Gazette* office to pick them up. She also wired away for additional copies of *Ten Nights in a Barroom* from the publisher. She read her latest issue of *The Temperance Banner*, taking notes, gathering ideas for her local. And she wrote two letters: one to Governor John P. St. John, supporting his introduction of a prohibition bill before the Kansas State Legislature; the other to the First Lady of the United States of America, Lucy Hayes, thanking her for her staunch support of the temperance movement, and for forbidding the serving of alcoholic beverages in the White House so long as her husband, Rutherford, was in office.

Agatha felt much better then. It seemed as if she'd been powerless against the many attractions innovated by the proprietor of the Gilded Cage Saloon. But the pamphlets would help. And anyone who read a copy of *Ten Nights* couldn't help but be moved by it. The letters, too, gave her a great sense of power: the voice of the American people at work.

It had been three days since she'd seen Gandy. Business at the millinery shop had picked up somewhat, too. A couple of cowpunchers had ordered wide-brimmed leghorns to be decorated for their "mothers"—Agatha smirked, recalling how serious the pair had looked when explaining who the hats were for. How gullible did they think she was?

No "mother" would wear a leghorn hat decorated with grosgrain "follow-me-lads" trailing off the back brim to the center of her back. She had no doubt she'd see her creations sashaying down the street on the heads of two soiled doves one day soon.

Agatha's thoughts were interrupted when someone pounded on her back door.

Before she could reach it, Calvin Looby, the station boy, stuck his head inside. He wore a white-and-navy-blue-striped railroad cap and small, round, wire-rimmed spectacles. His chin looked as if he'd rammed it into the point of an anvil and set it back a good two inches. He had teeth like needles and nearly nonexistent lips. She'd always pitied poor Calvin his bad looks.

"Delivery for you, Miss Downing."

"A delivery?"

"Yup." He checked his railroad bill of lading. "From Philadelphia."

"But I didn't order anything from Philadelphia."

Calvin removed his railroad cap and scratched his pate. "Funny. Says here plain as a windmill on a Kansas prairie: Agatha Downing. See?"

She peered at the paper Calvin extended.

"So it does. But there must be some mistake."

"Well, what you want I should do with it? Railroad delivered it to its destination. That's all we're responsible for. I'd have to charge you to haul it back to the depot again."

"Charge me? But . . ."

"'Fraid so. Regulations, ya see."

"But I didn't order it."

"How 'bout Miss Violet? Think she could've ordered it?"

"Most certainly not. Violet doesn't do my ordering for me."

"Well, it's a mystery." Calvin looked back over his shoulder into the yard. "What do you want me to do with it, then?"

"Do you know what it is?" Agatha went to the back door.

"Carton says: Isaac Singer Patented Treadle Sewing Machine."

"Sew—" Agatha's heart began to thud. She stepped outside anxiously. There stood a sleepy old piebald mare hitched to a parsley-green railroad dray. On the dray a huge wooden crate stood out against the backdrop of her shed and "the necessary."

"But how . . . who . . . ?"

Suddenly, she knew. She looked up at the rear of the building. The landing was empty but she had the feeling he was somewhere chuckling over her confusion. She glanced at the single window facing the backyard from his office. It was vacant. She turned back to Calvin.

"But if you take it back, what will happen to it?" She moved closer to the carton, drawn against her will.

"We'll put it on the next train heading back to Philadelphia. Can't let a thing that big lay around the depot takin' up space."

She walked to the wagon and reached up to lay her palm on the side of the carton. It was warm from the midday sun. She experienced a sharp stab of greed. She wanted this piece of machinery with a pagan intensity that yesterday she'd have thought it impossible to feel. She had the money, thanks to Gandy. But spending it seemed so final. Consorting with the enemy. But heaven knew her failing business would be miraculously revived by such a machine.

She turned to Calvin, wringing her hands. "What are the shipping costs, exactly?"

Calvin studied his paper once more. "Doesn't say here. It just says where t' deliver it to."

She'd had that catalogue clipping on her wall for so long—suppose the price had gone up appreciably?

She made a quick decision. "Could you bring it into the shop, Mr. Looby? Perhaps if we open the crate I can find the papers inside."

"Sure thing, Miss Downin'."

Calvin clambered onto the dray, pushed and shoved and unloaded the cumbersome crate onto a flat, wheeled conveyance, which he rolled through the back door of the hat shop. In the workroom, he removed the wooden cap with a claw hammer. Atop the packaging material was the bill. Stamped across it in neat black ink were the words PAID IN FULL.

Confused, Agatha looked from the bill to Calvin. "But I don't understand."

"Looks to me like somebody give you a gift, Miss Downin'. Well, what d'you know about that!"

She stared at the paper.

Gandy? But what was his motive? Three cancan dresses? Perhaps. But there could be several other motives in that shrewd mind of his. Bribery. Whitewash. Subversion.

If it was bribery, she wanted no part of it. She already felt uneasy about accepting the generous amount he'd paid her for making the red birdcage cover.

And if he were seeking to throw a red herring over his secret nighttime counterplays, it seemed odd he'd spend so much money to do so.

Subversion? Would he be devious enough to undermine her W.C.T.U. efforts by suggesting to the officials that she was doing business with the enemy? Oddly enough, she didn't want to believe it of him.

Perhaps he was still feeling guilty for pushing her in the mud. *Don't be silly, Agatha.* Yes, he had looked somewhat remorseful that day, but he was a gambler, well versed in assuming whatever face he thought it advantageous to assume.

There was, of course, one other possibility. Free enterprise. Jubilee and the girls most certainly would keep the edge of the mahogany bar belly-shined, especially in red cancan skirts. Perhaps Gandy's spirit of competition was aroused by the thought of doing all in his power to crowd his saloon with more men than it could comfortably hold. To lord it over the other ten saloon owners in town out of sheer contrariness.

The thought made her smile. She sobered abruptly. Whatever his motives, Agatha realized she could not be a party to them.

"Put the cover back on, Mr. Looby. Take it back to the station."

"As you say."

"I think I know who ordered it, and he can pay the return charges."

"Yes, ma'am." He matched the nail holes, lifted his hammer.

"Wait! Just a minute."

Looby scowled impatiently. "Well, what's it to be?"

"I just want to see it. One peek. Then you can pack it off."

That one peek was fatal. No one who'd worked with stitches as long as Agatha had could possibly glimpse that wondrous piece of American ingenuity without coveting it in a wholly gripping way. The black paint shone. The gilt logo gleamed. The silver flywheel tempted.

"On second thought, leave it."

"Leave it?"

"Yes."

"But I thought you said—"

"Thank you so much for delivering it, Mr. Looby." She led the way to the door. "My, haven't we been having some ideal weather? If this keeps up, the streets should dry in no time."

Looby glanced from her to the crate and back again. He took off his railroad cap and scratched his head. But it was beyond him to try to figure out the workings of the female mind.

When Looby was gone, Agatha checked the time—nearly eleven o'clock. Violet would arrive any minute. Hurry, Violet!

When the little white-haired woman stepped into the millinery shop, she found Agatha standing just inside the curtained doorway, her hands clasped excitedly beneath her chin.

"Oh, Violet, I thought you'd never get here!"

"Is something wrong?"

"Wrong? No!" Agatha flung out her hands and flashed a beaming smile toward the heavens. "Nothing could be more right! Come!" She turned toward the workroom. "Let me show you." She led Violet directly to the packing crate. "Look!"

Violet's eyelids sprang open. "Gracious sakes alive, if it isn't a sewing machine! Where did it come from?"

"From Philadelphia."

"You mean it's yours?"

"Yes."

Violet didn't remember ever seeing Agatha this happy. Why, she was actually pretty! Funny thing, Violet had never realized it before. Her pale green eyes were alight with excitement. And her smile—gracious sakes alive, what that smile did for her face. Took off a good five years from it and made her look the age she actually was.

"But why didn't you tell me?"

"It's a surprise."

Violet walked in a circle around the crate. Agatha's excitement was infectious. "But . . . but where did you get the mon—" She stopped, looked up. "The ten gold pieces from Mr. Gandy."

"Six. I gave four of them back."

Violet's eyes glittered with shrewd speculation. "We're going to make the cancan dresses, aren't we, Agatha?"

"My stars, Violet! I haven't had time to give it a thought. Come, help me get it out of the crate." Agatha lost all her usual reserve, hustling about like a carefree girl in search of a hammer and screwdriver. She looked so radiant Violet couldn't quit studying her and smiling. When she'd found the tools she set to work. "We'll just knock the front off the packing crate and pull the machine straight out. The two of us should be able to handle it."

Violet couldn't believe the sudden change in the woman she'd seen somber for so many years. "Do you realize what you're doing, Agatha?"

Agatha looked up. "Doing?"

"You're kneeling."

Agatha glanced down. Glorious day! She was! But she was too excited to stop wedging the screwdriver between two slabs of wood. "So I am. Hurts a little bit, but I don't care. Come on, Violet, get your fingers in there and pull."

Instead, Violet's fingers gently touched Agatha's shoulder.

Agatha lifted her face.

"You know, dear, you should do this more often."

"What?"

"Smile. Act young and coltish. What a pretty, pretty young thing you are this way."

Agatha's hands fell still. "P . . . pretty?"

"Most certainly. Why, if you could see your eyes right now, they're as bright as spring clover in the morning dew. And you have roses in your cheeks that I've never seen there before."

Agatha was stunned. *Pretty? Me?*

Not since her mother's death had anyone called her pretty. The roses in her cheeks grew brighter from self-consciousness. Uncomfortable with the unaccustomed praise, she turned to her work again.

"You know, Violet, I think you've been out in the noon sun too long. Now help me with this thing."

Together they worked to free the sewing machine and pull it onto the workroom floor. Agatha touched it reverently, her eyes still gleaming.

"Imagine what a difference it's going to make in the business. I *have* been worried lately, though I didn't want to admit it. Ends have scarcely been meeting. But now . . ." She tested the sleek steel flywheel, brushed her hand appreciatively along the smooth oak cabinet. "Let the hat business dwindle. We can make dresses, can't we, Violet?"

Violet smiled lovingly at the changed young woman before her. "Yes, we can. As fancy as anyone wants them."

Suddenly Agatha sobered. Her face turned worried. "I am doing the right thing, aren't I?"

"The right thing?"

"It really is Mr. Gandy's money that's buying this."

Violet turned realistic, pursing her lips. "You earned that money, didn't you?"

"I don't know. Did I?"

"You most certainly did, young lady. You did a rush job for him that nobody else in town could have done. And you did it with some of the best red satin he could have found. There should be a markup on the satin, shouldn't there?"

"You really think so, Violet?"

"I know so. Now, are you going to stand there all afternoon, or are you going to thread that thing and give it a whirl?"

With the help of the instruction book they loaded the bobbin, dropped it into the bullet-shaped shuttle, followed the diagram, and guided the upper thread into place. When the needle was threaded and a piece of cloth had been secured beneath the presser foot, their eyes met in anticipation.

"Well, here goes." Agatha placed both feet on the treadle, gave one pump, and jerked her feet and hands back. "Awk! It went backward!"

She looked up to Violet for guidance. Violet shrugged. "I don't know. Try it again."

Agatha tried it again. Once more the cloth moved backward. She got up from her chair. "Here, you try it."

Violet took her place and gingerly tested the foot treadle. Backward again. They looked at each other and giggled. "Forty-nine dollars for a sewing machine that only sews backward." The longer they giggled, the funnier it got. With their next attempt the machine took one stitch forward, one back, and another forward. The two women laughed themselves breathless.

Finally, Agatha exclaimed, "The book! Let's read the book."

Eventually, they figured out that the flywheel needed a boost in the right direction to get it going. Agatha sat with the long swatch of cotton flowing smoothly beneath the needle. The belt made a soft hum as it drove the mechanism. The needle arm created a rhythmic cadence. Beautiful, tight stitches appeared magically, at an almost dizzying pace. Agatha's hip hurt as her feet pumped, but she was too excited to notice. It was all she could do to give up her seat to Violet and let her give the machine a second try.

"Isn't it miraculous?" She leaned over Violet's shoulder, watching the blue cotton move smoothly, listening to the wondrous sound of well-oiled machinery working at an unbelievable pace.

Oh, Gandy! she thought. *How ever can I thank you?*

At five o'clock Agatha gave the sewing machine one last appreciative touch, carefully placed the boxy wooden cover over it, then closed the shop. She paused to glance at the rear door of the saloon. It was closed, but still she could hear the place was busy. Undoubtedly, it would get busier tonight. Now would be a far better time to speak to him. Perhaps she could slip in unobtrusively and signal him to the back hall for a moment.

She opened the door and stepped in. The music was absent, but the cowhands' voices created a steady chatter. Laughter and clinking glasses filled the place. Straight ahead she saw Dan Loretto at a crowded table, dealing cards. The smell of stale smoke and old liquor stopped her momentarily. But she gripped her hands and inched her way to the end of the short corridor, searching the main room for Gandy. The moment she came into view, Jack Hogg noticed her. She crooked a finger. He dried his hands and immediately left his post.

"Why, Miss Downing, this is a surprise."

"Mr. Hogg." She nodded in greeting. "I'd like to talk to Mr. Gandy."

"He's in his office. Top of the landing, first door on your right."

"Thank you."

Outside the air wasn't much fresher. Already the smell from the stock pens drifted over the town. The incessant sounds of lowing cattle and clattering trains carried through the late afternoon as Agatha took the stairs. Reaching the landing, she glanced at his window, but the rippled glass gave no more than a reflection of the blue-washed sky. The door squeaked as she opened it and peered along the shadowed hall.

So this was where the gilded cage rested during the day! She smiled at Gandy's ingenuity.

She'd never been upstairs in this half of the building before. Four doors on the left. Two on the right. A window at the far end of the hall overlooking the street. Everything quiet. She felt like a window peeper—why, she wasn't certain. Perhaps because people might be sleeping behind those closed doors at this very moment.

Gandy's office door was closed. She knocked lightly.

"Yes?"

She turned the knob and peeked timidly inside. Gandy sat at an ordinary oak desk in an austere office. He leaned forward, writing, a smoking cigar in an ashtray at his elbow.

"Hello."

He looked up. His face registered surprise before he poked the pen into its holder and leaned back on his well-sprung swivel chair.

"Well, bowl me over," he said softly.

"May I come in?"

Only her head showed around the door. The childlike entry was so untypical of her, he couldn't help grinning.

"By all means." He half rose as she slipped inside and glanced around with frank curiosity.

"So this is where you do business."

He dropped back into his chair, pushed away from the desk, crossed a knee with an ankle, and interlaced his fingers across his stomach.

"Not too fancy, but it serves the purpose."

Her gaze moved across the dull wainscoting, the drab green walls, the tiny stove, the unadorned window with its uninteresting view of the back alley and the prairie beyond.

"Somehow I expected to find you in more lavish surroundings."

"Why?"

"Oh, I don't know. The way you dress, maybe. Those bright vests." Today his vest was celery-green. His black string tie was loosened, his throat button freed, and his shirt-sleeves rolled to mid-arm. His black sack coat hung on the back of his chair. It was five in the afternoon and he needed a shave. She took a moment to appreciate his semitidiness. Heavens above, he *was* one handsome man!

"Funny, I never thought you noticed."

She met his eyes directly. "I work with clothing, Mr. Gandy. I notice everything about it." She continued scanning the room—the safe, the coat-tree. . . . an open doorway? Her eyes fixed upon it, her interest piqued. In his sitting room were the lavish surroundings she'd expected.

And a lady's turquoise-green dressing gown flung across the settee.

He studied her, amused by the interest she suddenly showed in his sitting room and the bedroom beyond. From behind, he catalogued her with a more critical eye than ever before. The elegant rear draperies of her garnet taffeta dress. The shapely "Grecian bend" lent to her lumbar region by unseen corsets. The attractive puff of her bustle, her narrow shoulders, neat hair, and graceful arms accentuated by tight, tight sleeves and a high clerical collar. She dressed with magnificent taste in genteelly elegant clothes. Forever proper.

But something was different about her today. He couldn't pinpoint exactly what.

Agatha realized her mistake only after staring too long into his private apartment. She turned to catch him watching her carefully.

"I . . . I'm sorry."

"It's quite all right. A little more roomy than yours, I take it."

"Yes, quite."

"Have a chair, Miz Downin'."

"Thank you."

"What can I do for you?"

"I believe you've already done it."

He cocked one eyebrow. One dimple pocked his cheek. "Oh?"

"You saw the advertisement for the sewing machine on my workroom wall, didn't you?"

"Did I?"

"Don't spar with me, Mr. Gandy. You saw it and you read my mind."

He chuckled. "Come to the point, Miz Downin'."

"The point is—there's a brand-new patented Isaac Singer sewing machine downstairs, and the packing slip claims it's already paid for."

His smile grew cheeky. "Congratulations."

"Don't be obtuse. I came to thank you for taking it upon yourself to order it, and to pay what I owe you."

"Did I say you owed me anything?"

She produced five gold coins and stacked them on the corner of his desk. "Fifty dollars, I believe, is the correct amount, isn't it?"

"I forget."

She tried to be harsh but her eyes sparkled too brightly, her lips refused to obey. "If you think I'm going to accept an expensive sewing machine from a saloon owner, you . . ."—How had Joe Jessup said it, again?—" . . . you have a wheel loose, Mr. Gandy."

He laughed, then tipped his chair farther back and linked his fingers behind his head. "But it's a bribe."

Her return laugh caught them both by surprise. Then they were laughing together. Gandy noted how her face had changed. That's what was different about her today! It wasn't her hair or her clothing; it was her mood. For once she was happy and it transformed her. The plain gray moth had become a bright, gay finch.

"You admit it?"

Grinning amiably, he shrugged, still with his elbows in the air. "Why not? We both know it's true."

He was an enigma. Dishonest and truthful at once. She found it increasingly difficult to rationalize him. "And what do you hope to gain by it?"

"For starters, three bright red cancan dresses."

A disquieting awareness of his masculine pose hit her like a fist in the stomach. The paler color of his bared wrists and forearms, the tendons running taut from the hands clasped behind his head, the crinkles on the armpits of his white shirt, the black boot resting casually across his knee, the smoke ascending from the ashtray between them.

"Ah," she crooned knowingly, "three bright red cancan dresses." She cocked one eyebrow. "And after that?"

"Who knows?"

She dropped the game-playing. Her voice turned serious. "I'm committed to my temperance work. You know that, don't you?"

He dropped his arms and studied her silently for several seconds. "Yes, I know."

"No amount of bribery can change my mind."

"I hadn't thought it could."

"Tomorrow night we'll be downstairs when your customers arrive, handing out pamphlets that we've had printed, passing out literature detailing the hazards of the fare in which you deal."

"Then I'll have t' think of a new way t' woo my customers, won't I?"

"Yes, I suppose you will."

"You haven't been around for a couple o' days."

"I've been busy. I wrote a letter to the First Lady, thanking her for keeping the White House dry."

"Old Lemonade Lucy?"

Agatha burst out laughing, then smothered the sound with a finger. "So disrespectful, Mr. Gandy."

Half the country called the First Lady that, but it had never seemed quite so funny before.

"Me and plenty of others. She keeps that place drier than the great Sahara."

"At any rate, I wrote to her. *The Temperance Banner* encourages its members to do so. I also wrote to Governor St. John."

"St. John!" Gandy wasn't so blithe about this news. Murmurings about the proposed amendment to the state constitution had more than one Kansas saloon owner nervous. "My, my. We are busy little beavers, aren't we?"

Studying her, he reached for his cheroot and took a deep draw on it. The smoke rose between them before he seemed to realize he'd exhaled it. "Oh, pardon me. I forgot—you hate these things, don't you?"

"After the sewing machine, how could I possibly deny you your pleasure, especially when we're on your battleground?"

He rose and went to the window, anchored the cigar between his teeth, and lifted the sash. She watched his satin waistcoat stretch across his back, wondering which of them would win in the final outcome. He stood looking out, smoking the cheroot, wondering the same thing. After some moments he braced one boot on the sill, leaned an elbow on his knee, and turned to study her over his shoulder.

"You're different than I thought at first."

"So are you."

"This . . . this war we're engaged in, you find it rather amusin', don't you?"

"Me?" She spread a hand on her chest. "I thought you were the one who found it amusing."

"Maybe. In a way. It isn't turnin' out anything like I thought it would. I mean—what general reveals his battle plan to the enemy?"

She smiled. Her face became transformed into the younger, pretty countenance Violet had remarked upon earlier. Her pale eyes softened. Her austerity dissolved.

"So tell me—what name did Mr. Potts give your 'Lady of the Oils'?"

"I'm surprised you didn't hear the other night when you swept in with your invadin' host." Again he made her laugh.

"There were only four of us."

"Is that all?"

"And, anyway, how was it possible to hear anything in that din?"

"Her full name is Dierdre in the Garden of Delight, but the men have nicknamed her Delight."

"Delight. Mmm . . . I'm sure Mrs. Potts is thrilled that Elias won your contest. Next time I see her, I must be sure to say congratulations."

Gandy replied with a full-throated laugh. "Ah, Miz Downin', you're a worthy opponent. I must say I'm comin' to admire you. However, y'all didn't last too long in the saloon the other night."

"We were crowded out."

"Tsk-tsk." He shook his head slowly. "Too bad."

She decided it was time to stop playing cat-and-mouse with him.

"You *are* my enemy," she stated quietly. "And in spite of how my personal opinion of you may be slowly altering, I must never lose sight of that fact."

"Because I sell alcohol?"

"Among other things." It was difficult to believe those other things when he leaned on the windowsill that way— all charm and humor and enticing looks. But she understood quite clearly how he shamelessly used his charm

and humor and enticing looks to sway her from her good
intentions.

"What else?"

Her heart thudded harder than normal. She didn't stop
to question the wisdom or the consequences of what she
was about to ask.

"Tell me, Mr. Gandy, was it you who pinned the threatening note to my door the other night?"

Amusement fled his face. His forehead beetled and his
foot hit the floor. "What?"

Her heart thumped harder. "Was it?"

"How the hell can you ask such a thing?" he demanded
angrily.

It thumped harder still. But she rose to her feet, plucked
his pen from its holder, and held it out to him. "Will you
do something for me? Will you print the words *good, stay,*
and *what* on a piece of paper in capital letters while I
watch you?"

He glared at the pen, then back up at her. He clamped
the cheroot between his teeth and yanked the pen from her
fingers. Leaning from the waist, he slashed the letters across
a piece of scrap paper. When he straightened, his eyes bored
silently into hers. He neither offered to hand her the paper
nor backed away, but stood so close to the desk she'd have
to brush him aside to reach it.

"Excuse me." She nearly bumped him, but he stood his
ground rigidly.

"Don't push your luck," he warned through gritted teeth,
just above her ear.

She picked up the paper and retreated. The smoke from
his cigar burned her nostrils as she studied his printing.

"Satisfied?"

Relief closed her eyelids, brought a light rush of breath
from her nostrils.

He stood before her seething with anger. What the hell
did this woman want from him?

She opened her eyes to confront him directly. "I'm sorry.
I had to be sure."

"And are you?" he snapped.

She felt her face color but stood her ground. "Yes."

He swung toward the desk, stubbed out his cigar in two angry twists of the wrist, and refused to glance her way again. "If you'll excuse me, I have a lot o' work to do. I was orderin' a shipment o' rum when you interrupted me." He sat down and began writing again.

Her heart turned traitor and flooded with remorse. "Mr. Gandy, I said I was sorry."

"G'day, Miz Downin'!"

Her face burning, she turned and shuffled to the door, opened it, and paused with her back to him. "Thank you for the sewing machine," she said quietly.

Gandy's head snapped up. He stared at her back. Damned infernal harpy! What was it about her that got beneath his skin? She took another shuffling step before his bark stopped her.

"Agatha!"

She hadn't thought he remembered her name. Why should it matter that he did?

"I'd like t' see that note if you've still got it."

"Why?"

His face tightened even further. "I don't know why in blue blazes I should feel responsible for you, but I do, goddammit!"

She didn't hold with profanity. Why, then, didn't she take him to task for it?

"I can take care of myself, Mr. Gandy," she declared, then closed the door behind her.

He stared at it, unblinking while he heard the outer door open and close. With a vile curse he flung down his pen. It left a splatter of ink on the order he'd been writing. He cursed again, ripped the paper in half, and threw it away. Then he balled his fists one around the other, pressed them against his chin, and glared at the office wall until her shuffling footsteps finally stopped sounding through his open window.

CHAPTER
7

The W.C.T.U. ladies learned a new song. They sang it with rousing enthusiasm at four saloons the following night.

> Who hath sorrow? Who hath woe?
> They who dare not answer no.
> They whose feet to sin decline
> While they tarry at the wine.

They handed out pamphlets to the men and continued soliciting signatures on pledges. To everyone's surprise, Evelyn Sowers stepped forward several times, boldly accosting saloon goers. With her intense eyes, her sometimes dramatic gesturing, she displayed an amazing oratory flair none had known she possessed.

"Brother, take care of your future now." She seized upon an unsuspecting cowboy who scarcely looked old enough to shave. "Don't you know Satan assumes the shape of a bottle of spirits? Beware that he does not trick you into believing otherwise. Have you thought about tomorrow . . . and tomorrow . . . and the tomorrow after that, when your hands begin trembling and your wife and children suffer without—"

"Lady, I ain't got no wife and children," the young cowpoke interrupted. With wary eyes he sidestepped Evelyn, as if she were a coiled rattler. As he made for the door of the saloon, Evelyn fell to her knees, hands lifted in supplication.

"I beg you, young man, stay out of that male refuge! The saloonkeeper is the destroyer of men's souls!"

The shiny-faced youth glanced over his shoulder and scuttled inside with a look that said he feared Evelyn far more than the dangers to be found behind the swinging doors.

Four more cowboys came along the boardwalk spiffed to the nines, their spurs shining, their jinglebobs ringing. Evelyn stopped them in their tracks with her emotional appeal.

"Do you recognize the evils of the vile compound you've come here to consume? It robs men of their faculties, their honor, and their health. Before you step through that door—"

But they'd already stepped through, looking back at Evelyn with the same trepidation of the young cowpoke.

Evelyn seemed to have found her true calling. During the remainder of the evening as the ladies made a sweep of four saloons, she embraced her newfound ministry with growing fervor.

"Abstinence is virtue; indulgence is sin!" she shouted above the noise from the Lucky Horseshoe Saloon. And when she couldn't outshout the noise, she led her troops inside, walked straight up to Jeff Diddier, and stated, "We've come on a mission of morality—to awaken your conscience." When Evelyn produced a temperance pledge and demanded that Diddier sign it, the ruddy-faced bartender answered by pouring himself a double shot of rye and gulping it down before Evelyn's eyes.

Though Agatha personally didn't hold with Evelyn's histrionics, the woman succeeded in shaming two of Jim Starr's customers into signing the pledge. This success prompted four of Evelyn's "sisters" to drop to their knees with her and begin singing at the top of their lungs. Agatha tried it. But she felt like a fool, kneeling in the saloon. Thankfully, after several painful minutes on the hard wooden floor, she was forced to stand again.

At the Alamo Saloon, Jack Butler and Floyd Anderson appeared to be so embarrassed by seeing their wives in the company of the fanatic Evelyn that they shamefacedly

slipped out the door and disappeared. Spurred on by yet
another victory, Evelyn grew increasingly flamboyant in
both speech and gestures.

By the time the W.C.T.U. contingent reached the Gilded
Cage, the place was going strong, and so was Evelyn. She
elbowed her way into the crush of men, raised both hands
to heaven, and bellowed, "What an army of drunkards shall
reel into hell!"

The dancing and singing stopped. Ivory turned from the
piano. The card games halted. Evelyn looked manic. Her
eyes blazed with unnatural fervor; her fists came down on
tabletop after tabletop. "Go home, Miles Wendt! Go home,
Wilton Spivey! Go home, Tom Ruggles! Go home, all of
you, back to your families, you sinful wretches!" Evelyn
grabbed a mug of beer and upended it at Ruggles's feet."

"Hey, watch it!" He came out of his chair.

"Filth! *Nux vomica!* Swill a man wouldn't feed to his
swine!"

Agatha felt her face coloring. The W.C.T.U. members
prided themselves on nonmilitancy and grace. She looked
up, found Gandy's eyes leveled on her, and glanced away
quickly, only to confront three other pairs of dismayed
eyes—Jubilee's, Pearl's, and Ruby's.

Into the sudden lull Gandy spoke with his usual *savoir
vivre.* "Welcome, ladies." He stood behind the bar, hatless,
dressed totally in black and white.

Evelyn swung on him. "Ah, the rum-soaked ally of Luci-
fer! The trafficker in ardent spirits! Beg the Lord's for-
giveness for the negligence and bestiality you cause to be
visited upon innocent families, Mr. Gandy!" Two cowboys
who'd had enough scraped back their chairs and headed for
the door.

Gandy ignored Evelyn's tirade.

"You're just in time." He raised his voice and called,
"Drinks're on the house, everyone!"

The pair of cowboys spun in their tracks. The roar that
rose nearly deafened Agatha. While it boomed around her
ears, she met Gandy's eyes again. Though the others might
be unable to read beyond his surface charm, she had seen
him grin too many times not to recognize the absence

of mirth in his expression tonight. His eyes pierced her like two icicles. Gone was the amusing glitter she'd come to expect. What passed for a smile was really a baring of teeth.

While their gazes locked, he found the neck of a bottle, filled his glass with amber liquid, and lifted it.

Don't, Gandy, don't.

He gave her a salute so slight nobody else noticed. Then he tipped his head back and changed the salute to an insult.

She had never seen him drink before.

It hurt.

She turned away, feeling empty for no reason she could explain. All around men pushed their way to the bar and raised their glasses for free drinks. Behind her the piano and banjo started up again. Jubilee and the Gems struck into a chorus of "Champagne Charlie," ending with the words, "Come join me in a spree." Evelyn knelt in the middle of the rowdydow praying for the depraved. With her hands crossed over her chest and her eyeballs rolled back, she looked as if she'd been bitten by a rabid dog. At the keno table, men jeered. From the wall, Delight smiled down benevolently on the chaos.

There simply had to be a better way.

Agatha signaled the others to follow her to the door, but only Addie Anderson and Minnie Butler did. As they reached the exit, Agatha turned for one last look. Gandy's obsidian eyes impaled her. She wheeled and pushed through the swinging doors.

And that's when she met Willy Collinson for the first time.

He'd been squatting down, peering beneath the shuttered panel into the saloon, when the door hit him in the forehead and rolled him over like a ninepins ball.

"Ooooowwww!" he howled, holding his head and bawling. "Oww-www-weee."

Agatha struggled to one knee to help him up. Addie and Minnie hovered, clucking with concern.

"I'll see to him. You two go home to your husbands."

When they'd gone, Agatha righted the boy. Standing, he was the same height as she was, kneeling.

"My goodness, child, what were you doing so close to that door? Are you all right?"

"My h . . . head," he sobbed. "You h . . . hit my h . . . head. Owww! It h . . . hurrrrts!"

"I'm sorry." She tried to see how much damage she'd done, but he clutched his head and pulled away. "Let me see."

"Nooo, I w . . . want my p . . . pa."

"Well, your pa's not here, so why not let me see if I can repair the damages?"

"Leave m . . . me al . . . alone."

In spite of his stubbornness, she forced his hands down and turned him toward the pale light coming from the saloon door. His blond hair could have been a sight cleaner. His overalls were soiled and too short. A trickle of blood ran toward his eyebrow.

"My heavens, child, you're bleeding. Come and we'll wash it off."

She struggled to her feet, but he jerked free of her. "No!"

"But I live right next door. See? This is my hat shop, and my apartment is right above it. We should take care of that head right away."

"Pa says I ain't supposed to go with strangers."

She dropped her hands to her sides. He was calmer now. "But what did he say about emergencies?"

"I don't know what them are."

"Getting bumped in the head by a swinging door—*that's* an emergency. It truly is. Your forehead needs washing and a touch of iodine."

He backed away, shaking his head no. His eyes grew round as horse chestnuts.

"Look out. Someone will come out and smack you again. Come along." She reached out a hand with a businesslike air. "At least move away from the door while we talk."

Instead, he knelt down and peered beneath it.

"You're too young to be peeking in there!"

"Gotta find Pa."

"Not that way, you won't." She stood him on his feet none too gently. He began to sniffle again. "There are things going on in there that a boy your age shouldn't see. How old are you, anyway?"

"None o' your business!" he said defiantly.

"Well, I'll make it my business, young man. I'll march you straight home to your mother and tell her what I found you doing."

"I ain't got no mother. She died."

For the second time that night, Agatha's heart felt pierced. "Oh," she said softly, "I . . . I'm sorry. I didn't know. Then we *must* find your father, mustn't we?"

He dropped his chin to his chest. "He ain't been home since after work." His chin began to tremble and he rubbed one eye with his dirty knuckles. "He said he'd come home tonight . . . b . . . but . . . he n . . . never come."

His voice quavered. Agatha felt sick with pity. Awkwardly, she touched his blond hair. She'd been around so few children in her life. How did one speak to a five-year-old? Six-year-old? Whatever his age, he wasn't old enough to be wandering in the street after dark. He should be in a warm bed after a warm bath and a hot supper. "If you'll tell me your name," she encouraged softly, "I'll try to help you find him."

Still scrubbing his eyes, he glanced up uncertainly, revealing wide glimmering eyes, a pug nose, and a trembling mouth. She watched him struggle with indecision.

"I'm really a very nice lady." She gave him a kind smile. "I have no little boys of my own, but if I did I'd never bump them over with swinging doors." She tipped her head to one side. "The lucky thing was, you rolled up just like a porcupine."

He tried not to laugh but couldn't stop himself. It came out as a reluctant snuffle.

"That's better. Now, are you going to make me guess what your name is?"

"Willy."

"Willy what?"

"Collinson."

Suddenly, she understood. *Take it slow, Gussie. Don't lose his trust now.*

"Well, Willy Collinson, if you'll sit down there on the step, I'll go back inside and see if I can spot your father and tell him you're waiting to walk him home. How's that?"

"Would you? He gets awful mad when I go in after 'im."

"Of course I would. You sit here and I'll be right back."

She paused at the swinging doors, looking over them at the revelry inside. Evelyn was gone. Behind the bar Gandy and Jack Hogg served drinks. Jubilee and the girls circulated, talking to the customers. In the near corner Dan Loretto dealt a game of blackjack. Agatha pushed the doors open and eased through the mob, searching for Collinson, unable to spot him. She tried to recall if she'd seen him earlier tonight but didn't remember. Passing a round table crowded with men, she felt a hand brush her thigh. Another reached out and clutched her arm. She jerked free, panicked, and advanced toward the bar. Gandy was laughing at something one of the customers said, looking down as he poured amber whiskey into a shot glass.

"Mr. Gandy?"

His head snapped up. The laughter fell from his face.

"I thought you were gone."

"I'm looking for Mr. Collinson. Is he in here?"

"Alvis Collinson?"

"Yes."

"What do you want with him?"

"Is he in here?"

"You've lived in Proffitt longer than I have—find him." His jaw tensed and his eyes remained hard with challenge.

Someone bumped her from behind. She lost her balance and caught at the back of a leather-covered shoulder to keep on her feet.

"Hey, what's this?" The cowboy turned lazily, slipped an arm around her hips, and flattened her to his side. His breath reeked as he leaned close. "Where ya been hidin', li'l lady?"

She pushed against him, straining away.

"Let her go, fella," Gandy ordered.

The stranger ran his hand up Agatha's ribs, squeezing. "Feels too good to let it go."

Gandy was over the bar so fast he kicked two glasses off and beat them to the floor.

"I said let her go." He grabbed the wandering hand from Agatha and flung it back. "She's not one of the girls."

"All right, all right." The cowboy raised both palms, as if Gandy had pulled a derringer. "If she's your own personal property, ya shoulda said so, buddy."

A nerve jumped in Gandy's cheek. Agatha's stomach trembled and she blinked at the floor.

Gandy plucked a bone-colored Stetson off the bar and shoved it against the cowpoke's belly. "There's plenty o' whorehouses down the street, if that's what you're lookin' for. Now, git!"

"Jesus, man, you're touchy."

"That's right. I run a clean saloon."

The cowpoke slapped his hat on, pocketed some change, and flashed Agatha an angry glare. She felt other eyes probing her from all directions and turned away so Gandy couldn't see the tears of mortification in her eyes.

"Agatha."

She stopped, squared her shoulders.

"What do you want with Collinson?"

She glanced back at him. "His little boy's outside waiting for him to come home."

Gandy's resolution faltered for an instant. A vein stood out on his forehead as his eyes locked on hers. He nodded toward a table in the rear corner. "Collinson's over there."

She turned away.

His hand caught her elbow again. She looked up into his displeased eyes. "Don't rile him. He's got the temper of a wild boar."

"I know."

This time Gandy let her go. But he kept a close eye on her all the while she worked her way through the throng past a surprised Ruby, who stopped her to say something. She nodded, touched Ruby's hand, then moved on. Collinson glanced up in surprise when she stepped to his elbow. He listened to what she had to say, glanced toward the swinging doors, scowled, then threw down his cards angrily. He nudged her aside rudely when he lurched from his chair. She wobbled and, across the room, Gandy took one quick step toward her. She caught her balance against the side of the table and he relaxed. Collinson elbowed his way through the crowd, leaving her to fend for herself.

When she started working her way toward the door, Gandy did the same. He wouldn't put anything past Collinson.

Outside, the son-of-a-bitch was laying into his kid. "What the hell ya mean comin' up here when I tole ya to keep outta the saloon?" He pulled the boy off the step by one arm. Agatha's hands closed over the tops of the swinging doors. Her body strained toward the boy, tensed with uncertainty. Gandy silently came up behind her and gripped her shoulder. Her head snapped around. Without a word he moved in front of her and led the way onto the boardwalk, already reaching for a cheroot.

"You winnin' tonight, Collinson?" he inquired, forcing a bantering tone. He lit the cigar with deceptive calmness.

"I was till the twerp comes badgerin' me t' git home."

"Who's this . . . ? Well, howdy, son. Kinda late for y'all t' be out, isn't it?"

"I came to git Pa."

"Boy, I tole you, I come home when I'm good and ready. Now, I left a winnin' hand layin' on that table. How come you ain't at your Aunt Hattie's?"

"She ain't my aunt, and I don't like it at her place."

"Then git on home to bed."

"I don't like it there, neither. It's scary there alone."

"I told you, boy, that's bullshit. Chickens is scared o' the dark."

Gandy stepped forward and spoke to the boy. "Oh, I don't know. I recall times when I was a lad, I used t' think I heard voices behind me in the dark."

"Butt out, Gandy!"

The two men stood nose to nose in the deep shadows. The little boy looked up at them. Agatha moved beside him and put her hand on his shoulder.

"Take the boy home, Collinson," Gandy advised in an undertone.

"Not while I got me a winnin' hand."

"I'll cover your bet. Take him." Gandy reached for Collinson's arm.

The larger man shook it off and pushed Gandy back a step. "I cover my own bets, Gandy. And the brat lays off me when I'm havin' a good time!" He took a threatening step toward Willy. "Got that, kid?"

Willy huddled against Agatha's skirt.

Gandy answered for him. "He's got it, Collinson. Go on back inside. Enjoy your game."

"Damned right I will." He plucked Willy away from Agatha and aimed him toward the street. "Now quit snivelin' and git home where ya belong." He gave Willy a shove that sent him scuttling down the steps.

Willy ran a short distance, then turned to look back at his father. Agatha heard his soft, muffled crying.

Collinson spun and stomped back inside, muttering, "Goddamned kid could give a man liver trouble . . ."

Willy turned and ran.

"Willy, wait!" Agatha struggled down the three steps, but she was no runner. She hobbled after him but made it only the length of the hitching rail before she gave up the hopeless pursuit. "Willy!" Her anguished cry blended with the noise drifting out of the saloon as she gripped her aching hip.

Gandy watched her struggle, heard the boy running off, crying in the dark.

Agatha spun around and appealed, "Do something, Gandy!"

In that instant he began to see too clearly what it was this woman wanted of him and he wanted no part of it. But he answered the tug of his own unwilling heart.

"Willy!" He tossed aside his cheroot, leaped to the street, and took off at a run, his heart already pounding. A five-year-old's legs were no match for Gandy's long limbs. He caught up with Willy in less than a dozen strides and plucked him from the middle of the street into his arms.

The child clung to Gandy and buried his face in his neck.

"Willy. Don't cry . . . hey, hey . . . it's all right." Gandy had no experience with comforting children. He felt awkward and slightly terrified. The child weighed next to nothing, but the skinny arms clung to Gandy as if he himself were the boy's father. Gandy swallowed hard, twice. The lump in his throat refused to budge. He carried Willy back to Agatha and stood before her, feeling out of his depth.

She touched Willy's shuddering back, rubbed it reassuringly. "Shh! Shh!" Her voice was low and soothing. "You're not alone, little one." She smoothed the cowlick on top of Willy's head. Gandy's hand spread on the child's rumpled shirt, over the thin ribs that heaved in rhythm with his sobs. Her hand moved down. Their fingers touched briefly. A spark of good intentions bound them in that instant and they each fought the urge to link fingers in their joint effort to help the boy. Together, they turned toward the steps and sat side by side, with Willy on Gandy's lap.

"Willy, don't cry anymore."

But the little boy could not be silenced. He burrowed into Gandy, who helplessly looked over the blond head at Agatha. He saw the glint of tears in her eyes as her hand rubbed Willy's thin arm.

"I'd take him myself if I could, but . . ." During her brief pause he remembered the pitiful sight of her trying to run after the boy. "Could you carry him up to my place?"

He nodded.

They went through the dark millinery shop, out the back door, and up the back stairs. It had never taken Gandy so long to make the climb. With Willy in his arms he adjusted his pace to Agatha's, watching her shuffling two-step as she clung to the rail. All the way up, he found himself recalling his youth at Waverley—healthy, hale, and surrounded by all the love and security a little boy could want to allow him to grow up happy.

At the landing Agatha unlocked her door and led the way into total blackness.

"Wait here. I'll light a lamp."

Gandy stood still, listening to the two of them—Agatha, shuffling away; Willy, sobbing against his neck.

A lantern flared halfway down a room with the proportions of a stick match. Gandy barely had time to form the quick impression before she spoke again.

"Bring him over here."

He set the boy on the tiniest gateleg table he'd ever seen.

"If I could impose upon you one more time, it will be the last." She handed him a white enamel pail. "Could you fill this for me?"

He hurried back downstairs and filled her water bucket from the barrel beneath the steps. As he headed back up with the weighty pail, he thought of Agatha instead of the boy. If it was that difficult for her to climb the stairs empty-handed, how did she manage it with a bucket of water?

When he returned Willy was calmer. The two of them were quietly talking. He set the bucket on a low stool beside her dry sink and turned to find Agatha wiping the boy's lower eyelids with her thumbs. Gandy moved to stand beside them, looking down on the blond head and narrow shoulders. Willy was undeniably dirty. Hair, clothing, fingernails, neck—all could stand more than a bucket of cold water. Gandy's eyes met Agatha's and he saw she was thinking the same thing.

"Now, let's take care of that bump on your head." She turned and grabbed a cloth from a towel holder on the wall, slung it over her shoulder, and scooped a dipperful of water into a basin. The water sloshed close to the brim of the basin as she brought it to the table. Gandy stood by, feeling oversized and useless as she dipped and wrung and applied the cloth to Willy's forehead.

The boy pulled back, whimpering.

"I know it hurts. I'll be gentle."

Gandy braced one palm on the table beside Willy and talked. "I remember once when I was about your size, maybe a little older. We had this river where I lived. The Tombigbee, it was called. My friend and I used to swim there durin' the summer. That was down in Miz'sippi, and it gets mighty hot in Miz'sippi 'round about July." He accented the "Ju" in July. Agatha glanced up and smiled.

"So hot, in fact, that sometimes we wouldn't wait t' shuck off our britches. We'd jump in clothes and all. Time I'm talkin' about, Cleavon and me—" He glanced at Agatha and told her, "Cleavon is Ivory's real name." He returned his attention to the boy. "Well, anyway, Cleavon and me went runnin' down to that river full tilt. Head first in the water we goes, and sure enough, I hit a rock and put a goose egg on my forehead the size o' your fist. Y' got a fist, don't y'?"

Willy proudly displayed one puny fist. He had stopped resisting Agatha and sat entranced. From the corner of his eye, Gandy saw her pick up the iodine. He rambled on.

"Knocked me out colder'n a clam, too. My friend Cleavon fished me out and went yellin' for help. My father came down to the river himself and carried me back up to the house. We had this old dictator called Leatrice . . ." Agatha smiled at the name: Lee-att-riss. "She was black as an eight ball and shaped about the same, only much, much bigger. Leatrice scolded me. Told me I didn't have a lick o' sense in my head.

"Well, now, Willy, I figured I was smarter than her." Agatha applied the iodine and Willy scarcely flinched. "After all, *I* went down to the river swimmin' when it got up to a hundred degrees in July. Leatrice, she stayed in the hot kitchen."

"How come?" Willy asked.

"How come Leatrice stayed in the kitchen?"

Willy nodded vigorously. Gandy's eyes met Agatha's briefly. Had she been for the North or South? he wondered. And fifteen years after the war, did it still matter to her, as it did to some?

"B'cause she worked for us. She was our cook."

"Oh." Willy was blessed with a child's ignorance of overtones. He went on with undisguised interest. "What happened to your goose egg?"

Gandy laughed. "Leatrice put a foul-smellin' marigold poultice on it and made me drink basswood tea for my headache."

"Did it go away?"

Gandy laughed. "Most of it." He leaned forward, touching a finger to his hairline. "Still carry a little scar right here to remind me never to dive into rivers without knowin' what's beneath the water. And my father had a swimmin' pool dug after that, and that's where I did my swimmin' from then on."

When he straightened, Agatha studied his hairline, searching for the scar.

His eyes roved in her direction. She dropped her glance. In the lull, Willy asked, "It still hurt?"

"Nah. Don't even remember it's there most times. Yours'll go away, too."

Willy gingerly tested the bruise on his forehead and declared, "I'm hungry."

If Agatha had had her way, she'd have had a pantry that was a child's delight, filled with tasty treats to make him forget his bumps and scrapes. If she'd had her way, she'd have stuffed Willy until his belly popped. As it was, all she could offer was, "How about some rusks?"

Willy nodded enthusiastically.

She found the dry cinnamon toast and left Willy sitting on the table edge with the entire tin.

"I wish I had a kitchen," she told Gandy. "I've always wanted one."

For the first time he took a good look at her lodgings. The apartment was half the size of his—and his seemed cramped. There was a stove, the dry sink, but no other signs of the domestic trappings necessary for cooking. Her furnishings were old and sturdy. A sampler hung on the wall, lace curtains on the windows. It was almost painfully neat.

"How long have you lived here?"

"Thirteen years. Since my father died. We lived in Colorado when he was alive. After he was gone, Mother wanted to make a new start, get away from bad memories. So we came here and she opened up the millinery shop. I've lived here ever since."

"But you don't like it?"

Her eyes met his. "Does anybody like what life doles out to them? It's where I live. It's where my work is. I stay, just like hundreds of others."

He'd always felt so free to come and go where he pleased, to pull up roots and plant them somewhere new. He couldn't imagine staying in a place he disliked for so long. He himself didn't think Proffitt was the Garden of Eden, but he intended to stay only long enough to make a killing. Then he'd move on.

While his gaze roved around her dwelling, hers rested on him. "Your collar is soiled."

Gandy came away from his musings to realize she'd spoken to him.

"What?"

"I said, your collar is soiled." He dropped his chin but he couldn't see. "A little of Willy's blood," she clarified.

Gandy spied a tiny oval mirror above the dry sink and went to peer into it. He had to dip his knees to do so. He rubbed the collar.

"I could try to get it out with a little cold water."

He turned. "Would you?"

No, she wanted to reply, sorry now that she'd made the offer. Whatever was she trying to prove, fussing over Gandy's clothing? It was having the little boy here, and the man—almost as if the three of them were a family. She'd best not carry the pretext too far.

But she'd offered, and he was waiting. "Let me get some fresh water." She took the washbasin to the dry sink and stopped before him. He stood directly in front of the doors. "Excuse me." She glanced down.

"Oh . . . sorry." He jumped and stepped back.

She poured the dirty water into a slop pail, closed the doors, and refilled the basin. When she turned to him with a damp cloth, their eyes met briefly, then flashed apart.

"Perhaps you should loosen your tie."

"Oh . . . sure." He gave it a yank, worked it free with a finger, whipped it off, then stood waiting.

"And the collar button."

He freed it.

Her hands lifted and his chin shot up. Oddly enough, she sensed that he was as uncomfortable as she. She inserted the corner of a clean towel behind the collar and soaked it from the front with a wet one. It was the first time in her life she had ever touched a man's neck. It was warm and soft. The whiskers on the underside of his jaw grazed the back of her hand, sharp but not unpleasant—another first. His beard was inordinately heavy and black. He nearly always appeared to need a shave. The scent of his tobacco clung to his clothes. In lighter doses it became distinctly pleasant.

Gandy studied her stamped-tin ceiling. *What in hell's name're you doin' here, boy? This woman is trouble. An hour ago she and her infernal "drys" were harassin' your customers and tryin' to get them to go home! Now you're standin' with your chin in the air, lettin' her mollycoddle you.*

"You know, it's funny," he commented, still studying her ceiling.

"What?"

"What we're doin' now, and what we were doin' an hour ago."

"I know."

"I have mixed feelin's about it."

Her hands dropped and so did his chin. Their eyes met. Hers wavered away.

"So do I," she admitted softly. Again she lifted her face and met his gaze. "This wasn't exactly our choice, though, was it?"

He glanced at Willy, then back at her. "Not exactly."

"And just because I've sponged your soiled collar doesn't mean I've joined your camp."

"You'll be back with more ammunition."

A tiny sting of regret coiled within Agatha as she answered, "Yes."

"And I'll keep sellin' whiskey."

"I know."

While Willy sat on the table eating rusks, Agatha and Gandy stood looking at each other. They were enemies. Or were they? Most certainly they were not allies! Yet neither could deny, through some mysterious means, that they had become friends.

There was something on her mind that she simply had to say. She lay the wet cloths over the edge of the dry sink, half turning from him. "I want you to know, I was embarrassed by what Evelyn Sowers did in your saloon tonight. She's turning into a radical, and I'm not certain if I can stop her." She swung around, revealing a troubled expression. "I'm not even sure if it's my job to try to stop her. I didn't ask to lead the W.C.T.U., you know. Drusilla Wilson finessed me into it."

In the narrow, quiet, lonesome-looking room, Gandy suddenly became aware of how clearly the sounds of the music and voices filtered through the walls into her apartment. She opened her shop early in the morning. He supposed many mornings she opened it tired and grouchy, while he and the gang slept soundly on the other side of the wall.

"Listen, I'm sorry about the noise."

She hadn't expected him to say such a thing. Neither had she expected to hear herself answer as she did.

"And I'm sorry about Evelyn Sowers."

It struck them both at once—they were smiling at each other.

Gandy recovered first. "I'd better get back. It's busy down there and they need me."

She glanced at the shadows thrown by the lantern light into the open neck of his shirt. "I couldn't get all the blood out of your collar."

He touched it and glanced down. "That's all right. I'll stop by my apartment and put on a clean one."

Gandy glanced at the table. Willy was munching, scratching his head and swinging his crossed feet. Gandy spoke to Agatha in an undertone. "What are you goin' t' do with him? You can't very well keep him here."

"I'll walk him home. I wish I didn't have to, but . . ." She glanced at the boy, then back at Gandy. Her face saddened. "Oh, Gandy, he's so little to be left alone that way."

He reached out and squeezed her upper arm. "I know. It's not our problem, though."

"Isn't it?"

Their eyes communicated for several long, intense seconds. He dropped his hand.

"I intend to ask Reverend Clarksdale to talk to Alvis Collinson," she said.

"Do you think it'll do any good?"

"I don't know. Do you have a better idea?"

He didn't. Furthermore, he didn't want to become embroiled in Willy's problems. He was no crusader. That was her forte. But he crossed to stand before the boy.

"You about full yet?"

Willy beamed and wagged his head no.

"Well bring one for the road. Agatha's goin' t' walk you home."

Willy stopped chewing. His face fell. He talked through a mouth full of rusks. "But I don't wanna go home. I like it here."

Gandy hardened his heart, handed Willy one rusk, put the cover on the tin, and lifted him from the edge of the table. "Maybe your pa is home by now. If he is, he's probably worried about you."

Fat chance, he thought, meeting Agatha's eyes, which reflected a similar thought.

They left the lantern glowing and walked out to the landing, all holding hands, with Willy forming a living link between Agatha and Gandy. She expected Gandy to leave them there and enter his apartment. Instead, he put his hands under Willy's armpits. "Up you go!" He carried him down the stairs, patiently keeping pace beside Agatha. At the bottom he set Willy down and squatted before him. "Tell y' what. Y'all come by and visit me some afternoon." He swiveled on the balls of his feet and pointed with a long index finger. "See that window up there? That's my office."

Willy looked up and smiled. "Really?"

"Really. You ever seen cotton—I mean real cotton just the way it grows?"

"Uh-uh."

"Well, I got some up there. Y'all come visit and I'll show it to y'."

Impulsively, Willy flung his arms around Gandy's neck and gave him an enormous hug. "I'm comin' tomorrow!"

Gandy laughed and turned the boy toward Agatha. "Go on home now, and sleep tight."

When Willy returned to Agatha, his hand reached for hers without hesitation. As she took it, her heart contracted, then felt an upsurge of happiness.

"Say good-night to Mr. Gandy."

Willy turned, still holding her hand, and waved over his shoulder. "'Night, Mr. Gandy."

"'Night, Willy."

Gandy had a sudden thought. "Agatha, wait!"

She stopped. He held up a finger. "Just a minute." He disappeared into the shadows beneath the steps and entered the rear door of the saloon. In only a moment he returned, stepping out into the moonlight. "All right," he said quietly.

So Alvis Collinson was still inside. Instinctively, she tightened her fingers around the small hand she held.

"Good night, Gandy," she said softly.

"G'night, Agatha."

Wearing a troubled frown, the tall man with the black whiskers watched them walk away into the dark, holding hands.

Collinson's house was a pigsty. It had a dirt floor and a rusting stove. Filthy dishes with spoiled food tainted the air. Soiled clothing lay wherever it had been dropped. Agatha had to close her mind to the condition of the bed into which she tucked Willy.

"You'll be all right now."

His luminous brown eyes told her his bravery was slipping, now that she was about to leave him.

"You goin', Agatha?"

"Yes, Willy. I have to."

His chin quivered. She knelt beside the bed and brushed the hair back from his temple. "When you visit Mr. Gandy, be sure to drop by my shop and say hello to me."

He didn't answer. His lips compressed. Tears formed in the corners of his eyes.

May your soul burn in hell, Alvis Collinson, for treating this beautiful child as if you wished he weren't alive, while I would give my one good hip to have one like him. It was all she could do to keep her eyes dry.

"You'll do that, won't you?"

He swallowed and nodded. A tear slipped down his cheek.

She bent and kissed it, feeling as if her heart would burst its bounds.

The stench of the bedclothes seemed to linger in her nostrils all the way home.

CHAPTER
8

Within a week Willy became a fixture at Agatha's millinery shop. She'd hear the back door open and a moment
later he'd be standing at her elbow asking, "What's that?"
"Why're ya doin' that?" "What's this for?" He had been
unfairly slighted in the education department. Though he
was curious about everything, he had basic understanding
of little. She answered each of his questions patiently,
pleased by the way his eyes lit up at each new tidbit he
learned.

"That's a thimble."

"What's it for?"

"Pushing a needle, see?"

"What's them?"

"What are they?" she corrected. Then she answered,
"Stones, just plain old stones."

"What y' gonna do with 'em?"

"Hold down the pattern while I cut around it . . . see?"
Since she'd acquired the sewing machine, she'd subscribed
to Ebenezer Butterick's fashion journal and had ordered
twenty of his tissue patterns, which had excited her customers and already brought in several dress orders. Today,
however, she was cutting out the first of three scarlet-and-
black cancan dresses. She selected stone after stone from
a tin washbasin, weighting the tissue into place. With his
chin on the edge of the high worktable, Willy watched
intently while she cut out the skirt. His eyes documented
how carefully she pushed aside each severed piece with the

138

pattern and stones still in place. He checked the washbasin, then the remaining pattern pieces.

"You're gonna need more stones, Agatha."

She peered into the basin. "So I am, Willy." She affected a frown. "Oh, bother, how I hate to stop working to go out and get them."

"I'll go!" He was heading toward the door before the smile lifted her cheeks.

"Willy?"

He spun, brown eyes eager, hair sticking up on end. "Huh?"

"Take the basin to collect them in." After dumping the remaining stones onto her worktable, she handed it to him. As she continued working, she looked up often and gazed out the back door to see him squatting in the dirt, his curved backside almost touching the ground, chin to knees, digging with a stick. He came inside five minutes later, proudly bearing a basin full of dirty rocks.

"Take them out back and wash them first or they'll soil the cloth."

He bounded outside but returned in seconds. "I can't reach."

She laughed and felt happier than she ever remembered feeling as she went outside to help him. While she bent to scoop water from the deep wooden barrel, she commented, "We'll have to get you a little stool to stand on, won't we?" Before she went back inside, she added sternly, "And make sure you get those hands clean at the same time."

When he came back in, his soiled clothes were covered with damp spots where he'd dried the rocks. He huffed and puffed, carrying the heavy basin, but set it down proudly at her feet.

"There! I done it!"

"I did it," she corrected.

"I did it," he parroted.

She made a great show of examining the rocks. "And a fine job, too. All clean and—my goodness!—even dried. Go out front and ask Violet for a penny. Tell her I said you earned it."

His face grew radiant, the cheeks rounded like October apples. Then he spun and darted through the curtain. Agatha smiled at the sound of his giddy, high voice.

"Hey, Vy-let, Agatha says to ast you for a penny. She says t' tell you I urnt it."

"She did?" came Violet's reply. "Well, now, just what did you do to earn it?"

"Picked 'er some rocks and washed 'em and dried 'em."

"She's right. That's hard work. I don't know what we did before we had you around here." Agatha imagined Willy's shining eyes following Violet's hands as she fetched a penny from the cash drawer of the desk. A moment later the front door slammed.

He was back in less than five minutes with a sarsaparilla stick. Sucking it, he took up his stand beside the worktable again.

"Wanna suck?" He pointed the stick in Agatha's direction. Knowing how rarely he got candy, Agatha realized the value of a lick. She hadn't the heart to say no.

"Mmm . . ."

"Sassparilly." He rammed it back into his mouth. A minute later he inquired, "What's that?" One stubby finger pointed.

"That's powdered chalk."

"What's it for?"

"Pricking."

"What's pricking?"

"That's what it's called when I mark the places where I must stitch this dart together."

"What's a dart?"

"A dart is a row of stitching that holds the cloth together and gives the dress shape."

"Oh." He scratched his head vigorously, working the sarsaparilla stick on his tongue as if it were the plunger on a butter churn. He watched her hands intently. "You gotta get that chalk through them tiny holes?"

"That's right." The only markings on the thin paper were holes of graduated sizes, each size having its own meaning. She carefully sprinkled fine powdered chalk across them and rubbed it in before fastidiously removing the pattern piece, leaving a series of clearly marked white dots. "See?"

"Garsh!"

"Isn't it remarkable?" She, too, was still awed by the new patterns and her sewing machine. Work had become exciting.

She curled the pattern piece and tapped the chalk back into the glass pot. Willy scratched his head and chewed up the last of his sarsaparilla. "Could I try doin' that sometime?"

"Not today. And most certainly not until you wash those sticky hands. *And* the edge of the table!" She looked pointedly at the smudged spots where his fingers had been resting.

After that day he began showing up with cleaner hands. But the rest of him was still a mess. He scratched his head constantly. He wore the same clothing day after day. He smelled abominable. Agatha spoke to Reverend Clarksdale, but it seemed to make no difference. Alvis Collinson paid no more attention to his son than before. But the attention Willy lacked at home he got in Agatha's workroom. The hours he spent there became the brightest of her day, and of his, too, she suspected.

At nighttime her W.C.T.U. work continued. She made it a practice to attach herself to any of the groups except that including Evelyn Sowers. She set up a routine of visiting four saloons each night, ending, regularly as clockwork, at the Gilded Cage. As time went on, more and more local men signed temperance pledges. Few of them, however, were Gandy's regular customers.

He was too innovative to lose any.

The night Agatha stationed herself outside his door and read aloud from *Seven Nights in a Barroom,* he hung out a shingle advertising free popcorn.

The night she distributed pamphlets entitled "Help the Heathen Cowboy of the West," he offered a token good for one free bath at the Cowboys' Rest in exchange for each pamphlet handed in at the bar.

The night she led the ladies in the song, "Lips That Touch Whiskey Shall Never Touch Mine," he posted a list of the newest drinks available at the Gilded Cage— concoctions with such intriguing names as gin slings, mint juleps, sangarees, sherry cobblers, timber doodles, and blue blazers.

The night she led the ladies in the old Christian standard, "Faith of Our Fathers," he nodded at Ivory, who immediately chimed in with a piano accompaniment. Then Gandy stood behind the bar and directed his entire clientele in the most rousing rendition of the song Proffitt had ever heard . . . in or out of church! When the "amen" faded, he grinned at Agatha and announced, "Free sardines at the bar! Come and get 'em, everybody!"

When she passed around a collection bowl seeking donations for the movement, he announced the keno pot would double that night.

Yes, Gandy most certainly was innovative. But Agatha had come to enjoy the challenge of trying to best him.

One evening, before his crowd arrived and before her constituents gathered, she walked into the Gilded Cage and headed directly for the bar. Gandy was on its near side, leaning back with his elbows resting on its well-polished edge, watching her approach. His Stetson was pulled low. He puffed on a cheroot without touching a finger to it. His ginger-brown waistcoat was immaculate. And his dimples were intact.

"Well, what brings you in so early, Miz Downin'?" He always called her "Miss Downing" when others were around.

She handed him a copy of "Help the Heathen Cowboy of the West."

"My free bath token, if you please, Mr. Gandy."

He glanced down at the pamphlet, removed the cheroot, and broadened his grin. "I have t' presume you're serious."

She nodded. "Most certainly. A pamphlet for a token, I believe the sign says."

He took the pamphlet and flicked through the pages. "I hope y'all don't expect me t' read it."

"Do as you like, Mr. Gandy. My token, please?" she repeated amiably, holding out a palm. She and Gandy hadn't the slightest problem confronting each other with the utmost civility even while issuing challenges back and forth.

Again he leaned back against the bar, elbows caught up as before. Over his shoulder he instructed, "Give the lady a bath token, Jack."

The cash register rang and Jack Hogg extended a round wooden slug. "Here ya go, Miss Downing."

"Thank you, Mr. Hogg."

"Best time to go down to the Rest is probably early in the morning before the cowboys are up."

Her neck grew pink; no respectable woman in the state of Kansas would be caught mummified in a place like the Cowboys' Rest. Still, she returned politely, "I'll remember that."

She turned to leave.

"Oh, Miss Downing?" She turned back to Jack. "I got a shirt ripped out under the arm that could use a little stitching up on that sewing machine of yours."

"Bring it over any time. If I'm not there, Miss Parsons is."

"I'll do that." He tipped his bowler and smiled. She no longer thought of the livid half of his face but imagined how handsome he'd been before it became scarred.

As she passed Gandy, he picked up a platter from the bar. "Have a sardine, Miz Downin'?"

She glanced at the platter, then up at him. His dimples declared very plainly that he expected her to decline.

"Why, thank you, Mr. Gandy. I don't mind if I do." She detested fish, but she plucked one from the platter and popped it into her mouth without hesitation. She chewed. Stopped. Chewed again and swallowed, then shivered violently and squinted hard.

"What's wrong? Don't like sardines?"

"Shame on you, Mr. Gandy! Have you no conscience at all, feeding your customers fish that are as salty as the seven seas?"

"None whatsoever."

"And popcorn, which I'm sure is the same."

"Next week we're bringin' in fresh oysters. Not as salty, but a delicacy nevertheless." He cocked one eyebrow and hefted the platter. "Have another?"

She glanced wryly at the lineup of slick fish. "Free enterprise, I suppose you call it." He set the platter down and laughed. She licked the oil off her finger and thumb. "What will you think of next, Mr. Gandy?"

"I don't know." His gaze was totally friendly and winning. "I'm runnin' out o' ideas. How about you?"

She didn't laugh. But it took great self-control not to.

Agatha decided it was best to be frank with her fellow W.C.T.U. members and tell them she was doing work for Mr. Gandy and his employees.

Evelyn Sowers puckered up and snorted. "Consorting with the enemy!"

Agatha had expected this. "Perhaps it is, but to a good end. Ten percent of all the profits I earn from Mr. Gandy will be donated to the cause. As you all know, our coffers are very slim."

Evelyn's mouth remained sour, but she offered no further argument.

Jubilee, Pearl, and Ruby came for a fitting. They sashayed through the back door in lazy fashion, chattering and laughing, wearing their dressing gowns. Pearl's was pink. Ruby's was purple.

Jubilee's was turquoise-green.

Agatha tried hard not to stare at it.

The three laughed and came inside the shop proper. "Hello, Agatha. Hello, Violet. Howdy, Willy."

Willy left Agatha's side to run and meet them. "You gonna try on your new dancin' dresses?"

Ruby tweaked Willy's nose. "Sho' nuff."

"I'm gonna peek under the door and watch you dance in 'em."

Jubilee affectionately turned him by a shoulder. "Oh, no, you're not, young man."

"Am, too."

"If I catch you, I'll paddle your backside."

Willy wasn't threatened. He smiled and shook his head confidently. "Uh-uhhhh."

"How do you know I won't?"

" 'Cause I'll run and tell Scotty and Agatha and they won't letcha."

With her hands on her hips, Jube leaned down and rested her forehead against Willy's. "Pretty smart little scalawag, aren't you, Willy Collinson?"

"Agatha says I am."

Everyone laughed. Pearl tousled Willy's hair.

He lifted brown eyes to her. "I been helpin' Agatha make your dresses, Pearl."

"You have!"

"Ain't I, Agatha?" He turned excitedly to her.

"Haven't I?" she corrected, beaming down at him. "He most certainly has. He puts the weights on the patterns after I lay them on the fabric."

Violet added, "And he helps keep the ruffles from curling while Agatha and I do the gathering."

Ruby rested a fist on one hip and assumed a falsely supercilious pose. "Well, would y' feature that now!"

"And Agatha says she's gonna get me a stool so I can see up on the table better and reach into the water barrel."

Another laugh.

Then Agatha got down to business. "The dresses are ready for fitting." She brought them out and hung them on a high rod. "They're going to be quite, quite stunning."

They were. Especially on three such exquisite bodies. Agatha couldn't help envying the girls as they slipped from their robes, displaying wasp waists shaped by flattering corsets with spoon busks running down the center fronts. Upon Agatha's request, all three had worn their high-heeled boots so the hem lengths could be properly adjusted. Agatha had never been able to wear high-heeled shoes. How shapely the women's ankles and legs looked in them. Watching was almost as much fun as wearing them herself.

Jubilee and Ruby stood atop the worktable while Agatha and Violet marked their hems with chalk. Pearl lounged on a chair, waiting her turn.

"You know that cowpoke named Slim McCord?" Jubilee inquired.

"That tall, skinny one with the nose like a carrot?"

"He's the one."

"What about him?"

"He tried to tell me it gets so hot on the trail sometimes that they have to dip the horses' bits in the water bucket to keep 'em from burning their tongues."

From the corner of her eye, Pearl flashed a glance to make sure Willy was listening. "You believe that?"

"Hmm . . ." Ruby appeared thoughtful. "I dunno. But what about old Four Fingers Thompson, who claims whenever the chuck wagon runs out of salt he licks the horse's sweat from his saddle?"

Willy listened to every word, enthralled.

"Listen to this one, everybody!" Pearl said excitedly. "Old Duffield asks me, 'Ya know how t' tell when the wind's pickin' up in Texas?'" Pearl let the mystery build, then angled a glance at Willy. "You know how, Willy?"

He shook his head, then scratched it.

"Well, accordin' to Duffield, you nail a log chain on top of a post, and when the wind blows it straight out—that's calm. When the last link snaps off, you can expect rough weather."

Everyone laughed and Willy plunged gaily against Pearl's lap. "Aw, you're just funnin' me, ain't you, Pearl?"

She tousled his hair and smiled.

The girls always brought an air of festivity, and they, along with all the other employees of the Gilded Cage, had taken an interest in Willy. Agatha loved having them in the shop. When the fitting was done and they left, it seemed dull.

Willy sat on the threshold of the back door, playing with a green worm and scratching himself. He bent at the waist, watched the worm crawl across his boot, and scratched his neck. He sat straight and watched the worm crawl from index finger to index finger, then gave his armpit a good workover. He put the worm on his knee and scratched his crotch. He set the worm on the ground and scratched his head.

"How would you like a bath, Willy?"

He pivoted on his backside. "A bath! I ain't takin' no bath!"

Agatha and Violet exchanged wry glances. "Why not?"

"Pa never makes me take none."

"Take *any*," she corrected, then hurried on. "Well, he should. Baths are important."

"I hate baths!" Willy declared emphatically.

"Nevertheless, I think you need one. I have a token. All you have to do is give it to Mr. Kendall at the Cowboys' Rest and you can have one free."

Willy jumped up as if he'd suddenly remembered something. "I gotta go down and watch 'em load the cows on the cattle cars. See ya, Vy-let. 'Bye, Agatha." He scuttled off without a thought for the worm, which by now was crawling up the doorframe.

At four-fifteen that afternoon, Agatha knocked on Gandy's office door.

"Come in."

"It's me." She entered to find him squatting before the safe counting a stack of bills. Immediately, he stretched to his feet.

"I thought you were fittin' the girls' dresses this afternoon."

"We're finished already."

"When will they be ready to wear?"

"Another day or so."

Everything looked the same, except for a tall glass jar of black licorice whips that hadn't been on the corner of his desk before.

"Is there some problem?" He nonchalantly flung the stack of bills onto his desk.

"Not with the dresses, no."

"Well, sit down. What is it?"

She perched on the edge of an oak armchair. He dropped into his swivel chair and unconsciously reached for his vest pocket. The cheroot was half withdrawn before he realized what he was doing and tucked it away.

"It's Willy I've come about."

A crooked smile captured Gandy's lips and his eyes dropped to the apothecary jar.

"Oh, that Willy, he's somethin', isn't he?"

Her eyes followed the path of his. "He's an angel. It appears he's been coming to visit you quite regularly."

Gandy nodded and chuckled. He cupped his fists loosely and rested his chin on them. "You, too?"

"Yes, every day."

He noticed her staring at the licorice and explained hastily, "They're not just for him. I like 'em, too."

She smiled, sensing his reluctance to seem too taken with the boy. "Yes, I'm sure you do."

As if to prove it, he lifted the glass cover and helped himself to one, then angled the jar her way. "Have one."

It was on the tip of her tongue to decline, but her mouth began watering. How long had it been since she'd had a licorice whip? "Thank you."

Gandy clinked the cover back on, took a bite of his candy, and sat back, chewing. Agatha nibbled hers, then absently studied the limp black licorice stick in her fingers. She glanced up and placed the wooden token on his desk. "I'd like to trade this in."

He gave it a cursory glance, then rested his gaze on her. His dimples appeared, along with a teasing grin. "I'm afraid you'll have t' go down t' the Cowboys' Rest for that. We don't give baths here."

"For Willy," she explained.

"Willy?"

"He smells." She paused eloquently. "And he needs a bath worse than any human being I've ever met."

"So send him down there."

"He won't go."

"Tell him—"

"I'm not his mother, Mr. Gandy, nor his father. Willy says his father doesn't make him take baths, which is altogether too obvious. When I suggested his going alone, he took off like a shot to watch the cowpokes load cattle."

Gandy took another chaw of licorice. "So what do you want me t' do about it?"

"He'd go with you."

"Me!" Gandy's eyebrows flew up.

"He worships the ground you walk on."

"Now wait a minute." Gandy rose from his chair and moved as far away from Agatha as he could get. In the corner near the window he turned and pointed at her with the floppy candy stick. "I'm not the boy's father either. If he needs a bath, let Collinson see to it."

Agatha spoke calmly. "That would be ideal, wouldn't it?"

She took another dainty nibble of licorice. He threw his on the desk.

"Why should *I* do it?" he asked in exasperation.

She continued reasonably. "I'd take him there myself, but it wouldn't be proper. Women don't go to public baths. You go there anyway on a regular basis, don't you?"

Gandy looked thunderous. "I don't mind havin' him come up here now and then, but I'm not goin' t' start squirin' that ragamuffin around as if he were my own. He could get to be an infernal nuisance. And I'm not goin' to be around this town forever, you know. It wouldn't be good if he grew attached to me."

Agatha brushed a nonexistent piece of lint off her skirt and said succinctly, "I think he has lice."

"Lice!" Gandy stared at Agatha, aghast.

"He scratches incessantly. Haven't you ever noticed?"

"I . . ." Damn the woman! Why didn't she leave him alone? Gandy took up pacing, running his fingers through his hair.

"Have you ever had lice, Mr. Gandy?"

"Most certainly not."

"Been bitten by a flea, then?"

She had the aggravating power to make him answer when he didn't want to. "Who hasn't? We had dogs and cats when I was young."

"Then you know it's not the most pleasant thing in the world to be infested. Fleas bite and jump away. Lice stay and suck. They're constantly on the move in a person's—"

"All right! All right!" Gandy's eyes slammed shut. He held up both palms in surrender. "I'll do it!" He opened his eyes, scowled at a corner of the ceiling, and cursed softly under his breath.

Agatha smiled. "His head will need scrubbing with kerosene first."

"Jesus!" Gandy mumbled disgustedly.

"And his clothes will need washing. I'll see to that."

"Don't put yourself out, Agatha," Gandy advised sarcastically.

"I've left the token to pay for his bath." It looked ridiculous lying on the desk next to his stacks of money. "Well . . ." She rose to leave. "Thank you for the licorice stick. It was a wonderful treat. I haven't had one in years."

"Humph!"

Amusement got the better of her and she smiled cajolingly. "Oh, come on, Gandy, it's not so bad. Just pretend the kerosene is that atrocious Kansas sheep dip you sell downstairs."

He stood with both fists on his hips. His dark eyes lost none of their attractiveness when his expression grew fierce.

"Agatha, *you're* the damned infernal nuisance, you know that?"

She looked at his mouth and burst out laughing.

His scowling lips were ringed with black, like a raccoon's eye. He bristled and tried to look mean. *Damned interferin' woman! Comin' in here with those unsettlin' pale green eyes and her maneuverin' ways, makin' my conscience act up, then laughin' at me t' boot.* "What in tarnation's so funny?"

She opened the door, still laughing, and suggested over her shoulder, "Wipe your mouth, Gandy."

When the tail of her bustle disappeared, he stomped into his apartment and peered at himself in the mirror above the washbowl. Angrily, he wiped the licorice from his mouth. But in a moment a willful chuckle threatened. He pondered silently for some moments. The damned woman was starting to grow on him.

He tallied up her physical attributes, one by one: the attractive mouth; the flawless skin; the determined jawline; the arresting opacity of her sea-green eyes; the surprising glint of mahogany-red in her artfully arranged hair; her mode of dress, always formal and superbly tailored, but somehow right for her; her high-riding bustles. He'd never much cared for bustles before, but on Agatha they took on a certain undeniable sense of class.

He studied his reflection in the mirror.

Be careful, boy, you could fall for that woman, and she's not exactly the triflin' kind.

The skinny little boy, smelling of kerosene, and the tall sturdy man, smelling of cigar smoke, stood in a room redolent of wet wood. Two wooden tubs of steaming-hot water waited in the middle of the damp pine floor. In one corner a scarred hoop-back chair held two dingy Turkish towels, a bowl of unrefined soft yellow lye soap, and a stack of clean clothing.

"Well, shuck down, boy. What're you waitin' for?" Gandy removed his jacket and draped it on the back of the chair.

Willy's lower lip protruded. "You tricked me."

"I did not. You lost that game of five-card stud fair and square."

"But I ain't never played before. How was I s'posed t' win?"

"That's luck, Willy. It just happened t' be with me durin' that particular hand. And I thought Agatha told you not t' say 'ain't' anymore." Gandy's vest joined the jacket. He pulled his shirttails out, unbuttoned the garment, and still Willy hadn't lifted a finger to undress. Gandy put the crock of soap on the floor and sat down to remove his boots.

"Boy, I been without a cheroot now for nigh on an hour, and if you don't want t' go up like a firecracker, you'd better get yourself in that tub and get rid of the kerosene."

Pouting, Willy dropped to the floor and began tugging at his curled-toe boots. Gandy watched from the corner of his eye and grinned. The boy's lip looked twice as large as usual. His chin was flattened with disgust. His disheveled hair made him look like an old blond hen that had taken more than her share of pecking from her coop mates.

"I gots a knot." Willy refused to look up as he grumbled.

"Well, untie it."

"I can't. It's too tight."

Dressed in nothing but a knee-length cotton union suit, Gandy went down on one knee before the boy. "Here, let's see . . ."

Willy had a knot, all right. All he had were knots. His bootstrings were a series of them. The boots themselves looked as if they should have been scrapped months ago. When they came off, the smell nearly knocked Gandy on his prat.

"Lord o' mercy, boy, you smell like a boar's nest!"

Willy snickered, burying his chin against his chest, and sheepishly tried to cover his mouth with a wrist. Then he reached out blindly and punched Gandy on the knee.

"Do not," he mumbled.

"Well, at least like a polecat, then."

Another punch.

"Don't neither!"

"Whoo-eee! Takes my breath away! If it's not you, who could it be?"

Willy's face hurt from holding in the laughter, so he punched Gandy again and knocked him off balance.

Gandy smirked at him, dimpling. "Yessuh, I think I see four she-polecats waddlin' toward the door right now."

This time Willy's laugh burst free before he could stifle it. His head came up and he thumped himself full-body against Gandy's chest. "I don't care. You still tricked me, Scotty."

It was the second time Gandy had had Willy in his arms. Even smelling of kerosene and sour feet, the boy made his heart melt. With their faces separated by only inches, Gandy grinned and inquired, "You ready t' get in that water now?"

"If I hafta." The angelic expression returned to Willy's face. "My head stings."

They stood side by side, stripping. When they were both naked they faced each other, man to man, Gandy looking down, Willy up. Willy, with a penis like a tiny pink acorn; Gandy's nothing whatever like a tiny pink acorn. Willy, with legs like white matchsticks; Gandy's long and hard and sprinkled with coarse black hair. Willy, with ribs like a marimba; Gandy, with a torso like a full bag of oats.

Their eyes—deep brown and long-lashed—were very much alike as Willy looked up appealingly. "When I get big, will I look like you?"

"Probably."

"Will I have me a big tallywhacker?"

Gandy laughed, arching backward, hands on hips. He grinned down at the face that was eye level with his navel.

"Willy, my boy, where did you learn a word like that?"

"Heard Ruby talkin'."

"Ruby? What'd she say?"

"She said she liked a man with a big tallywhacker, and Ruby's my friend, so I want her t' like me."

Gandy touched Willy's nose. "If you want the ladies t' like you, take a bath at least once a week. Now, come on . . ." Gandy dropped to one knee beside a tub. "Head first."

Willie knelt down, clutched the lip of the tub, and leaned over. His dirty gray ankles cradled a bare backside with buttocks as white and miniature as loaves of unrisen bread. Each vertebra stuck out like a pebble on a washed shore. And that hair—ye gods!

What a sight, thought Gandy, all skin and bones held together by goose bumps and dirt. Reaching for a handful of soap, he smiled, braced an elbow on one updrawn knee, and set to work.

There was something eminently satisfying about scrubbing the small head. Gandy's wide hands looked so dark against Willy's paleness, his forearms so powerful beside the skinny neck. He thought of his own child, wondered if he'd have done this for her, had she lived.

Forget it, Gandy, it's past.

He folded one of Willy's ears back, then stretched it to peer inside. "Boy, what you been growin' in here? Time t' harvest it, don't you think?"

Willy gurgled, his bony elbows pointed at the ceiling. "Hurry up!"

"I'm hurryin'. But I shoulda brought a shovel."

Again the boy giggled. "You're funny, Scotty," came his muffled words.

Odd, how such insignificant praise from a small boy made him feel profoundly happy. When Willy's hair was clean, Gandy ordered the tub removed and another of fresh water brought in.

"Jump in and warm up."

He himself shuddered with appreciation as he folded his long limbs into one tub, while Willy sank Indian fashion into the other. Soaping and rinsing, raising his arms and curving his shoulders, Gandy showed the boy how a real bath was handled.

"Ream those ears out good now, ya hear?"

"I will," the boy replied disgustedly, following Gandy's lead.

"And not only inside, behind 'em, too."

"What if I go deef? It ain't no good t' git water in your ears."

"I promise y' won't go *deef.*"

"That's what Gussie says, but—"

"Gussie?" Gandy's palms stopped scouring his chest.

"Yeah, she checked my ears and—"

"Who's Gussie?"

"Agatha. She says when she was little her ma always called her Gussie, an' she said I could call her it, too. Anyway, Gussie, she checked my ears an' said . . ."

Gandy heard only bits and pieces of what Agatha had said. *Gussie?* He sat back, thoughtfully ladling water over his chest, fitting the nickname to her face. His hands stopped moving. Why, of course . . . Gussie. He smiled and reached out one long arm, dried his fingers, then plucked a cheroot from his vest pocket. When it was lit, he lazed back contentedly with his knees sticking up like mountains, arms cradling the top of the tub, thinking of her.

A curious woman. Moralistic to a fault, but with an underlying respect for everyone and everything that won his respect in return. She had an amusing way of challenging him where temperance matters were concerned. He'd come to almost look forward to her appearance in the Gilded Cage each night. Yes, she crusaded beside all the others. But her campaign was tempered by an abiding belief in man's basic rights to live his life as he saw fit. When he thought about it, it became downright admirable; on the one hand, she could sing and hand out pamphlets and solicit signatures on a temperance pledge; on the other, she could allow that Gandy had a perfect right to run his business along with the other saloon owners in town.

Another of Agatha's dichotomies absorbed his thoughts. She was fascinated by Jubilee and the girls. Though she tried to pretend she wasn't, there were times when he caught her studying them as if she found them the most entrancing creatures on earth.

And the boy. She was particularly good with the boy. Too bad she never had any children of her own. She'd have done a much better job at raising them than would a reprobate like Collinson.

Gandy glanced over at Willy and chuckled. The lad was doubled forward with his chin and lips just below the water's surface looking as if he enjoyed every minute in the tub.

Gandy blew a puff of smoke toward the ceiling. "Agatha made you some new duds."

Willy's head popped up. His eyes rounded in disbelief. "She did?"

"Britches and a shirt." Gandy nodded sideways. "Over on the chair with mine."

"Garsh . . ." The water dripped off Willy's chin as he became transfixed by the stack of folded clothing. "She didn't tell me."

"Reckon she wanted it t' be a surprise."

Willy's eyes remained riveted on the chair while he stood up. "Can I git out now?"

"You sure you're scrubbed clean?"

Willy raised both elbows and gave each armpit a cursory check. "Yup."

"All right."

A glistening backside pointed Gandy's way as two wet heels thumped on the floor. Gandy reached for the towels, tossed one to Willy, and stood to use the other. Willy gave his body no more than a quick hit with the wadded-up towel before he dropped it in the puddle and headed for the clothing.

"Hey, not so fast there, sprout. You're still drippin'. Come here." Gandy slung his own towel over one shoulder and hunkered down with Willy between his knees. He grinned at the way the boy shivered and huddled. But Willie seemed unaware of anything except the fact that new clothing waited on the chair. While Gandy swung him this way and that, drying his back, armpits, ears, the boy craned toward the chair as if his head were mounted on a spring.

"Hurry up, Scotty."

Gandy smiled and released Willy with a pat on his backside. "All right, go."

The britches were blue muslin. Willy gave no thought to underwear. He hitched his buttocks on the edge of the chair seat and slipped impatiently into the new pants. Agatha had put a drawstring at the waist. Willy cinched it up and crossed to Gandy, staring down his belly. "Tie me up."

"Put your shirt on first and we'll tuck it in."

The shirt closed up the front with white mother-of-pearl buttons. It was made of blue-striped gingham and the sleeves were several inches too long. "Button me."

Gandy smiled secretly and did as ordered. The buttons held the cuffs from slipping over Willy's small hands. He tied the drawstring at Willy's waist and tucked the strings inside, then held him by both hips.

"You look pretty spiffy, boy."

Willy pressed the shirt against his chest with both palms. "Ain't they pretty?" He gazed down in wonder but suddenly spun from Gandy's hands. "Hey, I gotta go show Gussie!"

"Not so fast. What about your shoes?"

"Oh . . . them." Willy plunked backward onto the floor and slipped on his boots over bare feet—he'd come with no socks.

"And hadn't we better comb your hair?"

"I ain't got no comb."

"I do. Just a minute."

When Gandy was dressed, he sat on the hoop-back chair with an impatient Willy between his thighs. He parted his clean blond hair carefully and swished it into a perfect windrow above his brow, combed it back above his ears, and made a neat tail at his nape. When he was done he held Willy by both arms for inspection. "Agatha won't know you."

"Yes, she will—lemme go!"

"All right. But wait for me."

Outside, the man had to lengthen his stride to keep up with the boy.

"C'mon, Scotty, hurry up!"

Gandy grinned and hurried. The day was balmy. Agatha's front door was open. Had it not been, Willy might have broken the window throwing the door out of his way.

"Hey, Gussie, Gussie! Where are you?"

He ran through the lavender curtains as she called, "Back here!"

Gandy followed just in time to see Willy standing beside Agatha's chair, chest puffed while he inspected himself and boasted, "Lookit me, Gussie! Ain't I pretty?"

Agatha clapped once and rested her folded hands beneath her chin. "Why, for the love of Pete, who do we have here?"

"It's me, Willy!" He patted his chest convincingly.

"Willy?" She studied him dubiously, then shook her head. "The only Willie I know is Willy Collinson, but he doesn't look all shiny like you. He doesn't smell like fresh soap either."

Willy's breathless words tumbled out one atop the other. "Scotty an' me, we took a bath and washed our hair an' he brung me my new clothes you made an' he tied my string an' . . . well . . . but I couldn't button an' he helped me an' I love 'em, Gussie!" He catapulted himself into her arms and hugged her tenaciously.

Gandy stood just inside the doorway watching. Willy kissed Agatha flush on the mouth. She laughed self-consciously and flushed with happiness.

"My goodness, had I known I'd get all this attention, I'd have made them days ago."

"An' I cleaned my ears real good, just like Scotty said, an' I scrubbed everythin' an' he combed my hair. See?"

Willy raced back to Gandy, caught him by a hand, and tugged him forward. "Din't we?"

Agatha raised her eyes to Scott Gandy, standing above her. It was as close to being a wife and mother as she had ever felt. Within her heart fullness abided. At her knee the child leaned, touching her, smelling soapy, his shirt—with room for growth—standing out from his slight body in starched peaks. Close before her stood a man who, along with her, had made one small neglected soul feel happier and more cared about than he'd perhaps ever felt in his life.

She reached up a hand, unable to say all that flooded her heart. Scott Gandy took it, held it tightly, and smiled down at her.

Thank you, she mouthed silently above Willy's head.

He nodded and squeezed her fingers so hard the touch ricocheted off her heart.

Suddenly, they both became self-conscious. Gandy dropped her hand and stepped back. "He'll need new socks and underwear. I thought we'd go over to Halorhan's and pick some out."

As Agatha watched the two walk away, hand in hand, her eyes stung with joy.

At the curtains, the boy swung around and flashed a quick wave. "See y' later, Gussie!"

Gandy's brown eyes settled on her pale green ones. His wore an expression somewhere between a tease and a caress. "Yeah, see y' later, Gussie," he said.

She blushed and dropped her gaze. Her heart fluttered like a cloud of butterflies lifting into the air. When she looked up, the doorway was empty of all but the swinging lavender curtains.

CHAPTER
9

Alvis Collinson suffered from a perennial case of gout. On the morning following Willy's bath, he awakened with both big toes throbbing. He tended to blame everything on Cora's dying, his gout included.

Damn you, Cora, for goin' and leavin' me without no woman t' do for me! Toes throbbin' like a pair o' bitches in heat, and I have t' git up and fend for m'self. No hot breakfast waitin'. No clean shirts t' put on. No woman t' fetch the coal and heat the water. Goddamn women, anyway—no good when ya got 'em and no good when ya ain't. And goddamn Cora the most, always harpin' at me t' be somethin' better, do somethin' more refined than pokin' cows. Refined meanin' somethin' fancy like Brother Jim, who gits hisself a panty-waist job as Registrar of Deeds just about the time the land agents started blowin' up this part o' the country t' strangers. Brother Jim who dudes hisself up in fancy suits ev'ry mornin' and walks down the boardwalk t' his prissy office doffin' his hat t' the ladies as if his farts don't stink. Why, hell, Cora couldn't look at Jim without her eyes buggin' outta her head and her tits swellin' up.

And nobody was gonna convince Alvis Collinson that miserable brat wasn't Jim's bastard. More than once Alvis had come home unexpected and caught Jim sniffin' around Cora. And her nose was twitchin' too, goddammit to hell if it wasn't!

Not tonight, Alvis, I'm too tired. As if once she got a sample of Brother Jim her own husband wasn't good

159

*enough anymore. Then she had the nerve to drop her whelp
and check out for good.*

*Come on, Brother Jim, show your face around this town
once more—just once!—so I can whip the piss outta you
and dump your brat on you, where he belongs. I'm gettin'
tired o' bein' tied down by that little thorn in the side when
he ain't even mine.*

In the kitchen, Willy stood on a chair, on tiptoes, peering into a small milky mirror hung high on the wall. His
fine yellow hair gleamed with water. Painstakingly, he ran
the comb through it, parted it on one side, then sliced it
flat over the crown of his head from left to right. He
tried to swish it back just like Scotty had done, but it
wouldn't stand up in the sideways peak. He tried again
and failed. He clamped the comb between his knees and
used his palms this time, shaping the crest as if it were
made of piecrust dough. After several attempts, he had
finally done it fairly well. *Boy, is Pa ever gonna be surprised!*

He clambered off the chair, dropped the comb on the
table, and went to the bedroom doorway, beaming with
pride.

"Pa, look! Lookit what I got!"

Alvis scowled at the doorway, nursing one aching toe.
It was the brat, already up and dressed. "Lookit what?" he
growled.

"These!" Willy rubbed his breast pockets. "They're from
Gussie and Scotty. Gussie, she made me the britches and
shirt, and Scotty, he bought me the new boots after him an'
me took a bath together down at the Cowboys' Rest."

Collinson's eyes narrowed on the boy. "Scotty? Ya mean
Gandy? The one from the saloon?"

"Yeah. First he give me a goin'-over with kerosene. Then
we took our bath and—"

"And who the hell's this Gussie?"

"Agatha, down at the millinery shop. She gots this new
sewin' machine Scotty bought for her, and she made me
new britches and this new shirt, too."

The gout seemed to spread from Alvis's toes to the rest
of his body.

"Oh, she did, huh? And what right's she got takin' over my kid, huh? Wasn't ya dressed good enough t' suit her?" Alvis struggled to his feet. "She the one behind that damned snoopin' preacher man come pokin' his nose 'round here? Is she, huh?"

"I don't know, Pa." The light went out of Willy's face. "Don't you like my new things?"

"Git 'em off!" Alvis hissed. Then he rummaged through the clothes he'd dropped beside the bed last night, searching for his socks. "Just like Brother Jim, ain't ya?" he mumbled, while the confused child tried not to let his disappointment show.

"But they're . . ."

"Git 'em off, I said!" Barefoot, Alvis lunged to his feet. He stood before the boy with his fists clenched, dressed in a filthy union suit with the legs cut off at mid-thigh, the back hatch sagging. His whiskered face contorted with rage. "Ain't nobody tellin' me I ain't dressin' my own brat good enough, ya understand?" Willy's lower lip trembled and two tears formed in his eyes. "And quit that snivelin'!"

"I ain't takin' 'em off. They're mine!"

"Like hell ya ain't!" Collinson caught the boy by the back of the collar and tossed him onto a scarred wooden chair. It screeched, tilted back on two legs, then clattered onto all fours. "Where's your old boots? Git 'em on, and your britches and shirt, too. I'll show them uppity sons-a-bitches t' keep outta my bus'ness! Now, where's them boots? I told ya, boy, t' quit your snivelin'!"

"But I like th . . . these. They're a pre . . . present from Sc . . . Scotty."

Collinson dropped to one knee and jerked the boots roughly from Willy's feet. The angle of his big toe against the floor caused a shard of pain to shoot up his leg, incensing him further. "When I decide you need new boots, *I'll* buy you new boots, ya got that, boy?"

Willy's eyes streamed and his chest jerked as he tried not to sob.

"Now git on your old ones!"

"I ain't g . . . got 'em."

"What d' you mean, you ain't got em?"

"I j . . . just ain't."

"Where are they?"

"I d . . . don't kn . . . know."

"Goddammit to hell! How can ya lose your own boots?"

Willy peered up fearfully, his thin chest palpitating as he held in the sobs. Collinson's fists clenched and he yanked the boy roughly off the chair onto his feet.

"Ya lose your boots, ya go barefoot. Now gimme the rest."

Minutes later, when Collinson limped angrily out of the house, Willy threw himself on his bed and let the pent-up weeping escape. His hot tears wet the tender white skin of his freckled arm as he cried against it. One skinny bare foot curled around the opposite ankle as he rolled up in a ball. The crest in his gleaming gold hair, which Alvis hadn't even noticed, became disheveled by the sour bedclothes.

Agatha's heart slammed into her throat when the voice roared from the front room.

"Where the hell is ev'rybody!"

Violet hadn't arrived yet. Agatha had no choice but to answer the call herself. She shuffled to the curtains and parted them. Immediately, the gruff voice shouted again.

"You the one they call Gussie?"

She composed herself forcibly. "Agatha Downing is my name, yes."

Collinson squinted, recognizing her as that "temperance bitch" who was always stirring up trouble lately, the same one who had stuck her nose into his business once before when Willy had come looking for him at the saloon.

"You're outta line, missus." He flung down the shirt and pants on top of the aviary display case.

"Miss," Agatha retorted tightly.

"Aw, well, that explains it, then. Ain't got no whelps o' your own, so ya take over other people's." Holding Willy's new boots in one hand, he brandished them at her nose. "Well, git yourself some o' your own. My boy don't need your charity. He's got an old man, and I'll see after my own. Is that understood?"

"Perfectly."

Collinson glared at her hard, then headed for the open door. Before reaching it he turned back. "And one more thing. Next time ya go whisperin' things t' the preacher, tell him t' mind his own goddamned business." He started for the door again and once more stopped to demand, "Where the hell's Gandy? I got words for him, too."

"More than likely still asleep upstairs."

He threw her one last glare, shouldered around toward the door, then disappeared. Agatha's heart was still thudding sharply when she heard the sound of shattering glass. She hurried to the front door just in time to see Collinson fling the second boot through a window overhead. "Gandy, wake up, ya son-of-a-bitch! I'll buy my own boy's boots, so stop interfering! The next time ya take him to the Rest for a bath, you'll need one yourself t' wash off the blood—ya hear me, Gandy?"

Curious heads poked out of doorways all along the boardwalk. As Collinson limped down the middle of main street, he glared at Yancy Sales, leaning out the door of his Bitters Shop. "Whaddaya gawkin' at, Sales? Ya want a boot through your window, too!"

Every head withdrew.

Upstairs, Gandy awakened with the first crash. He braced himself up on his elbows and squinted into the morning sun beaming in the window on the far side of Jube.

"What the hell . . ."

Jube lifted her head like a prairie dog peeping from its hole. "Mmm . . . mmm . . ." Her face fell into the pillow and Gandy rolled across her to look at the boot lying beside the bed.

He flopped onto his back and uttered, "Oh, Jesus!"

"Wh . . . zz . . . tt?" came Jube's muffled voice.

"The new boots I bought yesterday for Willy." He closed his eyes and thought how long it had been since he'd gotten into a rip-roaring fistfight. It would feel mighty good again.

A quiet knock sounded on his door. He rolled from the bed, naked, and stepped into his black trousers. Barefoot, he padded to the sitting room and opened the door.

Agatha stood in the hall, hands clasping and unclasping nervously.

"I'm sorry to disturb you so early." Her glance flitted from his stubbled cheeks to his naked chest, then down to his bare feet, and finally to the end of the hall. She'd never seen him any way other than impeccably dressed. She was unsure of the rules of propriety when faced with a man's hairy chest and toes. Her face turned pink.

"Believe it or not, I was already awake." He combed his hair back with his fingers, giving her a flash of dark hair under his arms. "Collinson's a real sweetheart, isn't he?"

She met his eyes squarely, her brow wrinkled in concern. "Do you think Willy is all right?"

"I don't know." He, too, frowned.

"What should we do?"

"Do?" Dammit! He hadn't wanted to get mixed up with Willy in the first place. "What would you suggest we do? March down to Collinson's house and ask him if he's mistreated the boy?"

Agatha's irritation sprouted. "Well, we can't stand by and do nothing."

"Why not? Look what happens when we try to play the good Samaritan." Even as Gandy replied, he remembered Willy, naked as the day he was born, looking up with his liquid brown eyes, asking him, "When I grow up, will I be like you?"

Just then Jubilee shuffled up behind Gandy, yawning, her white hair bunched in disarray. "Who is it, Scotty . . . ? Oh, it's you, Agatha. Mornin'." She was wearing the turquoise dressing gown. It buckled open as Jubilee balled her fists and stretched both arms sleepily, tilting her head to one side. Agatha caught a glimpse of enough cleavage and flank to guess that Jubilee slept in the altogether. Her voice became sharp.

"As soon as you wake up, you can tell Mr. Gandy I'm sorry I got him out of bed."

Picking up her skirts, she turned and made an exit with as much dignity as she could muster.

* * *

Not five minutes later everybody arrived at the millinery shop at once: Mrs. Alphonse Anderton, for a fitting on her new dress; Violet, for work; Willy, bawling; and Gandy, still barefoot, buttoning a wrinkled shirt with its tails flapping.

"Listen here, Agatha, I resent your—" Gandy pointed a finger angrily.

"Well . . ." Mrs. Anderton pompously scrutinized them, ending with Gandy's bare feet. "Good morning, Agatha."

"*Tt-tt.*"

"My p . . . pa . . . he s . . . says I c . . . can't c . . . come here no more t' s . . . see youuuuuu . . ."

Agatha stood behind a glass counter, so Willy ran straight to Gandy. Gandy went down on one knee and hauled the sobbing boy tightly against him. Willy clung to Gandy's neck. Gandy forgot his anger and Agatha's chest felt as if it would crack as she listened to Willy's sobs. "He t . . . took away m . . . my new b . . . boots."

"Please take care of Mrs. Anderton, Violet," Agatha ordered quietly, then moved to Gandy, and he straightened with Willy in his arms.

"Bring him into the back room," Agatha said.

Even after they were alone the boy sobbed and sobbed and spoke in broken snatches. "M . . . my n . . . new sh . . . shirt and br . . . britches . . . he . . . t . . . told . . . m . . . me . . ."

"Shh!" Gandy whispered going down on one knee again. Willy burrowed his blond head against the man's sturdy dark chest and half-buttoned white shirt.

Agatha felt as if she were choking. She sat down on Willy's little stool beside them, petting his head, smoothing his hair, feeling helpless and woeful. Over Willy's shaking shoulder her gaze met Gandy's. He looked shaken. She reached out and touched the back of his hand. He lifted two fingers, hooked two of hers, and pulled them against Willy's neck.

Why couldn't this child have been ours? We would have been so good to him, so good for him. It was a fleeting thought, but it brought to Agatha a bitter realization of the injustices of this world.

In time Willy calmed. Agatha withdrew her fingers from Gandy's and pulled a scented handkerchief from a pocket concealed within the back drapes of her dress.

"Here, Willy, let me clean up your face."

He turned, dripping, eyes and lips puffy. As she mopped his cheeks and made him blow, she wondered what either she or Gandy could say to restore Willy's broken heart.

"You mustn't blame your father," she began. "It was our fault, Scotty's and mine." She had never called Gandy by his first name before. Doing so gave her strength and a feeling of communion with both him and Willy. "We hurt your father's pride, you see, by giving you new clothes, taking you for a bath. Do you know what that means—pride?"

Willy shrugged, trying not to cry again.

Agatha didn't think she could speak one more word without breaking into tears herself. She looked to Gandy for help and he came through.

"Pride means feelin' good about yourself." His long, dark fingers combed back the blond strands above Willy's ears. "Your father wants t' buy you things himself. When we bought them instead, he thought we were tellin' him that he wasn't seein' after you properly."

"Oh." Willy said the word so softly it was scarcely audible.

"And as for you comin' t' visit us—I don't see why you shouldn't. We're still your friends, aren't we?"

Willy gave the expected smile, though it was tentative.

"But it might be a good idea t' slip in the back door and make sure you don't come when your pa's in the saloon, all right? Now, how about a licorice stick?"

Willy's face remained downcast as he answered unenthusiastically, "I guess so."

Gandy got to his feet, lifting the boy on his arm. He waited until Agatha, too, rose, then hooked an arm loosely about her shoulders as the three of them ambled toward the back door. She felt awkward, bumping against his chest and hip with each clumsy step she took. But he didn't seem to mind. At the door he dropped his arm and told her, "Willy'll be down later, but send him back up at dinner time and I'll have Ivory go over to Paulie's and pick up some picnic food."

Perhaps that was the moment when Agatha first realized she was falling in love with Gandy. She looked up at him, his hair still tousled, his cheeks still shaded with a night's growth of whiskers, his shoulders and arms looking as if they could handle all the Alvis Collinsons of this world as they held Willy.

"Thank you," she said softly. "And I'm sorry I was short with you upstairs. I understand. I feel the same way at times."

For a moment his eyes lingered on hers, bearing a soft expression, while Willy glanced back and forth between the two of them, his freckled arm resting on the back of Gandy's neck.

"Ain't you comin', Gussie?" the child asked plaintively.

"No, Willy." She dried a lingering tear with her thumb. "I'll see you later." She raised up and kissed his shiny cheek. As they left she realized she had placed herself in double jeopardy. She was falling in love not only with the man, but with the boy as well.

Later that day the girls came to try on their finished cancan dresses and Agatha seized the opportunity to apologize to Jubilee for her snappishness that morning.

Jube passed it off with a wave of her hand. "I was still so sleepy I didn't even know what you were saying."

All the while Agatha buttoned Jubilee into the sleek-fitting bodice she couldn't forget the way Jube had padded to Gandy's door, all warm and tumbled from sleep, looking more beautiful in disarray than most women looked after an hour at their dressing tables. She recalled Gandy's bare chest and mussed hair, his trousers with the waist button still freed, his bare feet.

Then she glanced at Jubilee, twirling before the wall mirror. Radiant, beautiful Jubilee.

Gandy is spoken for, Agatha, she told herself. *Besides, what would he want with someone like you when he has a stunning gem like her?* "Will you dance the cancan tonight?"

"Tonight's the night," Jube answered. "Second show, though. We're going to make them wait till eleven so they'll be good and anxious."

"Will you be there?" Pearl asked Agatha. Nobody found the question the least bit odd. The girls had grown used to seeing Agatha and her troops in the Gilded Cage at one time or another each night.

"I'll be there earlier," Agatha replied, squelching her disappointment. After all the work she'd done on the dresses, she wanted to see them flashing to the music.

But that night, true to their word, the girls saved the best for last, and Agatha bade good-night to the W.C.T.U. ladies on the boardwalk without seeing a solitary flash of red or a single high kick. It was a warm, sultry night for mid-June. The saloons had been stuffier than usual. No wind blew under the doors. The odor of dung from the hitching rails seemed to permeate everything. She took the shortcut through her store, made her last trip to the necessary, then mounted the stairs.

Her tiny apartment seemed stifling. She carried a hard wooden chair onto the landing and sat listening to the music from below, fanning herself with a lace handkerchief. From the opened back door of the Gilded Cage came a lively new song she'd never heard before. The cancan, most likely. Her fingertips kept rhythm against her thigh and she tried to imagine Pearl doing her notorious high kick with the red taffeta ruffles rustling and frothing about her.

A coyote howled in the distance.

Yes, I feel the same, she thought. *Howlingly lonely.*

She thought of Gandy and Willy—it was insanity to become embroiled in the lives of two such unlikely candidates, yet she feared it was too late to extricate them from her affections. She was doomed to heartache on two counts, for Collinson had made it clear Willy was his, and Jube had made it clear Gandy was hers.

She thought of Jube, pretty, pretty Jube, dancing the cancan downstairs right now with Ruby and Pearl. She pictured their legs flashing through the air, and it made her feel weighted and unwieldy. She wondered what it felt

like to kick a man's hat from his head. She wondered what
the cancan looked like and had a sudden idea that left her
feeling nervous but determined.

She took her chair back inside, but instead of getting
ready for bed, she found one of her voluminous outdat-
ed petticoats and laid it on the table. Into it she put the
items she needed, then lay down on the bed fully clothed
to wait.

It seemed to take forever for the noise below to stop
and for the bar to close down. Then again forever before
Agatha heard everybody from next door make their way to
their rooms and retire for the night. She lay stiff and flat,
as if any movement would betray her plans.

She allowed a full hour to pass after all was quiet before
she cautiously sat up and slipped from her bed. In total
darkness she found the bundle she'd prepared beforehand,
plus a single candle in a holder and her sampler from the
wall. She moved down the outside stairs barefoot, making
no more noise than a shadow.

The dress shop was silent and dark. She felt her way
into the workroom, lay her bundle on the table and lit the
candle. She lifted it to check the shadowed corners of the
room, breathing shallowly.

*Don't be silly, Agatha, it's only your own conscience
you're scared of.*

Turning her attention to the bundle, she felt like a burglar.
She folded back the white petticoat to reveal a hammer,
nail, brace, and bit. She picked up the brace and bit and
Willy's stool and shuffled to the common wall between
the millinery shop and the saloon. From the corner she
measured off four paces, picturing the pine boards on the
other side of the wall, the places where occasional knots
had fallen out. She set the stool down and struggled up
onto it. Guiltily, she glanced behind herself—but of course
no one was there. Again it was only her conscience that
seemed to be watching from the shadows on the far side
of the room.

Determinedly, she braced the bit against the wall and
slowly, slowly began boring. She stopped often and lifted
the candle to check the depth of the hole. At last the far

end of the drill slipped through. She closed her eyes and sagged, resting a palm against the wall. Her heart hammered crazily.

Please, don't let there be any wood shavings on the saloon floor.

Agatha, you should be ashamed of yourself.

But I only want to watch the girls dance.

It's still eavesdropping.

It's a public place. If I were a man I could sit at a table and watch everything I'll see through this hole and nobody would think a thing of it.

But you're not a man. You're a lady, and this is certainly beneath your dignity.

Who will it hurt?

How would you like it if somebody looked the other way through the hole?

Agatha shivered at the thought. Perhaps she wouldn't use it after all.

The wood shavings all seemed to come her way when she withdrew the drill bit. She pressed her face against the wall and peered into the hole. Solid black. The wainscot felt cool against her hot, flushed cheeks and again she experienced the queer sensation that those upstairs knew what she was doing.

She set the drill down and with three sharp raps drove the nail into the wall. Holding her breath, she paused, looking up at the ceiling, listening for the slightest movement. All remained silent. Releasing her breath, she hung the sampler over the hole and put Willy's stool where he'd left it. Then she carefully swept up the wood shavings and hid them beneath some fabric scraps in her wastebasket, blew out the candle, and returned to her apartment.

But she could not sleep for the remainder of the night. Clandestine activities at three A.M. did not set well with Agatha. Her nerves jittered and she felt as if she had a touch of dyspepsia. She heard a train rumble through town. And near dawn the distant coyotes yapped in chorus. She saw the sky lighten from black to indigo to chambray-blue. She heard the lamp-lighter move down the street, snuffing the lanterns, closing their doors, growing closer and closer, until he passed beneath her window and then faded off in the opposite direction. She heard the town cowherd gather the local cows from backyard sheds and herd them down the main street toward the prairie to spend the day. The dull clong of the lead cow's bell became fainter and fainter and fainter . . . and at last Agatha slept.

She was awakened by her first customer of the morning rattling the shop door downstairs. After that the day was disastrous. She snapped at poor Violet and became impatient with Willy's questions. A fight broke out in the Gilded Cage in the late forenoon, and when Jack Hogg threw the two hotheads out onto the boardwalk their momentum carried them in the direction of the hat shop and a flying elbow broke one of the small panes of her front window. When Gandy came to apologize and offer to pay for the damages, she treated him abominably and he stomped out angrily with a scowl on his face. The mute man, Marcus Delahunt, brought over a shirt with a simple torn seam, but the bobbin jammed on her sewing machine and the thread formed a bird's nest of knots on the underside of her stitching. Delahunt watched her slam things around in frustration, touched her calmingly on the shoulders, then sat down himself to find the problem: two coarse blue frayed yarns caught in the bobbin race. He mimed a question: Did she have any oil? She produced a tin can with a long, skinny spout and he squirted oil into twenty places, worked the flywheel back and forth, rose from the stool, and flourished a palm toward the machine as if introducing it to Agatha.

It ran as if new. In no time she had his shirt mended.

She looked up square into Marcus's face, feeling small for her churlish behavior, not only to him, but to everyone all day long. "Thank you, Marcus."

He nodded and smiled and mimed something she could not understand.

"I'm sorry. Say it again?"

He glanced around the shop searchingly, spotted the calendar hanging beside the back door, and took her hand, leading her to it. He pointed to her, the oil can, and measured out seven days on the calendar.

"Every week. I should oil it once a week?"

He nodded, smiling, making a smooth-running driver of his elbow, illustrating how the machine would run if she'd follow his advice.

"I will, Marcus." She squeezed the backs of his hands. "And thank you."

He reached for his pocket, as if to extract money. She stopped his hands.

"No. It was nothing. Thank you again for fixing the machine."

He smiled, doffed his hat, and left.

After that Agatha's temper mellowed, but at suppertime, instead of eating, she napped, overslept, and was late joining the other W.C.T.U. members for their evening circuit.

By the time ten o'clock came she was in a state of intense anxiety.

Her conscience would not relent.

You were surly and short with everyone all day long, and you know why. It's because of that blame hole you drilled in the wall. If you can't live with it, patch it up!

But it drew her like an Aladdin's lamp.

In the dark of night she shuffled through the blackness of her familiar back room, then ran her fingers along the stamped wainscoting. Against her fingertips she felt the beat of the music sending tremors through the wall. The rhythm pulsed up faintly through her shoes. Carefully, she lifted the sampler away. Into her silent, lonely world streamed a tiny pinpoint of light. She leaned close and put her eye to the hole. There were Jubilee, Ruby, and Pearl doing the cancan.

Their magnificent skirts—shining black on the outside, ruffled red on the inside—flashed left and right. Their long legs created shots of black fishnet in triplicate. In ebony ankle-length high-heeled boots they pranced and strutted, wagged their calves and kicked. Their feet shot to the heavens. Their torsos leaned forward, then back, before they circled and shouted and tossed their heads until their red hair feathers trembled.

It was a bawdy dance, but Agatha looked beyond its lustiness to find in their leggy bodies the symmetry, grace, and agility she herself had not possessed since she was nine years old.

The music hushed and Jack Hogg was pressed into work as an announcer, calling out above the noisy crowd. Though Agatha couldn't make out the words, she watched everything. The girls circulated through the saloon, capturing the hands of six bright-faced, eager men whom they tugged along to the front of the bar. Ruby and Jube arranged the cowpokes in an evenly spaced line and flirtatiously squared the men's Stetsons on their heads. Jack produced a pair of cymbals and called out a verbal fanfare joined by that from the instruments.

Then up strutted Pearl, skirt caught up to her waist, her long legs supple and strong as she twirled like a top along the line of erectly postured men.

The cymbals crashed. Pearl's toe shot up in a swinging arc. The first hat tumbled to the floor.

She whirled, kicked, and another hat flew to the floor.

Down the line she went until six Stetsons lay strewn at the men's feet.

Agatha's heart pounded. Exhilaration made her double her fist and she punched the air along with the last two incredibly high kicks. Through the wall she heard the rumble of applause, men's sharp wolf whistles, and the stomping of feet.

Jubilee and Ruby joined Pearl for a final chorus, including a totally immodest pose in which the three of them spread their legs, flung their skirts up over their derrieres, and peered at the audience from between their knees. A last volley of breathtaking contortions, a final flourish of red ruffles, and the three of them fell to the floor with their legs split and their arms raised.

Agatha found herself as breathless as the dancers. She watched their bare chests heave beneath their brief silk bodices and saw beads of perspiration trickle down their temples. She felt as if she'd danced right along with them. Her body wilted against the wall. She slid down and slumped onto Willy's stool.

It was a wicked dance, suggestive and brazen. But spirited and filled with the zest of life. Agatha closed her eyes and tried to imagine kicking the hat off a man's head. It suddenly seemed a most desirable talent. Why, if she could do it—just once—she'd feel blessed. She rubbed her left hip and thigh, wondering what it felt like to be beautiful, and whole, and uninhibited ... what it felt like to laugh and whoop and raise a ruckus in flashing red-and-black skirts.

She sighed and opened her eyes to darkness.

Agatha, you're getting dotty, watching cancan dancers through a hole in the wall.

But for a while, watching them, she had become vicariously young and resilient and happy and filled with a joie de vivre. For a while, watching them, she had done what she had never done before. For a while, she, too, had danced.

CHAPTER
10

The summer moved on. Across the prairie the gama and buffalo grass grew tinder-dry. At night, heat lightning flashed, bringing only empty promises. Around the perimeter of Proffitt, the townsmen burned a wide firebreak. The dust created by the incoming cattle infiltrated everything: shelter, clothing, even food. The only damp spot for miles around seemed to be at the base of the windmill in the center of main street, where a pump kept the public watering tank full for thirsty stock. The flies increased; with so much manure everywhere, they thrived. So did a colony of prairie dogs that decided to make their village in the middle of main street. Occasionally, a cow broke its leg stepping into one of their holes and had to be shot on the spot and butchered. If this happened between Tuesday and Thursday, it became cause for celebration: Friday was the regular butchering day at Huffman's Meat Market, and with temperatures in the high eighties, nobody risked buying meat after Monday.

A band of Oto Indians came and camped on the south edge of town. To the north the prairie became dotted by the wagons of immigrants waiting to file claims on government land. Every day the land agents rented a steady stream of rigs from the livery stables and rode out to show the unclaimed sections to the eager-eyed immigrants. Drummers came in on the train, selling everything from patent medicine to ladies' corsets.

Gandy and Agatha saw less of Willy. He ran barefoot with a gang of boys who hung around the depot selling

175

cookies, hard-boiled eggs, and milk to the passengers while trains stopped for thirty minutes to take on water. Occasionally, he ate with Gandy, but Agatha suspected most of his nourishment came from filched cookies, milk, and hard-boiled eggs. Agatha's only consolation was that it wasn't really a badly balanced diet.

On the Fourth of July the "drys" had one parade. The "wets" had another.

On one street corner the editor of the *Wichita Tribune* spoke out in favor of ratification of the prohibition amendment introduced by Senator George F. Hamlin in February of '79 and signed by the governor the following March.

On another corner a liquor advocate bellowed, "The saloon is an indispensable fixture in a frontier town, and liquor itself proves as powerful an aid to communication as printer's ink!"

A white-ribboned temperance stalwart cried out, "The chains of intoxication are heavier than those which the sons of Africa have ever worn."

From the wet camp came: "Drinking symbolizes equality. In the bar, all men are equal."

As July progressed the issue of prohibition became hotter along with the weather. From the pulpit of Christ Presbyterian, Reverend Clarksdale called down blessings upon "all the noble actors upon the human platform of temperance."

The town assembly staged a late July debate between the temperance and liquor forces. Distinguished orator and Methodist-Quaker preacher Amanda Way came to town to speak for the drys. Miss Way proved so convincing that before the evening was over, the ladies of the Proffitt chapter of the W.C.T.U. had additional reason to celebrate: George Sowers signed the temperance pledge.

There was only one way he could possibly keep his promise, and that was to remove himself from temptation: George took to collecting buffalo bones. With seventy-five thousand of the creatures having been slaughtered in the fifteen years since the Civil War, the prairie now seemed like an immense boneyard waiting to be harvested. On the morning following the signing of the pledge, George was seen driving west with a swayback nag hitched to a weatherbeaten wagon. The next day he was seen heading east to sell his chalky pickings to the fertilizer and bone-china producers in Kansas City. Though the bone trade left George a far cry from the gold baron he'd once been, Evelyn seemed satisfied. For a while she mellowed.

During that summer the ranks of the W.C.T.U. local swelled. They outgrew Agatha's back room and began having their regular Monday evening meetings in the schoolhouse. Then in early August Annie MacIntosh showed up at a meeting with a black eye, a cut lip, and two cracked ribs. She fell into the arms of her "sisters" and sobbed out the truth: her husband, Jase, beat her whenever he hit the bottle.

That was the end of Evelyn Sowers's mellow period. That very evening she led the march on the Sugar Loaf Saloon, bearing Annie along, surrounded by a protective wall of frenzied, angry women. She marched up to Jase MacIntosh, made a powerful fist, and put every ounce of her two hundred fifteen pounds into a swing that caught Jase on the jaw and flipped him backward off his chair. She stood above him, planted one thick-heeled black shoe in the middle of his chest, and hissed, "That's for Annie, you rum-soaked ally of Satan! You're a gangrenous excretion poisoning the life of this community!" She pointed to Annie and bellowed to the customers at large, "See what this has done to a good wife who's done nothing to deserve it except raise his children, wash his clothes, and clean his house?" She glared down at Jase. "Well, no more. Annie will live with George and me now, and you'll never lay a hand on her again." On her way to the bar she planted her full weight on MacIntosh's chest, nearly breaking his ribs. "And as for you"—she confronted Mustard Smith with both fists on her beefy hips—"you swine! You destroyer of the home! You're the cause of the human wreckage you see before you day in and day out. It's a wonder you can look at yourself in the mirror every morning!"

Mustard Smith drew a Colt .45 and pressed the barrel to the end of Evelyn's nose. "Git out, bitch," he growled low in his throat.

Evelyn didn't bat an eye. She pressed forward until the

gun barrel flattened her nose grotesquely. When she spoke no air came through her nostrils.

"Shoot me, go ahead, you slimy lizard. I ain't scared of you or any of the other saloon owners in this burg. Shoot me and you'll see a thousand others like me crawlin' over you like vermin over a dead skunk."

Smith calmly pulled the trigger.

The chamber was empty.

Though Evelyn stood foursquare to the fearsome saloon owner, her union members sent up a gasp.

"Next one'll be loaded," Smith warned.

"You can kill one W.C.T.U. member, or a dozen of us, but you can't kill the whole legislature, Smith." With a satisfied smile, Evelyn turned away, the tip of her nose imprinted with a tiny red doughnutlike circle. "Let's go, sisters. On to the next dispenser of strychnine!"

When Agatha returned to her apartment at ten o'clock that night, she was weak from emotion and fright. Evelyn might be fearless in the face of enemies such as Mustard Smith and Jase MacIntosh, but Agatha wasn't.

As she climbed the backstairs she felt each tense minute of the past three hours in her aching limbs. It required a supreme effort to drag herself up the stairs. There were times when she grew unutterably weary of fighting the temperance battle. Tonight was one of them. She approached her door eagerly and reached out with the key in her hand.

The door was ajar.

In the dark her toe struck something that rolled in a circle. She reached down for it. It was her doorknob.

A brief cry of fright escaped her throat. She pressed a hand to her hammering heart and felt the sickening clench of fear grab her chest. Hesitantly, she reached out and pushed the door wider. It struck something and halted. A man? She didn't think, only reacted: whacked the door back as hard as she could with the full force of her body! Instead of hurting anybody inside, she missed a step and fell, injuring herself. She lay on the floor with pain shooting up her hip, fear exploding everywhere inside her body. Waiting for somebody to kick her, hack her, kill her.

Nothing happened.

From downstairs came the sound of "Pop Goes the Weasel." From inside her chest came the pop of her own thudding heart. She pushed herself up and made her way to the table, her feet shuffling through objects of soft and hard texture. With trembling hands she struck a match and held it above her head.

God in heaven, what a mess!

Everything had been ransacked. Clothing, knickknacks, bedding, papers. Broken glass and upset chairs lay strewn like flotsam behind a tornado.

The match burned her fingers and she dropped it. With the next one she lit the lantern. But she remained rooted, too stunned to cry, too petrified to move. Within thirty seconds shock overpowered her body. Chattering teeth, jolting limbs, glassy eyes. When she moved, she did so without conscious thought, radiating toward help not because it was the wisest thing to do, but because she'd lost the power to reason another course.

Dan Loretto was calling out keno numbers at the table nearest the back door as she shuffled in. He glanced up and immediately leaped to his feet.

"Miss Downing, what's wrong?"

"Somebody br . . . broke into my ap . . . partment."

He put his arm around her shaking shoulders. "When?"

"I don't know."

"Are you all right?" It felt as if she'd rattle her bones loose, she shook so hard.

"I . . . I . . . yes . . . I was out . . . I . . . I didn't know what to do."

"Wait here. I'll get Scotty."

Gandy was playing poker near the front, facing the swinging doors. Dan slipped up behind him and whispered in his ear. "Miss Downing is here. Somebody broke into her apartment."

Gandy's cards hit the table before the last word left Dan's lips. "Deal me out." His chair screeched back and he rose, ignoring the fact that he left money in the pot on the green baize tabletop. He took one look at Agatha, waiting near the rear hall, and swerved to the bar. Without breaking stride he ordered Jack Hogg, "Bring the shotgun and come with me."

On his way past the piano, he commanded quietly, "Keep playin', Ivory . . . you, too, Marc. Keep the girls dancin'."

Agatha looked like a ghost, glassy-eyed and pasty.

"Agatha," he said, even before he reached her, "are you hurt?"

"No."

With an arm around her shoulders, he swept her along toward the back door, followed by Jack and Dan. "Is somebody up there?"

"Not any . . . m . . . more." Why wouldn't her teeth stop chattering?

"You sure?"

She nodded, breathless, struggling to keep up with his long-legged strides. "I'm sure. But everything's t . . . torn up."

He charged out the back door, tugging her along by the hand, agitated at holding back to accommodate her. He'd seen her walk up steps before; there wasn't that much time to waste.

"Hang on," he warned, then unceremoniously plucked her off her feet into his arms. "Boys, go on ahead." She hung onto Gandy's neck with both hands, while Dan and Jack took the stairs two at a time. They flattened themselves against the wall on either side of her door. The barrel of the shotgun went through first.

"We got a loaded gun out here!" shouted Jack. "If you're in there, you better be spread-eagled on your belly!"

Riding in Gandy's arms, Agatha told him, "I've been in . . . side. They're gone already."

"You've been inside! All alone?" He mumbled a curse and plunked her none too gently on the top step. "Now sit there and don't move!"

Gandy came up short in her doorway. *Lord o' mercy!* he thought. *Somebody's really done a job on this place.* Dan and Jack had already made their way inside and turned, looking back at him.

"It's a real mess."

"Jesus!" exclaimed Jack.

Gandy stepped over a broken teapot, leaned to pick up a music box with the cover twisted and one hinge broken. In the silence it began tinkling out a soft song.

"What do you suppose they were lookin' for?" Dan asked, turning toward the bedroom, where a torn pillow had caused feathers to scatter like fresh snow over everything.

Agatha spoke from the doorway. "My cash from the millinery shop, I imagine."

Gandy spun to face her. "I thought I told you to wait out there."

She hugged herself and raised her green eyes appealingly. "I'd feel safer in here with you."

The music box still tinkled:

Beautiful dreamer, wake unto me,
Starlight and dewdrops are waiting for thee . . .

She came toward him with her broken gait, staring at the delicate metal box in his long, dark hands. On its cover was painted a white-wigged lady with one wrist draped over the back of a garden bench, her skirts swagging delicately, while willows wept in the background.

"It was my mother's," she told him softly, taking it, listening a moment, then closing the cover. She glanced away. Tears came to her eyes for the first time. She pressed the music box just below her breasts, covered her lips with trembling fingers, and said softly, "Oh, dear."

Gandy stepped over the teapot again and took her in his arms with the music box pressed between them. "Easy, Agatha," he soothed. She seemed unaware of his presence. He righted an overturned chair and forced her to sit, then stood with both hands gripping her shoulders. "Agatha, listen to me." She raised tear-filled eyes. "Where do you keep your cash box?"

"Downstairs . . . in a desk drawer. I just lock it up at night. I don't bring it up here."

"Where's the key?"

"With the rest of . . ." She looked around vacantly, as if expecting them to appear out of thin air. "Oh, dear," she said again. Her eyes grew wide and frightened as she looked back up at Gandy. "I don't know . . . oh, dear . . . where could they be?"

"Did you have them tonight?"

"Yes. I . . . I remember coming to the top of the steps and reaching toward the door to unlock it, only the knob was lying at my feet."

Gandy shot a glance at Dan. "Check the landin'. Jack, you'd better go for the sheriff." When they were both gone, Gandy returned his attention to Agatha. In the harsh lantern light her face appeared milk-white. She held herself unnaturally stiff. He kneaded both her shoulders, rubbing his thumbs hard along her tense neck. "We'll find out who did this . . . don't you worry." And a minute later: "You doin' all right?"

She raised her translucent green eyes and nodded.

Dan came in with the keys. "I found 'em. Want me to check downstairs, Scotty?"

"Do that, would you, Dan?"

When he was gone, Scotty picked his way about the apartment, stepping over Agatha's private possessions. He felt a lonely desolation looking at her clothing, her papers, her bedding—all the things that nobody but she should have access to. It made him feel as if he himself were guilty in some small way for laying siege to her private life. He turned and came back to her. "I don't think they were after money."

Startled, she gaped at him. "But what else?"

"I don't know. Did you find any note? Any clue at all?"

"I went only as far as the table." They both glanced around but spotted nothing except the rubble left by the ransacker.

"Do you think it could be Collinson?" he asked.

"Collinson?" The idea terrified her more than the notion that robbery had been the motive.

Dan clumped up the stairs and burst through the doorway, breathless. "Nothin' down there. Everything's locked up tight." He handed the keys to Agatha, then dropped back a step. "What do you think, Scotty?"

"Hell, I don't know. But I *do* know she can't stay here tonight. We'll take her next door."

Agatha couldn't believe her ears. "Next door?"

"You can bunk in with Jube."

"With Jube?" But Jube slept with him.

"It's not safe in here with that doorknob broken off. And, besides, you're in no emotional state to be alone."

At that moment Sheriff Ben Cowdry stepped to the open door. A singularly dour man who wasted little time on civilities, he surveyed the scene with both hands hooked on his hipbones, eyes narrowed, missing little.

"Hogg told me what happened here." He picked his way inside, raising his boot heels high to step over the articles on the floor. His eyes moved carefully from one spot to the next. He glanced at Agatha. "You're all right, Miss Downing?"

"Yes."

"Her money's still downstairs, locked up in a desk drawer," interjected Loretto.

"Hmm . . ." The sheriff stood with feet planted wide, swiveling slowly, his small black eyes searching from beneath the brim of his brown Stetson.

"Any ideas?"

"One," said Gandy. "Miz Downin' and I have taken Willy Collinson under our wing, and his old man doesn't like it much. He paid us each a visit, which I'm sure you heard about."

"The boot through the window?"

"That's right."

"What'd he say?"

Gandy related the story of what had transpired that day, while the sheriff surveyed the apartment, touching little, missing nothing. When he came to stand again before Agatha's chair, he minced no words. "It strikes me that you've got plenty of folks riled up around this town over that temperance group you started. Do you think it could be one of them?"

"I . . . I don't know."

Gandy spoke up. "Once before one of them paid her a call." He swung toward her. "Have you still got the note, Agatha?"

"Yes, it's in my top bureau door." She rose and got it, then brought it back to the sheriff. Her fingers trembled as she handed it to him. "I found it tacked to my back door one night after a temperance meeting."

He took his time reading it, studying the paper long after he must have understood the brief warning it contained.

"Do you mind if I take this?" he asked at last.

"No, of course not."

He folded it, slipped it into his shirt pocket, and once more went on the prowl around the perimeter of the apartment, glancing closely at the mop boards, the furniture, the bedclothes, then checking behind her small heater stove. When he reached the door, he hooked it with a single finger and slowly swung it away from the wall.

"I think I've found it."

Agatha's pulse quickened. Gandy squeezed her shoulder. "What?" Gandy asked.

With a jerk of his head, Cowdry advised Jack to move out of the way. Jack stepped in off the threshold and the sheriff closed the door without uttering a word. Into the dun paint on its backside was scratched:

TEMPERUNCE BEWARE

The sheriff appeared deceptively cool. Agatha and Gandy both knew that beneath his unruffled exterior a shrewd mind clicked.

"Got any ideas?" he inquired.

It could have been anyone—Mustard Smith, Angus Reed . . . any of the saloon owners of Proffitt. Or any of their libating regulars. The list was so long it dizzied Agatha to ponder it.

Gandy stood close beside her. He saw her eyebrows take on an expression of dismay. She was shaken, he could tell. A woman alone with a dangerous enemy—she had good reason to be frightened. He was surprised at the burst of protectiveness he felt toward her.

"Agatha?"

She raised her pale green eyes. They still expressed fright.

"It could be anybody," she admitted in a reedy, trembling voice.

Gandy turned to Cowdry. "She's right. It could be Mustard Smith, Diddier, Reed, Dingo—any of them. About the only one it wouldn't be is Jesus Garcia. I don't think he can write English."

"I'll have my deputy pass through the alley a time or two each night. Beyond that, there's little I can do until I get some positive proof. So keep me informed of any peculiar doings, if you will."

Agatha assured him she would, and he bade them good-night. When he was gone, Gandy sent Jack and Dan downstairs with instructions to send Jubilee back up. Then he turned to Agatha.

"Get whatever you'll need for the night. You're comin' with me."

"Please, Scott, I . . . I wouldn't feel right, intruding on Jubilee."

"I'm not leaving you here alone. Now do as I say."

"But there's nothing wrong with my bed. I have one pillow left and—"

"Very well. If you won't fetch your things, I will." He made a move toward her chifforobe. "Are they in here?" He began opening a door.

"All right, if you insist. But if I think Jubilee has the slightest objection, I'm coming straight back here."

He grinned and stepped aside to let her fetch her nightgown and dressing gown. His eyes followed as she moved toward her bureau. But its top had been razed, and she searched sadly through the mess on the floor for her hairbrush and picked up a hairpin dish. The latter was broken. She fit the two pieces together and held them for a moment. Her face was sad.

She looked up and their eyes met.

"I'm sorry, Gussie." She looked as if she might cry again, so he said, "Let's go," and took her elbow. She stopped beside the lantern on the table and turned to scan the room that she always kept so fastidiously neat.

"Who would do such a thing?"

"I don't know. But I don't want you worryin' about it tonight." He tugged at her arm. "We'll come over and help you clean it in the mornin'. Now douse the light."

She did, and darkness fell around them. They picked their way to the door, which Gandy closed as best he could before opening his hall door and letting her pass before him. "Jube's is the last on the left." The gilded cage was lowered and the trapdoor was open halfway down the hall. Through the hatch a cone of light lit the ceiling, bringing with it slow-moving curls of cigar smoke. The sound of the piano and banjo drifted up clearly. Agatha glimpsed the bar below as she shimmied past the opening. At Jube's door she waited. Gandy opened it and stepped inside without any apparent compunction. He knew precisely where to find the lantern. Agatha heard the match strike. Then his face burst into view above the flaring wick. He replaced the chimney and came back to her.

"Jube'll be up in a minute. Will you be all right?"

"Yes."

"Well . . ." For the first time that night Agatha felt awkward with him. Neither of them knew quite what to say. She had never been escorted to a bedroom door before. He had never escorted a lady there and left her. "I'll shut down a little early so the noise won't keep you awake."

"Oh, no . . . please. Not on my account."

"Jube will be up as soon as she finishes this song." He turned and disappeared before she could thank him.

Jube's room overlooked the street. The double front windows were open and the summer breeze billowed the white curtains inward like filled sails. Nothing was orderly, yet the disarray was soothing. Dancing costumes were draped over the edge of a brocaded dressing screen along with black net stockings and garters. The doors to the armoire were wide open. Inside hung Jube's many white dresses. Beside it a dressing table was strewn with hair feathers, creams, lotions, and face paint of various kinds. Agatha couldn't help smiling at the ashtray and a tin box of cigars, which looked so out of place among the otherwise feminine clutter. The bed was made of brass and had not been made up that morning.

The door opened and Jube bustled in. "Agatha, Scotty just told me! My goodness, you must be in a state of nerves. Imagine someone breaking into your place that way. But don't you worry about a thing. You'll be sleeping right here with me tonight." Her hug was swift and reassuring. Agatha suddenly found herself extremely happy to have Jube's talkative company. It would have been terribly unnerving to spend the night in the mess next door, listening to each creak of the building, wondering if it were a footstep in the dark.

"I really appreciate this, Jubilee."

"Oh, phooey! What're friends for?" She dropped to the chaise and began releasing her shoe buttons with a hook. "Besides, my feet hurt tonight. I was glad to get off a little early. Scotty says he'll kick the last customer out by midnight."

"I told him he didn't have to do that."

"I know, but you can't change Scotty's mind when it's made up. Might as well get ready for bed."

Agatha glanced around diffidently. Jube was already pulling the feathers from her hair, so Agatha followed suit with her hairpins. To Agatha's chagrin, Jubilee stood beside the chaise and stripped off her brief dancing costume, then glanced up to find Agatha standing uncertainly beside the bed.

"You can use the screen if you'd like."

While Agatha undressed she heard Jubilee humming "A Bird in a Gilded Cage," then lighting a cigar and clattering things around on her dressing table. The scented smoke drifted behind the screen and Agatha couldn't help smiling. She recalled the day she'd first seen Jubilee arriving on the wagon. If someone had told her then that she'd end up spending the night sharing Jubilee's room, she would have called him insane. Yet here she was.

She stepped from behind the screen dressed in a high-necked nightgown and wrapper trimmed in plain white eyelet.

And there was Jubilee. Standing before her dressing table mirror scratching her bare white belly and breasts, clad in nothing more than her pantaloons. The cigar was clamped between her teeth and she talked around it. "Damned corsets." She scratched harder, leaving red tracks in her pale skin. "Isn't it aggravating how they itch when you take 'em off? While you ladies are campaigning for women's rights, why don't you campaign to get rid of corsets forever." She held both plump breasts in her hands and pushed them high until the mole between them disappeared in her cleavage. "Imagine that." She chuckled, as if she were in the room alone. "Walking down the street in a dress without boned corsets. Wouldn't that be something now?"

She swung around and Agatha dropped her gaze. She had never seen a naked woman before, much less one who unabashedly displayed her breasts before another. Jube puffed on her cigar and crossed the room to the chaise. She leaned over, breasts hanging, and rifled through the accumulation of garments until she came up with her turquoise dressing gown. When she straightened to thread her arms through the sleeves, her rosy nipples seemed to flash like beacons in the room.

Nonplussed, Agatha didn't know where to look.

Jube didn't seem to notice. She carelessly looped her belt and exclaimed enthusiastically, "Why, Agatha, what marvelous hair you have! Could I brush it?"

"B . . . brush it?" No woman had brushed Agatha's hair since her mother died.

"I'd love to. And it'll relax you. Come on." Jube set her cigar in the ashtray, snatched a brush from her dressing table, and patted the seat of the low bench before it. "Sit down."

Agatha couldn't resist. She sat at Jubilee's dressing table and allowed herself to be pampered. It felt wonderful. At the first sensation of the bristles massaging against her scalp, shivers crept up the back of her neck and arms. Her eyes closed.

"Nobody's combed my hair since my mother was alive. And I was a child then."

"It's so nice and thick," she praised. "Mine is too fine and straight. I always wished I had heavy hair like this. And you're so lucky to have waves. I have to put mine in with the curling tongs."

"Isn't it funny?" Agatha opened her eyes. "I always wished mine were lighter and straighter and blonder."

Jube stroked the full length of the tresses, from crown to

shoulder blade. "Do you think anybody's happy with what they got?"

Agatha thought it a curious question, coming from a beautiful woman like Jubilee. Their eyes met in the mirror.

"I don't know. But everybody makes wishes, I suppose."

"What would you wish for if you could have anything in the world?"

It had always seemed the most obvious thing in the world to Agatha. It stunned her to think Jubilee didn't find it obvious at all. Her blond head was tipped to one side as she idly wielded the brush.

"Two healthy hips and legs."

Jubilee's response was not what Agatha had expected—no big-eyed look of dismay at having overlooked the obvious. Instead she seemed dreamy as she continued shaping and reshaping Agatha's hair, observing, "Yes, I suppose so. But isn't it funny? I never think of you as lame."

Jube's words were such a surprise! Agatha had always been so sure everyone looked upon her with pity, yet somehow she truly believed Jube. There had never been anyone with whom she could share her intimate feelings, anyone who'd share theirs, so Agatha asked, "What would you wish for?"

Jube set the brush down, drew the hair tight and high to the crown of Agatha's head, and shaped it like a bird's nest, holding it up with her hands. Only then did her gaze lift to Agatha's again. Very softly she answered, "A mother to comb my hair sometimes. And a father who was married to her."

For a long moment the two women communicated with only their eyes. Then Agatha swung around. "Oh, Jubilee." She took both of Jube's hands and held them fondly. "Are we foolish, do you think, sitting here wishing for what we can never have?"

"I don't think so. What's the harm in wishing?"

"None, I suppose." Agatha blinked rapidly, then made a soft sound in her throat—not quite a laugh. "It just occurred to me that a year ago one of my wishes might have been for a friend. And now I believe I've found several where I least expected to. Jubilee, I . . ." Agatha's voice choked with emotion as she searched for the proper words to say how much she'd come to value the friendship of Jubilee, Scott, and the others. Her feelings for them had sneaked up on her unaware. Only now, when she needed them and they were there with helping hands extended, did she recognize the depth of their friendship. "I mean it when I say thank you for taking me in tonight. I'm so glad you're here. I was very upset about what happened in my apartment, but I feel so much better now."

Jube leaned down and pressed her cheek to Agatha's. "Good. Then why not jump into bed? It sounds like the rest are coming up now, so you should be able to get some sleep. Then Scotty says in the morning we'll all pitch in and clean up your place." Jube flicked the coverlet back, then patted the sheets with her palm. "Come on, now."

Agatha complied willingly. She plumped the pillow, then sat against it, raising her arms to do her last routine chore of the day.

"What are you doing now?"

"Braiding my hair."

"Why?"

"I always braid it at bedtime."

"But why?"

Agatha tried to think of a good reason but could come up with none. "My mother taught me that's what a lady does with her hair at night."

"But then you have to lie on the lumpy braid. That doesn't make much sense to me."

Agatha laughed. She'd never analyzed it before, but Jube was right.

"That's the last thing I'd do with my hair at night—twist it up in kinks."

"Well, what would you do, then?"

"Do? Why, nothing. Sleep with it free." She ran the brush through her own hair, hung her head back, and shook it. "It's heavenly."

"Very well . . ." Agatha began combing out the half-formed braid with her fingers. "I will."

Still brushing her hair, Jubilee wandered to the dressing table and clamped her cigar between her teeth, puffing while she brushed. "Does the cigar bother you?"

"Not at all." Agatha found it was true. She had come to enjoy the aroma immensely from being around Gandy.

"It relaxes me . . . you know?" Jube explained. "After I finish dancin' I'm all keyed up. Sometimes it's hard to get to sleep right away." Jube crooked the thin, black cigar in her finger, walked around the foot of the bed and sat down, leaning against the brass footrail with the ashtray on her lap, still brushing her white-blond hair.

Somebody knocked on the door. "Hello. It's us." Pearl and Ruby came in without waiting for permission. "We heard the bad news. Don't you worry now. It'll probably never happen again."

They came in turns to press their cheeks to Agatha's and wish her good-night.

"If Jube gets t' snorin', y'all come in with me."

When they were gone, another knock sounded.

"Yes?" Jube called.

"It's Jack and Ivory."

"Well, come on in—everybody else has."

Agatha scarcely had time to draw the bedclothes to her neck before the two appeared.

"You calmed down now, Miss Downing?" Jack asked.

"Yes, thank you. Jube brushed my hair and it made me forget all my troubles."

"Jube's good with a brush, that's for sure," remarked Ivory.

Jube had brushed *Ivory's* hair? Before she had time to imagine such a sight, he said, "Well, g'night, Miz Downin'. See y'all in the mornin'."

"Good night, Ivory."

" 'Night, then," Jack added.

"Good night, Jack."

Just before the door closed Jack stuck his head back in. "Here comes somebody else."

He disappeared and Marcus came to take his place, bearing a steaming cup. His smile told Agatha it was for her.

"Oh, Marcus, how thoughtful." She reached for the cup. "Mmm . . . tea. Thank you, Marcus. It's exactly what I need."

He beamed, then made motions as if stirring in sugar and raised his eyebrows questioningly.

"No, thank you. Without is fine." She sipped and nodded approvingly. "Perfect."

He folded his hands beneath one ear and closed his eyes, as if sleeping.

"Yes, I'll sleep wonderfully after this. Thank you again, Marcus."

At the door he waved. She waved back. The door closed behind him.

Agatha's heart felt full to bursting, warmed by so much more than the tea. She wondered if perhaps she had stated her wish too quickly; perhaps what she wanted more than anything else was to keep this feeling forever, this wondrous familial feeling.

In companionable silence, she sipped and Jubilee smoked.

After some time Agatha remarked, "How thoughtful of Marcus."

Jube's face softened. She stopped puffing and watched the smoke rise. "He's sweet, isn't he? He's always doing something kind for someone. Marcus is about the kindest man I've ever known. Whenever I'm sick he brings me tea with honey and brandy. And once he gave me a back rub. That was heavenly."

"It bothered me at first that he couldn't talk," Agatha confided, "but I soon found out he can get his point across better than most people with voices."

"That's for sure. Sometimes I wish . . ." A wistful expression crossed Jube's face. Then she exhaled a cloud of smoke and murmured, "Oh, nothing."

"Tell me . . . you wish what?"

"Oh . . ." She shrugged and admitted sheepishly, "That he wasn't so shy."

"Why, Jubilee!" Agatha's eyebrows rose. "Do you have . . . feelings for Marcus? I mean, special feelings?"

"I guess I do. But how is a girl supposed to know when the man never makes a move toward her?"

"You're asking me?" Agatha spread a hand on her chest and laughed.

"Well, you're a girl, too, aren't you?"

"Hardly. I'm thirty-five years old. I no longer qualify."

"But you know what I mean. Sometimes Marcus looks at me . . . well, you know. Different. And just when I think he's going to—"

A knock sounded.

"Everybody decent?" came Gandy's voice.

Jube whispered to Agatha, "We'll talk more later." Then she raised her voice. "More than decent. Come in."

The door swung in slowly and Gandy leaned against the frame with his necktie loose and his jacket slung from one finger over a shoulder. He spoke to Jube but looked at Agatha.

"So, you got her all settled in, I see."

"Sure did. She's feeling much better now."

"She looks better." He brought his shoulder away from the doorframe and ambled inside, dropping his jacket across Agatha's feet. "You looked like a ghost when you came downstairs lookin' for me, did you know that?" He reached for her empty cup. "Here, I'll take that." He set it aside, then sat at her hip with one hand braced on her far side. "But your color is back."

She tried to tug the bedcovers higher, but his weight pinned them low. Her cheeks grew rosy-bright above the pristine white of her high-necked nightgown. And her hair was glorious, flowing free in rich, thick waves, catching the lantern light and tossing it back in highlights nearly the color of burgundy wine. He took a moment to let his eyes wander over it appreciatively before returning his gaze to her translucent green eyes. They were captivating eyes, unlike any he'd seen before, as pale as seawater. They had begun bothering him in bed at night, keeping him awake, as if she were in the room watching him. An unexpected stirring brought warmth to his chest as their gazes remained locked and his hip pulled the blankets down from her breasts.

"M . . . Marcus brought me the tea," she stammered, flustered by his nearness, by the fact that she was clad only in a nightgown, and could feel his body warmth against her hip. "And Jubilee brushed my hair." She touched it uncertainly, almost apologetically. "And all the others came in to wish me good-night."

"So, will you sleep now?"

"Oh, I'm sure I will." She tried to smile, but succeeded only in dropping her lips open and revealing the fact that her breathing was none too steady. Her fingertips fluttered to the buttons at her throat. Immediately, he captured the hand and drew it down. Then they sat with their fingers linked. Her heart beat like that of a captured bird, but there were so many things she wanted to say. "I don't know what I would have done without all of you tonight," she whispered. "Thank you, Scott."

"There's no need for thanks." He gave in to impulse and circled her with both arms, pulling her lightly against his chest. He held her that way, motionlessly, for several long, long seconds. "We're your friends. That's what friends are for."

Her heart slammed hard against him. She didn't know where to put her hands except against his shoulder blades. She was conscious of Jubilee watching them from the foot of the bed, and of the intensified scent of cigar smoke from Scotty's skin and clothing, and of the fact that her unbound breasts were flattened against his hard chest—the first time they'd ever found such a resting place.

"Good night, Gussie," he whispered, then kissed the tip of her ear. "See you in the mornin'."

"Good night, Scott," she managed to say in a whisper. While her heart still pounded within her breast, he rose, caught up his jacket, and moved around the bed. Standing behind Jubilee, he leaned over the brass footboard. Jubilee lifted her face and smiled upside down at him.

"G'night, Jube," he said.

They kissed upside down.

" 'Night, Scotty. I'll take good care of her for you."

He winked at Jube and grinned at Agatha. "Y'all do that."

Then he, too, was gone.

When the lantern was extinguished and the building

became silent, Agatha lay beside the sleeping Jubilee for a long, long time, as wide awake as she'd ever been in her life. She was confused and more aware of her own body than she ever recalled being. Not just the parts that usually hurt, but the parts that didn't. From head to foot she felt tingly. Within her breast her heart continued thudding as if it had been powered by some mystical force after lying dormant all these years.

How could Scott have done such a thing—nonchalantly sat down beside her and taken her into his arms without a thought for propriety? And she in her nightie! And Jubilee right there!

But when her hands had rested upon his shoulder blades and her heart lay against his, her own thoughts of propriety had fled. How good it had felt to be pressed to his solid bulk, held for a minute. How hot her face had felt, and how insistent her own pulsebeat. How full and heavy her breasts, when crushed. She remembered the smooth feeling of his cotton shirtback stretched taut as he held her. And his jaw against her temple. And his collarbone against her mouth. And the smell—ah, the smell—so different from her own violet water and starch.

In the wake of remembrance came embarrassment.

But he belongs to Jubilee—doesn't he?

Confused, Agatha tossed and turned to lie on her other hip. The same refrain kept spinning through her mind over and over again.

How can Jubilee belong to Scott if she has feelings for Marcus?

When she finally slept, it was fitfully, and without an answer.

CHAPTER
11

In the morning they all pitched in as promised. Marcus installed a new doorknob, and when Willy showed up they put him to work collecting feathers and stuffing them into a pillowcase. Agatha noticed he was scratching again and made a mental note to talk to Scott about it.

She'd awakened uncertain how to act around Scott this morning, but he treated her as platonically as always.

By ten-thirty Willy grew weary of chasing down feathers, so Agatha sent him off to Halorhan's to see if she'd received any mail.

He returned with the latest issue of *The Temperance Banner* and an envelope bearing a Topeka postmark and Governor John P. St. John's official return address.

"Why, it's from the governor!" she exclaimed.

"Oooo, the guv'nuh!" repeated Ruby. "My, ain't we in tall cotton!" She rolled her eyes and shook her fingers as if they'd been singed.

Agatha carefully slit the envelope and removed a letter engraved with the state seal, while they all gathered around: Marcus, with a screwdriver in his hand; Scott, with his elbow propped on a broom handle; the girls, perched on the edge of Agatha's tiny kitchen set; Ivory and Jack peeking over her shoulder; Dan with Willy climbing up on his boots to get a better look.

Agatha's eyes quickly scanned the sheet.

"Well, what's it say?" demanded Ruby.

"It's an invitation."

"Well, read it 'fore we git gallstones from frettin'!"

Agatha's glance flashed to Scott. Then she turned away nervously. Her mouth felt suddenly dry. She cleared her throat and moistened her lips.

Dear Miss Downing,

As an active member in the movement to prohibit the sale of intoxicants in the state of Kansas, your name has been mentioned to me by State Representative Alexander Kish, Miss Amanda Way, and Miss Drusilla Wilson. As you know, when I became elected governor of Kansas, I made a promise to my constituents to do all within my power to banish not only the consumption of alcohol, but its sale as well within the boundaries of our fair state.

To this end I heartily support the recent legislation passed by both houses of the legislature, proposing ratification of a prohibition amendment to our state constitution.

If those of us who in the past have worked with zeal toward this noble cause will clasp hands once again for more aggressive work than ever before, this amendment can and will be ratified by the voters of Kansas.

By way of expressing my appreciation for your work and encouraging your further support for the prohibition movement, I extend this invitation to afternoon tea in the rose garden of the governor's mansion on September fifteenth at two o'clock P.M.

The letter was signed by Governor John P. St. John himself.

When Agatha finished reading, nobody said a word. Her face and neck felt uncomfortably warm. She stared at the letter, afraid to look up and meet their eyes in the strained silence. The stiff paper crackled as she folded it slowly and then slipped it back into the envelope.

"What's wrong?" Willy's voice seemed to boom in the room as he glanced up from one face to another.

Finally, Agatha raised her eyes. She tried to think of an

answer, but the only one that came to mind was, "Nothing," and it wasn't true. Scott still leaned on the broom, frowning at her. Marcus worked a thumbnail over a blob of dry paint on the screwdriver handle. Jack scratched the back of his neck, avoiding her eyes, while Ivory's long black fingers played a silent song against his thigh. The girls sat dejectedly, studying the floor they'd just helped clean.

One could have heard a snake breathe in the room.

"What's wrong, huh?" Willy repeated, confused.

Dan came to the rescue. "Whaddaya say, buddy?" He dropped a hand to Willy's head. "Wanna come downstairs and help me sweep up the place?"

Willy obediently turned to leave, but he craned his neck to look back at the dismal group as he and Dan walked away. "Well, sure, but what's wrong with everybody?"

"Things you don't understand, pup."

When they were gone the silence hung long and heavy. Finally, Ruby asked Agatha, "You goin'?"

With an effort, Agatha raised her eyes to Ruby's—black and inscrutable. It struck Agatha that Ruby was the descendant of a long line of slaves, and slaves learned early how to hide their deeper emotions. Not a glimmer of emotion showed upon Ruby's face at the moment.

"I don't know," Agatha answered heavily.

Ruby looked away, leaned over to pick up a dustpan. "Well, bes' be gittin'. Everythin's done 'round here."

They drifted away one by one until only Scott remained.

Through the open window came the distant mooing of cattle, the sound of wagon wheels and hooves passing on the street below, a ringing game of horseshoes in progress outside next to the hotel. But within Agatha's apartment all was silent.

Scott dropped his elbow from the broom, took two punishing swipes at the floor, then gave up to stare at the toe of his boot. He shifted his weight to the opposite hip and looked across the room at Agatha.

"Well . . ." He drew in a deep breath, then blew it out.

A small fissure formed in her heart. "Scott," she appealed, "what should I do?"

"You're askin' me?" He laughed once, hard and harsh.

"Who else can I ask?"

His voice grew angry, exasperated. He pointed toward the street. "Try those crazy women you march into the saloons with!"

"They're not crazy! They have good cause."

"They're a bunch o' dissatisfied wives who're lookin' for a way t' get their men back home when all it'd take is a little cuddlin' t' keep 'em from leavin' in the first place!"

She couldn't believe his willful blindness. "Oh, Scott, do you really believe that?"

"My father never hung around a saloon in his life. That's because his wife knew how t' please him at home."

"Your father lived on a plantation. There were probably no saloons for miles around."

He bristled visibly. His eyes hardened to black marble. "And just how do you know so much?"

"The girls told me long ago. The point is, there *were* no saloons, so your father acted as provider and stayed at home, which is where more men should stay."

Scott snorted disgustedly. "You've been hangin' around those fanatics too long, Agatha. You're gettin' t' sound just like 'em."

"The truth hurts, doesn't it, Scott? Yet you know it as well as I do—alcohol is addictive and debilitating. It impoverishes entire families by destroying a man's ability to work, and it turns gentlemen into brutes."

Scott's scowl deepened. "What's worse is you're beginnin' to believe all those generalizations." He pointed a finger at her nose. "And that's just what they are! Half o' you women are kneelin' at every swingin' door in town singin' your damned self-righteous songs and you don't even have cause."

"What about Annie MacIntosh, with two cracked ribs and a black eye? Does she have cause?"

"Annie's a different story. Not every man who has a glass o' whiskey is like MacIntosh."

"And what about Alvis Collinson, who gambles away shoe money and grocery money and lets his own son sleep in a bed crawling with lice?"

Scott's teeth clenched. His jaw took on a stubborn jut.

"You really don't fight fair, do y'?"

"What do you think is fair? To take Willy to the Cowboys' Rest once every month or so to assuage your guilt?"

"My guilt!" Scott's face darkened, his fist tightened on the broom handle, and his head jutted forward. "I don't have any guilt! I'm runnin' a business down there, tryin' to keep eight people alive!"

"I know. And I appreciate what you're doing for all of them. But don't you ever have doubts about the men you serve all that liquor to? About the families who desperately need the money they lose at your gambling tables?"

His expression turned smug. "It doesn't keep me awake nights, no. If they couldn't get whiskey from me, they'd get it somewhere else. Ratify that amendment and the saloons'll close—sure enough—but Yancy Sales'll be sellin' the same stuff I'm sellin', only he'll call it bitters, and every lawmaker in the country'll be in there buyin' it and claimin' it's for *medicinal* purposes."

"That may be. But if prohibition straightens up even one father like Alvis Collinson, it will have been worth the fight."

"Then go, Agatha!" He flapped one hand toward the depot. "Go t' the governor's shindig! Have afternoon tea in his rose garden!" He stomped across the room and slammed the broom into her hands. "Only don't expect me t' come runnin' t' save you the next time a fed-up saloon owner ransacks your bedroom!"

He stormed to the door and slammed it so hard she cringed. The new knob worked perfectly; the door closed and stayed closed, but she stared at it through a film of tears. She lowered herself to a chair and dropped her forehead to her hands. Her heart ached and her chest hurt. The familial closeness of last night had been shattered by her own choice. Yet it wasn't her choice at all. She felt torn and confused and grieved that she was falling in love with the wrong man—heaven help her, with the whole wrong "family." But one did not always choose—she was learning—for whom one cared. Sometimes life made that choice. But it was what one did with that choice after it was made that brought happiness or grief.

* * *

The day hadn't gone Collinson's way. In the morning a wild fat-bellied cow had mashed his leg against the fence before he could draw it out of the way. In the afternoon the kid showed up with feathers stuck on his shirt and admitted he'd been hanging around that interfering hat builder again—helping her clean house, no less. And tonight his luck had soured.

Eight hands in a row he'd lost, while the duded-up cowpoke beside him beat the house on the last three pots. Even Doc, with his muddled-up brain, had managed to win two out of the last six.

Loretto had it in for him, just like the rest of them around the saloon, and Collinson had a feeling he was pulling face cards out of his sleeve somehow. *Smart-aleck punk!* Collinson thought. *Half a year ago he was still pissin' in his bed, an' now he sits gussied up in a fancy black jacket and string tie, double-dealin' them that he used t' call friends.*

Collinson counted his money. He had enough for two more hands, and if he didn't win he'd be busted flat. He downed another shot of whiskey and nervously backhanded his mouth, then turned to nudge Doc's elbow.

" 'Ey, ya got a spare cigar, Doc?"

"Doc" Adkins was no doc at all, but a self-proclaimed veterinarian who traveled around the country "pulling" calves and "worming" hogs by mixing wood ashes and turpentine with their feed. His business hadn't been too lively since he'd fed tincture of opium to one of Sam Brewster's sows, putting her to sleep permanently instead of curing her enteritis.

Some said Doc Adkins made a habit of sampling his own tincture of opium, which accounted for the distant expression in his yellow eyes and his torpid reaction to life in general.

But he was likable, nevertheless, and a faithful friend to the wretch Collinson. Doc found a cigar now and handed it to his drinking buddy. Lighting it, the florid-faced Collinson studied the dealer.

Loretto shuffled so slickly the cards hardly bent. He

arched them in the opposite direction and they fell into line as if by magic.

"So your ma ain't too happy 'bout you dealin' cards here," Collinson remarked.

"I'm twenty-one," Loretto responded flatly.

"He's twenty-one." Collinson nudged Doc's arm with his cigar hand. "Ya hear that, Doc? Got hisself a moustache an' everythin'." Collinson chuckled derisively and glanced at the blond swatch beneath Dan's handsome nose. "Looks like a patch of durum the grasshoppers found tasty, don't it?"

Dan had sensed undercurrents building all night. Collinson was spoiling for a fight, and Dan had his orders. He squared the deck and raised two fingers to Jack at the bar, who immediately poured two double shots of whiskey. Jack nodded to Scotty, who caught the signal and turned from his conversation with a cowpoke to bring over the shot glasses.

"You gentlemen mind if I sit in for a few hands?" he inquired with practiced indifference.

"Why, shore." The young Texan beside Collinson looked relieved as Gandy caught a nearby chair with a boot and slid it up to the table.

"Your drink, Dan." Scotty stretched to place one shot glass before the dealer, then set the other at his own elbow.

"What's the game?" he inquired, reaching into his ticket pocket and extracting some bills.

"Blackjack," replied Loretto. "Who's in?"

Collinson shoved his next-to-last dollar into the center of the table.

Loretto smacked the deck down on his left and Collinson watched to make sure all hands stayed on top of the table during the cut. The punk was good, but he'd make a slip sooner or later, and when he did, Collinson would be watching. Meanwhile, he could be as cool as a frog on a lily pad.

While the first two rounds were dealt, he struck up a seemingly idle conversation with the cowpoke. "What they call ya, boy?"

"Who, me?"

Collinson nodded and squinted through his own cigar smoke.

"Slip." The boy swallowed. "Slip McQuaid."

Collinson checked his down cards—a pair of aces. That was more like it. He split them up and noticed the dealer, too, showed an ace along with his down card. Goddamned punk had to get it from up his sleeve—nobody could be that lucky that often—but it riled Collinson that he wasn't able to catch him at it. He wiped his mouth with the edge of a rough finger and pushed his last dollar in to cover the double wager. Loretto hit him twice—a nine and a four.

Collinson's eyes grew beadier. He shifted his soggy cigar to the opposite side of his mouth, riveting his eyes on the dealer while he spoke to McQuaid. "Hope that ain't got nothin' t' do with how ya play cards. Wouldn't wanna play with nobody had the reputation for bein' slippery." Collinson gave a tight laugh, watching Loretto check his down card without clearing the green baize tabletop.

"N . . . no, sir. I slipped off a wet saddle when I was first startin' to ride and busted my collarbone. My pa give me that name."

"Cards?" Loretto inquired of McQuaid, ignoring Collinson's innuendo.

Gandy noted the slight shift of Dan's hips beneath the table as he crossed his left ankle over his right knee, bringing the concealed derringer within reach.

McQuaid took a card and pondered, while Collinson questioned him further. "What outfit ya ridin' with?"

Gandy refrained from interfering, though Collinson broke a cardinal rule: disturbing McQuaid during play.

"Rockin' J, outta Galveston."

"That where ya learned t' play cards?"

McQuaid tensed but tried not to let it show. "I played some in the bunkhouse with the boys . . . One more," he told Loretto, then cursed when he tallied twenty-two.

Gandy waved a palm over his resting cards as a signal that he'd stand pat. His eyes met Collinson's belligerent stare and he forced each muscle to relax. *Loosen up, Gandy, be ready.*

"And where'd you learn, Loretto? I'll take a hit—over

here." He knuckled the down four. Loretto upturned a seven. Collinson's brown teeth worked over the soaked end of his cigar while he considered and sweat broke beneath his arms. "Again." The king put him over. His temperature went up a notch. The goddamned punk couldn't be that lucky! Collinson still held twenty in his other set, but he'd been hoping to rake in double on this hand. "Yessir, I recall when Danny, there, was no taller'n an angleworm. Used t' wear *short* sleeves then." Collinson squinted pointedly at Dan's knuckle-length black sleeves. "You 'member, don't ya, Doc?"

"I remember," Doc replied vaguely, though it took him some time to do his recollecting. "Hit me, Danny."

Loretto deftly whipped a card his way.

Doc took a long time pondering.

"Hurry up!" snapped Collinson. "Don't see what the hell can take ya so long."

Again Gandy held his temper. When Collinson blew, he'd blow hard. Meanwhile, Doc finally decided.

"Again," he mumbled.

With a snap of his wrist, Dan sent another card to its mark.

Doc peered at it myopically, sighed, and folded. "I'm out."

Collinson's face turned bloodred. "That leaves me against the house, don't it? Now just how lucky would a man have t' be t' win around here?"

"You got something to say, Alvis, say it." Dan kept one hand on the table but dropped the other to his thigh.

"Let's see your cards, boy," Collinson challenged, biting hard on his cigar.

Dan took another hit with the hand that had never been out of sight, then showed three cards totaling a perfect twenty-one.

"You crooked sons-o'-bitches!" Collinson's face turned ugly as he produced a knife. "Don't tell me you ain't got no cards up your sleeves!"

Gandy rose slowly, each muscle tense, prepared, but his voice came out like slow honey. "I don't allow fightin' in here, Collinson, you know that. Now put the knife away."

Collinson crouched with the blade flashing in his hand. Doc and McQuaid backed off.

"Put it away before somebody gets hurt," Gandy warned.

Collinson swung toward him. "You, too! I'd be doin' this town a favor gettin' rid of both o' ya! Which one o' you wants it first?"

"Be sensible and drop it," Dan said, bringing the gun into sight. "I don't want to have to shoot you, Alvis. Dammit! I've known you all my life."

"I ain't droppin' nothin' but one o' you!"

"Four dollars is hardly worth gettin' shot over," Gandy cajoled. "Put it away and we'll have a round on the house." He began to signal Jack.

"This ain't just about four dollars, Gandy, an' you know it. It ain't enough you bastards take my money with them cards you keep up your sleeves; you turn my own flesh an' blood against me, too."

The place had gone silent. Every eye in the room watched warily.

"Go home, Alvis. You're drunk," Dan said reasonably, rising to his feet. "I told you, I don't want to have to shoot you."

"I ain't drunk. I'm broke is what I am, ya crooked—"

"Give it t' me." Gandy moved in, palm up. "We'll talk outside."

"Like hell we will, you fancy, no-good son-of-a-bitch, stealin' everythin' I got—"

Alvis drew back his arm and all hell broke loose at once. The knife plunged into Gandy's upper arm. The derringer exploded and Collinson fell facedown across the round, green tabletop. Customers dove to the floor. The girls screamed. In the sudden silence Gandy grimaced and grabbed his right arm.

"Damn! He got you anyway." Dan jumped forward to help and Jubilee came running, wild-eyed. But Gandy shrugged them both off and dropped to a chair.

"Check Collinson," he said quickly.

Dan rolled him over and felt for a pulse. He raised doubtful eyes to Gandy, who sat slumped and panting, still clutching his limp arm.

Dan raised his voice. "Somebody run and get Doc Johnson!" Then he turned to Adkins, who seemed to have come out of his stupor for the first time in years. His face was chalky, his eyes round with fright.

"Doc, get over here," Dan called. "He can use your help."

"Me?"

"You're a veterinarian, aren't you? See what you can do to keep him alive till Doc Johnson gets here."

"B . . . but I—"

"He's your friend, Adkins!" Dan bellowed impatiently. "For God's sake, quit sniveling and act like a man!" Then he turned to Scotty and went down on one knee beside him. He glanced up dubiously at Jubilee, swallowed hard, and fixed his eyes on the knife protruding from Gandy's arm. "What do you want me to do?"

Gandy was fading in and out from the pain. He lifted his head and stared dazedly into Dan's face. Sweat stood out in beads on his own. "Get . . . it . . . out . . ." he whispered, clutching his right biceps, where blood already had turned his black sleeve shiny.

At that moment Agatha reached the back door after hearing the shot. She entered, puffing, and paused near the keno table to survey the scene before her. She saw someone lying on a gambling table with blood soaking his plaid shirt, and Scott was lying slumped on a chair with a knife protruding from his arm.

"Dear God!" she whispered, hurrying toward him.

Marcus tried to stop her, his hands strong on her arms, his eyes begging her to heed his silent plea and do as he indicated.

She met them squarely, understanding afresh that he cared enough to be concerned about her welfare as well as Scott's. "Let me go," she ordered gently. "He helped me; now it's my turn."

Marcus reluctantly released her and she hurried forward, already issuing orders to Jack and Ivory and all the girls, who hovered undecidedly around Gandy's slumping form. "Lay him down before he falls off the chair."

Dan and Jack reacted without a pause. Gandy groaned

and his forehead grew shiny as they laid him on the raw pine floor. Agatha struggled to her knees beside him. She released his tight tie and collar button and touched his throat lovingly. "Oh, Scott," she whispered, her face drawn with concern, "oh, my dear."

He managed a faint smile. "Gussie . . ." he whispered weakly, fluttering the fingers of his bloody hand.

She clasped them tightly and pressed the back of his hand between her breasts, heedless of the fact that her own hand grew bloody.

Just then Doc Johnson burst through the swinging doors with his nightshirt tucked into his trousers, his suspenders trailing beside his knees, and his red hair standing up on end.

"Step aside!" It took him less than thirty seconds before he pronounced, "Collinson's dead."

The name penetrated Agatha's mind. Kneeling beside Scott, she fired a glance at Dan. "Collinson?" she repeated, shocked. "He shot Collinson?"

"No, I did," Dan corrected.

She looked down at Scott's blanched face, the knife protruding from his flesh. "Then how——"

"He tried to get Alvis to give over the knife . . . Alvis gave it over, all right."

"Move aside!" ordered Doc Johnson impatiently. He knelt down, took one look at the knife, and advised, "Better get this man drunk. And the drunker the better."

Jack fetched a full bottle of Newton's whiskey. Scott lay on the floor blearily smiling up at the bartender. "Make sure you got the ninety proof, Jack." He attempted a crooked smile, but it looked ghostly on his pale face.

Sheriff Cowdry arrived and made a silent inspection of Collinson's body, while Jack fed Scott more whiskey than Agatha thought one man could consume and still remain conscious. Jubilee sat on the floor with Scott's head in her lap while his blood dried on Agatha's palm.

Cowdry questioned the customers, then cleared them out. The undertaker came to haul away Collinson's body and two tables were pushed together to create an emergency operating room. Marcus, Dan, Ivory, and Jack lifted Scott gently and laid him down. He was grinning loosely, his lips wet, his face flushed. He beckoned Marcus with one finger.

"Listen . . ." he whispered mushily. "This stuff's damned good, but don't tell Agatha I said so." He chuckled drunkenly and craned his head to see Ivory, behind him. "And if I kick the bucket, none o' your Baptist dirges at my funerull, boy. I want the cancan, ya unnerstan'?"

Jack put the bottle to his boss's lips again. "One more, Scotty. That should do it." The liquor trailed down Scott's cheek and made a dark spot on the green baize. His eyes blinked slowly once, twice—but still didn't close.

"Gussie?" he whispered, his eyes suddenly searching. "Where's—"

"I'm here, Scott." She moved quietly beside the table and found his good hand. He clutched hers desperately.

"Willy . . . you've got t' tell Willy." His eyes were rimmed with red. Against his black brows and hair his skin appeared waxy, except for the unnatural tinge of red brought to his cheeks by the liquor. "I'm sorry . . . tell 'im I'm sorry."

She touched the limp hair clinging to his perspiring brow, brushed it back. "I promise."

Doc opened his black case and began threading a needle with a piece of horsehair. "Bring a fresh bottle of whiskey," he ordered. "And anybody that's queasy, get out."

Agatha stayed long enough to watch Doc pull the knife blade out of the bone in Scott's arm, and to see his body convulse and to hear him cry out in agony. Long enough to hear Doc order, "Give him another shot!" Long enough for her stomach to twist and her eyes to fill and her throat to thicken. But when Doc dipped the needle and horsehair into the whiskey, she slipped out the swinging doors to gulp the clean night air and sob alone.

CHAPTER
12

Agatha had not been back to the Collinson house since that first time. But the smell was the same: a combination of must, coal oil, sour linens, and unwashed bodies. Even before she lit a lamp she knew she'd find no improvement in her surroundings.

Groping at the kitchen table, she found stick matches and a lantern. When it was lit she avoided glancing around; instead, she headed straight for Willy.

He looked so small curled up in a ball with his chin on his chest. He didn't rouse, even when she brought the light near and set it on the floor. He was probably used to somebody stumbling around in the kitchen and lighting lanterns in the middle of the night. She stood a long time gazing down at him, swallowing the clot of emotion in her throat, wondering what would become of him. So young, so unloved, so alone. Tears burned her eyes. She clasped her hands beneath her chin and said a silent prayer for him. And for herself and the task she must perform.

Gingerly, she perched on the edge of his bed, forcing herself not to think of the other living things that shared it with him.

"Willy?" She touched his temple, the skull behind his ear. "Willy, dear."

He snuggled deeper into the caseless pillow and she spoke his name again. His eyes opened halfway and immediately she saw they were puffed from crying. When he was fully awake he bolted up, his eyes wide open.

"Gussie! What're you doin' here? If Pa sees you we'll both be in trouble!"

There were welts on the side of his neck and a red slash across his ear. Dried blood marked his dirty pillow.

"Willy, what happened to you?"

"Gussie, you gotta go!" His eyes grew frantic. "Pa'll—"

"It's all right. He's still uptown. Did he do this to you?"

When she tried to touch his ear, he shrugged away and dropped his eyes to his lap. "Naw. I slipped when I was climbin' on the cattle pens an' banged it on a rail."

She knew he was lying. He refused to meet her eyes, and he scratched at the bedclothes with one dirty index finger. She covered his hand and forced his chin up until she was looking squarely into his eyes. A child's eyes, she thought, should not have pillows of puffed skin beneath them.

"He did, didn't he?" she insisted quietly.

His eyes began filling. His lips tightened and his chin trembled in her palm. As his throat worked to repress the tears, she was torn between two fervid emotions: love for this forlorn orphan, and a heathen gratitude that his father was dead and could never hurt Willy again.

"He found some feathers stuck in my shirt and ast me where I got 'em, and when I told him he thrashed me good with his razor strop an' said I couldn't go t' your place or Scotty's no more. So you better git outta here, Gussie, or he'll take the belt t' me again." Though Willy managed the admission without breaking down, he came close. So did Agatha.

She drew a deep breath, squared her shoulders, and squeezed his hands hard.

"Willy, dear, I have some bad news for you."

He studied her blankly for a moment, then declared, "I ain't takin' no more baths."

"No . . . no, it's not that. Darling, your father died tonight."

Willy's eyes widened with bewilderment. "Pa?"

"Yes. He was shot about an hour ago in Scotty's saloon."

"Shot?"

She nodded, allowing him a moment to accept that.

"You mean he ain't comin' home?"

"I'm afraid not."

Willy's brown eyes stared straight into Agatha's.

"He's really dead?"

Her thumbs rubbed the backs of his thin hands. "You know what that means, don't you?"

His gaze dropped and settled on a spot in the shadows beyond her shoulder. "I had a cat once and it died. Pa kicked it an' it flew against the wall and made a funny sound, and then my friend Joey an' me, we buried it outside by the toilet."

Agatha's tears could be held at bay no longer. Willy looked up with dry brown eyes to find hers swimming.

"That what they're gonna do with my pa?"

"He'll be buried, yes, but in the graveyard where your mother is."

"Oh."

"Y . . . you're coming home with me tonight. Would you like that?"

"Yes." The word came out flat, expressionless.

"Willy, your father was probably a . . . a good man . . . deep inside. But he'd had a lot of sadness in his life, with your mother dying when she was so young."

Willy's mouth thinned and he stared at the tucks on Agatha's bodice. Muscle by muscle tightened until a look of defiance was etched across his entire face. "I don't care if he's dead," he said stubbornly. But his chin quivered. "I don't care!" His voice grew louder and he punched the mattress. "I don't even care if they bury him outside by the toilet! I don't care . . . I don't care . . . I d . . . don't . . . ."

By the time he plunged into Agatha's arms he was sobbing. His small fists clutched her dress and his scraggly head burrowed against her bosom. She spread her hand on his small back as it heaved.

"Oh, Willy." She cried with him, rocking him, cradling his head and pulling him against her aching heart. "Willy, darling . . ." She understood him absolutely. She empathized totally. She rested her cheek against his head as time spun backward and she, too, became a defiant waif, making the same declaration Willy had just made, meaning exactly the opposite.

"Willy, it'll be all right," she said soothingly.

But how? she thought. *How?*

She put him to sleep in a shakedown on her floor but awakened in the morning to find him curled on his side in her bed with his warm little buttocks up against her lame hip. Her first waking thought was that he was the only male with whom she'd ever slept; her next was that having him there even for so short a time was worth all the work she'd have to go through to delouse her bed.

She took him down to Paulie's for breakfast and watched him pack away enough pancakes to shingle a schoolhouse roof. Then she left him at the Cowboys' Rest with instructions that Kendall was to scrub him everywhere, mercilessly, then quietly dispose of his wretched clothes. She'd be back for him in thirty minutes with clean ones.

She found the britches and shirt she'd made for him still folded neatly in her bureau drawer. Carrying them, she went next to Gandy's apartment and tapped quietly on the door. Expecting it to be answered by Jubilee, she was surprised when Ruby appeared instead.

"How is he?" Agatha whispered.

"Middlin'. But he mule-strong, that one. He be fine."

"I've come for Willy's boots."

"Lemme have a look-see."

While Agatha waited outside she gazed at the picture of the white plantation house on the wall opposite the apartment door. Below it, a dresser held Scott's humidor and a hat block with his black Stetson. It was odd how the sight of a man's personal possessions, in his personal domain, made a woman feel as if she'd shared something intimate with him.

Ruby appeared with Willy's boots. "How's that li'l guy doin'?"

"At the moment, not so well. He's at the Cowboys' Rest getting a bath, and you know how he hates baths."

"He know about his pa?"

"Yes. I told him."

"How he take it?"

"He claimed he didn't care." Agatha met Ruby's dark eyes while her voice softened. "But all the while he cried his little heart out."

"Reckon you had the hardest job of all, tellin' him."

"It wasn't an easy night for any of us, was it?" The last time Agatha had talked to Ruby, the black woman had turned away with detached stoicism after Agatha had read the invitation to the governor's tea. How it had hurt. Agatha reached out to her now. "Ruby, I'm sorry I—"

"Lawd, I know it, woman. Ain't this a crazy mixed-up world, though?"

Ruby didn't take her hand. But it wasn't necessary. Agatha felt as if she had just shrugged out of a heavy yoke. She squared her shoulders and changed the subject.

"Willy wants to see Scott. Do you think it would be all right if I brought him up later today?"

"Don't see why not. Should take the boss's mind offa that throbbin' arm."

That afternoon at four o'clock, when Agatha knocked again on Gandy's door, she held the hand of a boy whose hair was neatly parted on the side and combed into a crisp gold wave above his brow. Along with a fresh barbershop haircut, he wore brand-new underwear and socks from Halorhan's Mercantile, shiny brown leather boots with unknotted strings, homemade blue britches, and a blue-striped shirt.

Ivory answered this time. He looked down at Willy and threw back his hands in feigned surprise.

"Well, what's this?"

"I had t' have another bath," the boy complained, putting on a sour expression.

"*Another* one?" Ivory looked properly shocked. "Tsk-tsk."

"We come t' see Scotty."

Agatha jiggled his hand. "We *came* to see Scotty."

"That's what I said, din't I?"

Ivory chuckled, then smiled at Agatha. "How're you, Miz Agatha?"

"How is Mr. Gandy?"

"O'nry. Doesn't much like bein' laid low."

She whispered conspiratorially, "We'll tread lightly, then."

His eyes were closed when they walked in. He lay in a curled-maple bed of masculine proportions, propped up against a bale of pillows with his arm bound in gauze. His chest was bare, the skin and black hair appearing dark in contrast to the white bedding. Agatha took one look at his face and recognized how much pain he'd suffered since last night.

Willy stood somberly at her side.

"Hi, Scotty," he said.

Scott's eyes opened and he smiled. "Sprout," he said affectionately, holding out a palm.

"Gussie says I can't hug you or jump on your bed or nothin'."

"She does, huh?" Gandy's brown eyes lifted to Agatha as she stood holding the boy's hand. The two of them looked right together. It felt right having them here. He had the insane urge to fold back the blankets and invite them both to lie down beside him and talk about foolish things and laugh with him.

"Hello, Agatha," he said quietly.

"Hello, Scott. How are you feeling?"

Confused, he thought. "I've had better days, but Ruby says, long as it's throbbin', y' know it ain't dead."

Willy looked up entreatingly, his hand still resting obediently in hers. "Can I go stand by him? I promise I won't jiggle nothin'."

"Of course you can." She released his hand and smiled as he crossed the room with uncharacteristic solemnity and inched as close to the bed as he could without touching it. Scott's good arm hooked him around the waist and pulled him against the edge of the mattress.

"You're lookin' mighty spit-shined there, sprout. Smellin' pretty, too."

"Gussie made me take another bath." His tone took on additional disgust. "*Then* she made me go to the barber-shop!"

"She's a nasty one, isn't she?" Scott teased, flashing Agatha a dimpled grin.

Willy stuck out his stomach and rubbed it. "Got my new britches an' shirt back, though, an' my boots, too. An' Gussie bought me new underwear!"

"She did, huh?" Scott's eyes wandered to Agatha while his large hand roamed the small of Willy's back. A lazy smile tipped up the corners of his mouth.

Agatha spoke up briskly. "Yes, she did." She brought a side chair and placed it next to the bed for herself. "But Willy's already paying it off by sweeping the floor in the workroom and running to fetch my mail. We've had a busy day." She sat down and folded her hands in her lap.

"Did you know my pa is dead?" Willy inquired without preamble.

Scott's hand stopped rubbing and rested along the boy's ribs. "Yes, Willy, I did."

Willy went on. "Was you there when he got shot?"

"Yes."

"Did . . . did *you* shoot 'im?"

"No, son, I didn't."

"Then who did?"

Again Scott flashed a glance at Agatha. Dan, too, was Willy's friend. Not wanting to disillusion the boy, Gandy answered evasively, "A man he was playin' cards with."

"Oh." Willy thought a moment, stared at Scott's bandage, and asked, "Did you get shot, too?"

"No, I had a little accident with a knife, that's all."

"Pa's knife?"

Scott cleared his throat and elbowed himself up a little straighter. "Listen, Willy, I'm really sorry about your pa, but I've got things worked out so you won't have t' worry." He patted the bed next to him. "Come on up here and I'll tell you about it."

Willy clambered up and sat beside Scott, his brown eyes intent on the dark face lying against the white pillows.

"I had Marcus clean out a corner o' the backroom downstairs. You know—the one where we keep the extra bottles and the brooms and things? He set up a little bed down there for you and that's where you'll sleep from now on. How does that sound?"

Willy's face lit up. "Really?!"

Agatha experienced a stab of regret even as her heart swelled with gratitude toward Scott. Reason told her she couldn't take Willy in to bunk beside her permanently, but she'd rather hoped his situation would remain unsettled for a few more nights. However, if there was one place Willy liked to be, it was with Scott. He'd be utterly happy in a shakedown, even in the backroom.

"But in the mornings you'll have t' get up and help Dan pile all the chairs on top of the tables while he sweeps. And you'll have t' help Jack wash glasses. And when the cuspidors need cleaning, that'll be your job, too. Agreed?"

"Gee, Scotty, really?"

"Yessir."

In his excitement Willy forgot himself and fell forward to give Scott a fierce hug. Scott winced and drew in a sharp breath.

"Willy!" Agatha hurriedly pulled him back. His expression immediately turned remorseful.

"Oh . . . I . . . I forgot."

"You'd better get down," she said quietly. "Another day when Scott is feeling better you can sit with him."

He clambered down and turned toward the bed with guilt drooping his boyish face. "I din't mean to hurt you, Scotty."

Scott forced himself to forget the sharp stabs of pain in his arm. "It's all right, sprout. You just gave me a twinge, but it's practically gone already."

Forgiven, Willy brightened immediately. "Can I tell Charlie an' the other guys where I'm gonna live?" he asked excitedly, referring to the boys who sold food at the depot.

"Don't see why not."

"An' can I tell 'em about the job you give me?"

"*Gave* me," Agatha corrected.

"Gave me."

Gandy managed a chuckle, though his arm still hurt like the devil.

"Go ahead, tell 'em."

"But, Scotty?" With quicksilver speed Willy's face became somber again.

"What now?"

"I can't help Dan with the sweepin' tomorrow, 'cause my pa is gittin' buried an I gotta go to the fune-rull."

Scott felt a lump form quickly in his throat. The boy's ingenuousness went to his heart like a hunter's arrow. "Come here," he requested softly, "but take it easy this time." Ignoring the pain in his arm, Scott stretched toward the edge of the bed and extended his healthy arm in welcome. Willy came carefully, as ordered, and when Scott's strong dark hand pulled the small body against his wide chest, when his coarse, unshaven cheek rested against Willy's blond hair, his voice grew low and unsteady.

"The day after tomorrow'll be fine, sprout. And I'll ask the doc if I can get up tomorrow so I can be at the funeral, too. How's that?"

"But Gussie's gonna take me."

Scott shifted his gaze to Agatha, still sitting beside the bed, watching Willy with a telltale tear in her eye and a sympathetic droop to her lips. At that moment her pale, pale eyes moved to Scott's very dark ones.

Gandy spoke softly, his bearded jaw catching strands of Willy's fair hair. "Gussie is a very dear lady. But I think I should be there, too."

The graveside of Alvis Collinson brought more mourners than he probably deserved. His friend, Doc Adkins, was there, and so was a fat, raw-boned woman named Hattie Twitchum, who wept noisily throughout the ceremony. Alvis had spent a lot of time at Hattie's since the death of his wife, and rumor had it that the last two of her seven children bore a remarkable resemblance to Collinson. Mooney Straub stood beside her, sober for the first time in memorable history. And every employee from the Gilded Cage was present: Jack, Ivory, Marcus, Dan, Ruby, Pearl, Jubilee. Standing in a tight little cluster of their own were Scott and Agatha, holding the hands of Willy between them. They looked very much like a mother, father, and son. Willy wore a brand-new store-bought suit, which was a miniature of Gandy's—white shirt, with everything else black. Agatha stood in a high-necked black bengaline dress with generous leg-of-mutton sleeves that narrowed sharply at the elbows, and a black shepherdess hat pitched forward on her head, crowned by a crisp black veil tied into a wide bow above the back brim. Gandy had one arm in his jacket sleeve, while the other hung against his ribs in a white sling.

Willy didn't shed a tear throughout the entire ceremony. When Reverend Clarksdale tossed a handful of soil on top of the coffin and quoted, "Ashes to ashes, dust to dust," Agatha glanced down at him, expecting him to crumble. But though he clung tenaciously to her gloved hand, and to Scott's much larger one, his eyes remained dry.

As the ceremony progressed, she glanced more often at Scott's uncharacteristic paleness. Even through his tanned skin, the pallidity was evident. When the service had begun, he held his hat in his right hand, reserving his good left hand for Willy. But after some time he placed it on his head, as if even the effort of holding it in the weakened hand grew tiring.

When the final prayer ended and the noisy weeping of Hattie Twitchum faded away, Agatha thanked Reverend Clarksdale, who inquired after Willy's welfare.

"For the time being, we'll look after him," she replied.

"We?"

"Mr. Gandy and I."

Reverend Clarksdale's protuberant green eyes seemed to pop out farther, but Agatha decided she owed him no explanations. Furthermore, she could tell Scott had over-taxed himself.

"Thank you again, Reverend Clarksdale. Now, if you'll excuse us, Mr. Gandy needs to sit down."

By the time they'd climbed aboard one of the waiting black carriages, Scott's color had faded to that of tallow. He leaned back into the corner of the seat. Ivory saw him droop and came to take the ribbons. Marcus saw, too, and nudged Jube and made motions among himself, her, the boy, and his own wagon, then pointed to the prairie and rocked as if taking off for a ride.

Jube pointed to herself. "Me, too?"

Marcus nodded and Jube smiled.

She went to tell Willy, "Marcus has a carriage all paid for for the whole day. Shame to take it back to the livery stable and not get his money's worth. What about the three of us taking it out for a little ride?"

Willy shrugged and glanced up first at Scott, then at Agatha.

"I'll bet we could find some jackrabbits or some prairie dogs," Jube cajoled.

They were a remarkable group, Agatha realized again. Scott needed rest. Willy needed diversion. Marcus and Jube stepped right in to provide both.

But Willy wasn't as enthusiastic as they'd hoped. Obviously, he was anxious to get settled into his new lodgings instead.

Agatha put her arm around Willy's shoulders. "Scott needs to go home and lie down," she explained. "His arm is bothering him. Wouldn't you like to go out with Marcus and Jube for a while?"

"I s'pose," he answered unenthusiastically.

Shading her eyes, Jube looked up at Willy. "You haven't had your dinner yet. Maybe we could all take a picnic."

The suggestion brought the first spark of interest to Willy's brown eyes.

"A picnic?"

"Why not?"

"With lemonade?"

"If Emma Paulie made some today. And if Marcus agrees." She turned a fetching smile on him.

"Hey, Marcus," Willy called, "can we take a picnic?"

Marcus agreed and within ten minutes the three of them were pulling up in front of Paulie's Restaurant in a rented Studebaker buggy with shining yellow wheels and a bouncy black leather seat.

Emma Paulie had not made lemonade that day. But she had baked chicken, fresh bread, and pumpkin pie. She packed these in a peach crate, and along with it they took a jug of sarsaparilla and Marcus's banjo.

They turned the wagon northward, crossing the Union Pacific Railroad tracks and setting off across the prairie, leaving behind cattle trails, the town, and the graveyard.

It was a clear day, and the sun was warm on their backs. Overhead lambs'-tail clouds dotted a true blue sky. Around them Kansas stretched as flat as a stove lid. The undulant grasses sang a sibilant song, while from overhead a circling hawk watched them pass.

A killdeer scuttled away from the wagon path, trailing its tuneless note, and Willy asked what it was. Jube said she didn't know, but later she pointed out a meadowlark perched on a hackberry bush.

Marcus was content, listening to Jube and Willy chatter, glancing now and then at the boy's blond head at his elbow, and Jube's white one on the far side of the seat. Today was one of the rare times when she hadn't worn white. Against her dress of somber indigo blue, her fairness shone like a star in the midnight sky. She was the most beautiful creature God had ever created. And she certainly had a way with Willy. The lad had totally forgotten his original hesitation about coming and gazed up at her now, enthralled, as she gestured at the clouds and sang robustly:

Oh, he flies through the air with the greatest of ease,
This daring young man on the flying trapeze.
His movements are graceful, all girls he does please
And my love he has purloined away . . .

"Sing it again, Jube!" Willy piped up when the song ended.

She looked down at him from beneath the brim of a high blue hat. "I will, but I'll need a little help."

"But I don't know it."

"It's easy . . ." She taught him the words.

Oh, once I was happy, but now I'm forlorn . . .

Soon the two of them were singing loudly, their voices ringing across the boundless prairie, Jube's rich and true, Willy's off-key, missing words here and there. When they ended the last chorus, he crinkled up his nose and asked, "What's purloined?"

"Stolen."

"Oh. Then how come we don't just sing *stolen* away?"

Jube considered a moment, then turned toward the driver. "I don't know. Marcus, do you know?"

Marcus didn't know, but he loved smiling into her almond-shaped eyes. And he loved the tilt of her small, pretty nose, and the mole on the crest of her cheek, and her heart-shaped mouth that seemed always to be smiling. He tried to remember a time when Jubilee had grown snappish or pouting, but he could recall none. Her temperament was as bright as the rest of her. Their gazes held for some moments across the top of Willy's head, their smiles half formed, their bodies rocking with the motion of the rig. He wondered if he'd ever been happier in his life. He felt alive and vibrant, and he gloried in each precious moment of her company.

The only thing that marred his bliss was the fact that he could not tell her how he felt. How beautiful she looked. How he revered her, would do anything for her, give her anything it was in his power to give.

They picnicked in the middle of the prairie amid the abundant blooms of late summer. Wild aster in pale violet, blazing stars in heliotrope, goldenrod in rich yellow. But no wildflower could ever match the beauty of Jubilee.

While she spread the blanket and knelt to unpack their food, Marcus sat cross-legged in the grass and took up his banjo. Immediately, Willy pranced over and hugged his neck from behind.

"Play somethin' fast, Marcus!"

He chose "Little Brown Jug," and soon Willy took up skipping in a circle around Marcus, in rhythm with the tune. Jube stopped unpacking and looked up. She smiled and began clapping. Willy giggled and lifted his new brown boots higher with each step.

She got up and stood close to Marcus, tapping one foot on the grass, dipping her shoulders as she clapped, laughing at Willy's antics.

"Hey, Willy, how 'bout a dance?" she teased.

Without missing a beat, he shouted, "Don't know how!"

"Aw, anybody can dance!"

"Not me!"

"You can, too—come on!"

She caught his elbow with hers and swung him in a circle, singing:

> My wife and I lived all alone
> In a little log hut we called our own.
> She loved gin and I loved rum
> I tell you we had lots of fun.
> Ha! ha! ha! you and me,
> Little brown jug how I love thee
> Ha! ha! ha! you and me,
> Little brown jug how I love thee.

Verse after verse she sang, with Willy joining in the chorus. Marcus picked up the tempo and laughed silently while the two joined hands and circled crazily until their heads hung back and Jube's hat fell off.

What a sight they made, carefree and exuberant, whirling and singing, then tumbling to the ground breathless and laughing. Willy fell to all fours, Jubilee to her back with an arm flung above her head.

"Hoo! What a time! Willy, you're some dancer!"

Willy popped up, grinning, swiping his brow with one small hand. "Wait'll I tell Gussie we was dancin' and singin'!"

Jube propped up on one palm, alarmed. "Willy, don't you *dare*—unless you want to get Marcus and me in trouble! A temperance worker like Agatha would be real mad if she knew we'd taught you such a song! Promise you won't tell!"

The words of the song hadn't fazed Willy. He was affected more by his thirst. "I want a sassparilly!" he demanded.

Marcus tucked away his banjo in its case and they all ate the main part of their picnic while lounging in the thick yellow Indian grass, after which Willy sat nearby eating too much pie and drinking too much sarsaparilla.

Braced on one elbow, Marcus gnawed on a drumstick and studied Jube at leisure. She sat so near that her skirts brushed his crossed ankles. She had let her hat lie where it fell, and its pin had pulled a piece of hair loose. The sun glanced off the drooping white strand as if it were spun of cobwebs. He imagined removing the remaining hairpins and letting it tumble to her shoulders, combing it with his fingers, burying his nose in it, then kissing her.

Willy brought Marcus back down to earth. "Feel my belly." He came waddling on his knees. "It's hard as a rock."

Marcus felt. Jube felt. "You're gonna get sick," she warned.

"Uh-uh." Willy waggled his head in big, wide sweeps. "I never git sick."

"But you'd better not have any more pie for a while. Or any more sarsaparilla, either."

Willy flopped on the grass, puffing, belly up. "Whew!" His mouth gleamed with grease. His shirt had worked itself out of his pants, leaving an inch of bare stomach showing. The strings of his new boots had come untied. He didn't care one bit. After several minutes a loud burp rumbled from him. Jube laughed, Marcus smiled, and Willy giggled.

"You're supposed to say 'Excuse me,' " Jube reminded him.

" 'Scuse me." Then he burped again, louder than before, adding an additional crack to the sound by forcing it. While everyone shook with laughter, Jubilee packed away the picnic articles.

The saloon would remain closed till evening. There was no rush to get back, so they sat listening to the buzz and hum of life around them.

"Are clouds soft?" Willy inquired after a while, staring at the fluffy white patches overhead.

"I don't know." Jubilee leaned back on both elbows to study them, too. "They sure look soft, don't they?"

"See that one?" Willy pointed. "Don't it look like a white hen with a dirty belly?"

"Mmmm . . ." She pondered it, letting her head hang back and the sun heat her face. A hairpin slipped and fell to the grass. "Maybe. Maybe like a teapot with a broken handle."

"Nuh-uh. It don't, neither."

She lifted her head and nudged him with a toe. "Well, it does to me."

He giggled and scrambled onto all fours above her, clowning, looking for more attention, more teasing. "Looks like a hen."

"It's a teapot."

"A hen."

"A teapot." She flattened his nose with the tip of one finger. "To me it's a teapot, Willy Collinson."

He plunked down across her torso and knocked her to her back, her head thumping Marcus's hip. Instead of moving away, she lay back against him.

"How come you're so pretty an' other ladies ain't?" Willy inquired with a silly twist to his lips and eyebrows.

"What a little flatterer you are. But how can I trust a boy who thinks a hen looks like a teapot?"

Willy flipped over to stare at the sky again. He ended up with his head on her stomach. The proper cradle for her head seemed Marcus's stomach, and he raised no objections when she settled more comfortably against it.

They lay in the thick prairie grass squinting at the clouds, fit upon each other like three notched logs. The breeze fluttered above them, tipping fronds of wild side oats into and out of their range of vision. A monarch butterfly fluttered past and perched upon a brown-eyed Susan, where it sat fanning its wings. Somewhere in the hidden turf a prairie chicken added its staccato cluck to the buzz of katydids. The warm earth reached up to them from below; the hot sun baked them from above. Content, they lazed.

Willy's fingers relaxed; his palms opened. In time he began snoring softly.

Marcus lay with his fingers locked behind his head, glorying in the weight of Jubilee's head on his stomach, feeling his heart thumping steadily through his shoulder blades into the virgin soil, which seemed to return the beat in kind.

He thought about reaching down, finding her throat with his fingertips . . . touching . . . just touching . . . nothing more.

But before he could, he felt her head move. He lifted his own and found her watching him, flawless and peaceful, her cheek turned against his belly. Then she did the most incredible thing: she reached up and touched *his* throat with her fingertips, a touch as tentative as the fanning of the monarch's wings.

She smiled gently.

And filled him with wonderment.

And sent his heart rumbling like summer thunder.

And raised a wild, reckless hope within him.

Jube, he thought. *Aw, Jube, the things I'd say to you if only I could. The things I'd do.* But she was Scotty's, wasn't she? Marcus imagined a man like Scotty would know everything there was to know about how to kiss and please a woman. How ever would Jube find his own kiss appealing after knowing a man like that?

So instead of kissing Jube, Marcus contented himself with a single consolation. He touched her hair lightly, felt for the first time the sun captured in its bounty and the silken texture against his fingers.

Jube. Though his lips moved, no sound came forth.

But she saw her name and said his in response. And though he could hear perfectly clearly anything she chose to say, she, too, only mouthed the word.

Marcus.

And for today—for this one golden day—it was enough.

CHAPTER
13

The day had been insufferably warm for September, hot and humid after two days of rain. Not a breath of wind stirred through the apartment. The sheets felt clammy and no matter how many times Gandy nudged Jube over, she sprawled back onto his half of the bed and edged her warm leg against him. His arm hurt and the damnable coyotes wouldn't shut up. Yip-yip-yip. They'd been at it for more than an hour now.

He nudged Jube's leg away again. Facedown, arms up, she crooked the knee and pressed it against him again. Agitated, he shifted over.

Things weren't good between himself and Jube. Something had gone sour, but he wasn't sure what. She slept in his room less often, and when they made love he had the feeling she didn't always want to. They'd done so earlier in the night, but when he'd asked her if something was wrong, she'd answered, "It's just the heat, and I'm tired."

"You wanna forget it, Jube? We don't have to."

"No . . . no, it's all right," she'd answered too quickly. Then when he'd reached for her, she'd gone on: "I just wish sometime we could do it when it wasn't one o'clock in the morning and I wasn't all tired out from dancing."

But it never used to matter whether it was one o'clock in the morning or one o'clock in the afternoon. Jube was ready. And enthusiastic.

Lying beside her now, Scott wondered if it was something he'd done. Something he hadn't done. Maybe she wanted to get married, was waiting for him to bring it up. He turned to study her in the dark. Her naked limbs were as pale as the sheets upon which she lay. Even her white-blond hair was indistinguishable from the bedding. She had blended into his life just as completely as her paleness blended with the sheets. It was a comfortable relationship, but not one he wanted permanently. Marry Jube? No, he didn't think so. The thought of marriage should bring a wild rush of eagerness, as when he'd been engaged to Delia. But it didn't. There were two different kinds of love, and the one he felt for Jube simply was not the marrying kind.

She rolled over and jostled his arm, sending a twinge of pain to his shoulder.

He sat up and found his trousers in the dark, slipped them on, buttoned all but the top fly button, then padded into the sitting room. Fumbling for his humidor in the dark, he found a cigar and a match, then left the apartment.

When he opened the landing door, a movement in the opposite corner startled him.

"Gussie, is that you?"

Agatha straightened in her chair and drew her wrapper together at her throat.

"Yes. I . . . I couldn't sleep, it was so hot."

He came out and quietly closed the door. "I couldn't either."

She wrapped one bare foot around the other and tried to hide them beneath her robe.

"You mind if I join you?" he asked.

"No, of course not. It's your landing, too." She noted that he, too, was barefoot, and shirtless. He crossed to the top of the stairs and stood with his legs spread wide, gazing out across the prairie. His skin appeared pale against the dark night sky. Overhead, stars twinkled, but the moon was too new to add much brightness.

"Damned coyotes. Once they start in, they don't know when t' stop."

"I've rather been enjoying them. They've been keeping me company."

He looked back over his shoulder. She sat on a hard kitchen chair, angled in the corner, holding her wrapper at the throat, the picture of threatened propriety. He compared her to Jube, sprawled naked in the bed he'd left. The comparison was almost laughable, yet he didn't feel like laughing. He felt troubled.

"You look so different with your hair down." More approachable. He wondered what she'd do if he walked over and touched it. Her hair had always attracted him, rich and lustrous as it was. She dropped her chin and reached up self-consciously, as if to hide the unrestrained mass.

"I . . . I should have braided it. I usually—" She bit off the words, realizing she'd been about to reveal a very personal bedtime habit, and that it was hardly a proper subject for conversation between a barefoot man and woman at three o'clock in the morning. "When I stayed with Jubilee she told me hair needs to relax sometimes, so I . . . well . . ."

"There's no need t' get nervous, Agatha. It was only an observation." To Agatha's relief he dropped the subject and asked, "Do you mind if I smoke?"

"No, not at all."

He ambled to the opposite side of the landing and sat on the railing with his back against the wall, one knee drawn up, the other foot on the floor. He struck the match on the narrow board beneath him, and when he cupped it, his face flared orange for a moment. He shook out the match, tossed it to the ground below, then took a deep drag.

"Isn't it funny?" she commented. "I used to despise the smell of cigar smoke, but I've grown to enjoy it."

He chuckled, leaned his head back. "Yes, that's how it is with most wicked things—they rather grow on you." As he puffed on the cheroot the scent drifted to her—acrid but pleasingly masculine. The coyotes yapped in the distance and she forgot to be self-conscious with him.

"Willy tells me you taught him to play five-card stud."

Scott laughed and expelled another cloud of smoke. "Why, that little tattletale."

"Scott, really . . ." Her tone became indulgently scolding. "Five-card stud. To a five-year-old?"

"Hey, the sprout is smart for a five-year-old."

"And I'm sure he grows smarter by the day, taking up with you."

"He'll do all right, as long as he's got you t' keep him on the straight and narrow after I fill his impressionable young mind with all my nasty habits."

She had never met a man who could make her forgive his transgressions quite as readily as Scott Gandy could. She was smiling as she asked, "And how can you explain the fact that he's been breaking into choruses of 'Little Brown Jug' lately?"

"Oh, no you don't." He pointed at her with the coal of his cigar. "You're not gonna pin that one on me. Ask Jube and Marcus about that."

"I will," she promised, a touch of humor in her voice.

"And while you're at it, ask the sprout *why* I taught him five-card stud."

"Why don't you save me some time and tell me yourself?"

She watched the coal of his cigar brighten while he considered the matter silently. Then at length he confessed, "We had a single game for high stakes and he lost."

"And?"

He grinned. "And he had t' accompany me t' the Cowboys' Rest for a bath."

Now it was Agatha's turn to laugh. The sound was soft and feminine, and he realized how few times he'd heard it. Southern women laughed like that—his mother had laughed like that, with a breathy sigh at the end, and so had Delia.

"You're resourceful, Scott Gandy, I'll say that for you."

He removed the cigar from his mouth, draped an elbow over a knee, and drawled, "Why, thank you, Miz Downin'."

"And entertaining enough that I find myself grateful Alvis Collinson didn't manage to do you in."

He studied the coal of his cigar in the dark, then rolled his head toward her. "I remember something about that night. I remember openin' my eyes and you were kneelin' beside me, touchin' my face." The only movement on the balcony was the rising coil of smoke. Even the coyotes had stilled, and in the silence her eyes met his and held. "You called me 'dear.' "

Her heart tripped in a light, quick cadence. She felt her cheeks grow warm but was unable to turn away from his scrutiny. Did he know what happened inside her each time she looked at him? Did he know what a picture he made—lounging on that railing, his head angled her way, his arm draped lazily over the knee, his bare feet and chest compelling in the starlight, the line of his black trousers accenting his masculine pose? If he knew, he'd probably run as fast as he could, back inside to Jubilee.

"I was very frightened, Scott."

"It just struck me as curious—you bein' a temperance worker and me bein' a saloon owner."

"Don't oversimplify. You're much more than a saloon owner to me, and I believe I'm much more than a temperance worker to you. By some odd twist of fate I think we've become friends."

"I do, too," he replied quietly. "So how can you go off to the governor's tea and talk about prohibition?"

She felt as if he'd tossed cold water in her face. She'd known the time would come when they'd have to talk about it further, but she hadn't been prepared for it tonight.

"Scott, you don't really think I want to shut down the Gilded Cage, do you? It would mean I'd lose you and Jubilee and Pearl and Ruby and Marcus and . . . well, all of you. And you've *all* become my friends—I thought you understood that. It's an unfortunate circumstance that if prohibition closes down the others, it'll close you down, too. Please understand."

He jumped off the rail and started pacing agitatedly. "I don't! Dammit! I don't." Close to her chair he stopped, gesturing with the cigar. "Why you? I mean, why not let those other women fight for the cause?" He waved an arm at the rest of the world. "At least they have reason—some of 'em. Their lives have been affected by liquor."

She wasn't sure she could make herself tell it; after all, she'd held it inside since she was nine years old. Not even when Annie MacIntosh had wailed out her pitiful story had Agatha been able to force herself to follow suit. The hurt was too immense. She had carried it too long, guarded it too closely to share it easily.

Within her nightgown and wrapper her skin suddenly felt clammy. Her heart thrust so hard within her breast that she heard it in her ears.

"Sit down, Scott. It's very difficult for me to talk to you when you're stomping back and forth as if you wish there were still public dunking stools for recalcitrant women."

He drew up short, glared at her for a moment, then plunked himself down on the top step, presenting his back.

"There are times, Scott Gandy, when you act the age of Willy." He snorted but said nothing. "May I come over there and sit, or will you bite my head off?"

"Come!" he snapped belligerently.

"Are you sure?"

He glared over his shoulder. "I said come," he repeated with strained patience. "What else do you want—an engraved invitation like the governor sends?"

She rose from her chair, tightened her belt, and fidgeted with her neckline. He sat hunkered on the step, his pique so evident she was reluctant to approach him. Her bare feet shuffled across the raw boards of the landing and she perched on the top step, as far away from him as she could get. Looking askance, she noted his resistant pose: facing the opposite direction, knees wide, shoulders curled, the cheroot clamped in his teeth.

She drew a shaky breath, then began.

"When I was a child we lived in Colorado. Never in one house for long because my father had gold fever. He'd stake a claim and work it until it proved worthless. Then we'd pull up roots and move to the next town, the next house, the next worthless claim. He was always so sure that he'd strike it rich. When a claim was new, he was happy—and sober. But as it continued showing no color, he'd begin drinking. Lightly at first, then more heavily as his disappointment grew. When he was sober, he wasn't really a bad man, only filled with self-delusions. But when he was drunk . . ." She shivered and hugged herself.

Gandy's shoulders uncurled and he half turned, captivated by her mellifluous voice and her straightforward gaze.

"He was one of four boys whose father had died, leaving them equal shares in a farm in Missouri. My father chose to sell out his shares to his brothers and make his way west instead of spending his entire life being a 'redneck dirt grubber'—as he put it." She laughed softly, sadly. "He only gave up one kind of grubbing for another. But he thought it preferable grubbing for gold instead of for rutabagas. That, he said, was woman's work, and he'd leave it to my mother.

"She was a hard worker, my mother. Wherever we moved she tried to make it a home, and at first the houses weren't so bad—we still had some of the money from the division of the farm to live on. But when it was gone the houses got older . . . colder . . . just as he did. And he got meaner."

Scott was studying her directly as she absently overlapped the panels of her wrapper upon her knees and smoothed them repeatedly. She lifted her face and stared at the invisible horizon.

"He began taking out his failures on my mother." She linked her hands and fitted them tightly around her knees. "When I was nine we moved to Sedalia to a pitiful little house with a drafty bedroom upstairs for them, and none for me. I slept in the kitchen on a cot." A winsome smile tipped up her lips. "At the foot of my bed, Mother had a rocking chair, right in front of a window, with an ivy hanging above it . . ." Her words trailed off and she turned her head away from him. She touched a wooden bar on the railing, picked at it absently with her fingernail. "I used to love that ivy."

He sensed there was more she wanted to say about her mother, but at present she kept the focus of her story on her father.

"He came home one night, drunk, angry, disappointed. It seemed he'd had the choice between two towns when we'd moved the previous time, and—typical of my father—he'd picked the wrong one. His friend Dennis, who'd staked a claim near Oro City, had struck gold, while my father's mine proved worthless again.

"He was so drunk that night. Cursing, throwing things. Mother was angry, too, accusing him of drinking up what little money we had when the house wasn't fit for mice and bats, and hadn't even a bedroom for me. She threatened to leave him, as she always did, only this time she headed upstairs to begin packing. I remember lying on my cot, listening to them fighting up there. The thumps on the floor, his cursing. I heard a muffled scream and ran upstairs with the childish wish to protect Mother. I know it was silly of me, but when you're that age you don't reason, you only react. They were at the top of the stairs, fighting. I don't remember much about those exact moments, except that I grabbed my father's arm, thinking to stop him from striking her, and when he shook me off I went backward down the stairs."

Gandy's heart began pounding as if he himself were tumbling down with her. *Oh, God, not that way,* he thought. Not by the hand of her own father. His cheroot suddenly tasted foul and he cast it aside. He wanted to tell her to hush, to halt the memories that must be excruciating for her to dredge up. But she went on in the same calm voice.

"Something . . ."—she clutched her knees and swallowed—". . . something happened to my hip. After that I had a . . ."

She could bring herself to say everything but the most painful word of all. Staring at her profile, so outwardly composed, Scott felt afresh the self-recrimination of the day he'd pushed her down in the mud. And contempt for the man who'd crippled her. And a choking sense of inadequacy because he could do nothing to reverse it. But he could say the word for her.

"Your limp?" he asked in a quiet, understanding tone.

She nodded, unable to look him in the eye. "My limp." She gazed off into the distance. "But the irony of it is that I did what I set out to do. I stopped their fighting—forever. She left him after that and we ended up here, where she opened the millinery shop. I never saw him again, but news came back to us when he died. I was in my late teens then. I remember the day Mother told me he was dead—he'd fallen off a mule and rolled down a mountainside. They hadn't found his body till some weeks later."

Scott's mind recaptured flashes of his own youth juxtaposed against hers. Secure, loved, knowing all the time he was both. He'd spent little time considering what it was like to grow up in any other kind of environment, until he moved to Proffitt and came up against Willy. And now Agatha.

"I told my mother I didn't care at all that he was dead." Her voice became lighthearted, but she rocked unconsciously, giving away the deeper emotions she concealed. "Not at all." He saw her struggling with tears for the first time since she had begun to relate her story. "Just like Willy the night his father died. He shouted it to me again and again, and ended up punching the mattress and sobbing in my arms."

"Oh, Gussie . . . Gussie . . . come here." He slid across the step and took her into his arms, stopping her pitiful rocking. She let herself be taken against him while she began to cry. But her weeping was silent and motionless. She acquiesced to his embrace but took no part in it. Her very stillness tore at his heart like a rusty blade. "Gussie, I'm sorry," he whispered brokenly.

"I don't want you to feel sorry for me. I never wanted that."

He pulled her face into the curve of his neck and felt her tears run down his bare collarbone onto his chest. "I didn't mean it that way."

"Yes, you did. That's why I never told you before. I've never told anyone before. Not even the women in the W.C.T.U. But I couldn't let you go on getting angry at me for what I must do. Please, Scott, don't be angry with me anymore."

She was small and narrow-shouldered, and fit perfectly beneath his chin. He stroked her hair, drawing it back from her face. There had been times lately when he'd wondered what it would feel like in his fingers. He scarcely noticed now, in light of his concern for her. "I'm not really angry at you. Maybe I'm angry at myself because half o' me agrees with you. Every time I took at Willy I know you're right. And I have t' force myself t' forget that there are thousands of other Willys in the world with nobody to help them out of a situation they don't deserve."

She closed here eyes and rested against him, absorbing the comfort he offered. His bare skin had grown sleek with her tears. He was hard and warm and smelled of the cheroots he smoked. And when his hand cradled her head and tucked her firmly against him, she went gratefully, her cheek pressed upon his chest with its coarse mat of hair.

He represented security, strength, and protection, and she'd had too little of all three in her life. She slipped her arms around his warm sides, spread her hands upon his naked back, and held fast.

And there in his arms, she began healing.

His fingers moved idly in her hair. His sure, steady heartbeat thrummed against her temple. The night shielded them. She wanted to stay that way forever.

But in time propriety interfered. She became aware that he was bare-chested and she wore only her nightclothes. She backed away to look up at him.

"Then you understand why I must go to Topeka?"

"Yes."

Meeting his direct gaze after crying in his arms became disconcerting. She groped for her lost sense of humor and told him, "I hate it when we fight."

She was rewarded with a small, sympathetic grin. "So do I."

She chuckled self-consciously and swiped her lower eyelids with the backs of her hands. "And I've never in my life dribbled all over a man's chest. I certainly don't intend to make a habit of it."

"Was I complainin'?"

"No, but it's not decent. You in practically nothing, and me in my night things. I've left you in a mess." She caught the edge of one sleeve, stretched it taut, and began drying his chest with it.

He caught her wrist. "Gussie, stop fussin' and listen."

His eyes were only dark shadows as she looked up into them. Her pulse suddenly drummed in her throat. She sensed that he'd become as discomposed as she by their brief intimacy, and the realization spurred her sexual awareness of him. He caught both her hands and held them loosely, dropping his gaze, then lifting it in a prolonged study of her shadowed features.

"Thank you for tellin' me. It means a lot t' me t' know I was the first one you trusted." Her chin dropped. She'd told him all that without blushing. Now, when there was nothing to be ashamed of, she felt herself get hot all over. He rubbed her knuckles with both thumbs. "And what I said before is true. When I say I'm sorry, I don't mean I go around feelin' sorry for you because you limp. You don't feel sorry for yourself, so others don't either. That's one of the things I admire about you. Long ago I stopped thinkin' of you as anything except Agatha, my spunky neighbor who's too much of a thorn in my side to be considered a cripple."

She couldn't help smiling sheepishly, still looking down at their joined hands.

"I don't mean to be a thorn in anybody's side, least of all yours." She withdrew her hands carefully before asking, "So, what do you intend to do with me?"

He leaned against the far rail and studied her from beneath lowered brows for some time before asking, "What are the chances this law'll pass?"

She was relieved that once again, though still members of opposing factions, they could discuss the issue without rancor.

"The latest issue of *The Temperance Banner* gives it about a forty percent chance," she answered honestly. "But that margin is narrowing all the time." He drew in a deep breath and ran a hand through his hair, then sat gazing distractedly at a point somewhere beyond the rooftop of the necessary. "What would you do if it passed?"

"Do?" He rested both elbows on his knees and swung his face toward her. "I'd pack up and leave Kansas. What else *could* I do?"

The thought sent a bolt of dread through her. "Where would you go?"

"I don't know."

A coyote howled. The lonely sound seemed a proper accompaniment to their morose speculations.

"What about Waverley?"

"Waverley?" He bristled. "What do you know about Waverley?"

"Please, Scott, don't get belligerent again. I'm your friend. Can't you talk to me about it?"

She saw him struggle with some inner turmoil before finally admitting, "I don't know where t' begin."

"Let me help you," she suggested softly. "You lived there before the war with a wife and a daughter."

He scowled sharply at Agatha and she sensed his surprise that she knew this much. He remained silent for so long that she thought he would refuse to talk about it. After some time he shifted on the hard step, and pressed his thumb knuckles against his chin. She waited, listening to the coyotes, supposing that whatever he held inside was as difficult for him to reveal as her own story had been. At last he let out a deep sigh, dropped his hands between his knees, and said, "My wife's name was Delia. She was . . ." He paused, stared at the night sky, then finished emotionally, "all I ever wanted."

Agatha simply waited. In time he went on.

"Her daddy was a cotton buyer who came to our plantation periodically and often brought Delia and her mama along. So I'd known her nearly all my life. They sometimes stayed the night, and we had the run o' the place, Delia and I. And how we ran. We explored the river, and the gin, and the hen coops, played with the black children and picked wild scuppernongs, and dipped our hands in the melted wax in the dairy on cheese day and stole molasses cakes from the kitchen out back and ran wild as deer." His recollections had brought a soft grin to his face. "Her daddy stopped all that, though, 'long about the time she started tuckin' up her pigtails and my voice started changin'. Seemed like from that time on I knew I wanted t' marry Delia. Our mamas and daddies knew, too, and favored the idea.

"We were married in Waverley—she'd always loved it—in what my mama called the 'weddin' alcove.' Mama insisted on havin' it put in when the parlor was built—it was an arched alcove outlined with decorative plaster leaves where Mama declared all her children would be baptized and married before she herself was laid out there in her casket."

He stopped and Agatha inquired, "How many of her children *were* baptized there?"

"Three of us. All boys. But two of us never made it t' the alcove in our caskets."

"You had two brothers?"

"Rafael and Nash. They both died in the same battle durin' the war. They're buried near Vicksburg instead of at Waverley beside the others." He mulled about it for a moment, then seemed to pull himself to a happier train of thought.

"So after we were married Delia and I lived at Waverley. Ah, it was somethin' then. I wish you could've seen it." He leaned back and gazed at the stars.

"I've seen the painting in your sitting room. It's beautiful."

"It was more than beautiful. It was . . ."—he paused, searching for words—" . . . majestic." He sat forward eagerly. "In its prime, Waverley supported twelve hundred people and had every facility t' make it self-sufficient. We had an ice house, a cotton gin, a tannery, a sawmill, a gristmill, a brick kiln, orchards, vineyards, stables, gardens, kennels, warehouses, a boathouse, and even a ferry."

"All that?" Agatha was awed.

"All that. And the house . . . everybody called it *the mansion* . . ." Again she saw a ghost of a smile on his lips. "The paintin' doesn't do it justice. It always reminded me of a proud eagle spreadin' its wings over its young ones with its head straight up and watchful."

"Tell me," she encouraged. "Tell me everything."

"Well, you saw the picture."

"Not very closely."

"Next time you're in my apartment, take a closer look. Waverley's unique. There's not another house like it in all the South. The eagle's wings, those are the actual wings o' the house, the livin' quarters stretchin' out on either side o' the center rotunda—or, as Mama liked t' call it, the cupola. And the eagle's head, that's the rotunda itself—a massive entry shaped like an octagon with twin curved stairwells that climb sixty-five feet to an observatory with windows on all eight sides. I can still see my daddy strollin' the catwalk around those windows, every mornin', surveyin' his holdin's. You know, Gussie, the cotton fields stretched as far as the eye could see in all directions. We had three thousand acres in cotton, food, and grain then. Fifteen acres of formal gardens, too."

In her imagination she could see Waverley, just as he described, proud and pillared and reigning above the lush green countryside.

"It was always cool in the house," Scott continued. "Every mornin' durin' the hot weather, Leatrice—she was the bossy old despot who ran the place—would climb those stairs and open all those windows, and the draft like t' tug the hair out o' your skull. And if that wasn't cool enough, off the end o' the drive there was a swimmin' pool made of brick and marble, with a roof t' keep the sun off the ladies."

"The one you told Willy about the first night we met him."

"The only one in all of northern Miz'sippi. Delia loved it. She and I used t' go down there and cool off at night sometimes when—" He suddenly halted and cleared his throat, then sat up straighter.

"I've never been swimming. What's it like?"

"Never been swimmin'!"

She shook her head. "Or dancing or riding a horse."

"Would you like to?"

She looked away, embarrassed. But she couldn't lie. "Most of all I'd like to dance. Just once." She faced him again, her voice brighter, and enthusiastic. "But swimming sounds grand, too."

"I'll have t' take you sometime. You'll love it. It's the freest feelin' in the world."

"I'd like that," she said softly. Then more loudly, she added, "But I interrupted you—you were telling me about Waverley."

"Waverley—oh, yes." He went on eagerly. "In the winter, when the fireplaces were lit, there was no place warmer.

And we had gaslights, too, fueled by our own gasworks and piped into the house."

"Your own gasworks?"

"It burned pine lighter—that's what made the resin gas."

She'd never heard of such a thing and had difficulty imagining the luxury of gaslights that would flare at the touch of a finger.

"Oh, Scott, it sounds wonderful."

"There's a chandelier in the middle o' the entry hall that hangs all the way from the cupola roof above." He looked up at the stars as if they supported the chandelier. "And over seven hundred walnut spindles outlinin' the stairway and cantilevered balconies. And Venetian glass sidelights around the front door, and plaster moldings on the ceilings, and brass cornices on all the windows and mirrors in the ballroom."

"It has a ballroom?"

"The main floor o' the rotunda. It's made o' the heart o' virgin pine, and the twin stairs come sweepin' down on either side. Delia and I had our weddin' ball there, and I remember many others when I was growin' up."

"Tell me about Delia."

He pondered for several seconds, then began: "Delia was like Jube. Always happy, never askin' for more than what she had. I never quite understood what it was about me that made her so happy, but I was grateful that both of us felt the same way about each other. She had blond hair and hazel eyes and this teasin' lilt of a laugh that could lift a man's spirits faster than a chameleon slitherin' up a post. And when Justine was born, she looked exactly like Delia. Except she had my black hair." He swallowed and cleared his throat. "Justine was baptized in the weddin' alcove, just like my mama planned. That was right about the time Lincoln was sworn into office. I saw her and Delia one time after I joined the Columbus regiment and marched north. I made it back for my daddy's funeral in '64. But by the time I made it back for good, they were all gone."

Now it was Agatha's turn to console. She laid her hand on his arm. "Ruby told me about them shortly after she came here. You don't know how they died?"

"No. Robbers, probably. The South was so poor then, people were desperate. Soldiers returned to find poverty where there'd been wealth before. Who knows? It could've been one of our own soldiers. They said it appeared as if Delia's wagon had been waylaid on the road." He chuckled bitterly. "Whoever it was didn't get much, 'cause Delia was no richer than anybody else by that time." He swallowed hard. "But why they had t' kill the baby, too . . . What kinda person would do a thing like that?"

Agatha could only rub his arm while his grief brought bitter words he'd been holding in so long.

"Do you know what it's like to go back and find everything changed? The people you loved, gone. The house empty, but everything inside lookin' just like it did before, as if it were waitin' for ghosts t' come and inhabit it again. Everything else was there, too—the gin, the tannery, the gasworks, everything. But the slaves had scattered, some o' them killed in the war, maybe on the same battlefield like my brothers. Others were gone to who knows where. A handful stayed, hoeing collard greens and livin' in the old quarters."

She searched for consoling words, but the picture he'd drawn was too bleak to be erased by mere words, so she remained silent and merely stroked his arm.

"I stayed there three nights, but that's all I could take. You know what, Gussie?" He shook his head slowly. "I couldn't sleep in the bedroom Delia and I shared. I just couldn't make myself do it. So I slept in Justine's room, and I thought I heard her voice callin' for help durin' the night. Now how can that be when she's been dead all these years?"

Her heart ached for him and she wished once again for the right words to help him. "Perhaps it was your own voice you heard, Scott."

He shook his head as if to rid it of the memory. He drove his fingers through his hair and clasped his skull. "I couldn't stand it there. I had t' get out."

"And you haven't been back since?"

Again he shook his head.

"Do you think you should go?"

He stared straight ahead and after a long silence answered, "I don't know."

"Your wounds were fresh then. It might be easier now."

"I don't think it'll ever be easier."

"Perhaps not. But going back might lay your ghosts to rest. And Waverley is your heritage."

He gave a single harsh laugh. "Some heritage. With vines growin' up over the front porch and the fields lyin' empty. I'd rather not see it that way."

"Isn't anybody there you used to know?"

"Ruby says old Leatrice is still there."

"But the house—you said it's just as you left it. Vines can be trimmed away and fields can be replanted. Isn't there some way you could make it thrive again?"

"It'd take twelve hundred people t' make Waverley what it was."

Twelve hundred, she thought glumly. Yes, she saw his point.

They sat silent for a long time, going over all they'd shared tonight. The coyotes had given up their night chorus as dawn drew near. In the cattle pens east of town the first restless shifting and lowing could be heard. The big dipper began dimming overhead.

"Isn't it funny?" Agatha mused. "When I first saw you, I looked at you and thought: There's a man with no troubles, no conscience, no morals. You came to Proffitt wearing tailored clothes, with enough money to buy this building and open up a business that was destined to make you a rich man quickly, and I looked at your perfect, healthy body and your handsome face and thought how you had the world by the tail. And I hated you for it."

Her summary brought him back from the past. He turned to study her as she looked up at the brightening sky, her wrists crossed on her good knee, while the other leg stretched along the steps in front of her.

He'd never before realized that she saw him as handsome or perfect in any way. To hear her say so gave his heart a tiny surge of weightlessness.

"And now?" he asked.

She shrugged, held the pose, and turned her chin onto her shoulder. It was a motion he recalled Delia making countless times, only when Agatha did it, it was thoughtful instead of coy.

"Now," she said, meeting his gaze squarely, "I see I was wrong."

Abruptly, she dropped the pose, breaking the momentary sense of intimacy. "You should think about going back, Scott. Whether or not the prohibition amendment is ratified you owe it to yourself. Waverley is your home. Nobody loves it as you do, and it seems to me it's waiting there for you. So many of the mansions like Waverley were burned in the war. It's a real treasure now. I think it deserves its rightful master back again."

She sighed and braced herself as if to rise. "Well!" She stretched, pressing her palms against the floor of the landing. "I've been sitting on this step until I'm not sure my one good hip will work anymore. I think it's time we go in and try to get some sleep before the sun comes up and catches us perched here like a pair of cats waiting for the morning cream."

She faltered, trying to rise, and he grasped her elbow to help her. Her limp was more pronounced as she crossed the landing toward her door. She stepped inside, then turned back.

"Scott?"

"Hmm?"

"Thank you, too, for telling me all that. I know it wasn't easy for you."

"It wasn't easy for you either, was it?"

"No."

He crossed his arms and tucked his hands against his ribs, then came toward her slowly, stopping only a foot away. Even in the shadows, she sensed his distraction.

"What do you suppose that means, Gussie?"

She was struck by the realization that more and more often lately he said things like that—leading questions intimating a change in his feelings toward her. But she caught, too, the hint of confusion each time those feelings surfaced, and she realized the hopelessness of their situation. They were nothing whatever alike. If, even for a fleeting hour, he thought he felt something more than friendship toward her, what could ever come of it? He ran a saloon and she wore a white temperance banner on her sleeve. He taught a little boy to play five-card stud on Saturday, while she took the same boy to church on Sunday. He slept with a woman to whom he wasn't even married, while her morals could not abide such an arrangement. He was as physically flawless a man as she had ever met, while her own body left much to be desired. And he was handsome enough to land any woman to whom he gave a second look, while she had never landed even a first one.

But most important, if the prohibition amendment was adopted by the people, he'd soon be leaving Kansas for good.

What end would it serve if she acceded to the hesitant invitation in his words? She was a woman with a broken body; she didn't need a broken heart, too.

"Good night, Scott," she said quietly, withdrawing into the shadows.

"Gussie, wait."

"Go to bed. Jube is probably wondering what happened to you."

When she had quietly closed the door, he stood staring at it, with his palms still tucked beneath his arms. What the hell was he trying to prove? She was right—Jube was sleeping in his bed right now, while he stood at Agatha's door thinking about kissing her.

He swung around angrily.

She's not the kind to take a kiss lightly, Gandy, so make damned sure before you do it that you mean it.

CHAPTER
14

If people thought it strange that one of the local saloon owners went to the railway station to see the local milliner off to a temperance tea at the governor's mansion, nobody said a word. After all, the newly orphaned Collinson boy was with them, and everyone knew they had taken him under their wing.

Willy was wearing his proudest possession: a pair of brand-new indigo-blue Levi Strauss britches with orange stitching and copper rivets—"just like the cowboys wear!"—as Willy had pointed out proudly when he came running into the store to model them for Agatha. "An', no suspenders, neither!"

"No suspenders!" She had turned him in a circle and duly admired him.

"Nope! Cuz they're choke-barreled."

Agatha and Violet had both laughed. "They're what?"

"Choke-barreled. That's what Scotty says the cowboys call 'em. Skinny-legged . . . see?"

He stood now at the station, seeing Agatha off in his choke-barreled blue denim pants, looking healthy and robust. His brown boots already had hundreds of scuffs, but his nails were clean, he had gained weight, and he no longer scratched.

Agatha, too, looked stunning. She had made herself a brand-new dress for the occasion, a gorgeous creation of tangerine faille. The jacket sported dolman sleeves, with a collar and trimmings of brown velvet. This summer's

Godey's dictated that no dress should be made of only one material, so she'd chosen a deeper melon-colored taffeta for the underskirt, and a stiffer silk faille for the sheath-fronted overskirt: handkerchief-styled—pointed in the front, with cascading rear draperies. At her throat billowed an ivory lace jabot of silk stockinet. Her outfit was completed by a tilted gable bonnet of melon and russet, forming a pointed arch over her face.

Watching her bid good-bye to Willy, Scott Gandy admired not only her dress, but the way its colors complemented the red highlights of her hair, which was coiled into a French twist up the back of her head. He admired, too, her pale green eyes with their mink-dark lashes, her apricot skin, and her fine-turned jawline, which he had liked from the moment he saw it. And her attractive mouth, smiling gamely, though he suspected she wasn't so anxious to go, now that the last minute had come.

"How long'll you be gone, Gussie?" Willy held both her hands and looked up angelically. Scott had combed the boy's hair with extra care that morning—and, for the first time, used a tad of Macassar oil. It gleamed brightly in the sun.

"Just overnight. Now you do as I said and help Violet sweep up before closing."

"I will."

Gandy watched her gloved hands adjust Willy's shirt collar, then brush something off his cheek. "And teeth, nails, *and* ears tonight at bedtime—promise?"

Willy's face skewed in disgust and he scuffled his feet. "Aw . . . I promise."

"I'll ask Scott when I get back." She touched the tip of Willy's nose to soften the warning. "Now you be a good boy and I'll see you tomorrow night."

" 'Bye, Gussie." He came at her with open arms.

"Good-bye, sweetheart." She bent forward in the constricting skirts and Willy kissed her flush on the mouth. She held him to her breast as best she could, while he balanced on tiptoes, stretched full-length. For a moment her eyelashes fanned her cheeks and Gandy saw clearly how she'd grown to love the boy. He thought of where she was going, and for what reason, and admired her for the kind of commitment it took to go. If the law passed, one of them would eventually have to bid Willy a final good-bye. She realized that as well as he.

Agatha straightened. Willy backed up and slipped his hand into Scott's. She looked up into the man's dark eyes. They appeared momentarily troubled and she wondered what had brought on the disturbed look.

"Good-bye, Scott."

He summoned a quarter grin, as if consciously shaking off whatever had been bothering him. "Take care of yourself. And I'll take care of Willy." He looked down and waggled Willy's hand. "We're plannin' t' go over to Emma's for supper tonight, aren't we, sprout?"

"Yeah . . . chicken and dumplin's."

Agatha watched the two of them smile at each other.

"Well, I'd best be boarding."

Scott reached down to pick up her small carpetbag and hand it to her.

"Don't worry about a thing back here."

"I won't."

For a moment his thumb pressed her gloved knuckles, then slipped away. They stood locked in a moment of uncertainty, a good-bye hug hovering on both their minds. Through her memory flashed the image of him greeting Jubilee on the day of her arrival—his bold caress on her buttocks, the kiss they'd shared while half the town looked on. But now he stepped back and Agatha realized how foolish she'd been even to think it. The hugging that night on the steps was one thing—that had been sympathetic sharing. To do it in broad daylight at the depot was quite another thing, she chided herself. She turned away quickly before either of them could give in to the urge.

From the window of her coach she watched Scott and Willy. Scott was wearing a trim suit of fawn-brown and a matching flat-crowned Stetson. His brown string tie lifted in the breeze, then settled back against his white shirtfront. He said something to Willy and Willy nodded enthusiastically. Then Scott reached into his ticket pocket and withdrew a cheroot. He patted his jacket searchingly and she could tell he was teasing Willy about something. Willy began searching, too, and came up with a wooden match. Scott clamped the cheroot between his teeth and leaned over while Willy lifted one knee and struck the match against the thigh of his new stiff denim britches. Three times he tried it; three times he failed. Then Scott adjusted the match in Willy's fingers and demonstrated for him. The next time the match caught and Willy held it gingerly while Scott leaned down and lit his cheroot.

Next he'll have the boy smoking, she thought. But instead of frowning at the possibility, her lips tipped up in a melancholy smile. Watching them together—the tall, uncondescending man and the happy blond boy—she saw a growing love flourishing between them. The train began moving and they both lifted their heads, waving—the two most important people in her life. Yet she stood to lose one, and maybe both of them, soon. In less than two months the decision about prohibition would be put to the voters of Kansas.

She rested her head against the seat and let her eyes slowly close. Her eyelids stung and a lump came to her throat. She almost wished the prohibitionists would fail.

The formal garden of the gubernatorial mansion was laid out in a diamond parterre design. Meticulously pruned privet hedges outlined the graveled paths between the profusely blossoming roses. Red, salmon, white, and pink, they scented the air with their inimitable fragrance. Chrysanthemums formed cushions of yellow and bronze at the junctures of paths. Stately yews stood as erect and uniform as a green picket fence around the boundaries, while scattered horse chestnut trees provided lakes of shade at strategic points within the formal design. Upon white iron benches, bustled women sipped tea from demitasse cups while bearded dignitaries in formal attire crossed their hands behind their back and discussed the political situation in harrumphing voices, their moustaches bobbing.

It was all very pompous, very elite. Dressed in her crisp, up-to-date finery, carrying herself with regal bearing and impeccable manners, Agatha fit right in. But all the while she discussed the format adopted by her W.C.T.U. local in combating demon rum, all the while she learned new methods of reaching voters and spreading antialcohol propaganda, she felt traitorous to the two who'd waved her off at the depot.

The governor was especially decorous, cinched tightly into a winged white collar and black Oxford tie. He bowed over the hand of each lady present, huddling solicitously with Baptist ministers, conferring with well-known illuminaries of the temperance movement.

Drusilla Wilson was there, and Amanda Way, and other notable leaders whose photographs Agatha had seen in the *Banner*. Meeting and visiting with them, Agatha again felt misplaced. Their ardor for the temperance cause ran hot in their veins, while hers had cooled considerably. Recalling her excitement the day she'd received the invitation to this event, Agatha wished some of it still bubbled within her. Instead, she thought about November 2 as the day the guillotine might very well fall—not on Scott Gandy, but on her.

She hired a carriage and driver to take her back to her hotel, ate dinner in the elegant dining room, and wished she were at Cyrus and Emma Paulie's restaurant eating chicken and dumplings with Willy and Scott. She settled into her tastefully decorated room with its screen-printed wallpaper and tasseled draperies and wished she were in her own narrow apartment with the piano and banjo thumping through the floor. She lay back in a bed lined with fat goose-down ticks and wished she were sitting on a hard wooden step looking up at the stars, listening to the coyotes howl and enjoying the scent of a man's cigar.

In the morning she shopped and found a harmonica for Willy and a carved ivory brooch for Violet. She passed a tobacconist's shop and paused.

No, Agatha, it won't do. You're a single woman and he's a single man. It simply wouldn't be proper.

Resolutely, she moved on, but a short distance beyond the shop she stopped and retraced her steps. She stood before the window, admiring cherrywood pipes, tulipwood humidors, and boxed cigars. She looked up and saw her reflection in the pane, lit by the early morning sun of the warm autumn day. She imagined Scott Gandy beside her, the two of them out for a stroll to the market, he in his flat-crowned Stetson and crisp fawn suit, she with her pert dress and gable bonnet, her hand caught in the crook of his elbow.

A horse and dray passed on the cobbles behind her. The clatter awoke her from her musing and she entered the shop.

Inside, it was dusky and aromatic, the smells heady, rich, and masculine. So different from the smell of dyes and starches and machine oil.

"Good morning, ma'am," the owner greeted her.

"Good morning."

"Something for your man today?" His handlebar moustache and rosy cheeks lifted as he smiled.

Your man. The thought was unduly provocative. Scott Gandy was not her man, nor would he ever be. But, for the moment, it was fun pretending. She knew nothing about brands, however, and realized she'd give herself away by questioning: What wife wouldn't know her husband's favorite brand?

"Yes. A pair of trimming scissors, perhaps."

"Ah, I have just the thing."

She left the store with a tiny gold blunt-nosed pair of scissors in a flat leather slipcase, wondering if when she reached home she'd have the nerve to give it to him after all.

How forward of you, Agatha. How unseemly.

But he has given me a Singer sewing machine. What is a tiny pair of scissors, compared to that?

You're rationalizing, Agatha.

Oh, go lick! I've been a prude all of my life, and what has it gotten me? For once I'm going to follow my heart.

Her heart led her home, hammering with expectation as the train pulled into the Proffitt depot late that day. Her heart told her she must not search the crowd for Gandy, must not expect him to be there. But she adjusted her hat and checked her hair and hoped her skirt wasn't too wrinkled and searched the depot for him in spite of herself.

He wasn't there. But Willy was—still in his stiff blue britches, standing on a bench of the depot veranda, exuberantly waving and jumping.

She stepped from the train and he came hurtling against her. "Gussie, guess what!"

"What?"

"I gots a cat!"

"A cat!" Her smile was radiant, though it took some effort not to search the platform in the hope that Scott might step out of the building belatedly. She told herself it was absolutely ridiculous to be disappointed at his absence.

Willy jabbered a mile a minute. "Vy-let, she said Miss Gill had a litter of 'em down at the boardin' house, and if she didn't git rid of 'em soon they was gonna have t' drown 'em, so I went over there and there was this one, he was purple and white—"

Agatha laughed. "Purple and wh—"

"And he was my fav-rite and I ast her if I could have it and she says yes, so I brung it to Scotty's and Scotty says I could keep it long as it slep' in my room nights so's it wouldn't get underfoot in the saloon, and during the day Moose can do mousin' in the storeroom."

"M . . . Moose?" Agatha chuckled.

"That's what I named him, cuz he's bigger'n all the others."

"And Moose is purple?" Agatha wondered how she'd ever made it through a day without Willy to brighten it. He scratched his head now from excitement, not even realizing what he was doing, till his hair stuck up like hard-crack taffy.

"Well, sorta—Scotty says he's gray, but he looks purple t' me, with white specks where his whiskers come out, and he slep' with me last night and I din't roll over and squash 'im or nothin'! Wait'll you see 'im, Gussie! He's the most beautiful cat you ever seen!"

"*Saw.*"

"Yeah, well, come on. Hurry up! He's at the saloon and Jack's takin' care of 'im for me, but I hafta get back and watch 'im."

She had little choice but to "hurry up." Willy picked up her carpetbag and ran.

"Willy, wait! I can carry that."

"Nuh-uh! Scotty says I'm supposed t' carry it for you."

Oh, he does, does he? she thought as she hurried after him, chuckling.

What a sight Willy made. The bag was bigger than he. He clutched the handle with both hands, his scrawny shoulders arched high as he struggled along cheerfully. Once it reared back and caught him in the knees and he stumbled, falling over it. But he didn't stop jabbering. Just popped up again and ran on while Agatha limped along trying to keep up with him, falling more in love by the second.

He led her straight through the swinging doors at the Gilded Cage. It was mid-afternoon, early enough that there were only a few customers. They were all gathered around the bar—Mooney Straub, Virgil Murray, Doc Adkins, Marcus, Jube, Jack, and Scott—laughing and talking and leaning on their elbows with entranced expressions on their faces. Between them, across the top of the bar, paraded an adorable eight-week-old kitten. It stepped in a puddle, shook its paw, then crossed to Mooney's beer mug, nosed the foam, shook its head, and sneezed.

"Gussie's back! I brung her t' see Moose!"

Every head turned toward the door.

"Moose is up here, entertaining us," Jube told him.

Willy dropped the carpetbag and snatched Agatha's hand. "C'mon, Gussie!"

Her eyes locked on Scott's as Willy tugged her across the floor. He stood behind the bar with Jack, dressed in a black suit and amber waistcoat, looking excessively handsome, as usual. Behind him Dierdre displayed herself in her Garden of Delights, but Agatha scarcely noticed. She saw only Scott. It seemed as if she'd been away from him for a week. The fleeting expression on his face told her he, too, was glad she was back.

Then Marcus caught Willy beneath the arms and sat him on the edge of the bar.

"See him, Gussie?" Willy's eyes gleamed with pride. "Ain't he cute?"

She turned her attention to the gray-and-white fuzzball. "He's adorable."

Jube shifted over to make room for Agatha, and she found herself, for the first time in her life, elbowing up to a bar. They all watched Moose sniff the beer in Doc's mug and take a delicate lap. Everyone laughed, but Doc pulled the mug back. "Oh no, you don't. Enough of that stuff'll kill a little thing like you."

Marcus extracted a coin from his pocket and spun it on the bar. Immediately, Moose poised himself, his eyes intent on the spinning gold piece. It lost momentum and rolled across the kitten's toes. He skittered backward, arched his back, and hissed comically. Everyone laughed. Then Willy took several turns spinning the coin and finally the kitten advanced cautiously and batted it over with its paw. Marcus rested a hand on Jube's shoulder and watched from behind her. Willy got right up on the bar and sat cross-legged. Jack drew himself a beer and took idle sips while the cat entertained them all.

Agatha looked up and found Scott watching her. All the others' attention remained focused on the cat. The coin whirred as it spun. They all laughed again, but neither Scott nor Agatha heard. Nor did they smile. His gaze was steady, his eyes as dark as the level brim of his hat.

Her entire body seemed to pulse.

God help me, I love him.

As if he'd read her mind, his gaze dropped to her mouth. She grew warm with physical awareness such as she'd never experienced. When his eyes reclaimed hers, she felt a blush forming and turned to Willy, tapping him on the knee.

"I have to go relieve Violet. Come over later. I have something for you."

He forgot the cat and snapped a bright-eyed look at her. "For me?"

"Yes, but it's packed in my carpetbag. Come over later after I've unpacked."

As she withdrew from the bar, he called, "How long will it take you?"

She smiled indulgently. "Give me a half hour."

"But I can't tell time!"

Scott chuckled and dropped a hand on the boy's shoulder. "I'll tell you when a half hour is up, sprout."

As Agatha picked up her carpetbag and left, she realized she and Scott had not spoken a word to each other. Not verbally, anyway. But something had passed between them that seemed more powerful than audible phrases. He had missed her—she was sure of it. He had feelings for her— his eyes seemed to say so. Yet how could that be? It seemed too incredible to believe. But if it were true, might that not be the very reason he had refrained from meeting her at the depot? If he was as confused about those feelings as she, it would be natural for Scott to exercise extreme caution in exploring them.

Violet was thrilled with her ivory brooch and immediately fastened it at her throat. As Agatha had known he would, Willy came long before thirty minutes were up. He gave one blow on his harmonica and Moose arched. Violet, who claimed to be Moose's "godmother," took him in hand and stroked him while Willy tooted some more.

"I thought Marcus could teach you how to play it properly. He's very musical. I'm sure he can play more than just the banjo."

"Gee, thanks, Gussie!" It took very little to light Willy's eyes with wonder and bring on a hug and kiss.

"I gotta go show Marcus!" He grabbed Moose and headed for the door.

Agatha made a snap decision. "Wait!"

Impatiently, he turned back. Violet looked on, but didn't that make it seem less . . . less personal? And somehow, after the graphic looks Agatha had exchanged with Gandy, she'd lost her nerve to give him the gift herself.

"I've bought something for Scott, too. Would you take it to him?"

"Sure. What is it?"

"Nothing much. Just a pair of cigar snips."

She handed the packet to Willy and he hit for the door. "I won't tell 'im what's inside till he opens 'em."

She smiled and watched him disappear, the cat climbing on his shoulder. If she'd expected Violet to take her to task for giving Scott a gift, she was wrong. Violet was too smitten with the man to claim good reason where he was concerned.

Agatha thought back to the time when Violet's titters over Scott Gandy used to irritate her. How featherbrained she'd thought her. Now she herself felt quite the same each time she was in the same room with him. She imagined that if people knew, they'd think she, too, was featherbrained. And probably she was. Probably she only imagined those pulse-raising looks of probing intensity. And even if they were real, how could she possibly guess what thoughts moved inside his head?

Her introspection was interrupted when Joseph Zeller entered the shop through the front door.

"Miss Downing, Miss Parsons, how're you?"

They exchanged civilities and eventually Zeller got around to the reason for his visit.

"Miss Downing, I understand you've been to Topeka to meet the governor."

Oh, no, Agatha thought. But while she struggled for an insipid answer, Violet bubbled proudly. "She most certainly was. She received an engraved invitation to tea in the governor's rose garden, didn't you, Agatha?"

Impressed, Zeller smiled. "It's not every day a citizen of Proffitt rubs elbows with the governor, now, is it?"

He stayed for nearly thirty minutes, asking her question after question, and there was little Agatha could do except answer. But the feeling of betrayal intensified with each response she gave. He extracted from her every innovative move under way to enhance the public's awareness of the dangers of alcohol.

The article ran, front page, in the *Gazette,* and it brought about a flurry of propaganda from unexpected sources, all strongly favoring constitutional reform.

The *Gazette* itself ran an editorial recapping how temperance was emerging as the first issue to unite women all over the country. From the pulpit of Christ Presbyterian, Reverend Clarksdale encouraged his fold to vote for prohibition, reasoning that the dangers of cholera, which had first prompted people to mix ale with their water—thus

beginning the alcoholic craze—no longer existed; thus, the
need for the "purifying agent" was past. Teachers began
lecturing in their classrooms on the danger of drinking
intoxicants, and children, in turn, repeated the warnings
at home, many of them badgering their fathers not only
to stop drinking liquor, but to vote in November for ratification of the constitutional amendment banning it. The
superintendent of schools announced an essay contest on the
same subject, the winner in each school to receive a bronze
medal and have his name engraved in a commemorative
plaque to be sent to Lemonade Lucy herself. The Proffitt
Literary Society announced a series of open debates at
their weekly meetings, inviting members of both factions
to participate.

Amid all this furor, Agatha and Scott avoided each other. Since her return from Topeka, she'd seen him only in
passing, or through the hole in the wall late at night. It was
from this vantage point that she first saw him use the gold
cigar snips, though he sent no word of thanks, nor even
acknowledged that he'd received them.

Agatha was chagrined. How humiliating to have given
a man a gift for the first time in her life and not receive
so much as a thank-you for it. Willy became their only
link. As the boy bounced back and forth between them,
he brought his usual enthusiastic reports on the every-
day occurrences in the two halves of the Gandy building.

"Scotty says . . ."

"Gussie says . . ."

"Me and Scotty went . . ."

"On the way to church yesterday, Gussie an' me . . ."

"I lost Moose, so Marcus an' Scotty had t' move the
piano . . ."

"Gussie an' Violet got this order for . . ."

"Pearl says if the probe-isshun law passes, she's goin'
back t' . . ."

"Violet says Gussie's sulled up . . ."

"Scotty an' Jube had a fight . . ."

"Gussie's makin' me some warmer shirts for . . ."

"Scotty an' Jube made up again . . ."

* * *

It was October. Less than a month to go before Election Day. The weather had cooled. The flies rarely bothered anyone at night, the cattle drives had dwindled to a near halt, the saloon closed earlier, but still Agatha slept poorly. She didn't have nightmares, exactly. But it seemed as if the Proffitt Literary Society debates were happening inside her head while she slept.

In her dreams she listened to one in which Mustard Smith argued vociferously with Evelyn Sowers, and when he realized he was losing, he gave way to hard agitated breathing, staring at Evelyn like an enraged bull getting ready to charge. The air seemed to hiss between his teeth: in . . . out . . . in . . . out . . .

Agatha came awake in a single second.

The breathing was real. Coming from right beside her bed. Heavy, hissing, asthmatic. Fear shot through her. Her palms turned to sweat. Her muscles tightened. She lay corpse-still, staring, wondering who it was behind her shoulder. *Oh, God, what should I do? Where is the closest heavy object? Can I reach it faster than he can reach me? What should I do first, scream or jump?*

She did both at once, closing her fingers around a pillow and swinging backward as hard as she could. It never even touched him. He ripped it from her hand and pounced. Her scream was severed as his palm clapped over her mouth. His opposite arm caught her across her breast and ribs and hauled her backward till she was half off the bed.

"I warned you, but you wouldn't listen," he hissed in her ear. "You're gonna listen now, lady. I got somethin' here gonna make you listen real good."

The pressure moved up to both breasts. Something pricked her beneath the left jaw.

"I can't see too good in the dark. Is it cuttin' you yet?"

It was. She felt the tip of the knife enter her flesh and screamed behind his hand, clawing at his knife arm.

"Be careful, lady."

She stopped clawing. If she pulled on him and he flexed against her grip, the knife could go in clear up to her eye.

She heard her own voice whimpering. "Hmp-hmp-hmp," with each panicked breath. Scott, help me! Sheriff Cowdry . . . Violet . . . somebody! *Pleeeeeease!*

"You're the one who started all this prohibition bullshit around here. Organizin' and preachin' and prayin' on the saloon steps. Then goin' to whine to the governor until you got this goddamned state in an uproar. Well, there's eleven of us in this town don't like it. Understand?"

His grip tightened. Her teeth sliced her lip and she tasted blood.

She tried to beg, but the sound came out in muffled grunts against his sweating, salty hand.

"Now, you're gonna back off, sister, you understand? Tell them women to quit their goddamned debates. Tell that mealy-mouthed preacher to shut his yap. And break up that temperance society! You understand?"

She nodded in a crazed, frantic fashion and felt something warm trickle down her neck. The sharp pain from the knife tip made it feel as if the blade had actually pierced her eyeball. She screamed again. He squeezed her face until she feared her jaw had broken. Each heartbeat felt as if it would explode her veins.

The whimpering hastened as she went past panic to mindlessness. "Hmp . . . hmp . . . hmp!"

The smell of cigar smoke and sweat entered her dilated nostrils.

"You think I'm afraid to kill you, think again." Her eyes felt as if they'd pop from their sockets. "One dead organizer could do wonders as far as puttin' the dampers on all them self-righteous reformers out there. But I'll give you one last chance, 'cause I got a big heart, see?" He laughed maliciously.

"Hmp . . . hmp . . . hmp."

"Say there, sister, what's this I feel?" The knife blade left her flesh and his hand closed over her breast. "You know, for a gimp, you ain't half bad. Maybe I got a better way to keep you in line than killin' you, huh?" His hand slid down her belly and he laughed evilly as her thighs involuntarily tightened. A moment later she felt her own nightgown pushed inside her body. She stifled the urge to scream again, but her eyelids slid closed and tears trickled from their corners. "I'll bet you ain't never had it, have you, gimp? Well, I ain't got time tonight, with that goddamned nosy sheriff walkin' the alley. But you better do right, or I'll be back. And it makes no difference to me whether you can wrap them legs around me or not. I'll make use of this."

He knocked her onto all fours on the bed, with her nightgown still inserted in her body, pushed her face hard against the mattress with one hand at the back of her neck.

"Now you stay just like that for five minutes—understand?"

She knelt on the bed like a Moslem facing Mecca, bleeding onto the sheets, her hip feeling as if it were breaking all over again. Five minutes or five hours, she was incapable of knowing which had passed. She only knew he'd thumped out the door and there was only one other way out of her apartment. She took it. Out the window, onto the narrow shelf behind the false storefront to the first window she found. She pounded, but Jube didn't come. Frantic, she groped her way to the next, pounded again, too dazed to realize it was still Jube's room. She groped to the next, banging on it with her fist, but it was the hall window. Crying, whimpering, she stumbled along the wall to the next window which was open several inches at the bottom. She pushed it up and went over the sill into Scott's bedroom.

She stood in the dark, chest heaving, hyperventilating, fighting for control of something more powerful than she'd ever faced before. "S . . . S . . . Scott . . . h . . . h . . . h . . . help . . . me," she pleaded. "S . . . S . . . Scott . . ."

Scott Gandy came out of a deep sleep at the sound of a whisper. He opened his eyes and wondered if Jube was mumbling in her sleep. No, she was crying. He rolled to look over his shoulder and saw a figure in white standing at the foot of the bed. His first instinct was to reach for his gun. But then the whimper came again, jagged, broken.

"S . . . S . . . Scott . . . pl . . . pl . . . please . . ."

Buck-naked, he leaped from the bed. "Agatha! What's the matter?"

"A m . . . m . . . m . . . m . . ."

In the grip of shock, she could only stammer. She quaked so violently he heard her teeth rattling. He took her by both shoulders, feeling his own heart jump with fear. "Easy, easy now, breathe deep, try it again."

"A m . . . m . . . man."

"What man?"

"A m . . . m . . . man . . . c . . . c . . . c . . ."

"Take your time, Gussie. A man . . ."

"A man c . . . c . . . came int . . . t . . . to m . . . my r . . . room and he h . . . had a kn . . . kn . . . kn . . . kn . . ." The longer she tried, the more the word stuck. "Kn . . . kn . . ." Tremors shook her entire body and she breathed as if she were thrashing in deep water.

He pulled her against him and held her steady, clasping her with hands and elbows, one palm on the back of her head. Still she panted in short, inadequate gusts, much like a winded dog. Against his chest he felt each sharp rise and fall of her ribs. "You're all right now. You're safe. Just take it a word at a time. A man came into your room and he had a—what did he have, Gussie?"

"Kn . . . kn . . ." She panted fast against his ear, as if summoning her vocal powers, then burst out, "Knife!"

"Sweet Jesus! Are you all right?" Each of his heartbeats felt like an explosion. He drew back but held her securely by her upper arms, bending close until he made out her wide, terrorized eyes.

"I d . . . d . . . don't kn . . . kn . . ."

Jube woke up and asked sleepily, "Honey? What's going on?"

Gandy paid no heed to her. "Did he hurt you?"

"I th . . . think I'm bl . . . bl . . . Hmp . . . Hmp . . . bl . . . bleeding."

He swung her into his arms just as her knees buckled. "Jube, get up! Agatha's hurt. Wake the men and run for the doctor!"

"Hmm?" she mumbled, still disoriented.

"Now, Jube!" he roared. "Get Doc Johnson!"

She pulled herself off the bed by her heels and found her robe on the way to the door.

"Send Jack in here!" he ordered as he laid Agatha on the warm bed. When he'd lit a lantern he immediately saw the blood on her white nightgown. Terror gripped him as he searched for its source and found the wound beneath her jaw. He scanned her body but found no tears in her nightgown.

She folded her arms up the middle of her chest, closed her eyes and shuddered. "I'm s . . . s . . . so c . . . cold."

He covered her to the neck and sat over her, feeling his own fear give way to rage. "Who did this?"

Still with her eyes closed, she stammered, "I d . . . d . . . hmp . . . hmp . . . d . . . don't kn . . . know."

"What did he want?"

"S . . . s . . . saloons . . . p . . . prohib . . ." She shook so hard the remainder of the word fell off into silence.

Gandy's words grew hard, clipped. "Did he hurt you in any other way?"

Her only answer was a tighter huddling and the tears that seeped from behind her closed lids as she ashamedly turned her head aside.

Through the covers he found her shoulder and squeezed it. "Gussie, did he?"

Biting her lips, squeezing her eyes closed, she shook her head violently.

Jack burst through the door dressed in nothing but his union suit.

"Somebody's attacked Agatha. Have a look out back."

Marcus and Ivory arrived, too, dressed in nothing but trousers.

"Is she all right?"

"She's been stabbed. Maybe worse."

Jack's teeth grated, his jaw bulged. "Let's go!" he ordered, and took off at a run with the other men at his heels.

Gandy looked down at Agatha, tightened the covers beneath her chin, and demanded, "He put more in you than just a knife blade, didn't he?" He leaped to his feet.

"Goddammit! I'll find out who the son-of-a-bitch is and he'll pay. I swear to God, he'll pay!"

Her eyes flew open and she sat up supplicatingly. "No . . . please, he's d . . . dangerous . . . and strong!"

Gandy stormed across the room, swiped up his trousers, and stepped into them, turning to face her as he angrily closed the buttons up his belly. He swallowed the epithets that bubbled in his throat and crossed hurriedly to the bed, pressing her shoulders down. "Lie back, please, Gussie. You're still bleedin'."

Her fingertips slipped up to test her wound. He caught them before she could touch it.

"Please . . . don't."

"But your sh . . . sh . . . sheets."

"It doesn't matter. Please don't move till Doc Johnson gets here." He put her hand beneath the covers and covered her securely again. Then he sat beside her, silent, staring into her wide, dazed eyes, stroking the hair back from her forehead again, and again, and again.

"Scott," she whispered, tears pooling in her eyes, making them appear transparent, like deep green water.

"Shh! . . ."

"He didn't . . ."

"Later . . . we'll talk about it later."

The tears ran in silver paths down her temples. He dried them with his thumbs.

"Don't leave me."

"I won't," he promised.

Her eyes grew wild with fright when Doc Johnson arrived and took Scott's place on the edge of the bed. He cleansed the wound with boiled saltwater, then announced no stitches would be necessary. He liberally dampened a gauze patch with tincture of arnica, then applied it to the wound and fastened it in place with another strip leading around the top of her head. Meanwhile, Ruby, Pearl, and Jube hovered anxiously in the doorway. The men reported they'd found nobody in the alley, nor in Agatha's apartment. Doc Johnson washed his hands at Gandy's shaving stand, and, drying them, advised, "She's going to be in some pain tonight. A touch of whiskey might dull it. She'll be chilled until the shock wears off, but other than that, she should recover nicely."

"Jack, go down and get a bottle, would y'?" Gandy said, without removing his eyes from Agatha's pale face.

Jack disappeared without a word.

"Marcus, Ivory, thank y' for lookin'. If one of you would get the sheriff, I think it's best if I talk t' him tonight."

"I already told him. He should be here any minute."

"Good." Gandy turned to the women. "Girls, go back t' bed. I'll stay with her."

Jube hovered a moment after the others had left. He cupped her jaw tenderly. "Sorry, Jube. She asked me not t' leave her. Do you mind goin' t' your own room for the rest of the night?"

She kissed his jaw. "Of course not. I'll check in on her in the morning."

Scott was the only other one in the room while Ben Cowdry asked his questions. Agatha had calmed down somewhat, and answered lucidly, repeating the threats her attacker made, recalling that he'd smelled of cigar smoke and seemed to have a big belly and a raspy voice. But when Cowdry asked if the man had harmed her in any other way besides the knife wound, her troubled eyes flashed to Scott's. He boosted himself away from the corner of the chifforobe and ambled forward.

"No, Ben, nothin' else. I already asked her."

Cowdry's eyes swerved from Gandy to Agatha, then back again. Rising, he adjusted his gun belt. "Good enough. I'll need to have you sign some papers regarding the attack when you're stronger. Don't worry, Miss Downing, we'll get him."

Gandy closed the sitting room door behind the sheriff and returned to the bedroom. Agatha's round, frightened eyes were trained on the doorway, waiting for him.

"I shouldn't be here, in your room."

He picked up the whiskey bottle and a glass on his way past the shaving stand. "Doctor's orders," he said softly, crossing to the bed, sitting on the edge of it with one knee updrawn. He uncapped the bottle, poured three fingers, then set the bottle on the bedside table. "Can you sit up?"

"Yes."

She struggled up, wincing as she strained her neck muscles, and he leaned close to stack the pillows behind her. She fell back with a sigh.

"Here." He held out the glass. She stared at it. "Have y' ever tasted it before?"

"No."

"Then be ready. It's fiery, but it'll help."

She reached out tentatively and took the glass into her delicate fingertips. She glanced up uncertainly.

He grinned. "What'd y' expect from a saloon owner?"

She braved a grin, but even that hurt her jaw. Clasping the glass firmly, she tipped it up and drained it dry in four gulps, squeezed her eyes shut, gave an all-over shiver, opened her eyes and mouth, and held out the glass for more.

"Whoa!" Gandy pushed her hand down to her lap. "Not so fast there. You'll be seein' pink prairie dogs if y' keep that up."

"I hurt. And my stomach is still jumping. And I'm not at all sure I still won't fall into a thousand pieces. If the whiskey will help, I'll take seconds."

She held up the glass and he eyed it dubiously, but reached for the bottle again. This time he gave her half as much. When she lifted it as if to swig it straight down, he stopped her. "Not so fast. Sip it."

She sipped, lowered the glass, and held it in both hands, then touched the bloody sheets and her bloody nightgown. "I've made a mess of your bed."

He smiled at her wan cheeks. "I don't mind if you don't."

"And I've chased Jubilee away."

Their eyes met directly and held. "It's all right. She doesn't sleep here all the time anyway."

She became aware of his knee flanking her thigh and lifted the drink as if in refuge. This sip drained the glass. Then she self-consciously backhanded the side of her mouth without looking up at him again.

"I feel better now. I can go to my own apartment."

"No. You'll stay here."

He reached for the empty glass but closed his fingers over both it and her hand. "What did he do to you, Gussie? I need t' know."

She raised her eyes and his were waiting, concerned, dark with emotion. She swallowed—it hurt terribly, all the way to the top of her skull. When she spoke, her voice trembled and new tears balanced on her eyelids.

"He didn't do what you think. He only . . . only t . . . t . . . t . . ."

Gently, he took the glass from her death grip and set it aside. "Lie down," he ordered, lifting the covers, adjusting the pillows while she slid into the warm security of his bed once again. He covered her to the neck, then stretched out beside her and rolled her to her side, facing him. He spread a hand on her back, feeling through the bedding how the shudders had revived. He rubbed the hollow between her shoulder blades and stared at her flushing face.

"Open your eyes, Gussie."

She did, and she met his fixed gaze, saw at close range his black spiky lashes and intent brown eyes, his well-defined eyebrows and somber lips. The whiskey had begun to relax her, though she huddled beneath the covers with her arms crossed protectively over her breasts. His Adam's apple rose and fell as he swallowed.

"I care about you," he whispered hoarsely. "Do you understand that?"

He moved not a muscle for several long, intense seconds. He stared into her distraught, green eyes until she, too, swallowed.

"He touched me," she whispered, "in an awful way that made me feel dirty. And threatened to come back and do worse if I didn't begin to discourage the local interest in the ratification of the amendment."

"But it's too late for that t' do any good."

"I know."

With pillows cradling their cheeks, they lay and stared into each other's eyes.

"I'm sorry," he said softly, wishing he had the power to wipe away the violation she'd suffered. She blinked once, slowly, and he saw that the alcohol was beginning to take effect.

"That's enough," she whispered contentedly.

"Is it?" It didn't seem enough, to be angry, to send the men out searching, to fetch the sheriff and the doctor and feed her a few glasses of whiskey. She was a good woman, and pure, and she'd undeservedly suffered again at the hands of someone who worshipped alcohol.

Beneath his hand, her trembling had stopped. Her eyes, wide and so mesmerizingly pale, refused to waver. His eyes dropped to her lips—what raced through his mind had been a long time coming. There were times when he was certain she'd thought about it, just as he had.

He lifted his head only enough to miss her nose and kissed her—like the brushstroke of an artist who wished to bring a canvas to life in pastels. She lay as still as a drawing of herself, her eyes closed, holding her breath, her lips still.

He lay back down, watching. Her eyelids fluttered open. She breathed again, as if testing her ability to do so. He tried to read those eyes, searching for willingness, then realized she would be too timid to grant it knowingly. But he saw the pulse beat fast at her temple, and it was answer enough. He didn't know where it would ultimately lead, only that they'd both wondered for a long, long time, and that their curiosity needed satisfying.

He braced himself up on an elbow, clasped her shoulder, and gently rolled her to her back. Leaning above her, he searched her eyes for a long, ardent moment. Then, slowly, slowly, he lowered his mouth to hers. His tongue intuitively reached, but though she lifted her face, her lips remained closed. He stroked her lightly—once, only to touch the seam of her lips. It struck him fully: she didn't know what was expected of her. He hadn't realized she'd been holding her breath until the kiss lengthened and it rushed out against his cheek. His heart felt an odd catch—she was even more innocent than he'd guessed. He thought of asking her to open her lips, but it would startle her. So instead he told her with his lips, his tongue, with soft plucking bites, deft, damp strokes, the slow waggle of his head—*Gussie, Gussie, open up t' me.*

He sensed the moment when understanding swamped her. And lightened his hold—waiting, waiting—the kiss turned invitation now.

A first hesitant parting. Then he felt his way across her lips with his tongue tip—*Wider, don't be afraid.*

She heeded, opened her lips farther, and held her breath again, waiting for his first faint touch within.

At the moment of contact he sensed her pleasure and her shock at this first elementary intimacy. Her tongue was warm and tasted faintly of brandy as he stroked it with his own and drew small persuasive circles, encouraging her to explore him likewise.

She answered with a first shy response.

Like this?

He answered with another. *Like this—deeper, longer.*

She tried it, cautious, reserved, yet entranced and willing. He sensed her awe building at the warm, sleek sensations and kept the kiss gentle. He lifted his head by degrees, giving her a parting, openmouthed nudge before looking down into her face.

Her eyes opened. She was still covered to the neck, her hands caught on her breast between them.

"So that's how it's done, then," she whispered.

"You've never done it before?"

"Yes. Once. When I was about eight years old, in the backyard of a little neighbor boy who said if I let him kiss me I could play on his swing. He was ten. You're much better at it than he was."

He smiled, the dimples forming in his cheeks. "Did y' like it?"

"I have not liked anything so much since you gave me my new Singer."

He chuckled and kissed her once more, longer than before, but with no more urgency, letting her explore his mouth as she would. Beneath his chest he felt her hands fidget and gave her space enough to free them. They came from beneath the blanket and rested lightly on his bare skin, just beneath the shoulder blades, fanning lightly.

He lifted his mouth from hers and rested his lips against her forehead while her fingers continued brushing. "Gussie," he said, "wherever we end up, you and I, remember that I never meant t' hurt you by this."

She was suddenly very certain where they'd end up, and it would not be together in Proffitt, Kansas. The thought hurt worse than the tip of her assailant's knife.

"I must be slightly inebriated," she ventured, "to be lying in a man's bed drinking whiskey and kissing him."

He lifted his head, held her cheeks between his palms, and forced her to meet his gaze. "Did y' hear me?"

She swallowed and replied soberly, "I heard you."

"You're not a woman who'd take a thing like this lightly. I knew that before I kissed you."

"So did I, before I let you."

He looked down into her face as the lantern light fired the tips of her lashes to deep umber and drew becoming shadows beside her nose and mouth. With his thumbs he drew light circles on her temples. He saw even more clearly what he had seen before—compelling green eyes, a straight, fine nose, and soft, kissable lips, all arranged in an utterly beguiling fashion. He found it hard to believe no man had ever been enticed by them before.

"You must have found it strange that I never came t' thank you for the scissors." She swallowed but remained silent. "Did you?"

"Yes. You're the first man I ever gave a gift to."

He kissed her chin and told her softly, "Thank you."

"Why didn't you come to tell me before?"

"Because tonight isn't the first time I've considered doin' this. I considered it that day. But, Gussie, I don't want y' t' think I'm takin' advantage of y' when you've drunk your first whiskey, and when you've been taken by surprise once already tonight. That's not why I did it."

"Then why?"

"I don't know." His eyes grew troubled. "Do you?"

"To comfort me?"

He searched her eyes and took the easy way out. "Yes, t' comfort you. And t' tell you the scissors have been in my breast pocket ever since Willy brought them t' me. They're beautiful scissors." He watched her expression change to one of imminent shyness. "You're blushing," he told her.

"I know." Her gaze fluttered aside.

It had been so long since he'd noticed a woman blush. With a finger he brushed the crest of her cheek where the soft skin had bloomed like a June rose. "Can I stay here? On top of the covers, beside you?"

Her eyes flashed to his. Pale green to stunning brown. She felt the weight of him pressing almost against her breasts. It would probably be as close as she'd ever get to the real thing.

"You can trust me, Gussie."

"Yes . . . stay," she whispered, then watched as he rolled away to lower the wick on the lantern and turn the room into a secure black cocoon. She felt him roll toward her again and settle onto his side facing her. Then listened to his breathing and felt it stir the hair above her ear. And wondered what it would be like to be able to share his bed like this for the rest of her life.

CHAPTER
15

True to his word, Scott remained totally trustworthy throughout the night. Still, Agatha slept little. Lying beside a sleeping man did nothing to promote it. Not until a gray dawn was lighting the night sky did she finally slip into slumber.

A loud whisper awakened her.

"Hey, Gussie, you awake?"

She rolled her head and opened her eyes. Scott was gone. Willy stood in the sitting room doorway with Moose in his arms. Outside it was raining and thunder rumbled.

"Hello, you two."

He smiled. "I brung Moose t' see ya. Moose'll make ya happy."

"Oh, Willy. *You* make me happy. Come here."

He beamed and came at a run, threw Moose onto the bed, then clambered up and sat beside her in his familiar pose, ankles out on either side of him. His eyes immediately took in her bandage and the dried blood. When he spoke, his voice held horrified respect. "Gosh, Gussie, did that man do *that* to you?"

She curled on her side and petted his knee. "I'll be all right, Willy. It scared me more than it hurt me."

"But g-o-o-osh . . ." He couldn't tear his eyes away from the sight.

Moose came pussy-footing across the blankets, nosed Agatha's lip, and tickled her with his whiskers. She giggled and rolled back, scrubbing at her nose. Willy giggled, too, watching. Then he offered, "Me an' Violet's gonna take care o' the store so you can rest today. Violet says t' tell you everything's under con . . . con . . ." He stopped, puzzled, and finally remembered the word. "Control."

"You tell Violet I'll be down shortly. I've never been a lazybones in my life, and I refuse to start now."

"So dat's where you are, you li'l rapscallion!" It was Ruby, swishing through the door with a covered plate in her hand. "Scotty know you got dat crittuh on his bed?"

"Yup. Moose is makin' Gussie happy again."

She chuckled in her dry, sarcastic way. "Moose is keepin' one young'un I know from helpin' with the sweepin' downstairs."

"Oh! I forgot!" Willy bounced off the bed and hit for the doorway. He caught himself on the doorframe and swung around, sending his feet flying. "Take care o' Moose for me, Gussie. He gets in the way when we sweep."

Ruby arched one eyebrow at the doorway when he was gone. "That chile evuh do anythin' slow?"

Agatha laughed. "You should see him on his way to the bathhouse."

"Eggs 'n' grits dis mornin'. Scotty says t' see ya eat 'em all. Emma says no rush returnin' the plate. I say, if I git my hands on dat no-count trash did this t' you, I'll pluck his balls bald, then grind 'em up for pig mash." She slapped the plate down unceremoniously. "Now eat."

Agatha couldn't help chuckling at Ruby's colorful language. There were times when she forgot about the girls' former lives, but reminders surfaced now and then in startling anecdotes or ribald language such as Ruby had just used. Eating her breakfast, after Ruby had exited, Agatha smiled to herself. *Oh, Ruby, I love you, too.*

Abruptly, Agatha turned thoughtful.

It was undeniably true. During the past six months she had grown to love all of Scott Gandy's "family." And they, in turn, loved her. They proved it in countless ways, by rallying around when she was in trouble, sheltering her while she feared, pampering her afterward. How miraculous. How sobering. Suddenly, she found herself toying with the grits, her appetite lacking. Supposing she lost them now, when she'd just found them?

Moose came sniffing. She set down the fork and fed him some scraps but found her eyes blurred by tears as she watched the kitten stand on her lap and lick the plate.

Petting Moose's tiny head, she prayed, *Dear God, don't let that amendment become law.*

The door between Scott's office and the sitting room was closed when Agatha rose. She paused in the nearer sitting room doorway, glancing at his sack coat tossed over an upholstered chair, a full ashtray beside it, a discarded newspaper, a discarded shirt collar beside his humidor. Once again she felt an unwarranted stab of intimacy, more poignant than before, as she realized their days together might be numbered.

The watercolor painting of Waverley drew her hypnotically. She shuffled across and stood studying it intently: a magnificent edifice any man would pine for, if forced to leave. Sweeping wings, Doric columns, and its crowning glory: the high, dominating rotunda studded by an eight-faceted peaked roof like a diamond in an elegant mounting.

She studied the broad entry door framed by top and sidelights, picturing Scott as a boy, charging through as Willy would. She pictured him as a young man marrying a beautiful blond woman somewhere inside, in a room with a wedding alcove. She pictured him as a new husband, reluctantly going away to war, galloping down the lane beneath the magnolia trees, turning for a last glimpse of his family, his tearful wife with their child on her arm, her hand raised above her head. She pictured him as a defeated "Johnny Reb," returning to hear the voice of his dead daughter haunting him in his sleep.

Agatha touched his rosewood humidor, let her fingertips linger upon the rich, polished wood he had smoothed so many times. She touched the worn collar that had circled his strong, dark neck.

You'll be going back, Scott. I know it. It's what you must do.

Leaving his apartment, she noted that the hall door to his

office was open. She tried to hurry past, but he was sitting at his desk and glanced up.

"Agatha?" he called.

Reluctantly, she returned to the open doorway, standing well out in the hall, self-conscious in her bloody nightgown and bare feet.

"How are you this mornin'?" he asked.

The look of him stopped her heart. Rumpled, unshaven, uncombed, as she'd never seen him before. His white shirt, minus its collar, lay open at the throat, the sleeves rolled back to mid-arm. The lantern was lit on his desktop, throwing flame across the dark skin of his face, while beside him the rain slapped the bare windowpane and ran down in rivulets. Instead of a cheroot, he held a pen in the crook of his finger.

Everything had changed in the course of a single night. She could no longer look at that finger without recalling the touch of it tipping her chin up. She could no longer look at the wedge of skin at his throat without recalling the texture of crisp, masculine hair beneath her fingertips. She could no longer look at his full, sculptured lips without recalling the thrill of being passionately kissed for the first time. Nor could she look at him without coveting and wanting more of the same.

Possessiveness was something new to Agatha. So was cupidity. How swiftly they controlled once a woman had had a taste of a man.

"I feel much better." It was an outright lie. She felt sick at the thought of losing him.

"I had Pearl change your beddin' and take the soiled sheets t' the Finn's."

"Thank you. And thank you for the breakfast. I'll send Willy up with some money for it."

A pair of creases formed between his eyebrows. "You don't need t' pay me back."

"Very well, then. Thank you, Scott. You've been—you've all been very good to me. I . . . I . . ." She stammered to a halt as tears collected in her throat. She swallowed them and forged on. "I don't know what I would have done without you."

He stared at her, eyes dark with consternation, while she searched for equilibrium but found only heart-wrenching dread. Suddenly, he dropped the pen and shot from the chair, swinging toward the window as he'd done once before in this room when they'd had words. Staring out through the runnels of rain at a jagged spear of lightning, he said tightly, "Agatha, what happened last night—I never should have done it."

The drone of thunder sounded while she wondered how to respond. How did one respond when a heart was shattering? She drew upon some hidden store of strength she would not have suspected she owned.

"Why, don't be silly, Scott, it was only a kiss."

He turned his troubled face to her and went on reasoning as if she'd argued with him. "We're too different, you and I."

"Yes, we are."

"And after November 2, everything might change."

"Yes, I know."

"Then . . ." The thought went uncompleted. He drew a deep breath and spun away, then caught his palms on the shoulder-high ledge where the upper and lower windows met. Letting his head drop, he stared at the floor.

A choking, exhilarating, chilling shaft of hope shot through her body. *Why, Scott, what are you saying?* Too confused to remain any longer, she left him staring out the window.

But if he'd been intimating what she thought, that rainy morning brought an end to any talk of it. While October waned and they waited for Election Day, he avoided her whenever possible, and when he couldn't, he treated her with the same friendly deference as he did Ruby, Jack, or Pearl.

Willy learned to play "Oh! Susanna" on his mouth organ and Agatha suffered moments of regret over her poor judgment in choosing such a gift. Its shrill sound began to grate on her nerves.

Sheriff Cowdry asked every bartender in Proffitt to print the word *temperance* for him, in hopes of discovering who'd left the note on Agatha's door. But four of them replied that they didn't know how to write, and of those remaining, five misspelled the word exactly as it had appeared on the note.

The weather stayed gloomy and the streets turned into a quagmire. The stomach influenza went around and they all got it, one after another. Willy said Pearl called it the "Kansas quick-step," which he found tremendously funny until it was his turn to suffer the malady. He made the worst patient Agatha could imagine, and with Violet home from work with the flu, too, Agatha was left both to see after the store and nurse Willy.

She herself caught it next, and though she recovered in time to be able to go to the polling place to pass out last-minute literature with the other W.C.T.U. members, she stayed at home instead, using the flu as an excuse.

November 2 was a bleak day. The sky was the color of tarnished silver and a cold wind blew out of the northwest, bringing beads of snow so fine they could only be felt, not seen. The cowboys were gone, the cattle pens empty. The ruts on the street had frozen into uneven knots that nearly shook apart the buckboards that came into town in a steady stream as outlying settlers came to vote. The saloons were closed. The sheriff's office—acting as a voting poll—was the hub of activity.

Agatha avoided the windows, sitting in the lamplit recesses of her workroom shut away from the world. She tried not to think about the decision being made by the voters all across Kansas. She tried not to think of the four men from next door crossing the rutted street and walking along the opposite boardwalk to cast their votes, nor her longtime neighbor women, who even now stood in the stinging sleet encouraging the male voters—in their stead—to stamp out alcohol once and for all.

It was a long, restless night for many Kansans. Those in the apartments above Downing's Millinery Shop and the Gilded Cage Saloon were no exception.

Nobody knew the exact time the news would tick along the telegraph wire the following day. Violet was back at work, but neither she nor Agatha could concentrate. They did little stitching and less talking. Mostly, they watched the clock and listened to the lonely sound of its pendulum ticking.

When Scott opened the front door shortly before noon, Agatha was seated at her pigeonhole desk and Violet was dusting the glass shelves inside the trimming display.

Gandy's eyes found Agatha immediately. Then he closed the door with deliberate slowness. But he remembered his manners and greeted Violet, who rose slowly to her feet.

"Mornin', Miz Violet."

For once she didn't titter. "Good morning, Mr. Gandy."

He crossed to stand beside Agatha, silent, grave, with his hat in one hand as if he were at a wake.

Her skin felt tight, even her scalp, and she found it difficult to breathe. She looked up into his solemn face and asked in a near whisper, "Which is it?"

"It passed," he said, his voice low but steady.

Agatha gasped and touched her lips. "Oh, no!" She felt as if the blood had suddenly drained from her body.

"Kansas is dry."

"It passed," Violet uttered, but neither the man nor the woman at the desk seemed aware of her presence. Their gazes remained locked while Agatha's face blanched.

"Oh, Scott." Unconsciously, she reached toward him, resting her hand near the edge of the desk.

His gaze fluttered to it, but instead of taking it, he tapped his hat brim upon his open palm. Their eyes met again, hers distraught, his expressionless. "We'll have some decisions to make . . . about Willy."

She swallowed but felt as if a cork had plugged her throat. Yes, she tried to say, but the word refused to come out.

His eyes, with all expression carefully erased, leveled on hers. "Have you thought about it?"

She couldn't stand it, analytically discussing an eventuality that would rip one of their hearts out. Covering her mouth, she turned her face to the wall, trying to control the tears that sprang to her eyes. Her throat worked spastically.

He glanced away because he could not bear to watch, and because his own heart was hammering as wrenchingly as he knew hers was.

Violet moved to the front window, holding the lace curtains aside, staring out absently. Somewhere in the store Moose chased a wooden spool along the floor. Outside, the sound of an impromptu victory celebration had began. But at the pigeonhole desk a man and a woman agonized in silence.

"Well . . ." Scott said, then cleared his throat. He fit his hat on his head and took an inordinate amount of time trimming the brim. "We can talk about it another day."

She nodded, facing the wall. He saw her chest palpitate, her shoulders begin to shake. Desolate himself, he wanted to reach out and comfort her, draw comfort in return. Ironic that he should be standing wishing such things about the woman who had fought actively to shut him down and had now succeeded. For a moment he strained toward her.

"Gussie . . ." he began, but his voice broke.

"Does W . . . Willy know?"

"Not yet," he answered throatily.

"You'd better g . . . go tell him."

He watched her control her impending tears, feeling desolate. When he could stand it no longer, he swung away and hurried from the shop.

It was the first time ever that Violet recalled his leaving without saying a polite farewell to her. When the door closed, she dropped the curtain and stood in the gloom beside the window, feeling forlorn. That nice Mr. Gandy—how she hated to see him go. What excitement would be left in the miserable little town when the saloons closed?

She heard a sniffle and glanced around to see Agatha's face turned toward the wall, a handkerchief covering her mouth and nose. Her shoulders shook.

Immediately, Violet moved to the desk. "My dear." She touched her friend's shoulder.

The younger woman swiveled suddenly in her chair and clasped the older one tightly, burying her face against Violet's breast.

"Oh V . . . Violet," she sobbed.

Violet held her firmly, patting her shoulder blades, whispering, "There . . . there . . ." She had never been a mother, but she could not have felt more maternal had

Agatha been her own daughter. "It will all work out."

Agatha only shook her head against Violet's lavender-scented dress. "N . . . no, it won't. I've d . . . done the m . . . most unforgivable thing."

"Why, don't be silly, girl. You've done nothing unforgivable in your whole life."

"Y . . . yes, I have. I've f . . . fallen in love w . . . with Scott G . . . Gandy."

Violet's eyes grew round and distressed as she looked down on Agatha's hair. "Oh, dear!" she proclaimed. Then, again: "Oh, dear." After some time she asked, "Does he know?"

Agatha shook her head. "Y . . . you heard wh . . . what he said about W . . . Willy. One of us w . . . will have to g . . . give him up."

"Oh, dear."

Violet's blue-veined hand spread wide upon Agatha's nutmeg-colored hair. But she didn't believe in platitudes, so there was little she could say to comfort the woman whose broken heart caused her own to break a little.

Heustis Dyar worked his cigar back and forth across his blunt, yellow teeth. Six hours since the news had come in, but it wasn't law yet! Not till they did the official paperwork and made it into a law! Till then—by God—he, for one, was going to make use of his time.

He filled his glass again and tipped it up. It warmed a path all the way to his gullet.

"What right they got?" a drunk at the bar demanded sloppily. "Ain't we got rights, too?"

Dyar took another swallow and the question seemed to burn deep within him, along with the liquor. What right *did* they have to take away a man's livelihood? He was an honest businessman trying to make a decent living. Did they know how many shots a man had to sell to earn enough for a horse? A saddle? A Stetson? He'd been patient, watching that millinery shop across the street where the drys had started the whole mess last spring. He'd been more than patient. He'd even been considerate enough to warn that damned gimp milliner who was responsible for all this.

Well, the warnings were done. She and her kind had howled and prayed and boo-hooed until they got their wish.

Jutting his jaw, Dyar bit the wax off the lower fringe of his red moustache. His eyes hardened and he stared out the small window at her darkened apartment. *What right, Agatha Downin', you interferin' bitch! What right!*

Dyar slammed his glass down, gave an enormous belch, and said loudly enough so everybody could hear, "I'd like drinkin' better if I didn't have t' stop t' piss so often."

Everyone at the bar chuckled, and Tom Reese refilled Heustis's glass as he headed for the back door. Outside, giving up the pretense of having to use the outhouse, he veered off the path and skirted the string of buildings between his back door and the corner. In less than three minutes he was mounting Agatha's back stairs.

Marcus had been the last one to get the flu, but when it hit him, it hit hard. Damned trots! He'd spent more time running out to the backyard privy than he did playing the banjo lately. And he hurt all over. Buttoning his britches and slipping his suspenders over his thin shoulders, he winced, then gingerly flattened a hand against his abdomen.

As he opened the privy door and stepped outside, he saw a movement at the top of the stairs. Quickly, he stopped the door from slamming, then flattened himself against the privy wall. Ignoring his painful stomach, he waited, gauging the exact moment when he'd make his move. He watched until the man at Agatha's door gave a furtive glance over his shoulder, then bent again to the lock.

When Marcus moved, he moved like a greyhound— full out, loping, taking the stairs two at a time, armed with nothing but anger. Dyar swung on the balls of his feet with the knife in his hand, but his reaction time was slowed by all the liquor he'd consumed, and his balance was precarious. Marcus flew across the landing, throwing his body into the attack. He kicked Dyar in the chest with both feet and heard the knife clatter to the decking. Never in his life had Marcus wished so badly for a voice. Not to yell for help, but to bellow in fury. *You bastard, Dyar!*

Lily-livered son-of-a-bitch! Preying on defenseless women in the middle of the night!

Though Dyar outweighed Marcus by a good seventy-five pounds, Marcus had *right* on his side, and the advantages of surprise and sobriety. When Dyar got to his feet, Marcus threw a punch that snapped his red head back so hard the neck joints popped. Rebounding, Dyer caught Marcus in his sore gut, doubling him over, then followed with a solid clout on his skull. Rage burst inside the mute man. Glorious, undiluted rage. The roar he could not release transformed itself into tensile power. He picked himself up, lowered his head, and charged like a bull. He caught Dyar in the belly and neatly flipped him backward over the railing. The big man's scream was brief, silenced when he hit the hard-packed earth below.

Agatha's key grated in the lock at the same moment Ivory and Jack came running out their door. Marcus sat cross-legged in the center of the landing, rocking and cradling his right hand against his stomach, wishing he could moan. Everybody else babbled at once.

"Marcus, what happened?"

"Who screamed?"

"Are you hurt?"

Others came out the apartment door.

"What's going on out here?"

"Marcus! Oh, Marcus!"

"Who's that layin' down there?"

Scott and Ivory ran down the steps and called back up, "It's Heustis Dyar!"

"He must have been trying to break into my apartment," Agatha elaborated. "I heard the scuffle, then the scream, and by the time I got out here Marcus was sitting in the middle of the floor."

Willy awoke and came out the downstairs door to squat beside Scott.

"He the one who's been pesterin' Gussie?"

"Looks like it, sprout."

"Good enough for him," the boy pronounced.

"Is Agatha all right?" Scott asked Ivory.

"She seemed to be."

On the landing above, Jube bent over Marcus, sympathizing.

For a moment he forgot the pain in his hand and concentrated on the feel of her silky robe brushing his shoulder, the sleepy, warm smell of her. If the hand was broken, it was a small enough price to pay for the consolation of having Jube fussing over him.

Agatha, also in a dressing gown, knelt on his opposite side. "Marcus, you *caught* him!" The one she'd have thought least likely to take on a man the size of Dyar, yet he'd done it and come out the victor.

He tried for a shrug, but the pain reverberated down his arm and he drew in a hiss through clamped teeth.

"You've hurt your hand?"

He nodded.

Jack found the knife and held it up.

Jubilee's soft palm ran down Marcus's arm. "Oh, Marcus, you might have been killed."

Though he delighted in Jube's nearness and attention, he realized Dyar still lay in the alley. He swung his worried eyes to the railing, gesturing with his head—what about Dyar?

Ruby called down, "How is Dyar?"

Scott answered from below, "Alive, but pretty well mashed up. We'll need t' call the doc again."

"And the sheriff, too," Jack added, still studying the knife.

"No-count redneck scum," muttered Ruby, then joined forces with the women who were lavishing Marcus with attention. They helped him to his feet, led him inside, lit lanterns, and checked the extent of the damage.

It turned out Marcus had broken a bone in his right hand. When Doc Johnson had secured a woodblock inside the palm and wrapped it in place with gauze, Marcus gamely displayed his agile left hand, fingering the frets of an invisible banjo—*At least it's not my chording hand,* his baleful expression said.

"Heustis Dyar will be wishing all he had was a broken picking hand," Doc Johnson noted wryly as Sheriff Cowdry carted Dyar off to jail.

As a thank-you, Agatha promised Marcus a free custom-made garment of his choice, as soon as he felt chipper enough to come downstairs and be fitted.

In his room, Marcus got a good-night kiss from Jube—a light brush on his lips that startled him, but before he could react, she said good-night and slipped out.

Scott, tucking Willy back into bed, had to bite his cheek to keep from smiling when Willy declared, "I heard most of it. Old Heustis sounded like fireworks comin' down before he went *splat!*"

"Go t' sleep, sprout. The excitement's over."

"Why would anyone wanna hurt Gussie?" he asked innocently, collaring Moose and falling back onto his pillow.

"I don't know."

The cat was so accustomed to sleeping with Willy that he flopped on his side with his head on the pillow as if he were human. Gandy half expected Moose to yawn and pat his mouth.

"It's b'cause o' the probe-isshun comin', ain't it?"

"I reckon it is, son."

"What're you gonna do when you can't sell whiskey no more?"

"*Anymore,*" Gandy corrected absently, scarcely aware that he'd picked up Gussie's habit of correcting the boy. Briefly, he rested a hand on Willy's head. "Go back t' Miz'sippi, probably."

"But . . . well, couldn't you be a blacksmith or somethin'? Eddie's pa, he fixes harnesses. Maybe you could do that; then you could stay here."

Gandy covered Willy and tucked the blankets around his chin.

"We'll see. Don't fuss about it, y' hear? We've got time t' decide. The law won't take effect for a few months yet."

"All right."

Scott began to rise.

"But, Scotty?"

The tall, lanky man settled back down on the edge of the narrow cot. "You forgot t' kiss me good-night."

Leaning to touch his lips to Willy's, Scott tried to hold

his emotions at bay, but the thought of kissing him good-bye for the last time tore at Gandy's innards. Suddenly, he clasped the boy tightly, holding him to his pounding heart for a moment, pressing his lips to the top of the short-cropped blond head. He thought of Agatha, with her face turned sharply toward the wall, her throat working. He thought of taking Willy away from her and didn't believe he could do it. Yet, when he imagined leaving the boy behind, with Willy's bright brown eyes filled with tears, as he knew they would be, he wasn't sure he could do that either. He had to force himself to press Willy back down and cover him up again. He had to force his voice to remain calm. "Now go t' sleep."

"I will. But, Scotty?"

"What now?"

"I love you."

A giant fist seemed to squeeze Gandy's heart. Sweet Jesus! What a choice lay ahead. "I love you, too, sprout," he managed to say. Just barely.

Scott Gandy and his employees had a meeting one morning in mid-November to discuss when to close the Gilded Cage and where to go next. It was decided there was no point in delaying since the flourishing business of the drive months had already been reaped. Between now and the time the law took effect, business would be slow at best, with Proffitt's population diminished to its original two hundred. The question of where to go next left everyone staring at Gandy for an answer. He had none.

"I'll need a little time alone t' figure things out. Where I want t' go, what I want t' do. Maybe I'll go south, where the weather is warmer, and try t' get my thoughts together. What do y'all say to a little time off?"

They all said nothing. Seven glum faces stared blankly at him. He felt the weight of responsibility for them and momentarily resented it. Tarnation! Couldn't they think for themselves? Would they always look to him as their savior, the one to deliver them to the next safe, profitable port? But the fact was, he felt dejected, too. The Gilded Cage was scarcely taking in enough to support eight people, and it was important that he preserve a big enough lump of cash to start them out again in a new place. So why should he feel guilty about needing a little time away from them, asking them to fend for themselves awhile?

"Well, it'd only be until the first of the year or so. Then I'll pick a spot where y'all can wire me and I'll wire back and tell you where we'll be settlin' next and exactly when to come."

Still nobody said anything.

"Well, what do you think?"

"Sure, Scotty," Ivory answered flatly. "That sounds good." Then, hearing his own lack of enthusiasm, he put on a false brightness.

"Doesn't that sound good, y'all?"

They murmured agreement, but the moroseness remained. It was left to Scott to feign enthusiasm.

"All right, then." He slapped the green baize tabletop and stretched to his feet. "No sense in hangin' around this dead little cow town any longer. Whenever you're packed and ready t' leave, y'all go ahead. I'll put the buildin' up for sale immediately."

"What about the sprout?" Jack inquired.

Scott did a good job of concealing his anxiety over the subject of Willy. "Agatha and I have t' talk about that yet. But don't worry. He won't be abandoned."

Quite the opposite. The sprout had two people who wanted him, and they'd put off discussing the subject as long as possible. But it could no longer be avoided.

For no good reason he could name, Gandy went upstairs to his office and penned a note to Agatha, then asked Willy to take it to her and wait for an answer.

Willy stared at the note as Scott held it out. "But that's dumb. Why don't you just go over there an' talk t' her?"

"Because I'm busy."

"You ain't busy! Heck, you've been—"

"I thought Agatha taught you not to say *ain't!* Now, will y' take the note, or won't you?" he demanded more sharply than he'd intended.

Willy's expression dissolved into one of dismay over the unearned scolding from his hero.

"Sure, Scotty," he answered meekly and headed for the door.

"And put on your new jacket. How many times do I have t' tell you not t' run up and down the stairs in the cold without it?"

"But it's down in my room."

"Well, what's it doin' down there? It's winter, boy!"

Mollified, yet further confused, Willy looked back at Scott with brown eyes that glistened. "I'll put it on before I come back up."

When he was gone, Scott fell heavily into his chair, then sat staring out the window at the snow, smitten by guilt for having been so curt with Willy. After all, it wasn't the boy's fault the saloon had to close, nor that he and Agatha were at this impasse.

Downstairs, Willy found Gussie in the workroom, pedaling on the sewing machine.

"Hi, Gussie. Scotty says t' give you this." He handed her the note.

The rhythmic rattle of the machinery slowed and the flywheel stopped spinning. Agatha's eyes dropped to the paper and a sense of foreboding flashed through her. *No, not yet,* she thought. *Please, not yet.*

"Thank you, Willy."

Willy tipped onto the sides of his boots and jammed his fists into the pockets of the new warm winter jacket Scott had bought him. "He says t' wait for an answer." While she read the message, Willy grumbled, "Garsh, how come he's so grumpy lately?"

A flood of dread hit her as she completed reading the message. It was the eventuality she'd known was inescapable. Yet all the mental preparation in the world couldn't make it less painful. She came out of a lapse to hear Willy saying her name.

"I'm sorry. What, dear?"

"Why's Scotty so grumpy lately?"

"Grumpy? Is he?"

"Well, he talks like he's mad all the time when I never done nothin' wrong."

"Did anything wrong," she corrected. "And adults get

that way sometimes. I'm sure Scott doesn't mean to be grumpy to you. He has a lot on his mind since the prohibition amendment passed."

"Yeah, well . . ."

She fondled the side of Willy's head, then ordered gently, "Tell Scott yes."

"Yes?"

"Yes."

"That all?"

"That's all. Just yes."

When he clumped out with none of his usual verve, she studied the back door and tried to imagine life without him bubbling in and out. She fully understood why Scott was grumpy lately. She herself was experiencing sleepless nights and worried days.

Drawing a deep, shaky breath, she reread the message:

Dear Agatha,
We must talk. Would you come to the saloon just after closing tonight? We won't be disturbed there.

                                                      Scott

Willy advanced cautiously as far as Scott's office door, but no farther. His chin thrust out belligerently.

"Gussie says yes."

Scott turned in his swivel chair and felt a catch in his heart. "Come here, sprout," he ordered softly.

"Why?" Willy'd been burned once this morning. Once was enough.

Scott held out a hand. "Come here."

Willy came reluctantly, wearing a scowl. He moved around the corner of Scott's desk and stood just beyond reach, dropping his gaze to the hand that still waited, palm up.

"Closer," Scott said. "I can't reach y'."

Willy stood his ground stubbornly, but finally laid his stubby hand in Gandy's long one. "I'm sorry, Willy. I made y' feel bad, didn't I?" He pulled the boy close, then hauled him up onto his lap and tilted his chair back.

Willy snuggled against Scott's chest with obvious relief.

"I wasn't mad at you, y' know that, don't you?" Gandy asked in a husky voice.

"Then how come you yelled?" Willy asked plaintively, his cheek pressed against Scotty's vest.

"I've got no excuse. I was wrong, that's all. Can we be friends again?"

"I guess so."

Willy's blond head fit snugly beneath Scott's chin. His small body in the thick woolen jacket felt warm and welcome, with one hand pressed trustingly against Scott's chest. The pair of short legs dangled loosely against the long ones, and even that slight pressure felt welcome to Scott.

Peace settled over the two of them. Outside, snow fell. In the small iron stove a cozy fire burned. Scott propped a boot on an open drawer and indolently rocked the swivel chair until the spring set up a faint noise. He found Willy's fine hair with his fingers and combed it up from his nape again and again.

After a long time, when their hearts had eased, the man asked, "You ever think about livin' somewhere else?"

"Where?" Willy remained as before, savoring the feel of Scott's fingernails gently scraping his skull, sending goose bumps throughout his body.

"Someplace where there's no snow."

"I like snow," Willy returned sleepily.

"You know what a plantation is?"

"I'm not sure."

"It's like a farm. A big farm. Y' think you'd be happy livin' on a farm?"

"I dunno. Would you be there?"

"Yes."

"Would Gussie be there, too?"

Scott's fingers and the chair paused for only a second, then began their soothing rhythm again.

"No."

"Then I don't wanna go t' no farm. I want us t' stay here, together."

If only it were that simple, sprout. Scott closed his eyes for a moment, feeling the reassuring weight of Willy stretched along his trunk. He was loath to move, to break the sweet contentment they'd found together. But he felt a twinge of guilt for asking Willy about his wishes, as if asking the boy to make a choice against Agatha. He hadn't intended it that way at all. He realized it would be the perfect time to tell Willy the Gilded Cage would be closing soon and all of them would be leaving town. But he hadn't the heart at the moment, and he thought it best if he and Gussie broke the news to Willy together.

"Sprout?"

When Willy didn't answer, Scott pulled his chin back and looked down. Willy was sound asleep, his head sagging low against Scott's chest. Gently, he picked him up, carried him into the sitting room, and laid him on the settee, then stood studying him for a moment: the long dark lashes lying against the fair cheeks; the soft, vulnerable mouth; the skinny neck hidden within the scratchy wool jacket that had worked up nearly to Willy's ears.

Sprout, Gandy thought wistfully, *we both love you. Will you believe that when this is over?*

CHAPTER
16

Scott was the only one in the saloon when Agatha entered by the rear door shortly before midnight that night. He sat at one of the green-topped tables, slouched negligently in his chair with one boot crossed over a knee, one elbow hitched on the table edge beside a whiskey bottle and an empty glass. Mechanically, he flipped cards at his upturned Stetson on a nearby chair. Five in a row hit their mark.

The only lamp burning in the place was a single murky coal-oil lantern directly above the table. It threw a pale smudge of light onto the top of his head and gave his eyes an obsidian glitter. Agatha halted at the end of the short hall.

Between cards, his glance flicked to her. "Come in, Miz Downin'," he drawled in a voice so low it scarcely carried across the room. *Flip. Flip.* Two more in the hat. She threw a cautious glance at Willy's closed door. "Oh, don't worry about the sprout. He's asleep." *Flip. Flip.*

She advanced to the edge of the circle of light and paused with her hands on the back of the battered captain's chair like the one in which Gandy slouched.

"Sit down," he invited without rising.

She cast a glance at the cards still sailing toward the hat.

"Oh, sorry." With a cold grin he stretched to pick up the Stetson from the chair, scooped out the cards, then settled the familiar flat-crowned hat low over his eyes, casting them into complete shadow. His apology held not

289

the slightest hint of contrition as he squared the deck and clapped it down beside the bottle.

She perched on the chair at his right, edgy because of his uncustomary arrogant manner.

"You wanted to talk to me."

"Wanted?" he bit out wryly. "Neither of us *wanted* t' have this conversation, did we?"

"Scott, you've been drinking."

He glanced ruefully at the bottle. "Looks like it, doesn't it?"

She grasped the bottle, sniffed its contents, made a disgusted face, and forcefully set it aside. "Rotgut!"

"Hardly. For this conversation I chose the best." He refilled his glass, then hefted the bottle her way. "Join me?"

"No, thank you," she replied tartly.

"Oh, of course not." He clunked the bottle down. "I forgot. Y'all don't touch the stuff, do y'?"

His drawl was very pronounced tonight. She'd thought at first he was drunk, but she realized now he was decidedly sober, which made his defiant attitude all the more distasteful. She stiffened and brought her chin up.

"If it's Willy you've brought me here to talk about, don't think you're going to cow me by brandishing your bottle in my face. I won't have it. Do you understand?" Her pale eyes snapped and her lips thinned with resolve. "We'll discuss it sensibly, without rancor, *and* without alcohol—or not at all."

His elbow was bent, but the glass stopped halfway to his lips.

"Put it down, Scott," she ordered, "or I'll go back upstairs right now. The answer to our dilemma won't be found in a bottle of fermented rye. I'm surprised you haven't learned that by now."

He considered downing it in one gulp, just to appease the unmitigated frustration she never ceased causing him, but in the end he set it down docilely, then slid it to the far side of the table, along with the bottle.

"Thank you," she rejoined calmly, holding his gaze firmly with hers. He felt suddenly childish, pulling such histrionics when she sat so unflinchingly, ready to meet him on equal terms. "Now," she added quietly, "about Willy."

He released a pent-up breath and informed her, "I'll be closin' the Gilded Cage by December first."

The starch left her in one second. "So soon," she said, mollified. Their animosity evaporated as if it had never existed. The rudeness with which he'd been arming himself, the obdurate primness with which she'd been doing the same, fled them both. As they sat in the dim circle of light they both became defenseless.

"Yes. There's no sense in us stayin' when we're not makin' any money. We have t' shut down eventually anyway, so why put it off?"

"But I'd hoped . . . I thought you might stay until after Christmas anyway."

"We've talked it over, all of us, and the others agree with me. The sooner we get out the better. We'll all be leavin' except Dan. He's decided t' stay here and live with his mother again."

"Where will you go?"

He picked up the glass he'd filled and took an idle sip; she made no objection this time. He rested both elbows on the table and drew circles on the green baize with the bottom of the glass. "I've thought a lot about what you said—about layin' ghosts t' rest, and I've decided you're right. I'm goin' back to Waverley, at least for the time bein'."

She reached across the table and gently squeezed his forearm. "Good."

"I don't know what I'll find there, what I'll do, but I have t' go back."

"It's the right thing for you to do. I'm convinced of it." His hat brim dipped slightly and she assumed he'd dropped his gaze to her hand. Immediately, she withdrew it and clasped it in her lap. The silence stretched long. "So . . ." she said at length, expelling a nervous breath. "We must make a decision about Willy. Do you want him?" She couldn't make out his eyes but felt them trained on her assessingly.

"Yes. Do you?"

"Yes." On her lap her fingers gripped harder.

Silence again, while they wondered where to go from there.

"So, what do you propose?" she asked.

He cleared his throat and sat up straighter, toying with the glass but not drinking. "I've thought and thought, but there doesn't seem to be any answer."

"We could ask Willy," Agatha suggested.

"I thought of that myself."

"But it doesn't seem fair to force him to make a choice, does it?"

He swirled the rye around and around. "This mornin' after I sent him down with the note, he came back up t' my office and we . . . well, we'd had a fight." He gave her a quick sheepish glance, then concentrated on the glass again. "Truth is, I snapped at him for no good reason. But we came t' terms and he sat on my lap a bit and we talked— about the plantation. I asked him if he thought he'd like t' live there. First he asked if I'd be there with him and I said yes. Then he asked if you'd be there, too, and I said no." Gandy looked up, but Agatha's gaze dropped to the green tabletop. "So Willy said no, in that case he didn't want t' go anyplace, just wanted us all t' stay here together."

She didn't move, just sat staring with her hands clasped in her lap. His gaze lingered on her eyelashes, and their elongated shadows reaching down her fair cheeks; her mouth, drooped in sad resignation; her fine jaw and stunning upswept hair, whose red highlights shone even in the murky light; her breasts, restricted by the stiff garnet taffeta of her prim, high-collared dress; and the arms she held militarily at her sides.

"No," she said faintly, "we cannot ask a boy of five to make a decision like that."

"No," he echoed. "It wouldn't be fair."

Still staring, she murmured, "What is fair?"

There was no answer, of course. Fairness was a thing neither of them had ever contemplated with such vulnerability before.

He loves Scott so much, she thought.

What would he do without his Gussie, he thought.

Every little boy needs a father.

A child needs a mother more than anything else, and she's the first one he's known.

He idolizes Scotty.

She teaches him constantly.

I'm too strict with him.

I'm too loose with him.

Waverley would be such a wonderful place for a little boy to grow up.

It wouldn't seem right t' take him away from everything familiar.

Around them, all was still. A winter chill crept along the floor. In the room at the rear a child slept, while Agatha and Scott decided his fate. The decision—either way—would be painful for all three of them.

Hesitantly, Agatha reached for the glass and took it from Scott's fingers. Her hand trembled and her eyes remained downcast as she raised it to her lips and sipped. Only then did her gaze meet Scott's.

"We must make an honest assessment about which home would be best for him."

He deliberated for a minute, his fingers linked loosely over his stomach, watching her. "There's no doubt in my mind. Yours. I don't even know where I'll be settlin' permanently."

"You'll settle at Waverley. I'm sure of it. You must—it's your birthright, and it would be a wonderful place for a boy to grow up. All that clean air and no rowdy cowpunchers around."

"But who'd see after him like you do? Who'd keep him on the straight and narrow?"

With a fey smile, she told him, "You underestimate yourself, Scott Gandy. You would. Underneath it all, you're a very honorable person."

"Not like you. And you could teach him. You've already started, with your constant correctin' and makin' him clean his nails and scrub his ears. I'm afraid I wouldn't have the patience for that."

"There are schools."

"Not nearby."

"And space. All that space. Why, Waverley has so many bedrooms he could sleep in a different one each day of the week. I have only a single room with no such thing as privacy for either of us."

"But you're the better influence on him. You make him go to church and mind his manners."

"Boys need masculine influence, too."

"Willy'll be all right. He's got a lot of spirit."

"Much of which he gets from you. Why, he's even affected a bit of a Southern drawl lately."

"But I have bad habits, too."

"Everybody has bad habits."

He didn't reply immediately, and she felt his eyes probing her. Unsettling. "Not you. Not that I've noticed."

"Fastidiousness can be a bad habit if it becomes fanatic. And sometimes I fear I get fanatic." She leaned forward eagerly. "Little boys need to . . . to . . . scuffle with one another in the dirt, and come home with bruised shins and climb trees and . . . and . . ." She ran out of ideas and spread her hands, then let them drop.

"If you understand all that, you won't be too fastidious with him."

It was her turn to study him, though she wished she could see his eyes. She had one last trump card. Playing it, her voice came out more softly, more intently. "I'm not certain I can afford to keep him, Scott. It's all I can do to keep myself and pay Violet's wages, even with the sewing machine."

"All you'd have t' do is wire me and there'd be any money you'd need."

His generosity moved her deeply. "He means that much to you."

"No more than he means to you."

For a moment they sat locked in the irony of the situation, two people who loved Willy so much they each tried to convince the other to take him.

"So," Agatha said at length, "we're right back where we started."

"It looks that way."

She sighed and her eyes drifted off to a dark corner of the room. When she spoke, it was wistfully. "A perfect mother, a perfect father—isn't it a shame one of us must live in Mississippi and the other in Kansas?" Suddenly, she realized what she'd said, and she feared he'd misinterpret it. She shot him a glance. "I didn't mean—" Her neck grew warm. Her eyes fluttered down.

"I know what y' meant."

Flustered, she searched for words to fill the awkward moment. "So how do we decide? We can't ask Willy, and we can't seem to agree who'd be better as a parent."

Zzzt! Zzzt! She heard the sound before she realized what it was: his thumbnail repeatedly riffling the edge of the cards upon the green baize tabletop.

"I have a suggestion," he said in a low voice that, at another time, under other circumstances, might have sounded seductive. *Zzzt! Zzzt!* "But I'm not sure how you'll take to it."

Her eyes dropped to the deck of cards.

"A single hand," he went on, "for the highest stakes ever."

She felt as she had the night she'd drilled the hole in the wall, as if she were contemplating something forbidden and would certainly get caught the moment she began. But who was there to catch her? She was a grown woman, an adult under no one's mandate except her own.

Not a muscle moved in his entire body, except for the thumb that kept flicking the edge of the deck. Sitting back easily, he watched her battle with her own stern code of ethics. "What do you say, Gussie?"

Her heart seemed to lodge in her throat. "W . . . Willy's future, decided by a game of cards?"

"Why not?"

"But I . . . I've never played before."

"Five-card stud. No draw. Read 'em and weep."

A faint line of confusion appeared between her eyes as they raised to his. "I . . . I don't understand."

"I'll explain the rules of the game. They're simple. What do you say?"

She swallowed and tried to probe the deep shadow cast by his hat brim. "Take off your hat."

His shoulders flinched. "What?"

"Take off your hat so I can see your eyes."

After a long pause he removed it slowly and laid it on the table. Her clear, true eyes pinned his cool brown ones with an unwavering look.

"When you and Willy played and the stakes were a trip to the Cowboys' Rest, did you cheat?"

His brows curled. Then he forcibly smoothed them and eased his shoulders back against the chair. "No."

"Very well." She turned all businesslike. "Explain the rules."

"Are you sure, Gussie?"

"I've done everything else this saloon encourages—watched women dance the cancan, drunk rye whiskey, even learned to like the smell of your cigar smoke. Why not poker, too?"

A lopsided grin tipped his mouth. A dimple appeared in his left cheek. Tarnation! She was some game woman! He turned the deck face up. The cards were numberless, difficult to read, but she concentrated hard as he explained the rank of poker hands from highest to lowest, rearranging the cards to illustrate each: straight flush, four of a kind, full house, flush, straight, three of a kind, two pair, one pair.

"Do you want me t' write them down?"

"No. I can remember." She recited the rank, perfectly. His eyes settled on her with undisguised admiration. Had the stakes been lower, he might have made a teasing comment. Instead, he scooped up the cards and began shuffling.

She watched his long, strong fingers manipulate the cards with economical movements. She listened to the crisp snap of the edges meshing before he scraped them together neatly and tapped them into line. The ring flashed on his finger and she recalled the day he'd first come to town—how little she'd suspected his coming would bring her to share a poker table in a dimly lit saloon with him at midnight.

He slapped the cards down before her and she jumped.

"What?" Her eyes flew up.

"You can deal."

"But I . . ." Her eyes dropped to the blue-and-white deck. *Samuel Hart,* she read on the top card.

"Shuffle, too, if y' still don't trust me."

"I do."

"Then deal. Five cards—one to me, the next t' you, face up."

She stared at him as if he'd suggested they remove their clothing alternately. He sat back and drew a cheroot from the pocket of his ice-blue vest, then the gold scissors with which he snipped the end. She watched, mesmerized, while he tucked the scissors away and lit the cigar.

"I never gamble without one of these in my hand," he enlightened her.

"Oh."

Silence fell and his smoke drifted to her nostrils.

"Go ahead, Gussie," he said quietly. "Deal."

She reached for the cards as if expecting a scorpion to appear from beneath the deck. They felt alien in her hands, slippery and new, yet oddly unthreatening, considering the potential havoc they might bring on her.

She dealt him his first card, without shuffling.

He withdrew the cigar from his lips and reminded her, "Face up."

Obediently, she turned it over. It bore three black clovers.

"Trey," he said. She glanced up in confusion and he added softly, "Three."

Her own card showed a crowned lady and a red heart.

"Queen of hearts," he explained. "Beats my trey."

His third card proved to be another three, but by the time she'd dealt four cards each, nothing else on the board showed promise. With trembling hands she turned up his last card: a seven of spades matching nothing. Before turning over her own last card, she stared at the figure on its back. It seemed to shimmy before her eyes. Her heart knocked in her throat. Her pale eyes met Gandy's dark ones across the table, while the smoke from his cigar rose between them. He sat as calmly as if waiting for dessert, while she trembled as if with the ague.

"No hard feelin's, whatever it is," he said.

She agreed with a silent nod of the head, not trusting her voice to come out steadily.

She took a deep breath, held it, and slapped the last card over.

It was a two. His pair of threes beat her pair of deuces.

She stared at it and swallowed. He let his eyes slide closed and expelled a soft breath through his nostrils, struck by the irony of winning Willy with one of the worst hands he'd ever been dealt. He opened his eyes to find Agatha looking gray and stunned. His strong hand flashed across the table, covering the back of hers and squeezing hard . . . hard.

The future of three people, decided on the turn of a card. What was it men found so God Almighty exciting about gambling? She felt sick, hollow, afraid to raise her eyes and see in Scott's the glitter of victory.

But no sign of victory glittered in Gandy's eyes. Instead, they looked bereaved.

"Gussie, I—"

"Don't!" She jerked her hand away. "Don't say anything noble. I lost fair and square. Willy's yours!"

She jerked to her feet. The chair squealed back, but she moved too quickly and rocked against the edge of the table. The liquor sloshed over the rim of the glass and made a black blot on the green cloth, but neither noticed as Gandy, too, lurched to his feet.

"Gussie, wait!"

She picked up her skirts and limped quickly for the back door before she disgraced herself by crying in front of him.

When she was gone he stood in the silent murkiness of the cold saloon, telling himself it had been a fair hand; she had even dealt it. Fate had made the choice.

Then he grabbed the table and with a vile curse over-turned it, sending chairs reeling and cards flying across the room. The glass shattered. The bottle rolled against a table leg, where it lay, gurgling its contents onto the raw floorboards.

Listening to it, he felt worse.

He sank to a chair, slumped forward, and clasped his skull. Lord Almighty! How could he take that boy away from her? She had nobody in the world. Nobody! And he had so many. He sat that way until somebody touched him lightly on the wrist. He straightened as if he'd been shot.

"What're you doin' up?" he demanded, none too gently.

"I heard a noise," Willy replied. "You all right, Scotty? You got the trots again or somethin'?"

"No, I'm all right."

"You don't look all right. You look kinda sick. What happened to the table?"

"Forget it, sprout. Listen . . . come here."

Willy padded toward Scott's outstretched hands, then found himself swung up onto his lap.

"I've got somethin' t' tell you." Scott's long hand ran up and down Willy's back, over the scratchy long underwear he wore now that cold weather was here. "Remember I asked you about the plantation—whether you'd like t' live there? Well, you're goin' to. It's called Waverley, and it's where I lived when I was a boy your age. I'll be closin' up the saloon any day now and movin' back there, but I'm takin' you with me, Willy. Would you like that?"

"You mean I'll live with you for ever and ever?"

"That's right. For ever and ever."

"Wow!" Willy cried, awed.

"Y' think you'd like that?"

"Sure—gee!" His face lit up.

"We'll ride on the train. It's a long way to Miz'sippi."

"A train—golly!" His delighted eyes grew as bright as a pair of Southern pecans. "I ain't never ridden on the train before." Then he tipped his head, closed his hand around one of Scott's lapels, and looked straight into his eyes. "Will Gussie be goin' with us?"

Scott had expected the question. Still, it hit him with the force of a fist in the solar plexus. "No, son, she won't. Gussie lives here. Her business is here, so she'll be stayin'."

"But I want her t' come along with us."

Scott wrapped both arms around Willy and tucked him against his chest. "I know y' do, but it just isn't possible."

Willy pushed himself away and glared into Scott's eyes again. "But she's our friend. She'll feel bad if we go away without her."

A lump formed in Scott's throat. He cleared his throat and clumsily closed the top button on Willy's underwear. "I know she will. But maybe y'all can come back sometimes on the train t' visit her. Would y' like that?"

Willy shrugged and stared disconsolately at his lap. "I guess so," he mumbled. His mood so reflected Scott's that when the man took the boy by the shoulders he spoke to soothe both their withered spirits.

"Listen, son, sometimes we love people, but we have t' leave 'em behind. It doesn't mean we forget 'em, or that we won't ever see 'em again. And Agatha loves you—you can't forget that. She'd keep you here if she could, but it would be very hard for her with such a tiny place to live in. At Waverley there'll be plenty o' space, and you'll have a room of your own in the big house—you know, the one on the picture in my sittin' room? You won't be sleepin' in the storeroom anymore. And there'll be lots t' see and do. We'll get you a horse and you can learn to ride. And there's a river where you can fish." Scott forcibly brightened his voice. "And wait till I show you the scuppernong vines you can swing on in the woods. Why, they climb up in the water oak trees so high y' can't see the tops of 'em!"

"Really?" Some of Willy's enthusiasm returned, but it was still underscored by a note of unhappiness.

"Really."

"But I could come back an' see Gussie?"

"Yes—that's a promise."

Willy thought for a moment, then decided, "She'll feel better when I tell 'er that."

Scott rested a hand on the boy's fair head. "Yes, I'm sure she will."

"I'm takin' Moose, ain't I?"

This one was tough. Scott had been anticipating it, too, but hadn't known how to answer.

Mistaking the reason for Scott's hesitation, Willy amended, "I mean, *aren't* I?"

Agatha's influence. The boy still needed it badly, and Scott was hit afresh by guilt for having held the winning hand. He took Willy lightly by both arms, running his hands up and down. "It would be hard on the train, son. We'll be beddin' down in a sleepin' car, and animals can't sleep there. But I was thinkin'. You're right—Agatha's gonna miss us. Maybe she'd like t' keep Moose for company."

"But . . ." Willy's eyes began to fill with tears, but he struggled to repress them.

He'd lost so much in the last half year. First his father, now Agatha, and even his cat. It was expecting a lot of a five-year-old to accept these losses stoically.

"As soon as we get t' Waverley, we'll get you another cat," Scott promised. "Deal?"

Willy shrugged and dropped his chin. Scott took him against his chest once more.

"Oh, Willy . . ." He ran out of false enthusiasm and sat a long time with his cheek against Willy's hair, staring at the floor. He realized the best thing for all concerned was to make the break clean, fast. He'd order everybody to pack tomorrow and by the following day they should be ready to go.

"It's late. Reckon we oughta catch some sleep?"

"I reckon," Willy answered glumly. Scott stretched to his feet with Willy riding his arm and reached overhead for the lantern. "Can I come up with you?" the boy requested.

Scott stopped in the doorway to the storeroom. "I think Jube is sleepin' with me tonight," he answered truthfully.

"Oh." Willy's disappointment was evident before he inquired, "How come she sleeps with you an' she kisses Marcus?"

"She what?" A line of consternation bisected Gandy's eyebrows.

"She kisses Marcus. I saw her the night he hurt his hand. An' the day we went for a picnic they almost did. I could tell."

"Marcus?" So that's what was wrong!

"Is Jube an' Marcus an' everybody else gonna come to Waverley with us?" Distracted, Scott took some time in answering. "Are they?" Willy repeated.

"I don't know, sprout." He entered Willy's room and tucked him in, still with his thoughts elsewhere. "Now, y'all go to sleep and before you know it morning will be here. We'll have plenty t' do t' get ready."

"All right."

Scott leaned to kiss him. Halfway to the door, Willy's voice stopped him. "Hey, Scotty?"

"What?"

"Are there cows in Miz'sippi?"

"You mean like here, durin' the drives?"

"Yeah."

"No. Only the ones we'll keep for milkin'. Now go to sleep."

Scott felt somewhat better as he left Willy, realizing the boy's thoughts were turning inquisitive. It was the first solid sign of enthusiasm since Willy had learned Agatha wouldn't be accompanying them. But by the time he'd reached his room, he'd traded thoughts of Willy for those of Jube.

She wasn't in his bed as he'd expected. It made sense, though. Now it all made sense.

Willy was on his stool beside Agatha's sewing machine early the next morning, holding Moose in his arms. With typical childish directness he told her, "I have to go away with Scotty on the train an' live with him in Miz'sippi an' he says you can't go with us."

She intentionally kept sewing. Somehow, fingering the moving fabric kept her from breaking down. "That's right. The prohibition law is closing the saloon, but I still have to make dresses and hats for the ladies of Proffitt, don't I?"

"But I told him you're gonna feel bad. Ain't you gonna feel bad, Gussie?"

She pedaled as if her very body drew life from the flashing needle. "Of course I will, but I'm sure I'll see you again."

"Scotty says I can come back on the train."

The pedaling stopped abruptly. Agatha reached for Willy's hand, unable to help herself. "He did? Oh, that's so nice to know." Her consolation prize. But it was of little value at the moment. So she forced herself to begin working again. "I'm making you a pair of warm woolen britches to send with you."

"But, it's warm there," he reasoned.

"You'll still need them."

"Scotty says there's vines to swing on an' he's gonna buy me a horse so I can ride."

"My, won't that be something?" *Yes, all the things this child deserves.*

"But, Gussie?"

"Hmm?"

"He says I can't take Moose. Will you keep 'im?"

Please, God, make Willy dash off to some other pursuit. Make this day rush past on wings. Let me get through it without breaking down in front of him.

But she had to stop sewing again because she couldn't see the needle through her tears. She bent to pick up a scrap from the floor, secretly drying her eyes before facing Willy and giving Moose a quick scratch beneath his chin.

"Why, of course. I'd love to have Moose. Who else would do the mousing around here if you took him?"

"Scott says I can get a new cat when we get there. I'm gonna name him Moose, too, prob'ly."

"Ah, a good choice." She cleared her throat and turned back to her work. "Listen, dear, I have a lot to do. I wanted to try to get a shirt cut out and stitched up for you, too."

"Could you make it white, with a collar that comes off, like Scotty's?"

Please, Willy, don't do this to me! "Wh . . . white— wh . . . why, of course."

"I never had one with a collar that comes off."

"By tomorrow you w . . . will, dear."

"I gotta go tell Scotty!" He jumped off his stool and tore off. When the door slammed, Agatha leaned her elbows on the machine and covered her face with both hands. Everything inside her trembled. How long would the pain continue to intensify before finally leaving her numb?

Shortly after noon Willy came down with a note for Agatha, but she was busy out front with a customer, so he gave it to Violet instead.

"I'm not s'posed t' bother her when she's busy," he confided earnestly.

Violet smiled shakily and produced a nickel from her pocket. "Very good, sir. I'll deliver the message when the customer leaves. Now you run along and buy yourself a sarsaparilla stick."

He looked from his palm up to Violet's watery blue eyes. "A whole nickel! Thanks!"

"Hurry along now. I've got things to do." She had very little to do, but it was a relief when Willy dashed out again and she could blot her tears in private.

When the customer left, Violet parted the lavender curtains and entered the front room.

"Willy delivered this for you a while ago."

Her eyes dropped to the envelope. She recognized Scott's writing by the single word: Gussie.

Violet stood smack before her, squeezing four fingers tightly with the opposite hand, watching Agatha's eyes as she read the message aloud:

Dear Gussie,
Willy and I request the pleasure of your company at Paulie's for supper tonight. We'll pick you up at your door at six o'clock.

Affectionately,
Willy and Scott

Violet was blinking hard. "Well . . . my . . . isn't that nice?"

Agatha serenely folded the note and slipped it back into the envelope. "Yes," she said quietly.

Violet fluttered a hand. "Well, you must . . . you must let me close up tonight, and go upstairs early to get dressed."

Agatha lifted sad eyes, and as they met Violet's the two women stood locked in a gaze that dropped all pretensions. They were both miserable and heartsore, and neither tried to hide it. Agatha pressed her firm cheek against Violet's soft, wrinkled one. "Thank you," she said softly. Violet hugged her hard for a brief moment. Then Agatha backed away and dashed the moisture from beneath both eyes as if irritated that it was there so often lately. "If I don't tend to business," she said brusquely, "I'll never get that shirt done for Willy in time."

They were all dressed in their best finery when Agatha answered her door at six that night: Scott in his fawn-colored suit and a thick brown greatcoat she'd never seen before; Willy in the Sunday suit he'd gotten for his father's funeral, and his new wool winter jacket; Agatha in the rust-and-melon dress she'd worn for the governor's tea, though she'd left the bonnet behind, which pleased Scott. Her hair was too beautiful to cover with birds' nests and plumes. He'd always meant to tell her that, but somehow he had never found the proper time.

"Good evenin'," he said when she opened the door. Their eyes met and held until Willy piped up.

"Hi, Gussie. I'm here, too."

Immediately, she bent to hold his cheeks and kiss him. "Of course you are. And, my stars, don't you look handsome!"

He smiled proudly and looked up. "Just as handsome as Scotty?"

She looked into the face of the man she would never forget as long as she drew breath. Her answer came out much more quietly than the question. "Yes. Just as handsome as Scotty."

She had always wanted to tell him that, but she had been bound by the proprieties of the single woman. However, with Willy putting the question to her, what else could she do but answer truthfully? It wasn't the way she'd have said it, had she been granted the choice of time, place, and situation, but at least he knew now.

His lips opened, then closed on a faint gust of breath.

She turned away. "I must get my pelisse." She hadn't expected him to be so near when she turned from the chifforobe with the garment in her hands. She swung around and bumped his arm. Her heart caromed at his nearness, his scent, his broadness in the heavy winter coat, the striking appeal of his face.

"Here, let me," he demanded softly, taking the pelisse from her hands.

"Thank you." She turned and he placed the brown velvet cape over her shoulders, then squeezed her arms tightly and pulled her back against him.

"Please don't put the hood up," he requested in a whisper, his lips brushing her ear. "Your hair is too lovely t' spoil."

The rush of her pulses seemed to flutter the very air around her. "Scott . . ." she whispered, closing her eyes, drowning in bittersweet emotions.

"Hey, I'm hungry!" Willy called from the doorway. "Come on."

Reluctantly, Scott released Agatha and stepped back, allowing her to lead the way out. Willy thundered down the stairs at breakneck pace. Agatha clutched the rail but found her free elbow held tightly by Scott. She could think of nothing to say as they reached the bottom and he let his hand slip all the way down to clasp hers. He held it tightly until they reached the end of the alley. On the boardwalk, he again took her elbow.

The meal was a farce she'd never thereafter recall clearly. She and Scott talked, but of what remained vague. Willy chattered with boyish enthusiasm and asked endless questions of Scott: "Where will my new cat sleep?" "What's a scuppernong?" "Are there snakes there?"

Scott answered succinctly—in the kitchen; a wild grape; yes—but rarely gave his undivided attention to Willy. He stared at Agatha instead, feeling restive and agitated, semiaroused and guilty. She was lovely. Why hadn't he *really* seen it before? What had taken him so long? And she was more of a lady than any woman he'd ever known.

She ate little, but with such incredible delicacy that each movement of her hands and jaws appeared more a dance than the banal acts of lifting food and masticating. He sensed how close to the breaking point she hovered, her tears so near the surface her eyes appeared the deep hue of a magnolia leaf in the spring rain. She was breathless, too, and flushed from trying to contain the emotions so close to welling over. Her fingers trembled and her voice shook, but she forced fleeting laughter for Willy's sake, whenever the child's comments demanded it. She seemed unable to meet Gandy's eyes, though he longed for her to do so throughout the meal. Not until their coffee arrived and he reached for the cheroot and gold scissors did she at last lift her luminous green eyes to his. And once, while he smoked, she closed those eyes and drew a deep breath through distended nostrils, as if savoring the scent for the last, last time. His eyes dropped to the hand she rested on her heart and he wondered if it raced like his. Then she opened her eyes and caught him watching her and hid her face behind her coffee cup.

He pulled out his pocket watch. "It's late," he noted.

"Yes." Still she refused to look at him. But she wore her hood down as they made their way slowly back to their lodgings. Approaching the stairs, she veered toward them, but he drew her back with a tight grip on her elbow.

"Come with me. We'll tuck Willy in together."

Her throat filled. Her heart hammered. But she couldn't say no. "All right."

The saloon was silent, dark, a bleak reminder of its former gaiety. Agatha was glad she didn't have to see into it in the dim glow of the lantern. Willy's wretched little cubicle was enough. She'd never been into it before and compared the stained wooden floor, the yeasty scents that permeated the room, to what it must be like at Waverley— bright windows and a high bed and more than likely a fireplace in each bedroom.

He shucked down to his woolen underwear and handed her each piece of clothing. She carefully hung them up for morning and smiled as she watched him leap onto his cot, shivering, the trapdoor of his underwear momentarily flashing into view as Moose appeared and leaped up, too. The room was drafty and far from warm. She felt the cold in the marrow of her bones, especially in her left hip, when she knelt down to Willy's outstretched arms.

"G'night, Gussie."

"Good night, sweetheart."

Oh . . . oh . . . the smell of him. She would never forget the smell of him, the little-boy smell she'd come to love. And the fleeting touch of his precious lips.

"You're comin' t' the train with us in the mornin', ain't . . . aren't you?"

She smoothed the hair back from his temple with one thumb and took a long, loving look into his heartbreaking brown eyes. "No, sweetheart. I've decided it would be best not to. The store will be open and—"

"But I want you to come."

Agatha felt Scott go down on one knee beside her, his thigh pressing against the thick draperies of her skirt. He rested one arm around her waist and the other on Willy's stomach, looking directly into the child's eyes.

Beneath his left arm he felt the trembling disguised by Agatha's loose pelisse.

"Listen, sprout," he said, forcing a grin, "y' didn't forget about Moose, did y'? She'll have t' be takin' care of Moose now, won't she?"

"Oh, yeah, that's right." Willy dragged the cat close. "I'll bring Moose down just before we leave, all right?"

She couldn't speak, could only nod her head.

"Well, g'night," he chirped, too young to realize the full import of last times, finalities.

She kissed him, letting her lips linger against his warm cheek. Scott kissed him, bending his dark head so close his shoulder brushed her breast.

"Sleep tight, sprout," he said throatily, then stood and reached for Agatha's elbow. Her heel caught in her bustle as she rose, and her hip sent out a shot of pain as she struggled clumsily to her feet. His hand tightened securely and guided her up.

When the lantern was out they moved through the dark to the rear door of the saloon, Scott's hand still clutching her arm. Up the stairs . . . slowly, reluctantly, counting the fleeting seconds until they reached the rough wooden landing. She moved to her door and stared at the knob unseeingly.

"Thank you for the supper, Scott."

He stood close behind her, uncertain of his ability to speak if he tried. His words came out deep and throaty. "May I come in for a while?"

She lifted her face. "No, I think not."

"Please, Gussie," he begged, this time in a racked whisper.

"What purpose would it serve?"

"I don't know. I just . . . God, turn around and look at me." He turned her by an elbow, but she refused to lift her eyes. "Don't cry," he pleaded. "Oh Gussie, don't cry." He squeezed her elbows fiercely.

She sniffed once and swiped beneath her eyes. "I'm sorry. I can't seem to help it lately."

"Aren't you really comin' t' the station tomorrow?"

"I can't. Don't ask it of me, Scott. This is bad enough."

"But—"

"No, I'll say my good-byes here. I won't make a fool of myself in public!"

He dredged up the words that had been haunting him all through the painful good-night downstairs. "Willy should be stayin' here, with you."

She pulled free of his touch and half turned away. "It isn't only him, Scott, and you know it."

She felt his surprise in the tense moment of silence before he swung her back to face him so abruptly the hood of her pelisse struck her ear. "But why didn't you . . ." He glowered down at her, holding her again by both arms. "You've never said anything."

"It wasn't my place. I'm the woman. Oh . . . I'm sorry, Scott." She turned her head sharply aside. "I shouldn't have now. It's just . . . I'll m . . . miss you so much."

"Will you, Gussie?" he asked with wonder in his voice, holding her in place and letting his gaze roam from her hair to her chin, then from ear to delicate ear. "Will you really?"

"Let me go," she entreated.

He drew her a fraction closer. "Let me stay."

She shook her head wildly. "No."

"Why?"

"Let me go!" she cried, whirling from him, stumbling toward the door.

"Gussie, wait!" Just as her hand reached the knob she was spun around and lifted bodily. Her pelisse twisted, binding her feet, catching one arm within its folds. The other groped for something solid and found his neck. Her feet hung a foot off the floor. Her trapped elbow dug into his ribs. They stared into each other's eyes while denial and arousal warred within them, colored by the awareness that in the morning a train would bear him away from her forever, along with the child she loved.

"Please, don't," she begged in a jagged whisper.

"I'm sorry," he said just before his lips covered hers. The shock of his open mouth sent a current straight to her core. Her own opened and their tongues meshed—

glorious, succulent, shattering. It was nothing like the other kiss they'd shared. This one was greedy and fated, desperate and clinging. He washed the interior of her mouth with his tongue, then, turning, made a soft noise in his throat as he pressed her against the wall. Even while he awakened a deeper yearning than any she'd imagined, she begged him silently to stop. Even while her own throat emitted a sound of passion, she willed him to relieve her of this torture before her heart burst.

She tore her mouth free. "Scott, if I—"

His mouth stopped her protest, stopped the soft open lips that threatened reason. She felt the flowering of passion as a gentle tug at her innards, an involuntary response plucked to the surface by the insistence of his tongue. Hers could do no less than answer, twine, explore, excite. New, delightful things happened in her body until she jerked her head back sharply and gasped for breath.

Her head hit the wall. Her captured arm ached. She couldn't reach the floor.

"Put me down," she begged.

He let her slip, freeing his hands. They threaded about her waist, inside the pelisse, learning the feel of her ribs inside their cage of steel and laces. His lips chased hers, but she rolled her head, avoiding further kisses that robbed her of ordinary sense. "If you have any feeling for me at all you'll stop." Her arm worked free and she captured his face in both hands, holding his head still. "You're making it harder," she whispered fiercely.

With his body bracing hers, he suddenly fell still. His eyes, only deep shadows, raked her face. A shudder of remorse quaked in him and he sagged against her. "I'm sorry, Gussie. I wasn't goin' t' do this. I was only goin' t' walk you t' your door." His hands left her ribs and, outside her cape, drew her lightly against his chest. With a sudden slump he spun them both about, leaning back weakly against the wall, bearing her weight.

"I don't want to go," he said thickly, looking up at the starless sky, with her head nestled just beneath his chin.

"Shh!"

"I don't want to take Willy away from you."

"I know."

"Jesus, I'm goin' t' miss you."

She rested her temple against his chest and tried to swallow the knot of love in her throat.

"S . . . Scott . . ." She pushed away, stood on her own again, and lay both palms on his vest. "It's still not proper, I'm still the . . . the woman. But there's something I must say or forever regret not doing so." She lifted a gloved hand to his jaw and looked at his lips as she said it. "I love you. No . . ." She waylaid his response by touching his lips. "It isn't necessary. It would only make life more unbearable without you. Just take care of Willy for me, and send him back whenever you can. Promise?"

He clasped the back of her hand and removed it from his mouth. "Why won't you let me say it?"

"You would only do so because you feel sorry for me. It's not reason enough. Promise me," she reiterated, "you'll send Willy back."

"I promise. And I'll come wi——"

This time it was her lips that silenced his before he could speak the lie. Once he left her he'd forget all about this night, when parting seemed so terrible. She flung her arms around his neck and kissed him once—just once as she'd dreamed of doing, holding his head, pressing her breasts against him, and feeling his arms take her—full length, nothing disguised.

"Good-bye, Scott," she whispered, pulling away. And in a flash she was gone, leaving him bereft and confused.

Inside, she turned the key in the lock, then fell back against it, listening.

"Gussie?" he called softly.

She clamped her upper lip between her teeth.

He rapped softly. "Gussie?"

After the third appeal went unanswered, she finally heard his footsteps cross to his own door.

That night was like a dress rehearsal for the ordeal of saying good-bye to everybody the following day. They came down, one by one, and each parting was harder than the previous one, until finally the one who poked his head around the door was Willy. He came last, after all the clunking and thumping of suitcases and packing crates had stopped next door. He was dressed in his Sunday suit again and clutched Moose against his shoulder.

"Gussie, we gotta go. We're nearly late."

"Come here, darling." She turned on her swivel seat before the sewing machine. He came into her arms, throwing one arm around her neck, the other maintaining a death grip on the cat.

"Scotty says t' tell you he'll write."

"You must write, too, as soon as you know how. I'm sorry I can't keep you."

"I know. Scotty says I hafta remember that you love me."

"I do . . ." She held his face in both hands. They were both crying. "Oh, I do. I'll miss you terribly."

"I w . . . wish you was m . . . my mother," he choked out.

Clasping him tightly to her breasts, she vowed, "So do I. I couldn't love you more if I were."

"I love you too, Gussie. Take good care o' Moose for me and don't feed him no milk. It gives him the trots."

"I won't." She laughed pitifully, taking the cat from his shoulder as he pulled away.

He paused uncertainly, clasped his hands behind his back, and shrugged. "Well . . . see ya."

She rested her face against the cat's warm fur but couldn't force a sound from her throat. Willy spun to Violet, waiting with tears running down her cheeks. "'Bye, Vy'let." She bent down for a swift kiss. Then he sprinted toward the door, paused, and turned, holding the knob. "'Bye, Moose," he said, then ran.

In their compartment on the train, while Scott stowed their carry-on luggage, Willy demanded, "But why wouldn't she come?"

"She didn't want t' cry where everyone could see her."

"Oh." Still feeling blue, Willy continued studying the busy train depot, hoping Agatha would change her mind after all. "She cried when I gave her Moose."

Scott settled into a seat, steeling himself against emotions he couldn't afford to feel. "I know." Though he knew it was useless, he found himself scanning the people seeing passengers off, and there were many, most of them former customers who came to wave a last good-bye to Jube and the girls.

He hated leaving Agatha this way, taking with him the memory of her tears as she ran into her lonely apartment. Outside, the wind buffeted the sides of the train, shredding the smoke from the engine, lifting the steam whistle's lonely shriek and throwing it back along the line, an eerie accompaniment to their departure from the place he'd always called a dreary little cow town. He'd never expected to ache so when he left it. But Proffitt had brought him Agatha, and leaving her did, indeed, make him ache. A deep furrow marred his brow as he stared out the window in silence. He saw the conductor stow the portable step, then disappear inside the train. He scanned the crowd hopefully. Just as the train lurched to life he saw her.

"There she is!" he exclaimed, grabbing Willy onto his knee and pointing. "There, behind all the others! See? In her brown cape."

She stood apart from the others, her gloved hands crossed over her breast. She wore the brown velvet pelisse with the hood up. He'd never seen a lonelier-looking picture in his life.

"Gussie!" Willy flattened one hand against the cold glass and waved exuberantly with the other. "'Bye, Gussie, 'bye!"

She couldn't have seen them board; she'd only appeared moments before the train began moving. And it was apparent as she scanned the flashing windows that she had no idea behind which they were. But as the wild wind caught at the hem of her pelisse and tossed it aloft, she lowered its hood and waved . . . and waved . . . and waved . . . until all the windows had streamed past and they lost her from sight.

Then Willy was crying quietly.

And Gandy lay his head back, closed his eyes, and swallowed thickly to keep from doing the same.

CHAPTER
17

None of Gandy's extended family seemed any less orphaned than Willy. Without loved ones or homes, and with Christmas coming on, anywhere they'd have gone would have been chosen against their will. By tacit agreement, they all went to Waverley together.

During the trip, they broke into smaller groups to share seats and berths, so Scott saw little of Jube. He spent much time wondering about her and Marcus, recalling what Willy had said. They didn't sit together much; Jube spent most of the time with Ruby and Pearl. But in the evening, after they'd been traveling several hours, Gandy needed to stretch his legs and, strolling down the aisle, he passed them sitting side by side. Marcus appeared to be asleep. Jube's head lay back against the seat but her face was turned toward him, and upon it Scott saw a winsome expression she'd never turned upon himself. She caught sight of Scott in the aisle and flashed him a quick self-conscious smile. Then her cheeks turned a becoming pink. To the best of his recollection, it was the first time he'd ever seen Jube blush.

Later, when he and Willy had retired to their bunks, he lay on his back behind the drawn curtains, one wrist behind his head, pondering the sleeping arrangements at Waverley. It was the perfect time to make the break. Whether or not Marcus and Jube had declared their feelings for each other, it would no longer be right for Jube to share Scott's bed.

How was it he and Jube hadn't talked about their deteriorating love affair? Because it had never really been a *love* affair. It had been a convenient arrangement that temporarily suited them both. Had it been anything more, he'd be jealous now, angry, hurt. Instead, he felt only relief. He hoped that Jube and Marcus would find in each other the perfect mate.

Wouldn't that be something? He smiled in the dark, thinking of it. Jube and Marcus, married. Maybe they could hold the service in the wedding alcove. Wouldn't that grand old house love to see life revived within its walls?

You're dreamin', Gandy. You can't keep the group there. How will they live? What will they do? Where will the money come from? You're a fool t' be goin' there in the first place. All it'll do is revive dreams of how it was, how it can never be again. And what about Willy? You promised him things you aren't sure you can give him. What'll he think if you inform him that he won't be livin' at Waverley after all? And what kind of life will he have traipsin' along after you and your troop, openin' saloon after saloon across the country?

Restive, he shifted, trying to get more comfortable. But the clatter and sway of the train kept him wide awake. He raised the heavy felt shade and tied it into place with its braided silk cords, then watched the countryside shimmy away beneath the glow of a winter moon. The train traveled southwest now. All traces of snow had vanished. Beside the tracks black snakes of water reflected the moon, while trees studded the landscape. Missouri? Arkansas? He wasn't sure. But already the flatness of the prairie had given way to gentle hills that swelled and rolled like a midnight sea.

He thought of Proffitt, the abandoned saloon, Agatha alone upstairs. *She cried when I gave her Moose.* A thick knot seemed to lodge in his chest as he pictured her curling up with Willy's cat, waking up tomorrow morning and going downstairs with no Willy to barge through the door and break the monotony of her humdrum life.

You did what you had to, Gandy. Forget her. You have enough t' worry about gettin' your own life in order, facin' the ghosts of Waverley again, deciding how to provide for a family of eight. Agatha's been on her own a long time. She'll make out fine.

But no matter how many times he reiterated these thoughts, he could not evict her from his memory.

On the afternoon of the second day the train carried Gandy and company into the town of Columbus, Mississippi, which had been a bustling cotton-trading center on the Tombigbee River before the war. The old cotton chutes were still there, like curved tongues waiting to drop bales again from the empty warehouses along the river onto the riverboats that were dying a slow death beside the railroad tracks, which carried everything faster, cheaper, safer.

"When I was a boy," Scott told Willy, "I used t' like t' watch the slaves load cotton on the riverboats just like you watched the cowpokes load cows on the train."

"Here?"

"Sometimes here. More often at Waverley. We had our own warehouses and the riverboats pulled right up t' shore t' load."

The comment released a torrent of questions. "How far away is it? How long before we git there? Can I fish in the river right away? What color will my horse be?"

Scott chuckled at the boy's excitement, which mirrored his own, as his first glimpse of Waverley grew closer.

They bought supplies at Sheed's Mercantile store. Old Franklin Sheed looked like a dried apple doll with white whiskers. He squinted at Scott from behind corrugated eyelids, withdrew a pipe from his mouth, and drawled, "Well, blezz mah soul. LeMaster Gandy, i'n't it?"

He extended a hard hand and clasped Scott's.

"Sure is, though nobody's called me that in a long time."

"Good t' see ya again, boy. Y'all back for good?"

"Don't rightly know, Mr. Sheed." Realizing Willy listened, he added, "I hope so. Brought my friends here t' see the old place." He introduced them all around, ending with the boy, upon whose shoulders Scott rested his hands.

"Well, it's still there," Sheed said of Waverley. "Nobody messes with it, 'cept a few o' the old slaves used t' work for your daddy. They're still out there, keepin' trespassers off the place. Be s'prised t' see you after all these years."

Something good happened inside Scott, clasping Franklin's hand. His roots were here. Folks remembered him, his people, his heritage. He'd wandered for so long, lived among strangers who cared little about his past or his future, once he parted from them, that coming back to a place where his name was remembered gave him an immediate pang of nostalgia. And here was old Franklin Sheed, who'd sold Scott's father cigars and his mother cotton cloth for the very diapers she'd used for his brothers and himself.

"What's it been now, since your folks passed on?" Franklin wondered aloud. But before Gandy could answer, a pinched-up octogenarian in a tattered gray bonnet limped in with a black cypress cane.

"Miz Mae Ellen," the store owner greeted her, "y'all remember Dorian and Selena Gandy's boy, don't you?"

She lowered her head and peered at Scott for a full ten seconds, resting both hands on the head of the cane.

"LeMastuh, is it?"

"That's right, Miz Bayles." He grinned down at the withered woman, remembering how much taller she'd been the last time he'd seen her. Or had he only been shorter?

"Used t' feed you peaches when your mama came t' visit me at Oakleigh."

"I remember, Miz Bayles." His grin remained. His eyes teased. "And some o' the tastiest molasses cookies anywhere this side o' the Mason-Dixon line. But y'all never let me have more than two, and I used t' stare at the rest on the plate and swear I'd get even someday."

Her laugh filled the store like the gobble of an old hen turkey. She rapped her cane on the floor, then shot a sly glance at Jube, standing nearby. "And I used t' look at that face o' his and think t' myself, that boy's too handsome for his own good. He'll end up in trouble over it someday." Her shrewd eyes pinioned Scott again. "Did you?"

Scott's dimples deepened to disarming depths. "Not that I recall, Miz Bayles."

She glanced from Jube to Willy to Scott. "So you married up again, did you?"

"No, ma'am." Scott gestured toward Jube, then looked down at Willy. "These are my friends, Jubilee Bright and Willy Collinson." The others were browsing throughout the store so he didn't bother to introduce them.

"Willy, is it?" She studied him imperiously.

Scott waggled Willy's shoulder. "'Member your manners, boy."

Willy extended a hand. "Pleased t' meet you, ma'am."

"Humph!" she snorted, shaking his hand. "Don't know why you should be—dried up prune like me, doesn't feed a boy more'n two molasses cookies at a time. But I have a grandson, A.J., and he's the one you'd like t' meet." She jerked a thumb at Scott. "You have this rascal bring you by someday and I'll introduce you two."

"Really?"

She poked Willy in the shoulder with the tip of her cane. "One thing you got to learn right up front, boy. Wrinkled-up old ladies don't say things they don't mean. They never know when they might drop over dead an' leave confusion behind."

Everyone laughed. Then Scott allowed Miss Bayles to make her purchases ahead of him. While she did, he inquired, "Y'all still live at Oakleigh, Miz Bayles?"

"Oakleigh is empty," she replied with stiff pride, carefully counting out her money from a leather pouch, then snapping it closed. "I live with my daughter, Leta, in town now."

For a moment Scott had been carried back into the past. Miss Bayles's revelation reminded him that Waverley wasn't the only grand mansion left derelict by the war. The turn of the conversation had put a damper on the subject, and when Miss Bayles turned with her purchases in hand, Scott politely tipped his hat.

"Greet Leta for me," he requested. "I remember her well."

"I'll do that, LeMaster. My best t' Leatrice. I remember her well, too."

Leatrice's name brought a resurgence of expectation to Scott. It remained within him as they bought ham and grits and flour and lard—enough food to feed a family of eight for several days. The good feeling stayed with him while they rented rigs at the livery—where again Scott was recognized and greeted enthusiastically by his given name—and while they set out for Waverley through the familiar Mississippi countryside.

Heading northwest, they rode through thick stands of oak, hickory, and post pine that opened into vast tracts of depleted cotton fields, few of which had been seeded in the last fifteen years. They passed Oakleigh, which appeared as only a faint white blur at the end of a long lane, half choked with underbrush and scuppernong vines.

The sky was clear but the breeze held a bite. The tips of the pines stroked the evening sky the way an artist's brush passed across a canvas, painting it the hue of a fading wisteria blossom. The carriages traveled upon a gravel road worn smooth by years of mule-drawn wagon wheels that had ground it down to fine silt. The scent of the earth was moist and fecund, unlike the dry, grainy scent of Kansas. Neither the sound nor odor of shifting cattle was anywhere to be heard or smelled. Instead, Gandy's senses thrilled to the sweet melodic trill of an occasional mockingbird rising from a thicket, and the scent of vegetation decaying now during the brief hiatus between growing seasons.

"Waverley land starts here," he said. Willy's eyes grew disbelieving as they rode on and on still farther.

"All this?"

Scott only smiled and held the reins loosely between his knees. They entered the last mile, the last half mile. Then ahead, on the right, a black iron fence appeared. As they approached it, Scott slowed the rig. Beside him, Willy looked up. Then his eyes followed the path of Scott's.

"Somebody's buried way out here?" Willy asked.

"My family."

"Yours?" The boy glanced up again.

In the back seat Jube and Marcus turned to glimpse the cemetery.

"Who?" Willy asked, craning to watch the gray headstones slip past.

"My mama and my daddy. And my wife and our little girl."

"You had a little girl?"

"Her name was Justine."

"And what's that?" Willy asked, pointing to a wooden structure on their right.

"Why, that's the bathin' house. Inside is the swimmin' pool."

"Wow!" Willy raised up off the seat in excitement. Scott pressed him back down. "Y'all can see it later." He went on quietly, "And this . . ." Scott turned left into the drive directly opposite the pool house—" . . . is Waverley."

The sight of it brought a leap to Gandy's heart, a thrill to his blood, even though, like Oakleigh, the house was glimpsed through snarls of vines and thickets of cedar and gum trees that had encroached upon the long lane, rendering it impassable. In its prime, the lane had been meticulously maintained. But today Gandy was forced to rein in after traveling less than a quarter of its length. In the early evening shadows the choking vegetation seemed to lend a menacing note to their reception. The overwhelming catlike smell of the gum trees seemed offensive, as if warning all mortals to keep away.

"Wait here," Gandy ordered, looping the reins around the whip bracket.

He went alone, picking his way through fifteen years' unchecked growth until he reached the massive magnolia—the one with the widest limb span in the state of Mississippi—that had dominated Waverley's front yard for as long as he could remember. But his disappointment redoubled at the sight of it, too, overrun by vines and hemmed in by his mother's precious boxwoods. She'd brought the boxwoods all the way from Georgia as a young bride and had nurtured them lovingly as long as she'd been alive. Their geometric perfection was long gone, for they'd been pruned by nothing but wild deer for years and years, leaving them grotesque and misshapen. Selena Gandy would have been appalled at their present disgraceful state.

Her son scratched his face on the unkempt bushes as he forced his way through them to the front entrance. The marble steps were intact, as was the iron grillework on the overhanging balcony and the ruby-red sidelights of

Venetian glass surrounding the massive front door.

But the door itself wouldn't budge.

He cupped a hand over his eyes and tried to peer inside, but the door faced south, and now in the descending twilight little light came through the windows around the matching north door across the entry hall. All he could make out were the carved lyre-shaped inserts on the insides of the windows. Beyond these, images appeared vague, translucent, as if viewed through a glass of burgundy wine.

He pounded on the door and called, "Is anybody there? Leatrice, y'all in there?"

Only silence greeted him and the sudden rat-a-tat of a woodpecker somewhere in the dense growth behind him.

The back door proved no more hospitable than the front. The two entrances were identical, with twin Doric columns fronting recessed porches two stories high. The only differences were the second, shorter pair of columns guarding the front door and the pair of familiar black wooden benches on either side of the back door. The sight of them brought another stab of nostalgia to Scott. They were thick, heavy, made of bois d'arc wood from the cypress swamps down by the river, bent and looped into the modified fanback design by the hands of slaves long before he himself had been born. It was upon the bois d'arc benches he remembered his mother and father sitting while Delia fed the peacocks.

Leaving the house behind, he followed a track showing evidence of recent use, past the old kitchen, the octagonal ice house, the gardens, the tannery, the stables, toward the slave cabins out back. He smelled Leatrice's woodsmoke long before he reached her door.

Knocking, he called, "Leatrice?"

"Who dat?" she called in a voice like flatulent wind escaping a bloated horse.

"Open up and see for yourself." He smiled, his face close to the rough door as he waited.

"Sumbuddy full o' sass, fo' sure." The door swung open and there she stood, nearly as big around as the century-old magnolia out front, her skin as coarse and black as its bark, and, like the tree, looking every bit as if she were here to stay forever.

"What kind o' welcome is that?" he teased, leaning an elbow on the doorsill and letting a grin slide up his cheek.

"Who . . . Lawd o' mercy"—her eyes flew wide. "Dat you, Mastuh?" She had never added the *Le* to LeMaster, and had always scoffed at the familiar *Scott.* "Praise mah soul, chile! It's you!"

"It's me." He lunged inside and scooped her up, though his arms reached scarcely two-thirds of the way around her. She smelled of woodsmoke and cracklings and poke greens, and her hug was mighty enough to threaten his bones.

"Mah baby come home!" she rejoiced, shedding tears, praising the heavens. "Lawd, Lawd, he come home at lass." She backed off and held him by the ears. "Lemme have a look."

Her voice was like no other in humankind, a deep rumbling bass that could not come out softly, no matter how she tried. She had smoked a corncob pipe all her days, and it was anybody's guess what concoctions she'd stuffed into it. Something long ago had damaged her larynx and left it able to emit only the grating sound no one ever forgot once they'd heard it.

"Jiss like I thought," she pronounced, "skinny as a sparrow's kneecap. What they been feedin' ya, pot likker?" She turned Scott around by the shoulders, inspected him minutely, then swung him again to face her. "Well, ol' Leatrice fatten ya up in no time. Mose!" she called without looking back over her shoulder. "Come see who's heah."

"Mose is here?" Gandy's face registered happy surprise as he glanced beyond her shoulder.

"Sho' is," said the aged black man who emerged out of the shadows and crossed the wooden floor with an arthritic shuffle. "Nevuh goed. Stayed right heah where I belonged."

"Mose," Scott said affectionately, clasping one of the old man's bony hands in both of his own. Mose was as thin as Leatrice was fat. His silver hair topped his head like Spanish moss, and, standing, he listed slightly to the left and forward, as if his spine refused to straighten completely anymore.

"Fifteen years," the old man mused aloud in a thin, wispy voice. "'Bout time ya was gittin' back heah."

"I may not be stayin'," Scott clarified immediately. "Just came t' see the place again."

Mose released Scott's hand to brace his back. "Y'all be stayin'," he said, as if there were no question.

Scott let his eyes slide assessingly from Mose to Leatrice. "So you two finally took up together."

Leatrice cuffed him none too gently on the side of the head. "Watch yo' tongue, boy. Ain' I taught ya t' respec' yo' elduhs? Me an' Mose kep' de place while y'all went gallyhooin' 'roun'." She turned away with an air of superiority. "'Sides, I wou'n't have 'im. He too lazy, dat one. But he company."

Scott rubbed the side of his head and smiled. "That any way t' treat the boy who used t' pick you wild blackberries and snitch roses for you from his mother's garden?"

When Leatrice laughed the rafters overhead threatened to split. "Set down, boy. I got warm cornbread an' black-eyed peas. Bes' get t' work hangin' some fat on dem bones."

Gandy stayed where he was. "I brought company. Think y'all could handle ham and biscuits for eight if I bring the ham and the fixin's?"

"Eight?" Leatrice humphed and turned away as if slighted by the question. "Like feedin' eight mosquitoes aftuh what I done feed in de good days. Y'all brung dat Ruby home, too?"

"I did. And Ivory, too."

"Ivory, too." Leatrice raised one eyebrow and added, sarcastically, "My, my, dat make four o' us. Soon we be raisin' cotton."

Gandy smiled. Being tongue-lashed by Leatrice was exactly what he needed to make him feel as if he were home at last.

"I left them stranded in the lane. Couldn't get into the big house."

"Key's right heah." Leatrice pulled it from between her ample breasts. "Been keepin' it in a safe spot. Mose, he open up." She drew the leather thong over her head and handed it to the old man.

But Mose gaped at it as if it had eight legs. "Me?"

"Yas, you. Now, git!"

Mose backed off, shaking his head, eyes bugging as they fixed on the key. "Ain't goin' in dere, nossir, not ol' Mose."

"What you talkin' 'bout. 'Cose you goin' in dere. Got t' open it up fo' young Mastuh an' his frien's."

Gandy watched the interchange with a puzzled frown.

"Git, now!" the black woman ordered imperiously.

Mose only shook his head fearfully and backed farther away.

"What is all this?" Scott demanded, frowning.

"Place got a hant."

"A hant!"

"Thass right. I heard her. Mose heard her. She in dere, whimperin'. Y'all go in, ya heah her soon 'nuff. What ya s'pose kep' folks out all dese years? Not jiss two old black folk goin' 'round checkin' de doors."

Gandy's neck stiffened even as he declared, "But that's ridiculous. A ghost?"

Leatrice picked up his palm and into it slapped the keys, still warm from her breasts. "Y'all open it up yo'self. Leatrice, she cook. Leatrice, she make biscuits, she make ham. Leatrice, she bring dem ham and biscuits far as de back door." She crossed her arms over her watermelon-sized breasts and gave one stubborn wag of the head. "But Leatrice don't go near no hants. Noooo, suh!"

As he picked his way back toward the house, armed with several tallow candles, Scott clearly recalled the child's voice he'd heard in the house after the war. Was it true, then? Was it Justine? Was she searching for her mother and father somewhere in the lofty, unoccupied rooms of Waverley? Or was it only the product of several overactive imaginations? He knew how superstitious black people were. Yet, he, too, had heard it, and he'd never had a superstitious bone in his body.

He shrugged aside the thought, rounded a corner of the house and bumped into something soft.

He gasped and let out a yelp.

But it was only Jack, prowling about the foundation of the old place, trailed by the others, who'd grown restless waiting in the carriages.

"She's a beauty," Jack declared, "and sound, too, from what I can see in this light."

"Let's go inside."

As he inserted the key into Waverley's front door, Scott found himself relieved to have the company of seven others, especially Willy, whose small hand he clasped tightly.

But once inside, all thoughts of ghosts fled. Even in the light of two candles, the massive rotunda welcomed him back. It smelled of disuse and dust, but nothing had changed. The Southern pine floors, the double staircase curving downward like two open arms, the giant pier mirrors reflecting the flickering candles, the hand-carved spindles lining the stairs, disappearing into the shadows overhead, the elegant brass chandelier dropping sixty feet from above—all waited to be polished and put to use again.

"Welcome to Waverley," he said softly, his voice echoing to the lookout four stories above his head, then dropping back down as if the mansion itself had spoken to him.

They lit a fire in the massive downstairs dining room and ate the supper Leatrice prepared, though only Ivory and Ruby caught a glimpse of her as she delivered the hot food to the back door. Afterward, discussing sleeping arrangements, both Ivory and Ruby said they'd be more comfortable away from the big house, which they'd scarcely seen before as slave children. Though Gandy tried to convince them they were welcome to sleep there, they prevailed upon Leatrice and Moses to put them up out back.

Gandy settled Marcus and Jack into one of the four massive second-story bedrooms, Pearl and Jube in another, leaving himself and Willy. Of the two remaining rooms, there was the one he and Delia had shared and the northwest bedroom, which had forever been known as the children's room. After inspecting them both he left the choice to Willy.

"That one." Willy pointed. "It's got a rockin' horse."

Scott, relieved that he need not face sleeping in his familiar rosewood bed without Delia, led Willy into the children's room. Together they turned back the dust covers, shucked down to their underwear, and settled down beneath the dusty coverlets.

"Hey, Scotty?" Willy's voice sounded smaller than ever in the big room when the candle was blown out.

"Hm?"

"I'm cold."

Gandy chuckled and rolled onto his side. "Then get over here."

Willy presented his back and burrowed his posterior into Scott's belly. Coiling an arm around him, Scott couldn't help thinking of Leatrice barking out the word "mosquito." It felt as if Willy had twice as many ribs as other people and half as much fat.

"This is nicer than the storeroom. Mmm . . ."

That was the last sound Scott heard from Willy. In minutes the boy was asleep.

But Scott lay in his childhood bed for hours, feeling Willy's heartbeat beneath his palm, listening to the regularity of his breathing, drawn back to Kansas by Willy's last remark.

He thought about Gussie, the empty town, the emptier saloon. He closed his eyes and pictured her at her sewing machine with Willy's empty stool beside her, limping down the street to eat alone at Paulie's, sitting on the top step in the winter wind, wrapped in her pelisse while snow fell on its hood. But the picture that burned brightest of all was none that he imagined, but one he recalled—Gussie with blood staining her nightgown as she lay in his bed and he kissed her.

He forced his eyes wide, as if attempting to transmute the memory into reality.

But around him pressed only unrelieved blackness. He tried to acclimate himself to its density, but it was difficult to do so. In Kansas there had been streetlamps. On the train the moon had lit the landscape. But here, at Waverley, beneath the giant magnolias and pines and creeping wisteria vines, the blackness was absolute. If there were a ghost, it could surely choose no better place. And if it wanted to make itself known, it could certainly choose no better time. After all, he already felt haunted by Agatha. What was one more ghost?

But none appeared. None spoke. And in the end, Gandy slept fitfully, warmed by Willy's small body.

*   *   *

He awakened early and lay for minutes recalling the past; remembering how his father had begun each day by surveying his domain from the very spot designed for it. That spot drew him irresistibly to follow in his father's footsteps. Quietly, he slipped from bed into his clothing and climbed up the stairs, up past the third floor, whose four closed doors led into the immense windowless attic beneath the main roof. The trunk room, they'd always called it, where Scott had often played with his brothers on rainy days and where members of the family had been isolated whenever they were ill.

He opened a door, unable to resist a peek into the dusky interior, cluttered with furniture, trunks, and flotsam from the past. Somewhere inside, Delia's clothing was stored, and his parents', too, he presumed. Someday he would explore it again, but now he closed the door and continued up the final sweep of stairs until he reached the railed catwalk that circled the octagonal rotunda, overlooking the entry below and the fields outside. Looking down the chain of the massive chandelier, he remembered nights when the doors of the twin parlors had been rolled back, transforming the area below into one vast, impressive ballroom. He and Rafe and Nash would creep from their beds after all the guests had arrived and from high in the shadows of the rotunda would look down upon the colorful hoop skirts of the ladies, while men in swallowtail coats guided them through the sweeping turns of the waltz.

He had a sudden vision of what Agatha's garnet dress would look like from above, with tier upon tier of rear draperies shot by gaslight as she glided across the pine floor below. He saw, too, her hair, neatly coiled up the back of her head, radiating the same red highlights as the taffeta she wore. Odd that he should envision her dancing when she herself had told him it was the one thing she'd always longed to do, but could not.

Whimsy, he chided himself. And useless at that. The problem at hand was figuring out how to make this place productive enough to support eight . . . no, *ten*—he had to include Leatrice and Moses now, too. To bring one more would be sheer stupidity when he'd have difficulty supporting those he already had.

Sighing, he turned to the windows that had once been kept sparkling but were now filmed with dust, their corners mitered by cobwebs. He scraped one aside and it stuck to his finger, trailing the dry husk of a dead mud dauber. Shaking it free, he forced himself to look beyond the disconcerting evidence of neglect to the faded empire that was now his heritage.

He lifted his eyes and there, for as far as he could see, lay Waverley Plantation. But the land that had once been brought to abundance by a thousand black hands now lay lorn and gone to weed.

He walked slowly, sadly, around the eight sides of the rotunda, as his father had done every morning after breakfast, surveying the fiefdom, which in those days had been self-sufficient. To the east the trees opened, forming a great green meadow that dropped in an impressive sweep to the Tombigbee River, visible in the distance. Cattle and sheep used to graze between the house and the river, but none was there now. The solid sheet of green grass was dotted with brush, which in time would give way to solid forest if not cleared. And in the remaining three directions, woods and fields stretched away to infinity, their chief product nothing but a tangled crop of kudzu vine.

How could a mere ten people make it pay?

His morose reflection was interrupted by a small voice echoing softly from below.

"Scotty?"

It was the sprout, standing outside the bedroom door on the opposite side of the rotunda two stories below.

"So you're up." Their voices carried like bells across a valley, though they spoke scarcely above a whisper.

"Whatcha doin' up there?"

"Lookin'."

"Lookin' at what?"

"Come on up. I'll show y'."

He watched Willy climb the impressive staircase, his bare feet padding softly, the trapdoor of his union suit flashing between the banister spindles of the cantilevered balcony.

By the time he reached the catwalk dust lined the edges of his toes.

"Whew!" he puffed, coming up the last step. "What's up here?"

Scott lifted Willy and perched him on an arm. "Waverley." He gestured, walking slowly from window to window. "All that."

"Wow . . ."

"I don't know what t' do with it, though."

"If it's a farm, don't you gotta plant stuff on it?"

It sounded so simple, Gandy chuckled. "Takes a lot of hands t' plant all that."

Willy scratched his head and looked through the dirty window. "Gussie says I'm lucky t' see it. She says there ain't . . . aren't many like it anymore, so I hafta learn t' up . . . up . . ."

"Appreciate?"

"Yeah—appreciate it. She says she wants t' see it someday 'cause she never saw no plantation before. She called it a . . . a way of life. What's that mean, Scotty?"

But Scott wasn't listening to the question, rather to what came before. Almost to himself he murmured, "She wasn't talkin' about the land, she was talkin' about the house."

"The house?" Willy craned his neck to look at the peak of the cupola above them.

"The house . . ." Scott threw a glance at the windows circling him, then at the ballroom floor below, the doors leading off the grandest staircase this side of the Mason-Dixon line.

"That's it!" he exploded.

"Where we goin'?" Willy bounced on Scott's arm as his black boots clattered down the stairs. "Hey, what're you smiling about?"

"The house. That's the answer, and it was so obvious, I overlooked it. Gussie told me the same thing she told you, last summer one night when I told her about Waverley. But I was too busy tryin' t' dream up a way t' raise cotton t' think about usin' the house t' make money."

"You mean you're gonna sell it, Scotty?" Willy asked, disappointed.

"Sell it?" As they reached the trunk-room level, where all those hoop skirts and swallowtail coats waited, Scott planted a loud, smacking kiss on Willy's cheek, but he was too excited to investigate now. "Never, sprout. We're gonna make it live again, and those Yankees who burned down damned near all the places like Waverley will pay a king's ransom t' see and experience one of 'em now. What you see around you, Willy, my boy, is nothin' short of a national treasure!"

They reached the sleeping level and, without breaking stride, Scott banged on doors, bellowing, "Wake up! Daylight in the swamp, everybody! Jack! Marcus! Jube! Pearl! Get up! We have t' get this place back in shape!"

His voice echoed through the rotunda, along with his footsteps, as he ran down the last curving section of stairs to the main entry. Sleepy heads began poking out from doors overhead as Scott, still with Willy on his arm, slammed out the back door.

"You're gonna meet Leatrice," Scott told Willy as they crossed the yard. "She believes in spooks, but other than that, she's all right. Y'all hear any spooks in the house last night?"

"Spooks?" Willy's eyes widened, but he grinned. "Weren't any spooks, were there?"

"I didn't hear none."

"*Any*. Then y'all tell Leatrice so, understand?"

"But why?"

"'Cause we need her to organize those slowpokes back there and make the dust fly. Nobody I know can do that better than Leatrice. Why, if we'd've had her commandin' the Confederate troops, the war would've turned out different!"

"But, Scotty, I'm still wearin' my underwear!"

"No matter. She's seen li'l boys in less."

Willy took to Leatrice like a tick to a warm hide. From the moment she ordered, "Come heah, chile, let Leatrice have a look at you," the bond was sealed. It made sense: she needed someone to fuss over, and he needed fussing. And being introduced to him while he wore only a scratchy woolen union suit endeared the sprout to her forever. The match seemed made in heaven.

But when it came to Scott's decree, she was far less enthusiastic.

"Ain't settin' foot in no house with no hants."

"Tell her, Willy."

Willy told her, but still she pursed her lips and looked mean. "Nuh-uh! Not Leatrice."

"But who's goin' t' get them movin'? The whole bunch is used t' sleepin' till noon. I need you, sweetheart."

At the word, her mouth loosened slightly. "Always was a sweet talkuh," she grumbled.

He went on while he saw her weakening. "And imagine the place full of people again, and music in the ballroom and every bedroom filled, and the old cookhouse fire stoked up and the smell o' sweet-potato pies comin' from the ovens."

She glared at him from the corner of her eye. "Who gonna cook?"

That took him aback. "Well, I . . . I don't know. But we'll think of somethin' when the time comes. First, though, we've got t' get the place waxed and polished again, and the grounds cleared and the outbuildin's cleaned up. What do you say, sweetheart? Will you help me?"

"Gotta think a spell," was all she would concede.

Leatrice thought for exactly four and a half hours. By that time Gandy's troops had arisen, eaten breakfast, and were desultorily following his inept orders. But the work they were producing, and the speed with which they produced it, was so disgraceful that when Leatrice glimpsed the clean-up crew carrying household items out into the yard for airing, she mumbled an imprecation about sweet talkers and threw up her hands.

Minutes later she appeared at the back door wearing an asafetida bag around her neck.

"Can't git dust outta rugs layin' 'em on d' ground," she announced imperiously, standing just inside the door with both hands on her hips. "Gotta git 'em in d' air an' whack 'em! Any fool knows ya don't start widda bottom layuh an' wuhk up. Time ya gits t' de top, d' bottom jiss as dirty as when ya commence."

Gandy came and gave her a grateful hug, but immediately backed off.

"Lord, woman, what've you got in that sack?" Gandy asked, almost gagging. "Smells like cat piss."

"None o' yer lip, boy. It's asafetida, keep de hants off'n Leatrice. You want I teach dose sorry white folk how t' clean, you leave off sass 'bout how I smell."

Gandy grinned and gave a teasing salute. "Yes, ma'am."

And from that moment on, Waverley's speedy, efficient revival was guaranteed.

CHAPTER
18

It was an immense undertaking, turning Waverley into a hotel retreat where Northerners would get the feel of a working plantation. But all the essential elements were there. They only needed dusting off and oiling and waxing and clearing and hoeing and mending.

Gandy's troop started with the rotunda and worked downward, as Leatrice dictated. And dictate she did, in a voice that carried like thunder and made the most dedicated sluggard straighten his spine and get his limbs a-flapping. Still, they could never have handled the massive job without the phenomenon that began the second morning. One by one familiar faces appeared at Waverley's back door—black, all of them, but with expressions telling how eager they were to lend a hand and see Waverley flourish again.

First came Zach, whose father had been a stable hand and had taught Scott all he knew. Zach set to work checking and mending harness, cleaning the old carriages and the stable itself. Then came Beau and his wife, Clarice, who smiled shyly when they greeted LeMaster Gandy, and obeyed without question when Leatrice told them they could begin clearing a spot to make the old vegetable garden bigger. A pair of brothers named Andrew and Abraham headed up a crew that cleared the long lane, and when it was passable, they went on to begin putting the yard and grand front lawn in shape. They trimmed the boxwoods and pruned the camellias and shaped the azalea bushes that had grown wild and rangy throughout the formal gardens. There followed general repairs on all the outbuildings, and thorough cleaning of their insides, where wild animals had nested, metal had rusted, and wood had warped. A black woman named Bertrissa came along and was put to work filling the black iron pot in the yard and beginning the massive job of washing dust covers and bedding. Her man, Caleb, became part of the crew that painted the mansion. Gandy himself headed it up, ordering four new ladders built, then scaling one to do the highest spot—the rotunda—himself. As the men swarmed over the outside of Waverley, the women swarmed inside.

Every drapery was aired and dusted, every inch of decorative brass cornice was polished. Rugs were hung and beaten, some scrubbed by hand. Interior woodwork was painted, floors waxed, windows polished, spindles washed and waxed, as were the decorative lyre inserts on the front sidelights. Every piece of furniture was either aired and beaten or scrubbed and polished. Every dish in the built-in china cabinet was removed from its shelf, washed, and replaced on a freshly lined surface. The closets were whitewashed, the chimneys swept, and the andirons polished until their brass knobs gleamed.

Scott himself checked out the old gasworks and got its burners working again. Ivory took a contingent—including Willy—off into the woods to search out pine lighter, and the evening they lit the jets in the great, gleaming chandelier for the first time they had a small celebration. Marcus played the banjo and Willy the harmonica. The girls danced around the ballroom floor, while the others sat on the stairs watching and teased them about soon having to give up the rowdy cancan in favor of the sedate mazurka, which would be more fitting for entertaining Northerners who would be paying a great deal of money to pretend they were elite Southern planters for a week or two.

There was business to attend to also. While the work crews continued, Scott drafted an advertisement to send to Northern newspapers, announcing the opening of Waverley Plantation to the public in March, the month of camellias. He made a trip to Memphis to secure a list of the country's one hundred most wealthy industrialists and sent personal letters of invitation to each. His idea bore quick results. Within two weeks he received reservation money from several who claimed their wives would be exceedingly grateful to escape the rigorous Northern climate and shorten the winter by spending its last weeks in the mellow atmosphere described by Gandy's advertisement.

It was a happy day when Scott purchased a reservations book bound in rich green leather, and along with it a ledger in which he logged the first income Waverley had made in well over eighteen years.

He'd taken as his office the same lower-level room his father had used for that purpose, the one just behind the front parlor. It was a bright, cheerful room with ceiling-to-floor jib windows that opened from the bottom up to provide a cool draft during the hot weather when the rotunda windows were opened high above. Now the jib windows remained closed, however, fronted by sea-green jacquard tiebacks that brought the color of verdant things into the room during this season when little grew. The walls were white plaster, as was the ceiling with its decorative sculptured work matching the moldings at the tops of the walls. No dominating bookshelves lined the wall; instead, the room was decorated with a set of mahogany shell-carved furniture: blockfront highboy, secretary, and flattop desk, and an assortment of upholstered wingchairs of rich taupe leather. The varnished pine floor held an Oriental rug with a pale pink dogwood design on a background of ice-green. The fireplace, with its decorative iron liner, kept the room cozy even when coals scarcely glowed.

Scott Gandy loved the office. He recalled his father sitting behind the mahogany desk, running the affairs of the plantation as he himself did now. Here, with pen and ledger in hand, he felt again a sense of continuity, but more—one of indomitable optimism.

The day he received the first advance deposits, he entered them in the books, stubbed out his cheroot, and went seeking Willy, determined to fulfill the promise he'd made to the boy before they'd left Kansas—to buy him a horse of his own. He charged through the house, calling, but it was a quiet afternoon, and if anybody was about, no one was answering. Scott took the stairs two at a time and charged into the children's room, which he still shared with Willy. But the boy wasn't napping, nor was he anywhere to be seen.

"Willy?" he called, stopping beside the bed with its ecru crocheted spread and matching tester.

It was then that he heard it—the soft whimpering of a child's voice and the single word, more a sigh than a cry: "Heeelp."

"Willy?" Scott spun about, but behind him the doorway was empty. The recently waxed floor gleamed, reflecting the unblinking eye of the rocking horse, the only one looking on.

"Heeelp." The word came again, soft, pleading, from behind him. He whirled and stared at the bed. The coverlet was rumpled, where a moment ago it had been smooth. He stared at the impression of a small body.

"Willy? Are you there?"

But it wasn't Willy's voice; it wasn't Willy's imprint. It was Justine's, Scott was certain. He waited, his eyes resting on the slight depression. The soft whimper sounded again, as if from the spot, but it brought no sense of fear or doom, only a strong wish to be able to ease whatever care it voiced.

The presence departed as suddenly as it had come, leaving Scott feeling certain he was again alone in the room. He felt helpless and guilty, as if he should have helped. But how?

He searched the other upstairs rooms, but all were empty, as were those on the lower level. At last he found Leatrice, out in the cookhouse in a rocking chair beside the fire with Clarice and Bertrissa, husking dried peas.

"Where's Willy?" he asked perfunctorily.

"Gone wid d' men."

"Where?"

"Out to d' woods someplace, puttin' up cordwood."

"How long have they been gone?"

"Lef' right aftuh breffus," she replied disinterestedly.

"Where are the women?"

"Down t' d' cabins, cleanin'."

* * *

Scott told no one about his encounter with the ghost, but the following day, when he took Zach and Willy to a stock auction, at which he hoped to bid on carriage horses and a pony for the boy, his mind was often distracted from the business at hand.

"Willy," he inquired in an offhanded manner while they strolled the barns, checking out horseflesh, "did y'all go out t' the woods yesterday right after breakfast?"

"Yup."

"And did ya come back t' the house before dinner?"

"Nope."

"Y' didn't take a nap in your room?"

"Nope."

"Had Leatrice made up your bed before y' left?"

"Nope."

So it hadn't been Willy's imprint on the coverlet. Then whose?

"Oh, lookit that one! That's the one I want. Can I have 'im, Scotty? Can I?" Willy's excitement and Zach's examination of a one-year-old strawberry roan gelding ended Gandy's speculation and forced him to turn his attention to the selection of Waverley's horseflesh.

He trusted Zach's judgment completely and when the day was over had bought the strawberry roan for the boy—"His name's gonna be Major," Willy declared—a team of skewbald carriage horses, and two full-grown riding horses—a stallion named Prince and a mare named Sheba.

It became a common sight after that to see Willy hanging around the stables, like a tick on Zach's pantleg, watering the horses, bombarding him with questions, bringing sweets from the house for Major, then turning circles in the middle of the corral as Zach taught him how to work the horse on a longe line.

Scott had almost forgotten the incident in the children's room until one day when he was heading up to the trunk room to check out the clothing he planned to disinter. As he passed the door of the bedroom, he heard Willy inside, talking to somebody. He backed up and glanced into the room. Willy sat on the floor, ankles out, build-

ing a tower of wood blocks, conversing with absolutely
nobody.

" . . . and Gussie, she lives in Kansas, where I used t'
live. She gots my cat. His name is Moose. Gussie's gonna
come for Christmas an' Zach says we're gonna shoot us a
wild turkey for Christmas dinner."

"Willy, who are you talkin' to?" Scott peered inside
curiously.

"Oh, hey, Scotty," Willy greeted, glancing over his shoulder before adding another block to his tower.

"Who were y'all talking to just now?"

"Justine," the boy answered levelly, then hummed several notes of "Oh! Susanna."

"Justine?"

"Uh-huh. She comes an' plays with me sometimes when
it's rainin' outside an' I hafta stay in."

Scott glanced at the windowpanes. A steady wash ran
over them, obscuring everything beyond. He moved into
the room and hunkered down beside Willy, bracing his
elbows on his knees.

"My daughter, Justine?"

"Uh-huh. She's nice, Scotty."

Scott experienced his first moment of fear, not because
the house might be haunted—after all, he was a reasonable
man who didn't believe in ghosts, did he?—but because
Willy seemed to believe this ghost was mortal.

"Justine's dead, Willy."

"I know. But she likes it here. Sometimes she comes
back for a visit."

Scott glanced around uncertainly. Willy's tower toppled
and he started rebuilding it, all the while humming happi-
ly. "Y' know the little cemetery across the road?" Scott
inquired.

"Sure. I been there with Andrew and Abraham when
they cut the grass and cleaned it up."

This was news to Scott, though he disguised his surprise
and went on. "Then you know Justine is buried there."

"I know," Willy replied blithely.

"If she's buried there, she can't come back here t' play
with you. It's just your imagination, Willy."

"She only comes t' this room. It used t' be hers."

Scott had never before disclosed the fact to Willy, though the sprout was certainly bright enough to associate a rocking horse with a nursery.

"Have you told Leatrice you've talked t' Justine?"

Willy laughed, a musical sound like the quick chatter of a tambourine. "Leatrice'd roll her eyes and run like a snake was loose, wouldn't she?"

Scott smiled and laughed, too. But then he turned thoughtful. "If y'all don't mind, son, let's not tell Leatrice about it. She's got enough on her mind, runnin' the place."

"All right," Willy returned, apparently unconcerned about the credibility of his experience.

"And one more thing." Scott stood and gazed at the top of Willy's head. "Who told you Gussie was comin' for Christmas?"

"You said I could see her sometime."

"But she's not comin' for Christmas, son."

"But, why not?" Willy lifted disappointed brown eyes and Scott groped for an answer.

"She just isn't, that's all."

"But, why not?"

"Because the house is crowded now until the cabins are ready. And we're all busy gettin' things ready for guests. There's a lot t' be done yet."

"But you said—"

"I'm sorry, Willy, the answer is no."

Willy leveled his tower with one angry sweep. "You lied! You said she could come!"

"Willy, that's enough!" Scott spun and stalked from the room, scowling, angered by the boy's insistence. Why not, indeed! Because Agatha was a complication Scott didn't need in his life right now. Because if he saw her again, saying good-bye would hurt worse than the first time. Because if Willy saw her again, there would be more tears and heartache when the two of them parted.

Besides, he had enough on his mind trying to reconcile himself to the fact that the house was being visited by a ghost. Common sense said it couldn't be Justine.

*　　*　　*

But three nights later, Scott was roused from a restless sleep by the impression of a voice echoing through the dark. His eyes seemed at first sealed, as if with wax, as he tried to open them. Someone was whimpering. Sad, childish whimpering. He must help . . . must help . . . must drag himself from this nether state . . . this drifting, misty cloud world . . .

The whimpering grew louder. His eyes opened. The room was pitch black.

"Heeelp . . ." a sorrowful voice beseeched.

Scott came awake as if thunder had struck. He braced up and leaned over Willy. But the child lay on his side with both hands softly curled in sleep, his breathing as regular as the beat of a metronome.

Again came the whimper, closer.

Scott braced up on both hands, peering into the dark. "Who's there?"

The whimper approached and brought the soft brush of breath on his cheek while he sat stock-still. A scent filled the room, unidentifiable, floral.

He tried to pierce the darkness with his eyes. Nothing moved. No shadow or pale image. Only the sound, pitiful, pleading, a girlish whimper, and the plea again, "Heeelp."

"Justine?" he whispered, glancing left and right.

A movement on the blanket over his chest, as if someone was running a hand over it, searching for the binding, as if to turn it down and get beneath the covers.

"Justine, is that you?"

The sound quieted but the scent remained.

"We're in your bed . . . is that it?" The room grew hushed, the silence broken only by the sound of Willy's regular breathing. Again Scott sensed no dire intentions from the presence, only a restlessness he longed to calm.

"Justine?"

It was winter, the windows and veranda door were closed, yet a soft breeze seemed to sigh through the room, whisking away the scent and the presence.

Scott sat up straighter, reached out a hand, and touched . . . nothing.

"Justine?"

Willy stirred beside him, snuffled, then rolled over. The presence was gone.

Scott fell back, lifting the covers to his armpits, running a hand over them, staring at the ceiling in the ink-black night. Who else could it have been? And if she'd meant them any harm, wouldn't she have related it somehow? He closed his eyes, thinking of her as a beautiful, dark-haired baby. *Justine, my daughter, how we wanted and loved you. You remember, don't you?*

He closed his eyes, but opened them momentarily to find himself restless and mystified, but no longer disbelieving.

As Christmas approached, Scott temporarily forgot about the ghostly visitations, while Willy began pressuring harder and harder to have Agatha at Waverley for the holiday or to go there. "But I miss her," he whined, as if that was the only thing required to bring about the granting of his wishes.

"I know you do, Willy, but I don't have time t' take you t' Kansas on the train, and you're too young t' go alone."

"You said I could!" Willy became obstinate, stuck out his lip, and stamped his foot. "You said I'd be able t' go see her whenever I wanted to."

Scott grew impatient. "You're twistin' my words around, boy. I never said you could go whenever you wanted. Lord sakes, it's only been a little over a month since you saw her."

"I don't care. I wanna see Gussie!" Willy put on his most repugnant face and enormous tears rolled over his eyelids. Scott had the distinct impression Willy had conjured them up on command. The damned little nuisance had never acted so demanding before.

"I don't know what's come over you, boy, that you think you can go around stampin' your feet and pushin' out your lip t' try t' get your way, but it won't work with me, so let's have an end to it, y' hear?"

Willy stormed out of Scott's office and slammed the door so hard the overhead light danced on its chain.

"What the hell's got into him?" Scott muttered.

*   *   *

Four days before Christmas Willy received a gift from
Gussie—a hand-made stuffed goose fashioned of soft white
flannel with an orange felt beak and embroidered eyes.
Willy again made demands, ending with another angry
exchange between himself and Scott before the boy ran
off crying. Scott glared at the door, then reached to the
floor for Agatha's note, which Willy had dropped. He read
it glumly. It was exclusively for Willy, with the exception
of the brief closing in which she'd added:

> Tell everybody hello from me and wish them all the
> merriest Christmas. Scott, too.

Scott, too—as if he were nothing more to her than an
afterthought. The idea raised a rage in him he didn't quite
understand and could not seem to quell.

Christmas of 1880 should have been one of the happiest
of his life. After all, he was back at Waverley. The mansion
was festooned with holly and mistletoe and every fireplace
was ablaze. The place gleamed with beeswax and bustled
with life. Zach had shot a wild turkey and Leatrice was
preparing it with chestnut stuffing and all the trimmings,
just as she had in the old days.

But Scott spent the holidays listless and bitter, slouched
in a leather chair in the front parlor, sipping eggnog and
staring despondently at the wedding alcove. He had everyone he loved around him, didn't he? Yet his mind wandered
back to a weatherbeaten clapboard building on a frozen mud
street in Kansas where the wind howled and the snow flew
and a woman without one soul to call her own spent the
holiday alone in a narrow, dark, cheerless apartment.

In January, Willy grew more cantankerous and demanding each day. He cried almost every night for Agatha and
spent more time talking to "Justine." Scott thought a friend
might help, so he took Willy into town to meet Mae Ellen
Bayles's grandson, A.J. But the two boys didn't get along
at all, and Scott's impatience with Willy grew.

In February, Scott and the women finally got around
to sorting out the collection of clothing in the attic. They

unearthed a veritable gold mine of dresses that the girls could wear to lend an air of authenticity when dancing in the ballroom with the paying guests. But none was generous enough for Jube's breasts, and when she tried altering one, she ruined it completely.

Scott's caustic remarks made everyone lay low for days afterward.

The stables were spotless, the stalls filled with enough horses to provide transit to and from the train depot and enough for the guests' pleasure riding, too. The equipage had been oiled and, where necessary, replaced. The ice house was stocked with ice, which had been transported from town after arriving on a freight car packed in sawdust. The smokehouse spouted a slow stream of hickory smoke. Two dozen Rhode Island reds pecked about in a screened pen, and a pair of black-and-white cows kept the front meadow evenly groomed and the table supplied with milk and butter. Even the ancient, creaking ferry had been rejuvenated, the idea being to take the guests across the river to picnic on the other side. And, as a final touch, Scott had found a pair of peacocks to adorn the emerald lawn. Everything was perfect . . .

Everything but Scott. He was fractious and unbearable. Not a person in the house could look at him crosswise without getting snapped at. He stalked around with his heels clomping on the hardwood floors, as if to warn everybody to get out of his way. He snapped at the men and glared at the women and told Leatrice if she didn't get rid of that "stinkin' piss bag" her neck was going to rot off.

Scott blamed his sore temper on Willy.

Willy was turning into an obnoxious brat! Probably from hanging around Leatrice so much and picking up her officious ways. His grammar was deteriorating into a deplorable state and occasionally he let fly with an unconscious profanity, learned from the girls, who didn't always guard their tongues around him as they should. Everybody spoiled him abominably, and when Scott crossed him he grew surly or mouthy or both. He had turned six in January and belonged in school, but short of taking him into town every day, there was no way to facilitate lessons, and nobody around the place was inclined to take up tutoring him or even to teach him to pick up after himself. When Scott ordered him to do so, Willy charged away and declared Leatrice would make up his bed or pick up his clothes.

Then one day the girls ruined another dress. When Scott heard the news he stomped into the downstairs parlor, which doubled as a sewing room, and lashed out at them.

"Dammit! How many dresses do you think I can dig outta that attic! If Agatha were here *she* wouldn't have made mincemeat o' this one!"

It was Jube who hurled back what they'd all been thinking. "Well, if Agatha can do them better, get Agatha! It's what's been under your skin ever since you left Kansas anyway, isn't it?"

Gandy's face turned formidable. His cheekbones seemed to grow sharp, his mouth thin, and his eyes deadly as rapiers. He pointed a finger at Jube's nose.

"You'd better watch yourself, Jube," he growled.

"Well, isn't it?" She thrust her face toward him and put both of her hands on her hips.

Gandy's jaw locked and a muscle twitched in his left cheek. "Y' know, you can be put off this place," he warned in an ugly voice.

"Oh, sure, as if that would solve your problem!"

He spun toward the door. "I don't know what the hell you're talkin' about!"

"I'm talking about one Miss Agatha Downing." She caught his elbow and spun him back. "You've been like a bear ever since you left her and it's getting worse."

He threw back his head and let out a sharp barking laugh. "Agatha Downin'. Ha!" He glared at Jube and spat out, "You're crazy! Agatha Downin', that . . . that prissy little milliner?"

"But of course you'd be too bull-headed to admit it."

He jerked his arm from her grip. "Since when am I bullheaded, Jubilee Bright?"

"Since when am I a seamstress, LeMaster Scott Gandy?" She kicked the dress that lay puffed on the floor, then swung on him with combat in her eyes. "You know, we've been working our private skin off around here, scrubbing floors and waxing wood—you wanna know how many spindles are in that damned railing out there?" Jube pointed at the hall. "Seven hundred eighteen, that's how many! We know, because *we're* the ones who oiled them! Your old slaves come back to help—fine, we appreciate the help—and we do what we're told and go out to make the cabins livable again. And we peel onions when Leatrice says peel, and wash bedding when Leatrice says wash, and we polish brass when Leatrice says polish. And now Ivory's got some addle-pated idea about all of us planting a cotton crop in one of the near fields this spring, just to lend a little touch of the pre-war South to this place. Well, I did all that, and I'll probably end up planting cotton, too. But I don't know possum-squat about sewing dresses, LeMaster Gandy!" She poked him in the chest. "And you'd best remember it!" Spinning away, she gave the dress a vicious kick, then fell to a nearby slipper sofa. Leaning back on both elbows, she caught one foot behind a knee, jutting out her breasts. "I'm an ex-prostitute, Gandy. Sometimes I think you forget that. I'm used to working in a reclinin' position in clothes that take a lot less upkeep than that." Her voice turned silky with challenge. "I'll wear it, honey, but you better get somebody else to make it fit me. And if that somebody is Agatha Downing, all the better. Maybe she'd have a sweetening influence on your sour temper."

Ruby sat in a nearby chair, legs crossed, one foot swinging, one magnificent eyebrow raised higher than the other. Pearl sat equally indolently, ignoring the dress she'd been working on when Scott entered.

He had never before seen three more ornery ex-prostitutes. They were harder than a ten-year drought. As his glance shot to the dress Pearl had discarded, he knew he'd be powerless against them as long as they all stuck together.

With a throaty curse he stalked from the room.

It was a day late in February with spring sending out feelers. Zach had turned out to be as adept a farrier as his father, and he was teaching not only Willy, but Marcus, too, all he knew about horses. Marcus had discovered he loved working with the animals. Like him, they were voiceless. But they conveyed messages just the same. Today the little two-year-old mare, Sheba, was anxious to get outside and kick up her heels. The staid pair of skewbald carriage horses blinked lazily in the sun that streamed through the window as he brought them water. And Scott's restless stallion, Prince . . . well, he had other things in mind. His sap was up. His nostrils flared. His ears stood straight and his chestnut tail arched at the whinny of Cinnamon, the brand-new mare Scotty had just bought, who was prancing around the paddock outside and tossing her head in invitation.

Four o'clock, Zach had said, as soon as Scott came back from town, where he'd taken the boy visiting while he checked the price of cotton seed.

It won't be long now, Prince, Marcus thought and wished he could say it to the impatient stallion, whose phallus was already partially distended and hung beneath him thick as a man's arm.

"Marcus?"

He jumped and spun toward the door. Jube stood in the flood of light wearing a blue dress as plain as any housemaid would wear. Her white hair was caught up in a loose drooping fold. A knit shawl was looped around her shoulders.

He raised a hand in greeting and hurried toward her, hoping to detain her at the far end of the barn away from Prince with his glistening member exposed.

"I was looking for you." Her face was somber as he halted before her, blocking her path.

She looked beautiful, with loose hair at her temples and her mouth soft. His heart hastened as he silently adored her.

"Can we talk?" she asked.

He loved her for saying things like that—as if he were no different from other men. He nodded and she took his arm and began sauntering along the stalls, eyes downcast. "I had a fight with Scott yesterday." Marcus stopped, frowned in question, and waggled a hand, catching her eye. She went on quietly. "We've never had a fight before, but this one has been brewing for a long time. It was over a dress I ruined when I was trying to alter it. Only it wasn't really over that at all. It was over Agatha." At his surprised expression, she laughed softly, then took his arm and sauntered on. "Yes, *that* Agatha. I think he's in love with her but he won't admit it to himself, so he's driving the rest of us crazy. Haven't you noticed how grouchy he's been lately? And how he's driving us? Well, I, for one, have had enough of it. I told him in rather unladylike terms that I'm not used to working as hard as he's asked us to lately. I told him I think he should bring her here and maybe it would make him more bearable."

Marcus squeezed Jube's arm. He pointed to Kansas, then to the spot where they stood.

"Yes, here." She lifted her face and placed her hands on his elbows. "Marcus, you've never asked, but I'm going to tell you. It's over between Scott and me. It has been since before we left Kansas. Does that make a difference to you?"

He swallowed and felt his face flood with heat, and his heart started slamming.

"I think you're too honorable to make a move toward me as long as you think Scott has any prior claims." Once the words were spoken she became self-conscious. Her cheeks grew bright and she tossed her shoulders, moving unconsciously toward Prince's stall. "Oh, Marcus, I know it's not my place to say this, but if I wait until—"

He lunged and grabbed her elbow before she could see into the stall. Her head swung around and their eyes clashed. Tightening his grip, he shook his head—an order.

"No?" she verbalized. "Don't say it? But, why? One of us has to."

His eyes darted from her to the stall and back. He shook his head more adamantly, unsure of how to make her understand it wasn't her words to which he objected.

"What?" She looked back over her shoulder and got a clear shot of the stall and the stallion within. "Oh!" she exclaimed, and her eyes widened.

Prince reared and pawed, his member bouncing lustily. Jube and Marcus stood locked in a moment of embarrassment so intense it seemed to stir the very air around them, lifting dust motes that drifted through the oblique shafts of light falling through the barn.

Then Zach spoke from the doorway and they leaped apart. "Better keep away from that stall. Horse like that's dangerous when he smells a mare in heat."

Suddenly, Scott followed Zach around the corner, entering the barn at a brisk clip, his mind obviously on the business at hand. "Better let him out, Zach. No sense gettin' the stall kicked apart. Marcus, Jube," he added, offhandedly, "if you're goin' t' watch y'all better get outside beyond the paddock fence. When he comes out he'll be in a hurry."

Marcus and Jube moved outside and stood at a white-washed fence—apart from the others who'd come down from the house to watch, too. The aroused stallion, Prince, came trotting down the stone rampway into the paddock, his tail arched and streaming like a willow in the wind, his mighty head held high, the nostrils dilated. He halted a good distance from Cinnamon, forelegs locked, eyes turbulent. Mare and stallion stood face to face, unmoving, for what seemed like minutes. He snorted once. She turned away. As if enraged by her indifference, he raised his head and trumpeted long and loud, then shook his head until his mane flew.

The sound brought a question from Willy, who sat on the fence while Scott stood behind him, an arm loosely circling the boy. "Why'd he do that, Scotty?"

"He's callin' her. They're goin' t' mate now, you watch. It's how foals get started in the mare's womb."

At the moment it appeared as if nothing would get started anywhere. Cinnamon remained aloof. At the far end of the paddock she pranced back and forth, as far as the fence would allow. Each time she turned it was with a lunge and a dip that tossed her mane aloft. Haughty yet restless, she stood Prince off, racking back and forth along the fence.

He snorted, pawed the soft earth, bobbed his majestic head and, with it, his majestic phallus.

She turned her rump on him, her vaulted tail exposing her swollen genitals, already glistening. Her scent reached him, strong and hot, and his nostrils pulsated, his hide quivered.

Six steps he took before she swung on him in warning. As he halted, his distended organ dipped as if mounted upon strong springs. She shifted left. He shifted with her. She shifted right. He thwarted her once again. Imperiously, he came on, lord to lady, sire to dame.

She would have none of it and, with a quick snort and lunge, shot around him, biting his flank as she sprinted away.

At his grunt, she turned and they eyed each other from opposite ends of the enclosure, standing erect and well matched, their dark hides gleaming in the late-afternoon sun, tails now still. A pair of neon-blue dragonflies hovered in tandem over the paddock as if showing the horses what to do.

Again Prince advanced, one cautious step at a time. This time she whinnied, raising her nose to the air, waiting, waiting, until he neared, nosing her hindquarters. His head dropped and she stood her ground just long enough for Prince to fill his nostrils. Then she turned and nipped him again before dancing away.

Those who watched felt the tension, drawn to its peak. Every palm along the fence was damp, every spine tense. As in human nature, there was a point beyond which the female could taunt no longer without arousing the male beyond endurance. When he rounded on Cinnamon again, Prince was engorged to startling proportions as he moved in for the coup.

Enough of this high-flown loftiness, madame, his approach seemed to say. *The time is here.*

He stalked in, indomitable, masterful, and caught her in a corner. After all the evasiveness she'd displayed earlier, Cinnamon's surrender was surprisingly accommodating. She stood as still as the earth itself, only her eyes shifting to follow Prince as he made his final overture. Their velvet noses nearly touched. The coarse hairs on their nostrils fluttered as they blew upon each other like bellows. Then he trotted around behind her and reared only once while she stood docile, waiting. His root found its sleek target and his powerful forelegs circled her sides as he immersed himself to the groin.

She called out at the moment of impact, a high vaulting screech that seemed to quake the budding trees in the orchard and lift shivers on every human hide within range.

There was a wondrous elemental majesty to their mating. It was felt deeply by Marcus and Jube, leaving them exquisitely aroused. They stood with their forearms lining the top rail of the fence, elbows touching, watching the mounting stud and grunting mare before them. Never had they been so aware of each other.

In a life filled with many occasions when arousal had been demanded, Jubilee had experienced none so extreme as the one that gripped her now. In a life filled with few such occasions, Marcus found himself in a similar predicament. As Prince had caught the scent of Cinnamon, Marcus caught the scent of Jube. From the spot where their elbows touched, a current seemed to sizzle to their extremities. He wanted her with a force as primal as Prince's. But if he approached her now, would she think it was nothing more than lust aroused in him by the horses? If only he could say to her, *It's not just because of them, Jube, it's because I've loved you for longer than you'd ever guess.* If only he could say to her, *I want solace of heart as well as body, and I believe you're the only one I can find that with.* If only he could say, *Jube, Jube, I love you more than any man has ever loved you and I can overlook them all, all the ones who pleasured you first and undoubtedly better than I.*

But he could say none of these things. His heart was locked within a voiceless body and he could only stand beside the woman he loved and throb.

Prince's seed was sown. He emerged from Cinnamon glistening, wet, leaving vestiges of their intercourse on her sheeny rump.

Pearl left the fence and ambled toward the house with Leatrice. Jack wandered off toward the woodpile. Ivory and Ruby went in opposite directions. Zach moved off toward his cabin. Gandy lifted Willy off the fence and took him away, answering questions. One by one they left until only Jube and Marcus remained.

Their silence was strained.

"I'll help you with whatever you were doing in the barn," Jubilee offered.

She turned and he followed at her shoulder as she sauntered toward the barn, wondering if he'd make a move at last. She'd made it as plain as the blue sky above that she had feelings for him and wanted him in every sense of the word, but he was shy and, in all likelihood, put off by her debauched past. Walking with him, she rued it.

There were ways—blatant ways—to touch a man, to entice him. She knew them all. But because she did, she didn't want to use them on Marcus. When and if they came together, she wanted it to be because of love, not just lust. And she wanted *him* to be the one to make the first advance.

The barn was quiet. Only the lazy dust motes drifted in the aisle between the stalls. It smelled of leather and hay and the pleasant fecundity that permeated old wood even years after horses were gone.

Jube stopped in the aisle with Marcus behind her. He watched her chin drop, the fine strands of her angel hair caught on the collar of her blue dress, the distortion of her crocheted shawl as she tightened it with knotted fists. In the rafters above their heads a pair of blue-winged swallows with apricot breasts fluttered about, building a mud nest.

"Marcus?" Her voice came, soft and pained. "Is it because I've been a prostitute?"

Is that what she thought? Oh, that she should have been laboring under the impression that it mattered to him.

He pivoted her by the shoulders and waved his hands before her eyes, shaking his head passionately. *No, Jube, no. It's because . . . because . . .* The ache in his body was nothing compared to his ache to put voice to all he felt. *Because I love you.*

When he told her, the motions were hard, muscular, tempered by a condensed anger at the slight that life had handed him. He touched his breast, thumped a fist on his own heart, and touched a fingertip to hers: *I love you.* He gestured wildly, as if to erase all they'd witnessed in the paddock—not that, this. Again he gestured: *I . . . love . . . you.*

She was in his arms so fast she knocked him a step backward. On tiptoe, she kissed him, flattening her body against his, even as his arms drew her close where he'd wanted her so long. And the tongue that could not speak spoke volumes as it learned the interior of her mouth. And the hands that had become the conveyor of his messages conveyed the most important one of all as they clasped her against his hammering heart, caressing her back, her waist, her head. She drew away and held his cheeks in both hands, her eyes intense and dark.

"Marcus, Marcus, I love you, too. Why did you wait so long to say it? I've loved you since that day of the picnic, maybe even before that."

He wished he could laugh, could know the heady release of the sound against her silky hair. Instead, he kissed her. Again and again and again—a league of impatient strokes that told her all he felt. And while they kissed, his hand fell to her breast, adoring, caressing. Hers stroked his hair, his back, his waist. He found buttons at her nape, freed them, and slipped a hand inside against her smooth skin. Her hands stroked his spine and, lower, until their bodies began moving against each other.

He loves me! she marveled. *Marcus really loves me.*

She loves me! he rejoiced. *Jube really loves me.*

But he wouldn't take her here in a stable, as if they, too, were merely animals in heat. She deserved better, and so did he, after all the time they'd waited.

Gripping her shoulders, he pushed her from him. Much like Prince's, his nostrils were dilated, his eyes turbulent. Much like Cinnamon, Jube stood docile, waiting, her lips open, the breath rushing between them in short, hard beats.

He pointed to a vacant stall and slashed the air with his hand—*not here, not like this.* He whipped her around and rebuttoned her dress, tucked two loose pins into her hair, then hauled her toward the door before she realized his intentions. With masterful footsteps and a firm grip on her hand, he led her across the beaten grass from the barn to the yard, along the worn wagon track past outbuildings, beside the formal gardens and the strutting peacocks, who lifted their heads to watch the couple pass. Up the back steps they went, across the deep veranda, and into the vast hall, where their footsteps echoed as they mounted the stairs.

Scotty stepped from his office, reading a letter. "Oh, Marcus, would you mind . . ."

The question died on his lips. His astounded eyes followed the pair, their footsteps reverberating from the magnificent staircase as Marcus tugged Jube along behind him. She glanced over her shoulder at Scotty—helplessly—and blushed to the roots of her hair. Then they disappeared above the turn of stairs and Gandy retreated quietly inside his office, closed the door, and smiled to himself.

Upstairs, Marcus took Jube straight to his room—the one he shared with Jack. He deposited her inside and without ado gripped an enormous armoire that appeared as if it would take Herculean strength to be budged. He slid it in front of the door as if it were a toy. But the screech echoed all through the house.

He turned, panting, and found a teasing smile on her face.

"You've scratched the freshly waxed floor," she said softly. "Leatrice will make us do it again."

His answer was to undo two shirt buttons, then jerk the tails from his pants before crossing the room to lift her off her feet. He carried her to the spooled bed and fell with her onto the soft coverlets. With his first kiss his hand found her breast, and before it ended he lay pressing her into the deep tick. As his body lay stretched upon hers, Jube learned that nothing had been lost between the barn and this room.

The only love Marcus had ever known had been bought. But this . . . this by some miracle had been won. With each caress he showed her how he prized her. His Jube, his beautiful, unattainable Jube, attainable, after all. She murmured in his ear, pouring out for both of them the words only one could say. He spoke with his roaming hands, his idolizing mouth, his eloquent eyes. When their clothing lay strewn, he worshipped her duly. Other men had words at their disposal, words that they might employ at will to seduce and tantalize. Because he had none, Marcus used only his body.

But he used it so adroitly that Jube heard his voice in each lingering touch.

Jube, my beautiful Jube. How I love your hair, your skin, your eyes, your dark lashes, darling nose, beautiful lips, soft neck, your breasts, the mole between them, the shadow beneath them, your white, white stomach, and this . . . this, too, Jube . . . ahhh, Jube . . .

Many times in her past she had produced counterfeit ardor, but with Marcus, sham was not necessary. What she felt for him turned this act, for the first time ever, into one of love.

And when he rose above her and linked their bodies with a single smooth stroke, it was as foregone as the mating of the swallows in the rafters, the dragonflies in midair, the horses in the paddock.

When it was over and the tumult had been reached and moved beyond, they rested with their sweating brows touching. Jack tried the door and went away grumbling, and the smell of freshly fried hush puppies drifted up from the dining room below, and Leatrice's voice thundered out a warning that they were late for supper, and they laughed into each other's eyes and draped their spent arms over each other. Then Marcus knew they were not like Prince and Cinnamon. They could not separate and trot their individual ways as if this meant little more than the sating of animal drives.

Excited, he scrambled off the bed, leaving Jube so suddenly she shrieked and clutched herself. He had to ask her now, quickly, before they even went down to supper. He rummaged frantically for a pencil and paper—through the armoire, the pockets of his discarded jacket, two drawers, the top of a refectory table between the windows. Finally, impatiently, he thrust the fire screen aside and found a chunk of charcoal, pushed Jube off the far side of the bed, threw back the coverlets, and wrote on the rumpled bottom sheet:

Will you—

"Marcus, what are you doing! Leatrice will behead you!"

marry me?

She stared at the question, so shocked her wide eyes seemed to tilt nearly to her hairline.

"Will I marry you?" she read, amazed.

He nodded, blue eyes bright, certain, blond hair mussed.

"When?"

He wrote on the sheet, underlining emphatically:

NOW!

"But what about a minister and a dress and a wedding feast and a—"

He landed on his knees in the middle of the bed, covering the word *marry*, grabbing her arms and tugging Jube to her knees before him. His eyes evoked a wondrous thump from her heart before he slammed his mouth down on hers and kissed her with the same authority he'd used when marching her up the stairs forty-five minutes ago.

He drew back, his unrelenting eyes holding her as forcefully as his grip upon her elbows.

"Yes!" she rejoiced, throwing her arms around his neck. "Yes, oh, yes, Marcus, I'll marry you. But in two weeks. Please, Marcus. I've never been courted before and I think I'm going to love it."

He kissed her again, starting hard, ending soft, wondering if joy this great could be fatal.

They were so late for dinner the hush puppies were all gone. Leatrice waddled around the table, collecting plates and scowling. She came to a halt at the sight of them careening to a breathless halt inside the dining room doorway, their faces shining with joy.

Scott looked up over his coffee cup and met Jube's eyes. Everyone else turned watermelon-pink and took a sudden interest in the crumbs on the tablecloth.

Where Marcus had towed Jube earlier, she now took the lead. Clutching his hand, she looked squarely at Gandy and announced, "Marcus and I are going to get married."

Six heads snapped up in surprise. Gandy set down his cup.

"In two weeks," Jube added quickly.

Every eye turned to Gandy, gauging his reaction.

A slow grin climbed his cheeks. When it reached his eyes and dimpled his face, the tension eased from the room.

"Well, it's about time," he drawled.

Jube catapulted into his arms. "Oh, Scotty, I'm so happy."

"And I'm happy for you."

He shook hands with Marcus and clapped him on the back, while Jube was passed around for hugs. When the congratulations ended, Scott stood with an arm around Jube's waist again. "I insist that the nuptials be spoken in the weddin' alcove," he told her.

Jube looked Gandy square in the eye and threw him into one of the major emotional upheavals of his life by declaring, "And I insist on inviting Agatha to the wedding."

CHAPTER
19

Oh, that winter, that endless unmitigated winter while Agatha's aloneness smote her daily. She had been alone before, but never as mercilessly as this. Before the advent of Scott, Willy, and Gandy's extended family into her life, her aloneness had been pacific. She had learned to accept the fact that her life would be a string of invariable days whose zeniths and nadirs fluctuated so minimally as to be almost indistinguishable, one from the other. She had learned to accept the blandness, the orderliness, the conformity. And the lovelessness.

Then *they* had come, bringing music and confusion and nonconformity and laughter. In terms of a lifetime, their presence had lasted but a brief heart flash, a few measly months out of years and years of solitariness. But in terms of living, she'd condensed more emotional vitality into those numbered days than she would experience in the remainder of her life, she was sure. Having lost it—and them—she was doomed to be forever aching.

Oh, the dullness after they were gone. The dullness had teeth and talons. It tore at her. She would never again be reconciled to it.

Sunset was the worst, that time of day between occupation and preoccupation, the time of long shadows and kindling lanterns when merchants drew their shades, women set their tables, and broods gathered in kitchens where warm fires glowed, fathers said grace, children spilled milk, and mothers scolded.

357

She watched the rest of the world end their days with these homely blessings and repined that they would never be hers. She bade Violet good-bye, went upstairs, lit her own lamp, and sometimes on a good day its shade would need washing. She sat down to read *The Temperance Banner* and sometimes on a good day one of its articles would interest her. She checked the clock after each article and sometimes on a good day she looked at it only five times before it was time to get ready to walk down to Paulie's. She touched up her already perfect hair and sometimes on a good day found enough strands out of place to justify taking it down and reshaping it. She limped down to Paulie's to eat her lonely supper and sometimes on a good day a child would sit at a nearby table and make eyes at her over the back of his chair. She drank her final cup of coffee with nobody to converse with and sometimes on a good day a man at a nearby table would light a cigar after his meal. And for a few moments she would gaze into the middle distance and pretend.

Then she went home with scraps for Moose and watched him eat, then wash himself, then curl into a contented ball and go to sleep. At bedtime she donned the nightgown she'd worn the night she slept in Scott's bed, then brushed her hair down, pulled the weights on the clock and, when she could avoid it no longer, climbed into bed—an old maid, getting older, sleeping with a spotted cat, while a pendulum ticked in the dark.

Most nights she lay awake listening for the tinkle of the piano and the ringing of the banjo, but the revelry was forever gone from below. She closed her eyes and saw long legs kicking toward the ceiling and red ruffles framing black fishnet stockings and a man with a cheroot between his teeth and a low-crowned black Stetson, and a little boy peeking under a swinging door.

One night when her restless recollections refused to desist, she rose from bed and crept downstairs with the key Scott had left her. She entered the back door of the saloon and stood motionless, holding the lantern aloft, watching light play along the short passage to the room where Willy had slept. Inside that room the cot was gone. The cradles that had held the kegs remained, along with the yeasty smell of old beer. But the boy was gone, and so were all reminders of his presence. She remembered the last night when she and Scott had tucked Willy into bed and he had kissed her. But the memory clawed at her heart and she left the storeroom.

In the main room of the saloon the chairs were upturned on the tables and the bar. But the piano was gone, and Dierdre, too, along with her Garden of Delights. The light from the single lantern created eerie shadows that crept along the walls and fell between the tables as Agatha moved among them. Here the scent of whiskey lingered, and perhaps the ineffable reminder of cigar smoke.

Something rustled and Agatha stopped, lifting the lantern high to peer into the murky corners. As if through a long tunnel came the distant tinkle of music, a lively song that wafted through the night with the tiny resonance of a harpsichord. Agatha cocked her head and listened. Now she recognized it—a piano and banjo together, and in the background the faint echo of laughter and feet tapping on a wooden floor.

> Buffalo gals, won't you come out tonight,
> Come out tonight, come out tonight . . .

She smiled and turned toward the spot where the piano was, where Jube and Pearl and Ruby were swishing their taffeta ruffles and lifting their heels in wondrous synchronization.

The sound stilled. The images vanished. It was only Agatha's imagination, the daft maundering of a melancholy and wishful woman standing alone in an abandoned saloon, shivering in a nightgown upon which a man had once pressed his body and a little boy had laid his head.

Go to bed, Agatha. There's nothing for you here, only heartache and the road to further unhappiness.

She never went into the saloon again after that, except once during daylight hours when she showed it to a party interested in renting it as a dry goods store. But when the man's wife lifted her nose and sniffed, she declared they would never get the whiskey smell out of the place. So they left without even checking out the back storeroom.

She wondered if others would come, new renters who'd spark her life with new friendships, new distractions. But who would come to this desolate little cow town anymore? Not even the cowboys now that the saloons were closed to them. Spring would arrive and the liveliness brought by the longhorns and their drivers would be absent. No noise, no commotion, no hubbub. How she would miss it, no matter what she'd said in the past. The cowboys and their disorderliness were as much a part of her life as the millinery shop. But without them and the prosperity they brought, the seasons would change and the town would wither, just as she and her business would, with nobody to care about either.

Christmas was an occasion to be suffered. Agatha's only delight—and it was a mediocre one at that—was making a stuffed goose for Willy and sending it along with her first letter to him. She filled the missive with idle chitchat about how big Moose was getting and how he had snagged the hem of her garnet dress with his claws, and what she was giving Violet for Christmas, and how beautiful the roof of Christ Presbyterian looked with its mantle of snow. She included no clue of her overwhelming loneliness and was careful to refrain from asking how Scott was or sending him too personal a message.

Whenever she paid the rent, she made out the check and addressed the envelope with more care than she used on anything else these days, forming each flowing letter in intricate copperplate that looked as if it should be embroidered upon a pillowcase. But the enclosed letter stated only that she was sending the month's rent in the amount of twenty-five dollars, followed by a report on whether any prospective buyers had looked at the building. Except for the month of January, when the sniffing woman and her husband came, that portion of the letter was negligible.

There were outpourings she longed to express. But for fear of sounding like a desperate, love-starved spinster— which was exactly what she was—she bridled the urge.

She made it through the days by wearing a false cheer-
fulness that vanished the moment Violet's back was turned.
But when she was in the shop alone she often found her
hands idle while she stared at Willy's little stool and wondered if he'd grown tall enough that he wouldn't need it
now; and wondered what it was like at Waverley, where
he and Scott lived; and wondered if they missed her, too,
sometimes; and wondered if she'd ever see either of them
again. Then Moose would come and preen himself against
her ankles and say, "Mrrr . . ."—the only sound in the
otherwise silent shop—and Agatha would have to force
herself out of a deep lassitude that seemed to pervade her
more and more often as winter slogged along.

December, with its unendurable Christmas.

January, with its biting cold that made her hip ache
worse.

February, with blizzards that blew down out of Nebraska
and coated the snow with topsoil, making it as brown and
forlorn as Agatha's life.

It was Violet who brought the telegram. Violet, with her
blue eyes lit like a pair of gas jets and her blue-veined
hands fluttering in the air and her blue hair trembling. And
her titter was back.

"Agatha! Oh, my! Agatha, where are you? *Tt-tt.*"

"I'm here. At the desk."

"Oh, Agatha!" Violet slammed the front door. The shade
snapped up and whirled on its roller but she took no notice.
"You have a telegram! From *him! Tt-tt.*"

"A telegram? From whom?" Agatha's breath seemed to
catch in her throat.

"*Tt-tt.* I was coming to work just as I usually do when
somebody called from behind me and I turned around and
there was that young man, Mr. Looby, the one from up at
the depot, and he—"

"From whom, Violet?"

"—said, 'Miss Parsons, are you on your way to the
millinery shop?' And I said, 'Yes, of course. Don't I go
to the millinery shop every morning at eleven o'clock?'
And Mr. Looby said—"

"From whom, Violet!" By this time Agatha's hands were trembling and her heart was making mincemeat of her chest.

"Well, you don't have to shout, Agatha. It isn't every day we get a telegram, you know. From Mr. Gandy, of course."

"Mist——" Agatha's voice refused to cooperate. "Mr. Gandy?" she managed on the second try.

"*Tt-tt.* Isn't it wonderful?"

Agatha stared at the piece of yellow paper in Violet's hand. "But how do you know?"

"Why, it says right here, plain as a barn fire on a dark night—L. Scott Gandy. *Tt-tt.* That's his name, isn't it? And he's asking if you'll—"

"Violet!" Agatha leaped to her feet and held out a palm. "Whose telegram is it?" Surprising, how calm that hand was when her body felt as if it contained a fault line that was separating.

Violet had the good grace to look contrite as she handed over the telegram. "Well, it was only folded in two. And, anyway, Mr. Looby told me what it said. Then he grinned and handed me this ticket made out for White Springs, Florida. *Tt-tt.*"

"A ticket—" Agatha's eyes dropped to the ticket and excitement made her body wilt into a chair as she began reading.

HAVE PROPOSITION FOR YOU STOP WILL DISCUSS ON NEUTRAL TERRITORY STOP MEET ME TELFORD HOTEL, WHITE SPRINGS, FLORIDA, MARCH 10 STOP TICKET INCLUDED STOP JUBE AND MARCUS ENGAGED STOP REGARDS STOP L SCOTT GANDY STOP

Each time Agatha read the word *stop,* her heart seemed to do just that. At the word *hotel,* her fingers covered her lips and she sucked in a quick breath. She was still staring, dumbfounded, when Violet tittered again.

"*Tt-tt.* That naughty Mr. Gandy. *Tt-tt.* He's sent a one-way ticket."

Agatha could scarcely breathe, much less speak. But she reached up woodenly and Violet placed the ticket into her trembling fingers—a stiff piece of white cardboard with black ink that seemed to dance before Agatha's confused eyes as she scanned the words *Proffitt* and *White Springs*.

"White Springs?" Shaken, she lifted her eyes to Violet. "But why White Springs?"

"Why, you just read it, didn't you? Neutral territory."

"But . . . but I've never even heard of White Springs, much less the Telford Hotel. Why would he ask me to go there?"

It was Violet's turn to cover her lips. Her blue eyes twinkled with illicit speculation. "Why, my stars, *tt-tt,* he's said it as clear as the Morse code can make it—to proposition you, my dear."

Agatha blushed and became flustered. "Oh, don't be silly, Violet. Having a . . . a proposition for me could mean anything."

"Then why is the ticket only one-way?"

Agatha's gaze fell to it. Within her body the fault line widened. "I . . . I don't know," she answered in a small voice. "But, my goodness. Jubilee and Marcus engaged to be married—imagine that."

"Do you think you'll see Willy?"

"I don't know. Scott doesn't mention him."

"Well, what are you sitting there for, child? The tenth is the day after tomorrow."

The realization stunned Agatha. "Oh, gracious, so it is." Pressing a hand to her hammering heart, she glanced around the shop, as if trying to recall why she was there. "But . . ."— she raised distracted eyes to Violet—"but how can I get ready to go by then . . . and how can I leave the shop for an indefinite length of time . . . and . . . and there's that dress I've been working on for—"

"Bosh!" Violet spat. "Put that ticket down in a safe place and get upstairs this moment, Agatha Downing. Don't ask yourself how or why or for how long, not when a man like that is waiting in a hotel room in Florida for you. Just stuff as many gowns as you can into your trunk and be on that train when it pulls out tomorrow!"

"But—"

"One more word and I'll quit my job, Agatha!"

"But—"

"Agatha!" For an elderly woman, Violet could muster remarkable choler.

"Oh, Violet, can I really do such a thing?"

"Of course you can. Now, up with you." Violet reached for Agatha's hands and assisted her from the chair. "Check your gowns and your petticoats and make sure you take plenty of clean underwear, and if anything needs laundering we'd best get it down to the Finn's immediately. There's not a moment to waste."

"Oh, Violet." Agatha would have been appalled at her lack of coherence had she realized how many times she'd already said "Oh, Violet." But this time she embraced the birdlike woman and said fondly against her temple, "You have a magnificent rebellious streak in you that I've always admired. Thank you, dear heart."

Violet patted her shoulder, then shoved her away. "Upstairs with you now, and use a little vinegar in your rinse water. It brings out the red highlights in your hair. *Tt-tt.*"

He'd booked her a berth in a sleeping car, but sleep was out of the question. During the night she spent in it, her eyes scarcely closed. Such brimming anticipation could not be squandered in sleep. Hours like this were too precious, too rare, to let them slip through unconscious fingers.

She watched the land change from brown to white to green, a green more verdant than any she remembered in her entire life. She recalled the semiarid climate of Colorado with its piñon pines and poplars, but the earth itself was sere. And in Kansas, though a veritable ocean of blue-stemmed bunch grass filled every vista, it was green for only a short time each spring. Beyond the plains, Kansas offered little verdure but for an occasional copse of cottonwoods and hackberries. But the farther south and east Agatha traveled, the greener became the view out the train window.

They crossed the Tennessee River on a majestic trestle so high above a canyon it felt as if she were looking down on earth from heaven. Near Chattanooga the tracks twisted and turned through verdant ravines and several times she glimpsed waterfalls in the distance. With the foothills of the Appalachians behind, the land began flattening. Then there was Georgia with earth as red as ten-year-old rust, and more pines than she'd ever imagined, straight and thick and secret.

She changed trains in Atlanta and the rumbling wheels bore her ever closer to Scott and an assignation whose outcome she dared not contemplate for fear it might be one she must refuse. She shunted the thought to the recesses of her mind and immersed herself in the childlike joy of discovery. When she saw Spanish moss for the first time, she gasped in delight and looked around for someone to share it with, but everyone was either dozing or disinterested. The pines gave way to water oak and live oak and soon the tracks were bracketed by black water from which cypress knees projected, and the foliage became so thick it seemed no creature could live in it. But she saw a deer on an emerald knoll and before it quite registered upon her brain, it had turned tail and disappeared into the wall of growth behind it. Something flashed past, an impression of candy-pink tufts on a ball of green, too fast to absorb. She watched for another and saw one in time to inquire of the conductor.

"A tulip tree, ma'am. We're just about to pass over the Florida border. Tulip trees bloom early down here. Watch for white flowers, too, big white flowers on spreading green trees. Those'll be magnolias."

Magnolias. Tulip trees. Spanish moss. The very words accelerated her heartbeat. But what accelerated it even more was the realization that with each passing mile she was being borne closer and closer to Scott. Would he be there at the station? What would he be wearing? Would Willy be with him? Whatever would she say to him? What did a woman say to a man to whom she'd confessed her love but from whom she'd received no similar response?

The conductor weaved his way along the aisle, announcing, "Next stop, White Springs. White Springs, Florida." He paused a moment, touched the bill of his cap and said to Agatha, "Enjoy those tulip trees, ma'am."

"Yes, I . . . I will," she replied breathily, surprised to find that she could speak at all. As the train began slowing she was deluged with a mixture of silly concerns: *Is my hat on straight?* (But there was no hat; she'd come bareheaded in deference to his wishes.) *Is my dress wrinkled?* (Of course it was wrinkled; she'd been riding in it since she'd left home.) *Should I have worn the blue one?* (The blue one! The blue one was a dairy maid's dress compared to the one she'd made for the governor's tea.) *If he kisses me hello, where shall I put my hands?* (If he kissed her hello, she'd be doing well to remember she even had hands!) *Should I ask him immediately why he's brought me here?* (Oh, Agatha, you're such a priss! Why don't you try to be more like Violet?)

After all her concerns, she stepped from the train to discover Scott wasn't there to meet her. Disappointment turned to relief and relief back to disappointment. But there were hack and baggage lines to transfer passengers and their luggage from the depot to the hotels. So many hacks! So many hotels! So many people!

She signaled to a Negro driver who pulled up and tipped his wide straw hat.

"Aftuhnoon."

"Good afternoon."

He got down with a great lack of haste and stowed her trunk and bandbox in the boot, then shambled back to the side of the rig. He wore maroon felt carpet slippers on misshapen feet. His legs were bowed, and his lips were swollen.

"Where to?"

"The Telford Hotel."

"De Telfund. Sho' 'nuff."

She sat behind him on a cracked black leather seat, while a clip-clopping white mare moved over the sandy streets with no more hurry than his driver. Agatha's head swung left and right, trying to take it all in. An offensive odor pervaded the air but she seemed to be the only one aware of it. Well-dressed ladies and gentlemen strolled everywhere, crossing streets and hotel verandas, along shaded paths all seeming to lead in one direction. A bunch of mounted men with guns on their shoulders and quail hanging from their saddles followed a pack of hounds down the street. The carriage passed a sign that read, HUNT CLUB—HOUNDS FOR HIRE. A woman in a cane-backed wheelchair crossed the street behind them, pushed by a portly man in a beaver top hat. A band of laughing men with fishing equipment strode toward them with creels strapped over their shoulders. Everybody seemed to be playing.

"Sir?" she called her driver.

"Ma'am?" He half turned as if he could crane no farther around. His neck was crosshatched with furrows deep enough to plant seeds in, had it been made of earth instead of skin.

"I've . . . I've never been here before. What is this place?"

"Minnul springs, ma'am," he replied, the words so abbreviated her brow furrowed.

"I beg your pardon?"

"Minnul springs. Healin' watuh."

"Oh . . . mineral springs." So that was what smelled like rotten eggs.

" 'S'right, ma'am. Rich folk come, play some, res' some, soak in d' watuh some. Go 'way feelin' fine as a frog hair." He chuckled and returned to his driving. Within three minutes they drew up before an impressive three-story white edifice with a deep front veranda where ladies and gentlemen sat on wicker chairs and sipped from tall glasses.

"Telford, ma'am," the old man announced as he backed down from the driver's seat with arthritic slowness. With equal slowness he fetched her trunk and bandbox from the boot and delivered them inside the busy lobby.

"Be twen'-fi'e cen', ma'am," he said, returning, shifting his hat brim left and right, as if scratching his temples with it.

"I beg your pardon."

"Be twen'-fi'e cen'," he repeated.

"I . . . I'm sorry."

A familiar deep voice drawled near her ear. "I believe the fare is twenty-five cents, ma'am." She had never before experienced such a stirring reaction at the sound of a human voice. She snapped around and there he was, smiling down at her with familiar brown eyes, a pair of familiar dimples, a wonderfully familiar mouth . . . and a totally strange moustache.

"Scott," she could only think to say because her breath was short, her head light, and she felt curiously weak.

He looked tropical, in a nankeen suit as pale as bleached bone, a matching straw hat with a wide curved brim, and a black band that matched his collar-length hair, eyebrows, and the new moustache. His waistcoat was tight, molding his ribs above the twinkling gold watch chain that spanned its two pockets. At his throat he wore an ascot of striped silk—white on wheat, pierced by a single pearl stud.

"Hello, Gussie." He took both her gloved hands in his bare ones and squeezed hard while they smiled at each other with wide, bold gladness.

He realized in a flashing moment how much he'd missed her. And that she'd worn no hat, and that her hair was as beautiful as always, and her face as becoming, her smile as rare. And that her breasts appeared ripe, her breath hard-driving within the boned, high-necked dress she'd made for the governor's tea. And that his heart was thudding to beat hell.

"Sorry I missed the train, but I wasn't sure which one you'd be on."

"It's all right. I've caught a hack."

Reminded that the driver waited, he released her hands to reach in his pocket. "Ah, the fare. Twenty-five cents, is it?"

"Yessuh."

He paid double that amount and the driver nodded twice while thanking him. Then Scott turned back to Agatha and retrieved both her hands. "Let me look at you." When he had, for so long her cheeks turned pink, he said, "No hat. Thank you."

She bobbed her head and laughed self-consciously, then lifted it to find his grin as delectable as ever and the scent of tobacco still marking him as the one she'd remember out of thousands.

"Thank heavens nothin's changed," he said.

She assessed him in return. "I can't say the same for you."

"What? Oh, this?" He touched the moustache briefly, then took her hand again. "Got lazy and left off shavin' awhile."

It was an obvious lie. The remainder of his face was shiny from a fresh blading, and the precise black moustache was trimmed as if to military specifications. She loved it immediately.

"Very raffish," she approved.

"I was aimin' for refined." But he was pleased that she liked it.

"Possibly raffishly refined," she concluded, and they laughed lightheartedly, then stared at each other again, ignoring the hotel bustle that continued around them while their joined hands hung between them.

He squeezed her fingers, hard. "You look wonderful," he said.

"So do you."

They stared some more. Then Gandy laughed, as if his cup of joy had just run over.

She laughed, too—there was no controlling it when a heart was this happy. Then she found it impossible to look into his eyes any longer. "Is Willy here?" She glanced around.

"No, just us." Again their gazes locked. They stood among bellboys and hack drivers, women and men with children in tow, and a trio of the quail hunters making their way toward the kitchen with their unplucked supper in hand. Yet it seemed as if Scott had spoken the truth: just them. The flurry around them receded and they basked in their reunion. He changed the position of their hands, lifting hers until their palms matched, then meshing his fingers between hers and squeezing. Their absorption in each other continued inordinately until finally Scott seemed to realize it, freed her, and cleared his throat.

"Well . . . uh . . . I take it you haven't checked in yet."

"No."

"Let's do that."

Let's? His ambiguity left her with a feeling of palpitating uncertainty as he escorted her to the desk, watched her sign in, then took the key. But the room she was given was private, not even on the same floor as his.

"I arrived yesterday," he explained. "Mine is on the third, yours is on the second, so you only have t' climb one flight."

But what a flight—triple-wide steps with heavy oak railings; a landing with an enormous oval window bearing a leaded spider web design; a sprawling fern on a pedestal table, then more stairs with their rich scarlet runner overhung by double-bracketed gaslights.

"It's breathtaking, Scott. The most beautiful place I've ever been in."

"Wait till you see Waverley," he replied.

She seemed to float up the remainder of the stairs. But she didn't ask when. Not yet. The anticipation was too heady.

"You're still living there?"

"Yes." He leaned to put the key to the lock.

"And the others—Jube and all the rest?"

The door swung back. "They're there, too. We're turnin' Waverley into a resort hotel. Your room, ma'am." He ushered her inside with a light touch on her elbow. The moment her toes touched the thick Aubusson rug she forgot everything else.

"Ohhh, Scott!" She turned in a circle, looking up, then down. "Oh, my."

"You like it?"

"Like it? Why, it's magnificent!"

Scott draped an elbow on a high footpost of the brass bed, tossing the key, watching her scan the room a second time, enjoying her smile, her delight. She moved to one of the twin windows overlooking the street, touched the rose-colored overdraperies and the white Austrian drapes behind them, the silky wallpaper with its tiers of trellised rosebuds. Turning slowly, her gaze passed the lacy fern on its three-legged pedestal, the glass washbowl with its rose design in red on white, the matching water dispenser with its brass spigot, the drinking glass beside it, the bed with its woven counterpane of shell-pink and neatly folded quilt over the footrail, just in front of Scott.

Her eyes—green as the leaves of the fern with the sun glowing through them—stopped when they reached his. She clasped her hands, thumb knuckles pressing her breastbone. Her smile dissolved into an expression that made him want to leave his post at the foot of the bed and take her by both arms and feel his mouth moving over hers. Instead, he stood as he was.

"I cannot possibly allow you to pay for all this." She stood still and prim with her white gloves carefully placed.

"Why?"

"It wouldn't be seemly."

"Who will know?" Unspoken came the question: *Who will know anything we choose to do in this room?* For a moment it seduced them both.

Having completed her study of the room, she realized the most breathtaking thing in it was Scott Gandy in his tailored tropical suit with the vest that fit his chest much as her glove fit her trembling hand, and his intense dark eyes leveled upon her from beneath the brim of the finely woven planter's hat. And the new moustache that drew her attention time and again to his mouth.

"I will. You will," she replied, unsmiling.

Muscle by muscle, he drew himself away from the bedpost, unsmiling, too. "Sometimes you're too rigid with yourself, Agatha." He had taken a single step toward her when the bellboy spoke from the doorway.

"Trunks here."

Disappointed, Gandy turned, forcing a lightness to his tone. "Ah, good. Bring 'em in. Put 'em here." He tipped the bellboy, who left the door open as he went out. But the interruption had broken the spell. When Gandy turned back to Agatha she was strolling the perimeter of the room, carefully keeping her eyes on things other than him.

"The room's already been paid for, Gussie."

"I shall reimburse you, then."

"But it was my invitation."

"Why?" She stopped strolling, facing him from the diagonal corner of the bed. "I mean, why here? If Waverley is a hotel, then why the Telford in White Springs, Florida?"

He expelled a breath and consciously brought his grin back into place. "Because I remembered that you said you'd never been swimmin'. What better place t' learn than in a mineral spring of the first magnitude?"

"Swimming!" She pressed her chest. "You brought me all this distance so I could go swimming?"

"Don't look so surprised, Agatha. It's not just a pothole in a Kansas creek. *First magnitude* means the springs spout thirty-two thousand gallons of water an hour, and when you hit those bubbles you'll feel like you're floatin' in champagne."

As if she were doing so now, she laughed. "But I've never even seen champagne, much less floated in it."

"Looks exactly like spring water, but tastes much worse. Oh, by the way." He pointed to the spigoted dispenser and the drinking glass beside it. "Be sure you drink plenty of the water while you're here. They see to it y' have an ample supply in your room at all times. And they claim it does all kinds o' miraculous things t' your body. Cures gout, goiter, colic, constipation, cretinism, corns, catarrh, dandruff, and deafness. *And* makes the blind t' see and the lame t' walk."

She was smiling as he began, but when he'd finished, the last three words lingered as if they'd been repeated aloud.

"Does it really?" she commented quietly, dropping her gaze.

He came around the bed to stand before her. "Yes, really." He lifted her chin with the tip of the key and forced her to look at him. "I thought it would be good for you, Gussie. And I wanted a chance t' talk t' you . . . alone. There's no privacy around Waverley. People underfoot everywhere."

His dark eyes refused to waver from hers. The key was cold and sharp. Her heartbeat was unsteady. Gazing into his eyes, she felt the unwanted weight of propriety pressing hard upon her vitals and knew if he'd brought her here to seduce her, she would have to say no. Now that she was here, in this private bower where they answered to no one but themselves, she realized she couldn't settle for an illicit liaison, no matter how strong her feelings for Gandy. When he reached for her wrist, her heartbeats swelled to the point where they caused an actual pain in her chest. But he only placed the key within her gloved palm, then folded her fingers over it and stepped back, dropping her hand.

"And, anyway, Waverley is my territory. It strikes me that wherever we've been, any time we've been together, we've been in somebody's territory. The millinery shop was yours. The saloon was mine. Waverley, too, would be mine. But White Springs is neutral, just as it was durin' the War Between the States. I thought it seemed like the perfect place for two scrappers like us t' meet."

"Scrappers—us?"

"Well, aren't we?"

"We used to be, but I thought we'd become friends."

He knew now he wanted to be much more than her friend, but he saw her nervousness reappear every time the notion transmitted itself to her. So he kept the mood light.

"Friends it is. So . . ." He stepped farther back. "As a friend, I wanted t' give you the waters of White Springs." He tugged his waistcoat into place as if preparatory to leaving. "I've already taken the waters earlier this afternoon, but I thought you might enjoy a bath before dinner. There's time yet and I'll walk you down t' the springhouse, or we can catch a hack if y' rather. Ladies bathe on the even hours, men on the odd, no mixed bathin' allowed, of course, except parents with children twice a day. Now, what do you say?"

"I have no bathing costume."

"Available at the springhouse."

She spread her palms, then joined them, her smile back in place. "Then what can I say?"

"Good. I'll give you time t' get unpacked, hang up your things. Then I'll be back for you." He checked his pocket watch. "Say in thirty minutes?"

"I'll be ready."

He crossed to the open door but stopped before leaving the room and turned to look back at her.

"It's good t' see you again, Gussie," he said simply.

"It's good to see you, too."

When he was gone she pressed both hands to her cheeks. They were warm as sun-baked stones. She sat on the edge of the bed, then fell back, placing her fingertips to the underside of her left breast, where her heart thrust with a mighty insistence that was becoming harder and harder to fight.

Closing her door, Scott remained with his fingers on the knob for long seconds, staring absently at the scarlet runner in the hall, asking himself again why he'd brought her here since he'd known all along it wouldn't work. A quick roll in a rented bed wasn't at all what he wanted from her, nor she from him. But if not that, what?·

He drew in a deep breath, proceeded along the hall, and decided to let time answer the question for him.

Thirty minutes later they descended the grand staircase together, with her hand formally grasping his elbow.

"By foot or hack?" he asked when they reached the deep hotel veranda.

It was such a beautiful afternoon she said, "Let's walk. I've been riding for two days."

After the dismal winter in Kansas, the balmy temperature felt glorious. Birds sang and blossoms billowed, and once again she was struck by the lush greenness of everything.

"What are those?" she asked, pointing to a bush laden with pink blooms that looked much like roses.

"You mean you've never seen a camellia before?"

"I'm beginning to think I've never seen much of anything before. This place is wonderful. How ever did you find it?"

"I was wounded during the war and sent here t' recuperate."

She flashed him a startled glance. "Wounded?"

"Nothin' serious. A leg injury. But it got infected and the waters helped. There's a legend about the springs that goes back to the Seminole Indians. They recognized the medicinal value of the waters and it's said that the Indian wars were started when a papoose was shot off the back of a brave who was kneelin' at the springs t' drink. After that, Osceola declared that Indians from all tribes should be free t' use the springs without fear for their lives, and he banned all fightin' within a seven-mile radius. That tradition, as I said earlier, was carried on durin' the War

Between the States. White Springs was declared neutral territory and soldiers from both sides were allowed t' come here t' recuperate from their battle wounds without fear o' retribution." He slanted a dimpled grin down at her. "Rather an appropriate spot for a whiskey peddler and a temperance fighter t' meet, wouldn't you say?"

She smiled and felt proud holding his arm, while strolling women gave him a second, then a third, glance. She pretended they were courting and even smiled sympathetically at the other women whose escorts, no matter how handsome, were eclipsed as Scott Gandy passed. Sometimes his elbow bumped the side of her breast. She loved the feeling. It reverberated down to her toes.

Within minutes they approached an impressive eight-sided structure. Agatha inquired admiringly, "Oh, my, what's that?"

"That's the springhouse."

"But it looks like a grand hotel." The three-story pavilion of white clapboard with latticed foundation and black shingles rose majestically like an eight-sided doughnut whose hole held the bubbling white springs of the Suwannee River. Six facets of the octagon, three on each side, held changing rooms. These were connected by a promenade on the top level, where the continuous roof shaded white observation benches.

"One of the reasons I've always liked it," remarked Scott, "is because it's built in an octagon, like the rotunda at Waverley."

The approach was landscaped with more camellias, azaleas, and banana trees between which a wooden boardwalk led to the main door. Just inside, Scott turned Agatha over to an attendant, a young white woman with coal-black hair and a nose like a gravy ladle.

"It's her first time," he told the girl. "Give her the entire treatment."

"But—" Suddenly, Agatha hated being left in the hands of a stranger.

"I'll be back in an hour. Enjoy yourself."

Whatever she had expected, it wasn't the royal treatment that she received.

"My name is Betsy," the flat-nosed girl said when Scott was gone. "Follow me and I'll take you to your changing room." Betsy led her to the center of the building, where a wide opening gave a view of the actual waters within. But before Agatha had time for more than a glimpse, she was ushered in the opposite direction, into an elevator operated by a pulley and rope system to which Betsy applied herself. The way she strained upon the cables it appeared an enormous amount of work, but Agatha surmised that Betsy's biceps were even broader than her nose. She took Agatha to the third floor with no visible breathlessness. There they emerged from the elevator onto an outside railed veranda overhanging the springs, and along it Betsy led the way to the changing room. Inside, Agatha was given a pair of woolen knit drawers, a blousy top banded at the thighs, and a white cotton mobcap. When she emerged, barefoot, Betsy led her back to the elevator and lowered them to the ground level and finally the springs themselves. "It's icy year-round and it'll chill you to the marrow of your bones, but after several minutes you get used to it, and remember, when you're done here there'll be a hot bath waiting inside. Enjoy yourself, ma'am."

The smell was ghastly in the confines of the octagonal bathhouse. But the gurgling water sounded inviting.

"Cold" scarcely did credit to the first shock Agatha felt as she stepped into the water. Shivers raced up the backs of her legs and seemed to raise the hair off her skull. It felt awkward to be walking into a pool fully dressed, but she did it. To the knees (hugging her arms). To the thighs (stretching as tall as possible). To the waist (gasping). To the neck (chattering).

Sweet Savior, this was madness!

But other women bobbed in the water with only their heads showing. One nearby smiled at Agatha. Nonplussed, she returned the smile with a far less decisive one.

"It can be wonderful once you get used to it," the stranger remarked.

"I'm s . . . sure. B . . . but it's s . . . so c . . . cold."

"Revivifying," the woman returned and seemed to lie back in the water, suspended.

Agatha glanced down. Tiny bubbles rose all around her. A chuckle formed in her throat as the bubbles, like inquisitive minnows, played along her limbs and slipped beneath her bathing costume to work along her skin. They touched her in all her private places, popping along like a series of unending explosions that brought her flesh alive.

It tickled. It soothed. It came very close to arousing. But at the same time it relaxed. How could it create all these feelings at once?

She brought her arm just beneath the surface and watched the bubbles climb over it and erupt on the surface with a sound like meat frying in the other room. She spread her fingers and watched the air pockets rise between them. She need not have seen champagne firsthand to imagine she was floating in it. The continuous bubbles created an uninterrupted effervescence. She felt as if she herself had become champagne—airy, delectable, even drinkable.

She closed her eyes and steeped herself in the sensation of movement along the insides of her thighs, up the center of her spine, and between her breasts. She breathed deeply and let the feeling supplant all worldly cares.

And in those moments she came to understand sensuality in a natural, yearning way.

Later, when she became accustomed to the novelty of the bubbles, she experimented with a tiny bounce and was surprised by the unexpected buoyancy of her body. Never in her life had she felt buoyant; the sensation was infectious. She bobbed again, using her arms, feeling wondrously free and weightless. She followed the example of the friendly woman, resting on her back, lifting her feet, and for several seconds floated free of the restraints of gravity. How perfectly glorious!

When her feet drifted down to the bottom again, she glanced around to find no one paying particular attention to her and realized with a pleasant shock that here, in the water, she was no different from anybody else. Its buoyant properties made everyone equal. Suddenly, she realized, too, that her teeth were no longer chattering, the hairs on her arms no longer standing on end.

All too soon Betsy came to summon her from the water

and escort her to the private bathing room where there waited a tin tub of hot water along with thick white Turkish towels. She was allowed to bask in the warm mineral bath for ten minutes before Betsy knocked and ordered her to dry in preparation for her massage. When Betsy reentered the room she told Agatha to lie facedown on a slatted wood bench, with one Turkish towel beneath her, the other covering her from the waist down.

The mineral rubdown was more restorative than anything Agatha could imagine. She closed her eyes while deft hands worked her muscles in ways that made her feel as if she were floating on a magic carpet. Neck, shoulders, arms, buttocks, legs—all were attended with equal expertise.

When Agatha was dressed again and stepped off the elevator, some miracle seemed to have taken place in her body. She still limped—yes—but all vestiges of discomfort were gone. She felt limber, tensile, and utterly revivified. She felt as if she could walk miles and not tire, as if she could jump fences, race up stairs, skip rope! She couldn't, of course, but feeling as if she could was nearly as good.

Scott was waiting at the main entry, smiling.

"How was it?" he asked as she approached.

"Oh, Scott, it was extraordinary! I feel reborn!"

He took her arm and chuckled in deep satisfaction at her exhilaration. She was usually so reserved, it was fun to see her bubbling like the spring water itself.

"Nothing hurts! And look! I feel like I could walk back to Kansas. But in the water—oh, it was heavenly—I floated! I actually floated! There was a woman there who smiled at me and said something friendly and I watched what she did and tried it. I bounced! *I truly bounced!* All it took was a nudge with one foot and there I was, just like everybody else around me, bobbing like a cork. Oh, Scott, it was glorious. I've never felt so unencumbered in my life." She turned to look longingly over her shoulder at the bathhouse. "Can I come again tomorrow?"

He laughed and squeezed her elbow, then transferred her hand to the crook of his arm. "How can I refuse?"

"Oh, but . . ." Her brow curled in consternation. "Does it cost a lot?"

"You let me worry about that."

"But—"

"Hungry?"

"But—"

"I am. And White Springs is famed for some of the best cuisine in the Deep South. Quail is a specialty. I'm gonna take you back t' the hotel and stuff you with breast of quail sautéed in butter with black mushrooms and walnut sauce and steamin' saffron rice."

"But—"

"And afterward a wedge of Black Forest torte piled high with whipped cream. And plenty o' mineral water t' drink."

"But—"

"I don't mean t' sound critical, Gussie, but you're bein' terribly repetitive. Do you know how many times you've said *but?* Now, I invited y' here as my guest, and that's how it'll be. Not another word about it."

The dining room of the Telford was elegant, the linens starched to perfection, the service real silver. It was a far cry from Cryus and Emma Paulie's. Gandy was gratified to be able to treat Agatha to an elegant supper in such a place. He enjoyed watching her dine upon quail with black mushrooms and the other foods he'd suggested. She did so with great relish, as if her hour in the mineral baths had sharpened her appetite immensely. Somehow he'd expected her to eat with the picky affectation of most modern women. The fact that she didn't charmed him more than any silly dissemblance she might have practiced.

Her hair was wet around the edges, and as it dried, strands shrank from their restraints and formed miniature coils behind her ears. The gaslights lit them and formed shadows upon her neck and on the shoulder of her emerald-green dress. Likewise, her eyelashes upon her cheeks, shading her pale eyes.

He thought once more about kissing her. Her lips gleamed as she bit into the buttered quail, but each time she looked up and caught him watching her she carefully applied the napkin and glanced down.

He took up pondering his motives for bringing her here.

Yes, he'd wanted to give her the waters themselves and all they could do for her physically. But if he were honest with himself, there were other physical experiences he wanted to give her. He took a bite of tender, succulent quail and let his eyes drift down her full breasts to her trim ribs. She wasn't the kind of woman a man compromised under the false pretenses of "taking the waters." When and if he ever touched her in an intimate way, he would feel compelled to do the honest thing.

She took a bite of meat, looked up, and caught him in a deep study of her feminine attributes. She stopped chewing. He took a gulp of mineral water. Tension buzzed around them for the remainder of the meal.

She wiped her lips for the last time and lay her napkin aside. He pushed his dessert plate back, ordered a cup of coffee, and lit a cheroot, after snipping it with the pair of miniature gold scissors.

"You're still carrying them, I see."

"Yes, ma'am."

As he lit the cigar, she watched his lips and moustache conform to the shape of it. Then she became immersed in the pungent aroma, relishing it again. A memory came back, clear as a reflection in still water.

"I remember the day that oil painting of Dierdre was delivered to Proffitt. You paid for my supper at Paulie's and I was so put out with you I wanted to . . . to ram your money down your throat."

"And you were so prim and proper and I was embarrassed as hell about pushin' you down in the mud."

"Embarrassed? You?" Her eyebrows rose.

"I was."

"I didn't think you were capable of being embarrassed about anything. You always appeared so . . . so cocksure. And so aggravatingly adept at teasing. Oh, how I hated you."

Scott leaned back casually in his chair and laughed. "I reckon y' had good cause."

"So tell me," she said, changing the subject abruptly, "how is Willy?"

Scott's eyebrows knit and he leaned forward, tapping the

ashtray distractedly with his cheroot.

"Willy's not the boy he was when he left Proffitt."

Her happy mood vanished, replaced by concern. "What's wrong?"

"He's turnin' into a brat, that's what's wrong. He's hangin' around with too many of the wrong people, if y' ask me. A riverboat gambler, a bartender, a roustabout, three ex-prostitutes, and a black mammy with a mouth as sassy as a hissin' goose. The only one he doesn't seem to pick up bad habits from is Marcus. The girls spoil him terribly and he occasionally lapses into some of their gutter language. Leatrice gives him his way all the time, and when he goes off with the men into the woods it's hard t' tell what kind o' talk he's exposed to. He's even gotten demandin' with me. When I don't give him his way, he pouts or gets mouthy. I tell you, Gussie, sometimes when he talks back to me . . ."—he made a fist in the air—" . . . I want t' turn him over my knee and tan his backside."

"Well, why don't you?"

The fist relaxed. Scott's expression softened. "I guess because he got enough o' that kind o' treatment from his old man."

"But Alvis Collinson never loved him, Scott. You do. He would surely know the difference."

He knew she was right and shook his head despairingly. "I can't do it, Gussie. I'll never be able t' raise my hand t' that boy."

In her chest she felt the lump of love expand, recognizing in those few words the kind of father he was; the kind she'd always wished for herself.

"But Willy must be reprimanded when the occasion calls for it or he'll only continue to get worse, and there's nothing more unlikable than a willful child."

"He's willful, all right. But it's not really his fault. Part of the problem is that he has nobody his own age t' play with. I've taken him into town a couple times t' spend an afternoon with a little boy his own age, named A.J. Bayles, but Willy is so insufferable t' A.J. that he hasn't been invited back again. And he's started talkin' to an imaginary friend."

Agatha didn't appear to be fazed a bit. "That's not unusual. I did that a lot when I was a child. Didn't you?"

"I wouldn't be so concerned if it weren't this particular friend."

"Who?"

Gandy frowned at the ashtray and tamped out his cigar more times than necessary. "Gussie, you're goin' t' think I'm mad, but the bedroom where Willy and I sleep is . . . well, that is . . . it seems t' be haunted."

Instead of looking bemused, Agatha asked seriously, "By whom?"

"You believe me?" he asked, amazed.

"Why not? By whom?"

"I think it's Justine, my daughter."

"And she's the one Willy talks to?"

"Yes." Almost unconsciously, he reached across the table for her hand. His eyes were dark, worried. "Gussie, I've heard her, too. She calls for help. Never anywhere except in the northwest bedroom on the second floor, the one we call the children's room. But it's as clear as any human voice I've ever heard, and several times I've seen the imprint where she—or somebody—has lain on the bed, when nobody else has been in the room t' muss it."

"Does it frighten you?"

He considered a moment. "No."

"Is Willy frightened?"

"No. Quite the opposite."

"Then what harm can come of it? You seem to have a friendly ghost. And if you're her father, she surely wouldn't harm you or anyone close to you."

He looked at Gussie as if in a new light. "You're amazin'."

"My father was a miner. There are no more suspicious people in the world than miners. If they hear so much as a falling pebble in a deep shaft they attribute it to ghosts. And there are plenty who'll swear they were right, especially after cave-ins."

He was so relieved at her acceptance of his tale that he felt guilty for having tried to reason with Willy. "I told Willy it was impossible for him t' have seen and talked t'

Justine. I suppose that was the wrong thing for me t' do."

"Maybe. If it were me, I'd allow him to talk to her all he wants. What harm can come of it? If she's just a figment of his imagination, he'll outgrow it in time. If not, he's no more deranged than you, is he?"

"Ah, Gussie, I'm so relieved. It's been on my mind so much lately, but I was afraid t' talk t' anybody at Waverley about it. I thought if I did, it might get back to Leatrice, and she's already wearin' a smelly asafetida bag around her neck t' ward off hants, as she calls 'em. If she finds out there really is one, we'll never get her inside the mansion again. And even though she's outrageously insubordinate, I need her there t' keep the place runnin' smoothly."

"This Leatrice sounds somewhat like Ruby."

"She is. But, as I said before, she's started to influence Willy. He's pickin' up her bossiness and her bad grammar. Which leads us to another point. Willy is six already. He should be goin' to school, but the closest one is in Columbus, and it's a ten-mile drive, one-way. I don't have the time t' make that trip twice a day, and there's certainly nobody on Waverley qualified t' tutor him."

Agatha's heartbeat accelerated even before Scott went on.

"Which is why I've brought you here, Gussie." He still held her hand, their fingers linked, palms down. "He needs you, Gussie, more than he needs anyone else right now. He cries for you at bedtime, and at Christmastime he raised a regular stink because I didn't bring you t' Waverley or send him t' Proffitt. I try t' do the right things for him, but after talkin' with you such a short time I realize my judgment isn't nearly as good as yours. He needs your steady, dependable sense of right and wrong. And someone who knows how to say no to him and make it stick. Somebody t' monitor what he picks up from the girls and Leatrice . . . and even me. He needs a teacher, daily lessons. You could do all those things, Gussie, if you came to Waverley."

So there it was—his proposition. So much for her foolish misconception that he'd brought her here with anything so tempting as seduction on his mind. She need not worry herself about it further. Neither need she waste even the briefest moments supposing that he'd brought her here to ask her to marry him. He didn't want her as a consort or a wife, only as a governess for Willy.

The picture of Willy crying for her at bedtime raised a surge of maternal caring within her breast. But it could not quite quell the disappointment she felt. She withdrew her fingers from Scott's and folded her hands in her lap.

"I would be a governess, then?"

"Why does that sound like such a cold word? You mean as much to Willy as any real mother could. That makes you so much more than a governess. Say you'll do it, Gussie."

And live in your house, longing for you for the remainder of my life?

"When would you want me to come?"

He sat forward eagerly. "Jube's taken that decision out of my hands by demandin' that I get you to Waverley with all due haste, t' start makin' her wedding gown. She and Marcus are plannin' t' be married on the last Saturday in March, and she said she wants you at the weddin'. Now what do you say?"

She felt obliged to put up some resistance, no matter how weak. "But I have a business. I can't just up and leave it."

"Why not? It's slowly dyin' anyway. Y' told me yourself hats will soon be a thing of the past. And with factories on the eastern seaboard turnin' out ready-made clothin', the seamstress's trade is sentenced to the same demise. It's only a matter of time."

"But what about Violet?"

"Ah, Violet." Gandy paused to recall the glinting blue eyes of the wrinkled little woman. "Yes, it would be hard for you t' leave Violet." He quirked one eyebrow. "Unless, of course, you left the entire business t' her."

"The whole business?"

"Well, what else are you goin' t' do with that . . . that aviary of birds' nests and butterflies, and those cubbyholes full of ribbons and lace, and that enormous rolltop desk? Why, you could even leave her the furniture in your apartment—that is, if you don't object. We certainly have all we need at Waverley. And wouldn't it be a nice change for Violet t' have a place of her own instead of only a tiny room at Mrs. Gill's boardin' house?"

The thought of Violet gave Agatha pause. Violet had become a true friend. Leaving her would be very sad, indeed.

"I think," Scott said, "that Violet would be the first one t' encourage you to say yes. Am I right?"

As if Violet were here, Agatha heard her titters at Scott's sudden appearance in the store, saw the little woman blushing as he leaned over her blue-veined hand and brushed it with his lips, heard her breathlessness as she sank to a chair and fanned her flushed face with a lavender-scented hankie.

"You never came within a country mile of Violet Parsons without her wishing she were forty years younger. How could I expect an unbiased opinion out of a woman like that?"

He laughed. "Then you'll do it?"

She might be a virgin, a virtual innocent. But there were vibrations between Scott Gandy and herself that could not be mistaken. She might vacillate between believing and disbelieving them, depending on her state of emotions. But in her saner moments she realized full well that within them both an undeniable physical attraction was being nurtured with each hour they spent together.

She should ask him—should she not?—what his intentions were on that score. Was she then, in time, meant to become his live-in mistress now that Jube was marrying Marcus? A man like Scott would not do without a woman for long, and though he hadn't said he loved her, love seemed unnecessary to him when considering consortium. After all, he hadn't loved Jube either. Yes, she should ask him, but how did a woman broach a subject like that with a man who hadn't even kissed her after a five-month separation? A woman like Agatha Downing didn't.

In the end she drew a quavering breath, held it a moment, then released it in a rush. "I will. On one condition."

"Which is?"

"That I leave Violet with everything except my Singer

sewing machine. If she wants one, she'll have to buy her own. Mine was a gift from you and I think it's only fitting that I bring it to Waverley to make Jube's dress."

"Very well. Consider the freight paid."

When he saw her to the door, it was not with the good-night kiss for which she'd hoped, but with a firm handshake on the pact they'd made.

He took her to the springs twice each day for the next two days while they stayed to enjoy the spa, and though they grew friendlier than ever in terms of conversation and companionableness, not once during those two days at White Springs did he make the slightest advance toward her . . .

Until they were at the train depot and he was seeing her off again.

What was it about train depots that made hearts grow desolate even before good-byes were said?

Just before she boarded, he took her by both arms and kissed her squarely on the mouth. She sensed when he did it that he was determined to keep the kiss short and friendly. But when it ended and he looked into her eyes and her gloved fingertips rested against his breast, the temptation became too great and he drew her to him, more gently this time, and kissed her once—a moist, voluptuous kiss with his tongue saying good-bye inside her mouth—and made her knees go watery and her heart detonate like cannon shot.

When he set her back and looked again into her eyes, she had the awful feeling that men and women kissed this way all over the world, at moments such as these, and it was only her lack of experience that made her believe this was special between her and Scott, that it meant something more than it actually did.

Why did you wait three days to do that? she wanted to ask. But a woman of propriety didn't ask such things.

"Good-bye," she said instead. "And thank you for giving me swimming in White Springs. I'll never forget it."

"I didn't give you anything. White Springs was always here for you t' take."

But he had and they both knew it. He had given her more

than any other human being had ever given. He had given her, if not his own love, then hers for him. And giving it, she discovered, was the next best thing to having it reciprocated.

CHAPTER
20

There was a mood created by rocking trains that lent itself to introspection—the landscape moving faster and faster until it became a smear of green in the distance; the incessant thunder of metal on metal shimmying up from below until its vibrations became as much a part of the rider as his own heartbeat; the keening whistle carried on the wind as a faint sigh; outside, the green turning to black, and a face looking back at the rider, and that face her own. It was like having one's subconscious staring back, demanding examination.

On her way back to Proffitt, Agatha spent the hours thinking about the gamble she was taking—and it was a gamble, wasn't it? Purgatory against heaven. For to live in Scott Gandy's house as nothing more than a governess was to deliver herself into eternal purgatory. She loved him, she wanted him, she wanted a life with him, but as his wife and nothing less. Yet he spoke of neither love nor marriage. Living in his house, keeping her feelings silent—would it truly be preferable to staying in Proffitt alone?

Yes. Because at Waverley there was Willy, too, and Willy's love meant almost as much to her as Scott's.

So what about the chances for heaven? Everything she'd ever wished for, that one day Scott would look her squarely in the eye and say he loved her, wanted to marry her and make Willy their own forever. That was really how it ought to be. Would he ever see that?

Ah, but that was the gamble, for she didn't know.

She had gambled once before with Scott Gandy and lost, and it had hurt. Hurt. But love was an infectious thing and a smart person would bet on it every time.

And Agatha Downing was one smart lady.

Leaving Violet turned out to be less painful than Agatha had anticipated, chiefly because Violet was thrilled with the new status of her life as a merchant businesswoman. And, as Scott had predicted, after having lived at Mrs. Gill's in a single room, Violet felt as if she were inheriting a villa in Agatha's apartment. Also, she maintained a breathless sense of awe at Agatha's having won a place in the household of LeMaster Scott Gandy, the man whose reckless smile had made her blush and titter so many times.

But at the last moment, when Agatha's things were packed, her sampler carefully tucked away between layers of clothing in a trunk, her older hats donated to Violet, her apartment ransacked of all meaningful personal possessions, the sewing machine carted off to the depot on a dray, the final instructions given regarding the status of the shop's books, Agatha looked around the building and her eyes met Violet's.

"We've spent a lot of hours here together, haven't we?"

"Most certainly have. We sewed plenty of stitches inside these walls. But then we did some laughing, too."

Agatha smiled sadly. "Yes, we did." Beside her, Moose let out an abused yowl from inside a poultry crate. "Are you sure you don't mind my taking the cat?"

"Of course I'm sure. That creature of Mrs. Gill's was gone for three days again last week and came home stinking to high heaven with her fur all matted down and limping, mind you! I'd like to have seen that. *Tt-ttt.* Anyway, in nine weeks there'll be a new batch of kittens at the boardinghouse, and Josephine won't know what to do with them when they start climbing the drapes and sharpening their claws on the furniture. No, you take Moose back to Willy. That's where he belongs." Violet paused and glanced around. "Well, now, we'd best get you two down to the depot just in case that train comes a bit early. Wouldn't want you to miss it, not with Mr. Gandy waiting at the other end. *Tt-tt.*"

Agatha closed the door of the dress shop behind her for the last time, turning to glance at the green shade she'd raised each morning and drawn each evening for more years than she cared to count. She glanced at the apartment windows overhead. The nostalgic remark she'd made inside had been voiced because of her affection for Violet. But not a twinge of regret troubled her as she turned her back on the building. It had been a lonely place all the years she'd lived there, and leaving it was a pleasure.

But when she and Violet said good-bye beside the steaming train, a sudden sharp stab hit both of them. Their eyes met and they both realized that it could in all likelihood be the last time they ever saw each other.

They hugged hard.

"You've been a dear friend, Violet."

"So have you. And I shan't give up hope that Mr. Gandy will see the light and take you for a lover, if not for a wife."

"Violet, you're outrageous." Agatha laughed with misty eyes.

"I'll tell you a secret, dear, one I've never told anyone before. I had a lover once when I was twenty-one. It was the most wonderful experience of my life. No woman should miss it." She shook a crooked index finger under Agatha's nose. "Now, you remember that if the chance comes up!"

Still chuckling tearfully, Agatha promised, "I will."

"And tell them all hello from me and give that handsome Gandy a kiss on the cheek and tell him that's from Violet, who wanted to do it every time he walked into the millinery shop. Now get on that train, girl. Hurry!"

And so parting was easy; Violet made it so with her unfailing spirit. It wasn't until Agatha was half a mile down the track that her tears fell freely. But they were happy tears, somehow. And Violet had certainly given her something to think about!

She thought about it during her brief waking hours on the long trip south, wondering about Violet and who her lover had been and if he was someone Violet had been running into all through the years. And how long had the affair lasted? And why hadn't they married? And what was it that made it the most wonderful experience in her life?

Agatha had always thought only wicked women coupled with men outside of marriage. But Violet was far from wicked. Violet was a good Christian woman.

The thought roiled around and around in Agatha's mind while the familiar transformation took place beyond the train window, while she gave up winter for spring, cool weather for warm, mud for blossoms. While the images of Scott and Willy danced before her eyes . . .

Then they became more than images. They were real, standing side by side on a red-cobbled depot yard, searching the windows that flashed past; Scott raising a finger and pointing—there she is!—and both of them waving, jubilant, smiling. Agatha's heart swelled at the brief glimpse of her two loves, and though she'd never before been in Columbus, Mississippi, the sense of homecoming was strong and sharp and sweet. They were at the foot of the steps when she emerged, Willy perched on Scott's arm.

"Gussie, Gussie!" he called, reaching.

He hugged her and knocked off the hat she'd worn only because she owned so many it was one less to carry in a bandbox. Scott caught it in his free hand while she and Willy hugged.

"Oh, Willy, I missed you." She closed her eyes to seal in tears of happiness. They kissed and he tasted of sarsaparilla. She brushed back his hair and held his face and couldn't get enough of looking at his beloved freckled cheeks and his precious brown eyes.

"Scotty says you're stayin' for good. Are you really, Gussie, are you?"

She smiled at Scott. "Well, I guess I am. I've packed up everything I own—even my sewing machine and Moose."

"Moose! Really?"

"Really. He's in a poultry crate in the baggage car and the porter has been feeding him."

Willy peppered her face with noisy kisses that landed anywhere and everywhere. "Garsh!" he rejoiced. "Moose! Did you hear that, Scotty? She brung Moose!"

"*Brought* Moose," Scott corrected. When Agatha would have smiled at him, Willy held her cheeks between both his hands, demanding her undivided attention. "Wait'll you see my horse. Her name is Cinnamon and she's pregnant!"

"She is!"

"Scotty let me watch her get bred."

"I see I'm just in time to get your education on the proper track for a boy of five."

"Six. I had a birthday."

"You did! I missed it?" She twisted her expression into one of exaggerated dismay.

"It's all right. I'm gonna have another one next year. Let's go get Moose. Zach is waitin' at the wagons."

Willy squiggled out of Scott's arms to the cobblestones and scampered off, leaving Gandy and Agatha facing each other. With no barriers between them their eyes met and held. The sense of rush dissipated.

"Hello, again," she said.

"Hello. How was the trip?"

"Fine. Rushed. Thank you for the fine accommodation. This time I actually slept."

"This time?"

"Last time I was too excited to sleep. This time I was too exhausted not to."

"No trouble gettin' things settled in Kansas?"

"Everything went fine." It was so hellishly tempting to touch him that she suddenly gave in to the urge. She went up on tiptoes, clipped an arm behind his neck, and kissed him on the cheek. "That's from Violet. She said I should tell you she wanted to do it every time you walked into the millinery shop." The hand holding her hat came around her back as he dropped his head obligingly.

When she would have backed away, his arm tightened. The dimples appeared in his cheeks, his voice softened. "That's from Violet. What about from yourself?"

She had the presence of mind to smack him blithely on the other cheek and make no more of it than a joke. "There. That's from me. Now give me my hat."

He placed it on her head. "I thought you gave up hats."

"That's asking a lot of a woman who's worn them all her life. I kept a few of my favorites, and this was the most convenient place to carry one of them." She reached to adjust it but he did it instead, studying the results critically.

"Uh-uh. I don't think so," he decided and removed it. "You always did look better without one."

"Hey, come on, you two," Willy interrupted. "Zach's waitin'."

Scott reluctantly shifted his attention to the boy. "All right, all right. Go tell Zach t' pull the wagon up t' the baggage car at the other end and we'll meet him there."

Gandy took Agatha's arm and they sauntered along the cobblestones toward the baggage car.

"You left the store in Violet's hands?"

"Yes. She was ecstatic. Who is Zach?"

"The son of one of our old slaves. He's very good with horses and is teachin' Marcus how t' be a farrier. So y' brought the sewing machine."

"Of course. I wouldn't want to make a wedding dress without it. Did any of the others come to town with you?"

"No, but they're all at home waitin'. Do y' need anything from town before we head for Waverley? It's an hour's ride and we don't make it every day."

She needed nothing. She felt as though she had everything in the world she'd ever need or want as she watched the reunion between Willy and Moose—face to face, whiskers to freckles, the cat suspended as Willy held him beneath his front legs and kissed him, then squeezed him far too tightly, scrunched his eyes shut, and said, "Hey, Moose! Garsh, I missed you."

Agatha was introduced to Zach, who pulled up in a weatherbeaten wooden wagon upon which was loaded the empty poultry crate and the sewing machine and all of Agatha's gear, including the hat, which Gandy tossed through the air at the last minute.

Then she and Willy and Scott and Moose boarded a black well-sprung rig and headed for her new home. On the way Agatha saw her first redbud in bloom—clouds of rich heliotrope. And dogwood—clouds of cottony white. And wisteria—cascades of pure purple. In the ditches beside the road wild jonquils bloomed in patches so large it looked as though pieces of sun had dropped to the earth and shattered upon the grass. Here, as in Florida, the scent of the South prevailed—rich, moist, fecund. Already Agatha loved it.

They passed Oakleigh and Willy told Agatha that was where A.J.'s grandma and mother had lived before the war. They passed a little white church in a copse of pines and he told her that was where Leatrice went on Sundays. They passed the cemetery and he told her that was where Justine was buried.

They turned into the lane and Gandy told her, "This . . . is where I was born."

Waverley.

More grand, more majestic than Scott's watercolor had been able to depict. Waverley, with its towering pillars and magnificent rotunda and its wrought-iron lacework. Waverley, with its massive magnolia out front and the boxwoods trimmed to match their names. She looked up and her heart hammered—she was really here at last. She looked down and saw the peacocks on the lawn!

"Oh!" she exclaimed breathlessly.

Scott smiled, watching her, filled with pride at the appearance of the place, decked out in its floral finery, lustrous as a pearl on its emerald lawns.

"You like it?"

Her reply was all he could have hoped for. She sat speechless, with a hand pressed to her thrumming heart.

Jack saw the carriage and came hurtling across the grounds from the tannery, bellowing at the top of his lungs, "They're here, everybody! They're here!" And before the carriage stopped, the front door flew open and voices were whooping and people were barreling toward the rig with arms uplifted.

Agatha was passed from Pearl to Ivory to Ruby, getting hugs from all. Then came Jack, puffing from his run across the yard, sweeping her in a circle and making her laugh. Then Jube, radiant even in a cleaning dress of washed cotton.

"Jubilee, congratulations!"

The two women backed off and smiled at each other. Then Jube captured Marcus's arm to tug him forward. "Isn't it wonderful? If he says anything different, don't believe a word of it."

Marcus, always the perfect gentleman, smiled at Agatha but held back. She gave him an impulsive hug.

"Congratulations, Marcus! I'm so happy for you."

He made motions as if he were squirting oil and raised a questioning brow.

"Yes, it's all oiled and ready to go. We'll have her dress made in no time."

There was one other person waiting on the front steps with hands crossed over her bulging stomach and a leather pouch suspended from a thong around her neck, a woman shaped like a water buffalo, who could only be the indubitable Leatrice.

Everyone except Leatrice talked at once. Everyone except Leatrice hugged Agatha or kissed her on the cheek. Everyone except Leatrice smiled and laughed. Leatrice waited like a queen on a dais for her subject to be announced.

When the initial hubbub had died down, Scott took Agatha's elbow and escorted her up the marble steps.

"Leatrice," he said, "I'd like you t' meet Agatha Downin'. Agatha, this is Leatrice. She's cantankerous and unreasonable and I don't know why I keep her. But I've been farther underwater than she's been away from Waverley, so I guess she's here to stay."

Leatrice spoke in a voice like an engine with gear trouble. "So you here at las', d' woman from Kansas. Maybe now we get sumpin' 'sides growlin' outta dis one heah." She curved a thumb toward Gandy. "Boy's been one bodacious bear t' live wid."

Gandy grew red around the collar and studied his feet. Agatha politely refrained from looking at him. "I've heard a lot about you, Leatrice."

"I jus' bet ya have, an' ain't none of it good, izzat right?"

Agatha laughed. The woman did, indeed, stink like a polecat, which Gandy had warned she would. "Well, I've heard that you rule with an iron hand, but I have a feeling there are times when *some*body needs it."

"Humph!" Leatrice readjusted her crossed hands over her barrel belly. "An' I know who."

Zach arrived with the baggage and the men began unloading it. Jack and Marcus came up the steps bearing the sewing machine. Zach and Ivory followed with a trunk, the latter with Agatha's pink-flowered hat perched on his head.

"Where you git dat hat, boy?" Leatrice demanded.

Agatha snatched it off. "It's mine, but the master of Waverley has issued his first order—no hats for me."

"Where to with these things?" Jack asked.

"The right parlor," Gandy answered, and the men moved inside.

Willy came by, lugging a hatbox nearly as big as he, while Jube and the girls followed with additional luggage. As they disappeared inside, Agatha plucked at the petals on the hat and peered up at Gandy with a teasing light in her eyes. "And where to with this thing?"

Gandy glanced wryly at the hat with its pink cabbage roses and whorl of net and its cluster of cherries in a sprig of green leaves.

"No offense, Agatha," he said, "but that is the singularly most ugly thing I've ever seen. Why any woman with hair like yours would want t' cover it with cabbage roses and cherries is a mystery t' me."

Agatha stopped plucking at the silk petals, sighed, and quite by chance won the black woman's heart forever by inquiring, "Would you have any use for one slightly used pink hat, Leatrice?"

Leatrice's eyes widened and fixed upon the gaudy creation. Her hands reached out slowly, reverently.

"Dis? Fo' me?"

"If you don't mind it being slightly worn."

"Lawdy . . ."

Gandy grinned at Agatha and said, "Come on. Let me show you the house."

They left Leatrice on the front steps, wearing the abominable-smelling asafetida bag around her neck and the pink hat on her head.

Scott took Agatha through a door wider and higher than any she'd ever seen into the grand rotunda, where she stood a moment to catch her breath. It was majestic. Spacious and bright with paneled doors rolled back revealing twin parlors on either side and the sweeping twin staircases twining down from overhead, forming a graceful frame for the matching back door across the shiny pine floor. She looked up and it was just as she'd imagined: the cupola roof overhead, the graceful brass chandelier, the catwalks and windows, the doors leading to the upper-level rooms, and the spindles—all seven hundred eighteen of them—like the ribs of a massive living thing.

She had that impression right from the start—that Waverley had a life of its own, apart from those who lived in it. It had dignity and a touching air of defiance, as if having survived the war gave it the right to feel superior. It dominated, too, its sheer scale dwarfing those who moved within its walls. But that dominance was tempered by an air of protectiveness. Agatha had the feeling that, should one need refuge, one had only to step between the twin staircases and they would embrace like powerful arms, holding any threat at bay.

"I love it," she declared. "How ever could you have stayed away all those years?"

"I don't know," Scott replied. "Now that I'm back, I really don't know."

"Show me the rest."

He took her into the front left parlor, a beautiful room with four high, dramatic windows, a large fireplace, and to the left of the doorway a graceful depression in the wall, surrounded by decorative plasterwork.

"The weddin' alcove," he announced.

"About to be used again," she noted. "How nice. I'm sure she'll be pleased."

"Jube is ecstatic."

"No. Not Jube. I meant the house." Agatha lifted her eyes to the high ceiling. "It has a . . . a presence, doesn't it?" She walked around a drake-footed Chippendale chair, trailed her fingers over the waxed surface of a Pembroke table, the back of a graceful sofa, then passed the piano, where she played a single note that hung in the air between them. "A personality."

"I thought I was the only one who believed that anymore. My mother did, too."

Through the low front windows they could see the box-woods his mother had brought from Georgia.

"Perhaps she's looking over from her grave across the road and nodding in approval at how you've revived the place."

"Perhaps she is. Come, I'll show you my favorite room."

She, too, loved his office on sight. So much more personal than the front parlor, and bearing a more lived-in look, with his ledger left open on the desk, a crystal inkwell and a metal-nibbed pen waiting to be put to use again; his humidor undoubtedly stocked with cigars, the remains of one in a free-standing ash stand near his desk chair. The smell of him permeated the room, cheroots and leather and ink.

"It fits you very well," she told him.

She glanced up and found him watching her, not exactly smiling, but looking as pleased at having her here as she felt at being here at last.

"I'll show y' the dinin' room," he said, turning to lead the way across the hall. It, too, was huge, with a great built-in china closet and a massive rectangular table beneath another gas chandelier. The floor was bare and gleaming beneath the table and their footsteps echoed as they stepped farther into the room.

"Breakfast is at eight, dinner at noon, and supper at seven. Supper is always formal and all our guests share the meal with us."

"And Willy?" she asked.

"Willy, too."

So Scott Gandy would gift her with yet another thing— that ineffable sense of family that thrived around no place so heartily as around a supper table. Her sunsets need never be lonely again.

Her heart was full. She wanted to thank him, but he was already leading the way to the other front parlor.

"And this is your room," Gandy told her, stepping back to let her enter.

"Mine?" She stepped inside. "But . . . but it's so big! I mean, I wouldn't need half this space." Her sewing machine and trunks were already installed in the spacious room. Brightness everywhere—four gleaming windows—a south view of the front gardens, the drive, his mother's boxwoods, and, to the east, the river. Too much to take in without being overcome.

"I wanted you t' be on the main floor so you wouldn't have t' climb the stairs so much. If it's all right with you, we'll use a corner in here for Willy's classroom."

"Oh, it's more than all right."

This room was the twin of the first parlor, without the alcove, but with that rarity, a walk-in closet bigger than any two pantries she'd ever seen. There was a pretty bed with a white brocade tester, a chaise upholstered in multicolored floral, a small chest-on-chest, a five-foot freestanding cheval mirror on swivel brackets, and a library table holding a large bouquet of golden forsythia.

"I'm sorry, Gussie. You won't have much privacy, except at night. Durin' the day, to add to the feelin' of intimacy around the place, it would be nice if you kept the doors rolled back while you're workin' in here. That way our guests feel like they're one of the family."

She stood before the cheval mirror, catching his gaze in the glass. She turned slowly, wondering if he had the vaguest notion of what it meant to a woman like her to have a room like this in a house like this.

"I've had privacy, Scott. It's not all that desirable. All those years I lived in that dark, narrow apartment above the shop with nobody to come to my door and interrupt me or disturb me. You cannot guess how awful it was." She smiled, a smile of the heart as much as of the lips. "Of course I'll leave the doors rolled back while I work here. But I feel a little guilty about taking one of the loveliest rooms in the house that could be bringing in money from paying guests."

"Your job is seein' after Willy. I don't see how you can do that from one of the slave cabins. Besides, there are three guest rooms upstairs, equally as large as this one."

"But this is more than I'd hoped for. The nicest place I've ever lived."

He came several steps into the room and stopped beside the foot of the bed. "I'm glad you're here, Gussie. I've thought—"

Suddenly, Willy came charging through the doorway, claiming Agatha's hand.

"Come and see my room, Gussie."

He tugged her along impatiently and Scott followed to stand at the bottom of the right stairway, watching them ascend. "Can you make the stairs all right?"

"Nothing could stop me," she replied, looking back over her shoulder.

On her way up Agatha was surprised to meet a middle-aged couple coming down. They were dressed for riding.

"Hello," the woman said.

"Hello."

Immediately, Gandy sprinted up the steps. "Ah, Mr. and Mrs. Van Hoef, off t' the stables?"

"Indeed," replied the man.

"A perfect day for a ride. Mr. and Mrs. Van Hoef, I'd like you t' meet Agatha Downin', the newest permanent resident of Waverley." To Agatha he explained, "Robert and his wife, Debra Sue, arrived yesterday from Massachusetts. They're our first official guests."

Agatha murmured a polite response. Then the Van Hoefs continued down the stairs.

"Guests already?" Agatha remarked.

"Van Hoef runs a successful milling operation and is reputed t' be one of the five most wealthy men in Massachusetts. Do y' know why he's here, Gussie?"

"No."

"Because of somethin' you said t' me one time when we were talkin' about Waverley. You called it a national treasure, do you remember?" She didn't. He went on. "I had no idea when I left Kansas how I was goin' t' make Waverley pay its way again. Then one day I was lookin' out the rotunda window"—he looked up to it, then back down at her—"and your words came back to me. I realized then what potential the place held. If it hadn't been for you, insistin' I come back here, I probably never would have. I just wanted to say thank you for badgerin' me into it."

"But I've done nothing. You and the others did it all."

Willy had gone ahead and was draped over the balcony railing, balancing on his belly. "Hurry up, Gussie!"

She lifted her head and caught her breath. "Willie! Get back!"

He cackled, the sound resonating through the great dome. "I ain't scared."

"I said get back—and I mean it!"

He thought he was funny, teetering on the banister, showing off.

"Scott, get him down from there."

It took Scott only seconds to pluck Willy off the rail and plant him on his feet. When Agatha reached him she was exceedingly angry. "Young man, if I ever catch you doing that again you'll be polishing these spindles all the way from the bottom to the top. Every one of them—is that understood?"

Willy grew sullen. "Well, golly, I don't know what you're so mad about. Nobody else gets mad. Heck, Pearl teached me how t' slide down the banister."

"She what!"

"She teached me—"

"*Taught* me. And you've done that for the last time, too. You can tell Pearl I said so. Now, how about showing me your room?"

Willy decided retaliation was a better course. "I don't wanna! You can look at my dumb room by yourself!"

"Willy, come back here!" Scott shouted.

Willy continued marching down the stairs. Scott began to head down after the boy but Agatha gripped his arm and shook her head. Her words carried clearly throughout the rotunda. "Why don't you show it to me instead, Scott? It's the room where Justine comes to visit Willy, isn't it? I'd like to hear all about it." She moved to the doorway. "Oh, isn't it lovely." They heard Willy's footsteps slow and pictured him gazing up longingly. They moved about the room, Scott giving a cursory tour, mentioning every item he was certain Willy had been eager to tell Gussie

about—all his toys, the rocking horse, the view of the
stables. When they emerged from the children's room and
moved on to the guest room next door, they knew Willy
had been listening and saw him dip out of sight beside the
curved stair extension downstairs.

"When we first reopened Waverley we used all the rooms
up here for ourselves, but one by one we improved the
slave cabins so everybody has a house of their own. Jube
and Marcus are fixin' up the old overseer's place and will
move in there after they're married. The Van Hoefs are
stayin' in here." He indicated the east front bedroom. "And
tomorrow we have guests arrivin' from New York who'll
take that room." He indicated the rear one opposite Willy's.
"And this . . ."—he stopped in the doorway of the bedroom
above the main parlor—" . . . this is the master bedroom."

For some reason, Agatha hesitated to step over the threshold. "You were born here."

"Yes. My mother and father shared it, then Delia and
I."

Delia, his lost Delia. Did he ever long for her?

"But you aren't using it for yourself?"

"No. I share Willy's room. That way we can rent this
one out."

The master bedroom was done in the same ice-blue as
the vest Gandy wore today. A tall rosewood tester bed
with hand-carved posts dominated the space. Incorporated
into the intricate carving upon the center of its headboard
was the convex oval that marked it as an original Prudent
Mallard piece. Billows of white netting were tied back to
its corner posts and beside it sat a set of three portable steps
for climbing up to the mattress. A matching dresser took up
nearly an entire wall. On the windows, tiebacks of ice-blue
with an apricot bamboo design matched that of the heavy
counterpane and tester. The design was picked up in a pair
of Chinese Chippendale chairs that faced each other before
the twin front windows with a low marble-topped table
between them. The fireplace was done in Carrara marble
with a decorative iron liner. The brass andirons gleamed,
matching the chandelier with its etched-glass globes overhead. A hand-tied rug of a deeper teal-blue with a rust

border design covered the center of the virgin pine floor, leaving the varnished edges exposed.

"Will guests be coming soon to use this room?"

"Next week."

"Ah." She hated to see it happen. Somehow it felt as if the room would be desecrated by having strangers sleeping in the big Mallard bed where Waverley's heir had been conceived.

"Would you like t' see the view from the top?" he asked, to all outward appearances unruffled about giving his bed to strangers. "It's grand, but there are a lot of stairs."

"I want to see it anyway."

They climbed the single staircase leading from the second to the third floor, where they passed two closed doors. "This is the trunk room. I'll show it to y' some other time."

She saw his chin lift, his eyes drawn to the octagonal summit that topped the mansion like a gleaming crown on a monarch's head. She sensed his pride, his eagerness, to have her see all he owned. They mounted the last single stairway that brought them at last to the catwalk. And there below lay Scott's heritage. Agatha stood with her fingertips on the window ledge, staggered.

"It's breathtaking."

"See that field down there?" He pointed.

"Yes?"

"We've put in cotton. Just enough t' recapture the old days for the guests. And see the meadow leadin' down t' the river?" They gazed east now. "I plan t' fill it with more horses as I can afford them." They walked around until they were looking straight south along the driveway.

"And see that buildin' across the road?"

"Uh-huh."

"That's the swimmin' pool. Want t' see it?"

"I'd love to!"

When they reached the main floor they found Willy, pouting, on the bottom step.

"We're goin' t' see the swimmin' pool. Would y' like t' come with us?"

At Willy's continued sullenness, Gandy merely turned away and touched Agatha's elbow, indicating the front door.

"All right! I'll go!"

Scott and Gussie exchanged a secret grin.

They walked three abreast down the gravel drive, between the formal gardens and the spreading lawn. Gandy said, "Tomorrow, Willy, you'll be startin' lessons with Gussie."

"Lessons! But I was gonna—"

"And y'all be ready at whatever time she says and—"

"How can I be ready when I can't tell time yet?"

"Then that'll be one of your first lessons. Now stop makin' up excuses and listen t' me. I've made it clear to all the rest, there is one person and one person only who gives you orders around here—and that's Gussie. Understood?"

"What about you?"

"Me? Oh, well, sometimes maybe from me. But before you make plans t' go off with Zach in the stables, or out t' the woods with Jack, or into town with the girls, you make sure it's all right with Gussie. And if she gives you an order and you don't obey it—like up on the balcony today—there'll be trouble. If y' want t' grow up t' be a gentleman, and be smart and well liked by others, you have t' learn how. It doesn't just happen. And that's the reason Gussie is here."

They reached the pool area then, a white-painted wooden building beneath the oaks and hickories on the opposite side of the road. Inside, it was cool and shaded, lit by a few small windows. The pool itself was constructed of red brick and at one end a set of wide marble steps led into it.

"Not as fancy as White Springs, but in the middle of the summer it's a welcome relief at the end of a hot day."

"It smells much better than White Springs."

Scott laughed. Agatha recalled the feeling of weightlessness and marveled that she could experience it again any time she chose.

"Where does the water come from?"

"Artesian springs."

"Is it cold?"

"Like ice . . . touch it."

He was right.

"Ivory says he's gonna teach me how t' swim," Willy announced.

"Really swim?" inquired Agatha. "I mean, not just splash around, but really swim? In water over your head?"

Scott answered. "Ivory and I used t' swim in the river together when we were boys, before they built the pool. He's a strong swimmer. That's why he used t' get the job of checkin' underwater damage when he worked as a rooster on the riverboats."

"So it's all right with you if he teaches Willy?" Agatha asked.

"Absolutely. As long as Willy's with Ivory, he'll be in good hands."

"Very well, then. We'll set aside some time each day for the swimming lesson."

And so it was that an unconscious cooperation began between Agatha and Scott in matters concerning Willy. Though he had said she'd be solely in charge of Willy, it never turned out that way. As in the days when they all lived in Kansas, they consulted each other about anything that directly affected his upbringing or his welfare.

At supper that first night she sent Willy off to rewash his hands when they weren't clean enough the first time, and when he complained, Gandy reinforced her order by snapping a single word: "Willy!"

Willy grumbled his way from the room but returned with spotless knuckles. Agatha looked across the table at Gandy and thought, *We'll be better parents than most, married or not.* And she cherished the moment and the man and the little boy and being part of the camaraderie around a dining room table at sunset.

The following morning Agatha inquired if it would be all right to let Willy sleep later and begin his classes at ten A.M., since she had plenty of other work to keep her busy until then and there was no sense in rousing him inordinately early—she planned only three hours of schoolwork each day at the beginning.

"Three hours? That's all?" Scott responded.

"Three hours for a boy of six can seem like two days to an adult. I'll increase the time gradually."

"All right, Gussie, whatever you think is best."

On Saturday she approached him and asked, "What about church tomorrow?"

"Church?" he repeated, caught off guard.

"Yes, church. Willy has been going, hasn't he?"

Gandy cleared his throat. "Well . . . uh . . ."

"He hasn't." She looked disappointed in him and he chafed under her somber regard. "Oh, Scott, you can't neglect a boy's spiritual upbringing."

"Well, it's not that I didn't want him t' go, it's just that the nearest church is clear in Columbus."

"What about the little white one we passed on our way?"

"That's the black people's church."

"Black people's? Baptist, you mean?"

"Well, yes, Baptist, but it's for the blacks."

"Does Leatrice go? And Ruby?"

"Leatrice does, not Ruby."

"Then I'll see Leatrice about Willy and me going along."

"But, Gussie, y' don't understand."

"We all pray to the same God, don't we? What does it matter if it's Baptist or Presbyterian?"

"It doesn't. But it's *theirs!*"

"Will they throw me out?"

"No, they won't throw you out. It's just that the whites and blacks don't mix in church."

"How odd. Now wouldn't you think that would be the natural place for them to do so?"

And so she and Willy went to church with Leatrice and Mose and Zach and Bertrissa and Caleb. Leatrice, proudly wearing her bright pink hat, took charge of introducing them. "This heah's the master's li'l adopted boy, Willy, an' Miz Agatha Downin' from Kansas. She Presbyterian, but she willin' t' put up wit us."

It didn't really surprise Gandy that Agatha managed it. After all, it was women like Agatha who'd gotten the entire state of Kansas to change its mind about prohibition. He was waiting when they returned, sitting on one of the bois d'arc benches on the north veranda.

"Y'all enjoy yourself?" he inquired, rising as Agatha came up the steps.

"It's a lovely little church. You must come with us next time."

And to Gandy's surprise, the idea became unexpectedly inviting.

He grew used to glancing up from the desk in his office and glimpsing Gussie at work in her room, diagonally across the rotunda from his. There was a satisfying feeling knowing she was there, steady, dependable. The guests loved her. She exuded an air of breeding of which the other girls fell just short. In her fine, rich gowns, with her hair always meticulously groomed, her nails buffed and trimmed into neat ovals, she was the picture of gentility the guests had all imagined when making their reservations for Waverley Mansion. She grew accustomed to greeting them when they arrived, coming out of her room to meet Gandy in the foyer, and together they'd open the front door and welcome whomever was stepping off the carriage. It was a logical mistake that more of them than not mistook her for his wife and greeted them as "Mr. and Mrs. Gandy." The first time this happened Gandy noted a blush color her cheeks and her eyes flashed briefly to his. But after that she took it in stride, allowing him to straighten out the misconception with a quick correction.

She assigned Willy the job of escorting each new arrival to the proper room, realizing that Willy's charm in itself would probably bring people back again. He could talk to anyone, familiar or strange, and much as he'd captivated her heart when she'd first met him, Willy won over wealthy industrialists and their wives within minutes after they set foot in the place. Realizing this, she broadened Willy's job to include giving a tour of the stables and the grounds for each incoming party. Afterward, he invariably received a tip. She had Marcus make him a little wooden bank shaped like a banjo with the strings stretched across the slot so whenever a coin was dropped the elastic strings twanged. Willy was so enchanted each time he dropped the money into it that he didn't mind saving. She made a miniature account book for him and taught him to enter each tip he made, including the date, the amount, and the name of the person who'd paid him. (Until he learned to write, she agreed to write the names for him, though he already knew numbers so could enter them himself.) She explained to him that when he grew up, undoubtedly he'd be running Waverley instead of Scott and he'd have to know how to keep books, just as Scott did. Also, simultaneously, she taught him to count dollars and cents, and to add. But more importantly, she taught him the value of a penny saved.

The three hours' formal work she did with Willy each day didn't begin to cover the time spent educating him. Manners were taught whenever and wherever the occasion called for it. How to use a measuring tape was taught when she cut out Jube's wedding dress; oiling the sewing machine was demonstrated when Marcus, at Gussie's request, allowed Willy to do the job, showing him how instead of just telling him. If some of the men went fishing, she sent Willy along to learn the sport. If Leatrice skinned catfish, Agatha had her show Willy how it was done. When Zach trimmed hooves or shod horses, Willy learned the names of the tools, the proper angle of the hoof, the fit of the shoe.

She taught him that play was the reward for work, making certain he had enough of each for him to grow up industrious, yet fun-loving.

He taught her, too. All about how Prince and Cinnamon had nipped at each other and played hard-to-get before Prince had mounted the mare with his long penis hanging nearly to the ground.

And all about how he'd come upon Jube and Marcus down by the old tannery one day and how Marcus had Jube's dress pulled up around her waist and Jube was giggling and bucking like a wild bronc.

And all about how the girls sneaked out to the brick pool at night sometimes and went swimming in nothing but their underwear.

Agatha was appalled at the earthy things Willy had witnessed around the place while he'd run roughshod with nobody monitoring him. She spoke to Scott about it. For the first time ever she failed to receive his support.

"Those things are natural, Gussie. I see nothin' wrong with him watchin' the horses mate."

"He's only six years old."

"And he's learned beside me that that's the way nature goes about propagatin'."

"And he's seen Jube and Marcus. What kind of lesson is that for a six-year-old?"

"They're in love. Isn't there a lesson in that, too?"

Too uncomfortable to face him any longer, she fled from his office. She lay awake nights wondering what Willy had seen when he'd watched the horses mate, and Jube and Marcus. The images in her mind made her restless and uncomfortably warm and she rose to open her window and saw lights flickering down in the pool house. She wondered what it would be like to experience that unearthly buoyancy wearing nothing but a thin piece of cotton. One day shortly before the wedding, when she was fitting Jube's dress, she asked her if it was true that the girls swam after dark. Jube said yes, and Agatha asked if they'd let her sneak out with them next time.

They went that very night, slipping down the driveway like four wraiths, their dressing gowns pale splotches of white beneath the giant magnolias. It was decidedly unladylike, walking barefoot at night with only a single thin garment underneath her gown, but Agatha had done so few forbidden things in her life, it was a pleasure to break the rules, just once.

They reached the pool house giggling, and they felt their way inside its black recesses—cool, damp dirt against their feet, then the colder, smoother marble at the edge of the pool. Jube teased, "Look out for water moccasins now." Two high-pitched squeals echoed eerily off the walls and the surface of the lightly gurgling water. Then a match caught and flared and the single lantern cast a thin orange light over one corner of the large enclosure. Jube turned, pulling the knot from her belt. "Anybody scared?" she inquired innocently.

Ruby pushed her in, robe and all. "Why, shucks, no, we not scared. Any snakes in dere, ya got 'em all out by now."

Though Jube came up gasping, she wasn't in the least angry. "Come on, you high-handed nigger woman. Get in here so I can get even with you!"

Ruby laughed, slipped from her robe, and walked down the marble steps like a naked ebony goddess, followed by Pearl. Jube splashed them and they gasped. Then the pair piled in to get revenge on Jube and soon the three of them were romping like children.

Agatha was much slower getting wet. She wore her cotton combination—a sleeveless garment that buttoned on one shoulder and at the crotch, combining pantaloons and chemise into one.

As Gandy had said, the water was icy. But once in it, she adjusted to the temperature just as she had at White Springs. The remembered weightlessness and grace returned—heavenly. The girls knew how to swim in a rudimentary fashion. They taught her to roll onto her back, flutter her feet, and use her hands like a fish's fins. And how to do a surface dive and come up nose first. And how to blow out through her nose to keep the water from getting into it. And how to rest in the water and pull in a deep lungful of air and hold it and feel herself lift, lift, lift to the surface and hang there as if floating upon a puffy cloud in the sky.

It ended altogether too soon. But Agatha promised herself she'd go again, soon.

Meanwhile, the plans for the wedding progressed. It took longer than expected before Jube's wedding dress was done and the overseer's cabin was livable. But finally everything was ready and the minister from Leatrice's Baptist church agreed to perform the ceremony.

They gathered in the front parlor on a late golden afternoon in early April—Gandy's family, and all the current guests at Waverley Mansion (all three rooms were filled now), and every former slave who'd returned to help the place thrive again. The room created a splendid setting for the bridal couple, with the sun slanting in through the tall west windows and the azalea bushes in profuse bloom, both outside and in. Enormous bouquets of pink ones had been placed on the piano and on tables throughout the room.

In the wedding alcove, Jube, dressed totally in white—her color—stood beside Marcus, wearing elegant dove-gray. Jube held a cluster of white azaleas bound by a single white satin ribbon. Marcus held Jube's free hand.

Ivory played the piano while Ruby and Pearl harmonized on "Sweet Is the Budding Spring of Love."

The Reverend Clarence T. Oliver stepped forward and smiled benevolently at the bridal couple. He was a spindly man, with too much height and too little breadth, upon whose lanky frame clothing hung like a flag on a windless day. He wore round spectacles and couldn't seem to stand still, even when speaking. But the moment he opened his mouth one forgot about all this. His voice, a deep basso profundo, resonated like a jungle drum.

He opened his Bible and the ceremony began.

"Dearly beloved . . ."

Gandy stood nearby, recalling the day he and Delia had heard the same words in the same alcove. They'd been bright with happiness then, too, just as Jube and Marcus were now. Their future had lain ahead of them, mapped out like a golden road upon which they had only to walk, hand in hand, to eternal happiness.

How brief that happiness had been and how relatively little he'd known in the years since. He envied Marcus and Jube, radiant with love, committing themselves to a future together. It was what he, too, wanted.

Between himself and Agatha, Willy fidgeted. She leaned over and whispered something to him and he settled down.

The minister asked who witnessed this union and Gandy spoke up. "I do."

Pearl and Ruby, together, said, "We do." (Jube had adamantly insisted on two female witnesses, declaring she could absolutely not choose one over the other, and the minister had finally given in.)

The minister asked, "Do you, Marcus Charles Delahunt, take this woman, Jubilee Ann Bright, to be your lawfully wedded wife, to have and to hold from this day forward, for better, for worse, for richer, for poorer, in sickness and in health and forsaking all others till death do you part? Signify by nodding yes."

Marcus nodded, and from the corner of his eye Scott saw Gussie pull a handkerchief from her sleeve.

The question was repeated to Jube.

"I do," she answered softly.

Scott watched Gussie dab the corners of her eyes.

"In the presence of these witnesses and with the power invested in me by God, I now pronounce you man and wife."

Willy looked up at Gussie and whispered, "What're you cryin' for?"

Gandy nudged the boy's shoulder.

Willy transferred his uplifted gaze to Scott. "Well, she's cryin'. What's she cryin' for?"

But the boy received no answer. Scott was engrossed in watching Agatha dry her eyes. Engrossed in the play of golden sun on the glossy red-tipped waves of her hair. And the curve of her jaw as she refused to turn and look at him. And the puffiness of her lips as she half covered them with the handkerchief. And the sudden crazy thumping of his own heart.

The conviction hit him as abruptly as if the ancient magnolia had suddenly toppled in the yard and crashed through the roof: *It should be us standin' in that alcove. It should be Gussie and Willy and me!*

CHAPTER
21

He pondered for two days, stunned by the realization that Agatha Downing had worked her way into his heart, a heart that had remained indifferent since Delia. Yet how could he remain indifferent to one who'd brought so much happiness into his life? Before Agatha there'd been no Willy, no Waverley. He'd been drifting, always drifting, searching for contentment in an unfulfilling affair with Jube, in the surrogate family with which he surrounded himself, in the string of riverboats and saloons where he gambled and sold whiskey and substituted the superficial gaiety of night life for the true contentment of family life. During those years he'd thought himself happy. Only in retrospect did he realize how shallow that happiness was. His "family" had been nothing more than a sad troupe of malcontents, searching for roots, for constancy, for purpose in their lives.

Jube and Marcus had found theirs in each other. And unless Gandy missed his guess, it wouldn't be long before Ivory and Ruby did the same. And what about himself and Gussie? When had he been happier than since she'd been at Waverley? Who had ever done more to lead him back to the values on which he'd been raised? When had he last felt the elemental familial security that he had since she'd arrived? Having her here, a mother to Willy, a hostess to their guests, a quiet influence on the girls, had completed the picture he'd had of Waverley revived. Only after she'd come had it been as he'd imagined. And now that she was

413

here, he never wanted her to leave again.

He wanted to watch Willy grow to be a bright and honorable young man, guided always by the two of them; to watch their business prosper and share its success with her; to raise a batch of their own babies who would romp on the lawns with the peacocks and fill the rooms until he was forced to add a wing on to the house; he wanted the assurance that he'd retire with her and awaken with her and glance across the corner of the dining room table to find her sipping her soup with the impeccable manners he'd come to admire; he wanted to watch her magnificent mahogany hair fade to gray along with his own, and sit on the bois d'arc benches in their dotage, while their grandchildren fed corn to the peacocks.

LeMaster Scott Gandy wanted Agatha Downing for his wife.

Evenings were her favorite. Evenings, when the girls came across the lawn in their hoop skirts, gliding as if upon air. Evenings, when everyone gathered on the deep back veranda for mint juleps, while Willy fed the peacocks and the guests sat upon the bois d'arc benches and the smell of fresh-scythed grass filled the nostrils with green. Evenings, when they retired to the great dining room table and shared a meal amid happy chatter. Evenings, when the gas jets were lit and the house glowed with mellow light. Afterward, there was music in the parlor—Ivory on the piano, Marcus on the banjo, and the girls singing pastorale songs.

And sometimes they would dance gracefully with the guests on the polished pine floor of the great rotunda while the chandelier threw amber light upon their shoulders and their skirts swished with a sound like long grass soughing in summer wind. Then Scott and the other men would invite the lady guests to waltz, while Willy sat on the third step and played his harmonica and tapped his foot to Ivory's quiet renditions. And Agatha would look up from her embroidery and drop her hands to her lap and become lost in the enchantment of the graceful couples that never failed to raise a wellspring of longing in her breast.

Then one evening shortly after the wedding, Scott stood before her, bowing from the waist. "May I have this dance, Miz Downin'?"

Her heart fluttered and her neck grew hot.

"I . . ." To save face she chose to play it like a game, affecting a rich drawl, using her embroidery hoop as if it were a fan. "How kind, sir. Howevuh, Ah've danced til' mah feet ah simply fallin' off."

He laughed and captured her hand. "I refuse t' take no for an answer."

Her eyes flashed to the rotunda. Her cheeks flared. "No, Scott," she whispered anxiously, "you know I can't dance."

"How do you know? Have you ever tried it?"

"But you know—"

"We'll take it real slow." He plucked the hoop from her fingers and set it on the sofa. "I assure you it'll be totally painless. Come."

"Please, Scott . . ."

"Trust me."

He tugged her to her feet and linked their fingers firmly while escorting her to the rotunda, where three other couples circled slowly. How awkward she felt, facing him with her cheeks the color of ripe tomatoes and her hands unaccustomed to taking the waltz position.

"One here," he said, placing her left hand on his shoulder. "And the other here." He lifted her other palm on his own. "Now, relax. You're not expected t' prove anything, only enjoy yourself."

He began by swaying, smiling down at her, while she refused to lift her face. She didn't ever remember being so embarrassed in her life. But the others went about their dancing as if unaware that a lame woman groped in their midst.

He took a small side step and she moved too late, lurched, and was forced to grab his palm to keep from falling. His grip was sure and supportive. He stepped the other way and she preguessed him, finding that moving in that direction was much easier, much smoother. He took one step for every three the other dancers took. It was nowhere near a waltz, but he didn't seem to mind. She struggled along to his patient swaying—one awkward step left, one smooth step right. And when at last her face cooled she lifted her eyes. He was smiling down at her and she smiled back uncertainly. And suddenly it didn't matter that she really wasn't waltzing. It didn't matter that she had to clutch his hand and shoulder a little harder than the others. It only mattered that she was on a ballroom floor for the first time in her life. And that Scott looked beyond her clumsiness to her yearning and had given her a gift of more worth than all the crown jewels in the world.

Her heart filled with gratitude. Her eyes filled with love. She wished fervently that she could be graceful and unbroken for him, that she could whisk around the dance floor laughing, leaning back from the waist while she watched the chandelier go around and around above them. He was such a beautiful man, he deserved a perfect woman. It struck her that he was beautiful not only without, but within. He was one of those rare beings who measured people not by what he saw, but by what he learned of them. He was benevolent, generous, judicious, and honest. And he was all of these things to all people. He didn't put on one hat to please one person, and another to please the next. He expected people to accept him as he was, because that was his own way. He was the first person with whom she'd ever been able to relax fully, to whom she could admit her frailty and the extent of its emotional drain upon her. And knowing this, he had brought to her the gifts of swimming and dancing, two freedoms she had never hoped to know.

"Gussie, I didn't know you could dance!" Willy piped from his spot on the step.

She smiled at him with cheeks now lit from happiness instead of embarrassment. "Neither did I."

"Think I could do it?"

"If I can do it, anyone can."

He barreled off the step, brushing his way between two hoop skirts. Scott leaned over to pick him up. "Give Gussie your left hand," he ordered. "No. Palm up." Willy turned over his palm and Agatha placed hers on it. With Scott's left hand still around her waist, the three of them danced, Willy giggling, Agatha beaming, and Scott looking pleased.

This is how it should be, she thought, *the three of us together.* She savored the happy moments, storing them in her memory to take out and examine later—the warmth of Scott's hand on her back, the firmness of his shoulder beneath her palm, Willy's happy giggle, his small damp hand beneath hers, the play of amber light falling upon Scott's face from above, his dimples as he smiled, his dark, merry eyes.

When the dancing stopped she went upstairs with Willy. It was the only time each day she climbed the stairs, at his bedtime. He had come to expect it and she to enjoy it. She found his nightshirt and laid out a clean shirt and underwear for the next day, then watched as he folded his pants neatly, as she'd taught him. While he changed into his bedclothes she wandered to the dresser, glancing at Scott's things as she often did. Humming the song they'd danced to, tilting her head, she picked up his hairbrush, flicked her thumb over the bristles, then ran it through the hair just above her right ear as far as the French knot permitted.

"Need any help up here?"

She dropped the brush with a clatter and spun toward the doorway. Scott leaned against the frame with his weight on one hip. His eyes moved lazily from her flaming face to the hairbrush, then back again. His dimples looked as deep as the tufts on a chaise. He'd never come up before when she tucked Willy in. Willy generally scampered downstairs to find him in his office, give him a peck good-night, get a last drink of water, and delay bedtime as long as possible. She'd call over the rail, "What are you doing down there?" And he'd come trudging upstairs with an air of persecution. Then she'd plump his pillow, kiss him good-night, adjust the netting around his bed and extinguish the light. It was her custom to retire to her room immediately afterward. Scott would always be in his office as she passed his door. And when she'd turned to roll her own closed, she'd look up to find him watching her, smoking a cheroot or toying with a pen.

"Good night," she'd say.

"Good night," he'd answer.

Then the doors would roll and thump quietly between them.

But tonight he sauntered into Willy's room and adjusted the netting on the far side of the bed, then came around and sat down on the edge of it.

"'Night, sprout," he said. Willy went pell-mell into his arms and gave him a reckless kiss.

"I like dancin'!"

Scott laughed and rumpled Willy's hair. "Y' do, huh?"

"Can we do it again tomorrow night?"

"If Gussie wants to."

"She will. You will, won't you, Gussie?"

Scott studied her, still wearing the grin. Tiny shocks of awareness buzzed up the backs of her legs.

"Of course." She busied herself with Willy. "Now, down with you, young man."

"Kiss first," he demanded, kneeling beside Scott, lifting his arms to Agatha.

She leaned down for the customary hug and kiss. Her leg bumped Scott's knee, her skirts buried his pant leg. The awareness trebled. Willy flopped back and the two of them stood up. Watching Scott close the netting, she was gripped by a fantasy as vital as air—that Willy was theirs, that as they exchanged good-nights with him, Scott would take her hand and lead her from the room, along the cantilevered balcony to the master bedroom. And there she would take down her hair and preen it with the brush they shared, and don a fine lawn nightgown with open lacework across the top, and look across the room and find his dark eyes following each movement, while he slowly unbuttoned his shirt and pulled it from his trousers. And they would meet on the big tester bed where he'd been conceived and he'd say "At last," and she would do with him the thing that Violet said no woman should miss.

But what happened was that they walked down the curving stairway with Scott adjusting his single step to her step and a half. And he turned into his office and she into her bedroom. But when the doors had rolled within a foot of each other, she paused and looked up to find him standing in his office doorway, watching her again.

"What?" she asked.

"Do you sleep when you go t' bed so early?"

"Sometimes. Not always."

"Then what do you do?"

"I read. Or work on my stitchery. The lighting is so good here, it's a pleasure, even after dark."

"I find it hard t' sleep if I go t' bed before eleven."

"Oh," she said, then stood there like a dummy, wondering if he could see her pulse race from clear across the rotunda.

"Are you sleepy?"

"Not in the least."

"Would you like t' come into my office for a while? We could talk."

Like they used to do on the steps, listening to the coyotes. How many times had she longed to do it again? "I'd like that."

He stepped back and allowed her to enter the office before him and she felt his eyes on her back as she circled the room, examining the furniture, the portrait of his parents on one wall, a set of clay pipes inside one of the glass-fronted cabinets. Behind her she heard the humidor close, a match strike. She smelled his tobacco even before she turned.

"Would you mind if I have a glass of brandy?" he asked.

"Not at all."

"Sit down, Gussie."

She chose a wingchair of sea-foam green, while he filled a tumbler and crossed to a leather chair no more than three feet away. As he settled down he freed the bow from his tie and unfastened his collar button.

"I see a lot of improvement in Willy since you've been here."

"I meant to thank you for giving me jurisdiction over him. I think it helps if he knows from whom to get his instructions."

"No need t' thank me. You were the natural one."

"He's very bright. He learns fast."

"Yes, he's come in here when I'm workin' and read things aloud over my shoulder."

She laughed softly. "He does like to show off, doesn't he?"

Gandy laughed, too. The subject seemed completely covered.

"Marcus and Jube seem happy," she said, voicing the first topic that came to mind.

"Yes, very."

"Does it bother you?"

"Bother me?"

Whatever had she been thinking to ask such a question? No matter how many times she'd wondered about it, she should have guarded her tongue.

"I mean . . . well, the fact that Jube was . . ." She came to an uncomfortable halt.

"My lover, and now she's Marcus's wife? Not at all. Does it bother you?"

"Me!" Her eyes snapped to his. He took a slow sip of brandy.

"Well, does it?"

"I . . . I'm not sure what you mean."

He studied her with distracting totality for several seconds, a half-puzzled expression about his eyebrows. Then he glanced aside and rolled his loose ashes against the ashtray. "Forget it, then. We'll talk about safe subjects. The cotton. Have y' seen the cotton? Why, it's up to my knees already."

"No. I . . . I haven't been out that way."

"You should take a walk out there. Or if you prefer, you could ride. Have you ridden yet since you've been here?"

"I've never ridden—in my life, I mean."

"You should try."

"I don't think I could."

"You didn't think you could dance either, but you did."

"I didn't really dance and we both know it. But it was so kind of you to let me pretend."

"Kind?" He studied her unwaveringly. "Did you ever stop t' think that maybe I *wanted* t' dance with you?"

No, she hadn't. She had thought of it only as something he gave, not something he enjoyed.

The front door opened and their guests, a railroad baron and his wife, Mr. and Mrs. DuFrayne of Colorado Springs, came in. As they passed Scott's office door, Jesse DuFrayne said, "We were out for a last walk. Beautiful night."

"Yes, it is," Gandy returned.

"And there's the sweetest smell in the air," Abigail DuFrayne added. "What is it?"

"Jasmine," Agatha replied. "It's new to me, too. Isn't it heavenly?"

"This whole place is heavenly," Mrs. DuFrayne returned. "I've told Jess we must come back every year." She smiled back over her shoulder at her husband and Gussie felt a pang of jealousy as he rested his hand on the back of her neck and smiled into her eyes as if the rest of the world had suddenly faded away. They were expecting their first child, yet they acted like newlyweds.

Agatha thought, *If Scott were mine, I'd treat him exactly the way Mrs. DuFrayne treats her husband.*

The couple in the doorway brought themselves forcibly from their absorption in each other and Abigail said, "Well, good night."

"Good night," Scott and Agatha said in unison as the couple linked hands and headed upstairs.

They were both aware that the DuFraynes were the last ones up. Nobody else would be coming through the foyer anymore tonight. When their footsteps disappeared overhead the office grew silent.

Scott finished his drink and tamped out his cigar.

"Well, I really should be going to bed, too." Agatha moved to the edge of her chair.

"Just a minute," he said, stopping her as she began to rise. "There's one more thing."

He rose casually, stepped before her chair, leaned forward, and rested both hands on its arms and kissed her indolently. She was so surprised that her eyes remained opened while his closed and he took his time, brushing her skin with his moustache, touching his smoky tongue to her lips. The only other place he touched her was at the knees, where his legs flattened her skirts. The kiss was lingering but soft, and it left her feeling stunned.

He locked his elbows and looked in her pale eyes.

"Sleep well, Gussie," he murmured, then straightened and saw her to the door.

All the way across the rotunda she resisted the urge to touch her lips, and the even greater one to turn back for more. Standing between the rolling doors, she turned, studied him with wonder, their expressions intent. Then, wordlessly, she backed into her room, rolled the doors closed, and let the shock waves build. She spun and leaned back against the doors and wondered what in the world had prompted him to do such a thing in such an offhanded way—*Just a minute . . . there's one more thing*—as if he were going to remind her to buy one last item of groceries as long as she was going to town anyway. She lifted her face to the ceiling, rested her fingers over her hammering heart, and let out a brief, silent laugh. Was this how courtships started? Or seductions? And did it matter to her anymore which it might possibly be?

She arose the next morning excited, expectant, and dressed with infinite care only to learn when she went to the dining room for breakfast that he'd left at dawn and wouldn't be back for two weeks. He was buying horses in Kentucky.

Two weeks! Kentucky!

Her world turned blue and empty.

Those fourteen days seemed endless. On the thirteenth evening she washed her hair and put vinegar in the rinse, and on the fourteenth day she styled it high, tight and becoming, and dressed in an ice-green day dress that made her eyes look paler, her lashes darker, her hair redder, and her skin fairer.

And every time the front door opened her heart seemed to slam into her throat and her pulse went crazy.

But he didn't come home.

On the fifteenth day she went through the same ritual again, only to go to bed deflated and worried.

On the sixteenth day she wore a plain gray plaid dress with a simple white collar because she and Willy were studying herbs in the garden while she gathered them for

Leatrice. It had rained during the night and she had forgotten her hat. The sun was fierce, the humidity sapping, raising sweat on her brow that immediately brought flies buzzing. Slapping one away, she caught her wrist buttons on her hair and pulled the neat French twist askew, after which an irritating strand kept falling down across her jaw.

Of course, that's how he found her, sitting on a low "weeding chair" between the rows of basil and comfrey with sweat darkening her underarms and her hair untidy and a smear of dirt on her chin and a flat basket on her lap. The garden was on the opposite side of the house from the driveway, so she didn't know he'd returned until his shadow fell across her.

"Hello."

She looked up and felt the familiar earthquake in her chest at the sight of him standing above her with his hands on hips and one knee cocked.

"Hello," she managed to say, lifting a hand to shade her eyes. "You're back."

"I missed you," he said without prologue.

She flushed and felt sweat running down her sides and wished terribly that she could dip in the pool and not see him again until she looked as she had the day before yesterday in the cool green dress with her hair glossy and high.

"You're two days late."

"Have you been countin'?"

"Yes. I was worried."

"Hi, Scotty!" Willy interjected. "We're studyin' herbs."

The tall man rubbed the boy's head affectionately, but he gazed at Agatha all the while.

"Herbs, huh?"

"Uh-huh."

Scott dropped to one knee, curled a finger beneath Agatha's chin, and brushed the dirt with his thumb. Holding her so, he kissed her, a light, brief graze, while the scent of dill and angelica and saxifrage and spearmint lifted from the steaming earth and steeped like potpourri around them.

"I've brought you somethin'," he told her softly, while Willy watched and listened.

"Me?" It came out in a whisper.

"Yes. The calmest horse I could find. Her name is Pansy and you're goin' t' love her. Can the herbs wait?" She nodded dumbly while his thumb continued brushing her chin. "Then, come. You have t' meet her."

And so he gave her the third gift of the three unattainables she had mentioned so long ago on a landing in Kansas. Agatha was terrible at riding, stiff and tense and frightened. But he put her in the saddle and led Pansy around the paddock and taught Agatha to loosen up and enjoy the easy walk of the mare. In time she took the lines herself and guided the horse beside his, always at a sedate walk, beneath the shady trees in the pecan grove and along the grassy verges between the unused cotton fields and through the thick green shade of the wild magnolias that pressed close to the Tombigbee, where the horses dipped their heads to drink.

May turned to June and they rode each day, but the fleeting kisses were not repeated and she was left to wonder to what end he wooed her.

June came on torpid, sticky.

Gandy had spent one morning clearing the riding trails with a scythe. He'd forgotten how fast kudzu vines grew in the summer. They could strangle an entire garden in a matter of days. Out in the woods, where they were often forgotten, they could get a tenacious foothold if not discouraged regularly.

Riding in on Prince, with the scythe handle across his thighs, he pulled a handkerchief from his pocket and swabbed his neck. Sweat ran down the center of his back. His trousers stuck to his thighs. He wore a dusty broad-brimmed black hat with a sweat-soaked band. It was deadly hot for June. He left Prince at the watering trough and checked the thermometer on his way to the ice house. Ninety-two degrees already and it wasn't even eleven o'clock. He descended five steps to a submerged stone building and from its wooden doorframe pulled an ice pick. Inside, it was dark and cool and smelled of wet sawdust. With a dusty boot he scraped some aside and gouged out a sharp wedge of ice, kicked the sawdust back into place, and emerged into the blinding midday light, sucking. He rammed the ice pick into the doorframe, left it twanging, and took the steps two at a time. At the top he almost knocked Agatha off her feet.

He grabbed her to keep her upright. "Gussie, I didn't see you."

"You didn't look."

He smiled down at her from beneath the brim of the dirtiest hat she'd ever seen him wear. She smiled up at him from beneath the brim of a simple wide sunbonnet of unadorned straw.

"Sorry. Y'all right?"

"I'm all right."

"You comin' out here for the same thing I just got?"

"I needed *something*. Gracious, but it's hot." She plucked at her dress as if to free it from her chest.

"You're in the South now. Gotta expect it to be hot." Suddenly, he slipped his ice into her hands. "Here, hold this while I get y' some." His hands were none too clean and she caught a whiff of sweat—half man, half horse—as he turned and headed back down the steps. As he yanked the ice pick from the doorframe, she noted the rings of dampness beneath the arms of his loose white shirt, and the long line of moisture running down its center back. In the year-plus since she'd known him, she'd never seen him so dirty. It felt intimate to see him so and did strange things to her insides. She heard the dull, rhythmic thud of the pick on the ice. Then he came back out, stabbed the doorframe, and closed the door.

"Here. Got you a nice pointed one, easy for suckin'."

They traded ice. His hands were no cleaner than before. Neither was his face. It was streaked with sweat, grimy in the cracks at the corners of his eyes. He made no apologies but sucked his own ice chip while it melted between his fingers and made rivulets of mud on his hands. She stood watching him with great fascination, her pale eyes fixed upon the springing black hair on his chest where the water dripped from his ice chip. She forgot that her own hands were freezing.

He pulled the ice from his mouth, backhanded his lips, and said, "Go ahead. It's good."

She took a lick and got some sawdust. When she spat, he laughed.

"A little sawdust never hurt anyone."

She licked again and smiled.

"Well, listen," he said offhandedly, "I'm goin' t' see if Leatrice has some cold tea. See y'all at dinnertime."

He dropped a kiss on her mouth with even less forethought than either of the two times before. His tongue took a single cold swipe at her lips. He backed up, stuck it out, and picked a piece of sawdust off it.

"Sorry," he said, grinning. And left her standing there, stunned.

Courtship or seduction? Either way, it matched none of her preconceived notions, but the chances of an unexpected kiss made her blood course each time she encountered him.

Gandy found Leatrice in the cookhouse with Mose, smoking her pipe and husking corn. It had to be one hundred five degrees inside.

"Lord, woman, you're goin' t' die of heatstroke."

"Heatstroke ain't nowhere neah as scary as what Mose just told me. Tell 'im, Mose."

Mose didn't say a word.

"Tell me what?"

"Hants is in de pool house now," Leatrice stated, too impatient to wait for Mose.

"In the pool house!"

"Mose see 'em. Carryin' light, too, and lookin' for folks to pull unduh de watuh."

"What's she talkin' about?"

"I seen 'em. Lights flickerin' roun' down dere deep in de night when de res' o' de house asleep. Seen 'em floatin' in, like swamp mist, all white an' shiftin'. Ain't got no shape atall. Heard 'em laugh, too, high, like screech owls."

"That's ridiculous."

"Mose seen it."

"I seen it. Come up from de buryin' groun', dey did."

"You claimed there were ghosts in the house, too, but you haven't seen any since you've been in there, have you?"

"'Cause I wear my asafetida, dat's why."

"Mebbe dey move out. House too crowded, so dey tuk to de pool house instead."

Maybe they had. It had been some time since Gandy had experienced any manifestations of spirits in the big house.

It lay on his mind the following night when he couldn't sleep. Beside him, Willy was restless and he wished for a room of his own. But he and Willy doubled up to free more rooms for guests. The sultry weather continued. The sheets felt damp and the mosquito netting seemed to block out any moving air.

Scott rose, slipped on his trousers, and found a cheroot in his coat pocket. Barefoot, he padded out onto the upstairs veranda. He propped a foot on the rail, lit the cheroot, and thought about a night when he'd sat just like this on the sorry little landing he'd shared with Agatha in Proffitt. Lord, it seemed such a long time ago, yet it was less than a year. August, it had been. August or September with the coyotes howling.

An owl called softly and he lifted his head.

At the far end of the driveway a tiny light flickered.

His foot dropped off the rail and he pulled the cigar from his mouth. Hants? Maybe Mose and Leatrice were right again.

He was downstairs in a trice. Not until he was reaching for the derringer in his desk drawer did he realize it would do little good against hants. He took it just the same—hard telling what he might run into at the pool house.

Outside it was no cooler than inside. The air was motionless, thick. Down by the river frogs sent up a full range of notes, from the shrill piping of tree frogs to the basso bark of bullfrogs. Walking barefoot through the damp grass, he stepped on a snail, cursed softly at the squish, and moved on soundlessly. The light was steady. He could see now that it came from a window of the poolhouse.

He approached the building stealthily, backing up against the outside wall—cold against his bare shoulder blades—holding the derringer in his right hand.

He listened. Sounded like someone was swimming. No voices, no movement of any other kind, only the soft lap of parted water.

He eased himself into the lighted door space. His gun hand relaxed and he breathed easy. Someone was swimming, all right. A woman, dressed in nothing but a white combination, and she had no idea he was here. She was on her stomach, heading for the far side of the pool with slow, easy strokes. A lantern sat on the marble steps. He moved beside it, curled his toes over the sleek stone edge, and waited. At the far end she dipped beneath the surface, came up nose first, smoothed the water from her face, then headed for him, on her back.

He waited until she had nearly reached him before speaking.

"So this is our ghost."

Agatha thrashed around, found her footing, and gaped up at him.

"Scott! What are you doing here?" She crossed her arms over her breasts and ducked below the surface. He stood stiffly, dressed in nothing but a pair of black trousers, his feet widespread, a gun in one hand, a scowl on his face. Lit from below, his expression appeared devilish.

"Me! What in tarnation are *you* doin' here in the middle of the night?"

She brought one hand from underwater to smooth her hair nervously. "Aren't I supposed to be here?"

"Hell's afire, Gussie, there could be snakes in that water!" He gestured impatiently with the gun. "Or you could get a cramp—and who'd hear you yell for help?"

"I didn't think you'd be angry."

"I'm not angry!"

"You're shouting."

He lowered his volume but propped both hands on his hips. "Well, it's a damned dumb idea. And I don't like you bein' here alone."

"I don't always come alone. Sometimes I come with the girls."

"The girls. I should've known they'd be behind it."

"They taught me to swim, Scott."

He softened somewhat. "So I saw."

"And it's been so hot, I've had trouble sleeping."

So had he—wasn't that what brought him onto the veranda in the first place? "Doesn't that icy water bother your hip?"

"Sometimes. When I first get in. But since I've been swimming regularly I think it's better."

"Regularly? How long has this been goin' on?"

"Since right after I first got here."

"But why do it at night? Why not durin' the day?"

She crossed her arms tighter, gripped her collarbone and looked away. Water dripped from her hair in magnified dribbles, while across the wooden ceiling shards of reflected lantern light danced like fireflies. Scott's glance dropped beneath the surface, but her bare legs were an indistinct blur.

"Well?"

"We . . ." She stopped guiltily.

"Gussie, I'm not upset about your usin' the pool, only about your usin' it at night when it's not safe."

"During the day the guests are around, and we don't have proper bathing costumes, so we . . ." Again she stopped, but her eyes came back to his.

A half grin touched his face.

"Ah, I see."

"Please, Scott. It's not proper for you to be here. I'll come out if you'll go back up to the house."

He dipped a bare toe into the water, wiggled it. "I have a better idea. Why don't I come in? It's a hot night and I couldn't sleep either. I could use a dip myself."

Before she could object, he laid the gun aside and splashed down the steps into the water.

"Scott!" she shrieked.

But he paid her no mind whatsoever. He made one clean dive and came up ten feet beyond her with a roar of shock.

"Waaaah!"

She laughed but stayed where she was while he headed for the far end in a powerful overhand crawl. He turned and came back her way, passing her without pause. On his third lap, he said, "Come on."

"I told you, I'm not properly dressed."

"Oh, hell, I've seen you in your nightgown." He struck out again and left her behind, absorbed in the physicality of the exercise. He was using one side of the pool. She decided it would be all right if she used the other.

But only her head showed above water while they shared the pool for the next ten minutes.

She was paddling idly on her stomach when his head popped up beside her like a turtle's.

"Had enough?" he inquired, smiling.

She backed off and clasped her collarbone again. "Yes. I'm cold now."

"Come on, then. I'll walk y' back t' the house."

He grabbed her by the wrist and began hauling her out of the pool.

"Scott!"

He just kept hauling.

"Do you know how many times you've said my name since I discovered you in here?"

"Let me go!"

Instead, he picked her up and climbed the marble steps and stood her on her feet at the top, where she shivered in a scrap of white that turned transparent the moment she left the water. He glanced once down her length and let her see the grin of appreciation before doing an about-face.

"I'll keep my back turned."

He did, while she executed a slapdash job of drying her face and arms, then slipped into her dressing gown with skin that was still damp and underwear that was soaked.

He smoothed the water off himself with his palms.

"Here, you can use this before I dry my hair with it."

He glanced over his shoulder and accepted the towel. "Thanks."

She watched covertly as he whisked it over his bare skin and gave his head a quick once-over, leaving the hair sticking up in spikes. Men were certainly more brusque about their toilette than women, she thought, amused.

He handed the towel back and combed his hair in a single swipe with both hands. Then he gave an all-over shake and grinned at her. "Never saw you with wet hair before."

She immediately grew self-conscious, bent at the waist, and wrapped the towel around her head. Straightening, she twisted it and secured the ends at her nape.

His eyes made another pass down her body before picking up the gun and the lantern. "Ready?"

She nodded and preceded him outside. On their way up to the house he said, "Leatrice thinks you're a ghost. Mose saw the lantern down in the pool house and must've heard y'all laughin' down there. He told Leatrice the place was haunted."

"Must I stop going down at night now?"

"I'm afraid so. But we can set aside a time durin' the day for you and the girls t' have the pool t' yourselves."

"Could we really?"

"Why not? It's much more sensible than in the dark. Would y' listen t' those frogs?"

They walked the remainder of the way to the house without talking, the chorus of frogs accompanying them. A thin sliver of moon lit the road to a dim ribbon of gray. From the gardens came the scent of night-blooming stocks. Beneath the spreading boughs of the magnolia tree Agatha looked up at the branches lit from below by lantern light. Stepping between the boxwoods, they moved into pale moonlight again. Their bare feet fell like soft drumbeats upon the hollow wooden floor of the veranda. The wide front door swung silently on oiled hinges.

Then they were inside, in the massive rotunda, which swallowed up all but a tiny circle of light from the inadequate lantern that Scott still held. One of her double doors was pushed back. They stopped beside it. She turned and lifted her face, with her arms crossed over her breasts.

"Well, good night," she said, unable to dream up an excuse to keep him a while longer.

"Good night," he answered.

Neither of them moved. She stood feeling her heart thump beneath one wrist, and warm water was dribbling down the insides of her legs, forming a puddle on the floor.

Her face was lovely and stark, framed by the white towel, wrapped turban fashion around her hair. He was conscious of the fact that her dressing gown had become soaked wherever there was underclothing beneath it, and that his own trousers clung and formed a puddle that crept along the waxed floor to pool with hers. He wanted to do the same thing himself—cling, pool himself with her.

His eyes dropped to the hollow of her throat, where a pulsebeat fluttered far faster than normal, as did his own.

"It was fun," she whispered.

"Was it?" he replied, holding the lantern high so it lit their faces to a rich apricot hue. He watched her eyes, wide, uncertain, realizing she was out of her depth in situations such as this, that her guarded posture had come from a life guided by stern moral codes.

Give me a sign, Gussie, he thought. *You stand like St. Joan, waitin' for the fire starter t' touch his flint.* But no sign came. She appeared scared to death, staring up at him with eyes as pale and clear as peridots. A droplet of water fell from his disheveled hair onto his naked collarbone. Her gaze snapped down to follow it, trailing lower and lingering on the wedge of coarse hair upon his chest. He saw her swallow, and the gravity that tugged him toward her became too powerful to fight.

He took her by both wrists and drew them away from her breasts.

Her eyes flew up. "I . . . should . . ." she whispered, but the rest went unsaid.

He lowered his head to kiss her, finding open lips, cool yet from the water. He touched them with his tongue and she responded timidly—a soft kiss of introduction and expectancy. He straightened and they studied each other's eyes, searching for and finding mutuality.

She twisted her wrists slowly until his grip relaxed, then with calculated deliberation curled her hands over his shoulders, looking at them there as if the sight awed her.

He stood stock-still, letting her adjust. "Are you afraid of me?" he whispered. "Don't be afraid."

"I'm not." To prove it, she raised up on tiptoes for a second, longer kiss. Her elbows rested on his chest. When the kiss ended she stood just so—eyes closed, forearms against him, breathing as if a fire had suddenly consumed all the oxygen around her.

She opened her eyes and met his. Her voice was uneven as she whispered, "What I told you the last night in Kansas was true."

"I know. It's true now for me, too."

She held his cheeks. "Then say it."

"I love you, Gussie."

Her eyes closed once more and her nostrils flared. "Please, oh, please, tell me once more so I'll know I'm not dreaming."

His hands closed tightly on her shoulders. "I love you, Gussie."

She opened her eyes and ran her fingertips over his lower lip, as if absorbing the wonder of his words. "Oh, Scott, I've waited so long to hear that. All my lonely life. But you must not say it unless you're certain."

"I am. I've known since the day of the wedding. Maybe even before that."

She looked pained. "Then why have you waited all this time to tell me?"

"I didn't know what you wanted first, t' be told or shown. And you're so different. You're fine and special and pure, the kind of woman a man woos for a while."

"Then put the lantern down, Scott . . . and the gun . . ." she begged softly. "And show me."

He stooped and in one fleet motion left them in the dark. When he came back up their embrace was immediate, their kiss intemperate, all seeking tongues and circling arms and driving breath—a clinging desire filled with impatience and a need to make up for lost time.

She threw her arms up and her head back, and the towel came loose from her head. He plunged one hand into her damp hair while hers spread upon his shoulder blades, running their width to learn the exquisite feel of his cool skin and taut muscle. He clamped an arm around her waist and drew their bodies so close the dampness from his trousers seeped through the dressing gown along her thighs.

One kiss followed another, growing more ardent, slanting this way, then that, while he found her breast with its cold, puckered nipple pressing against the wet garments. The moment he touched it she caught a breath in her throat and held it.

He fondled her until she began to breathe again . . . as if she were running uphill.

He reached for her belt and she thought of Violet's words and put up no resistance. The belt joined the towel on the floor and he parted the dressing gown, running his hand inside. She shivered.

"You're cold," he murmured against her forehead.

"Yes."

"I can warm you."

"Shall I let you?"

He kissed her and found the buttons at her shoulder. The wet undergarment folded beneath its own weight, exposing a single breast. Cupped, it filled his palm, the skin still cold, beaded, drawn. She shivered again from the transfer of heat as much as from the response that skittered down her stomach. Inside her wet clothing he found her other breast, puckered, too, with cold, and warmed it. Warmed her mouth with his tongue. Her wet stomach with his own. Her thighs with his thighs.

So fast, she thought, *so fierce the transition from want to wanton. So this is how it happens, not in a marriage bed, but in a hall, standing at a doorway while your knees turn to pudding and your skin to embers and you experience for the first time a man's turgid body impressing yours.*

Ignorant but eager, she lifted to him, took her fill of kisses, touched his damp hair as he'd touched hers, followed the tutelage of his tongue and lips, wondering if in a lifetime she would ever be able to make him understand what he meant to her. Words seemed paltry, yet she whispered, clasping his cheeks and letting her breath mingle with his.

"When you left Kansas I wanted to cry but I couldn't. My sorrow went too deep. But I grieved daily, and it could have been no harder had you died."

She kissed his chin, felt his jaw move as he spoke in a voice thick and gruff. "I asked myself over and over why I was leaving you. I didn't want to, but there was nothing else I could do."

"I thought about dying," she whispered. "Sometimes I wished I would."

"No, Gussie . . . no." He kissed her in quick hard motions, as if to force the memory from her head.

"It seemed preferable to living without you. I had always been lonely, but after you were gone I thought I'd never before guessed the true meaning of the word. I despaired of ever feeling this with you, and you were the first man I'd ever lain beside and I knew there could be no other. Not for me. Not ever."

"Shh! Love, that's over."

Again they kissed while his hands moved over her with new urgency, as if to reiterate the promise. Her breasts warmed, his caress grew gentler.

"That night we kissed on the landing it was hard for me to keep from doin' this."

"I wouldn't have let you then."

"Why?"

"Because you were leaving."

"But I didn't want t' leave you. At the last minute I was sick at the thought."

"Sick? Were you really? I thought I was the only one who felt like that—sick, from longing, from emptiness."

"No, you weren't the only one."

"But you had Jube. You didn't have to be alone."

"When you don't love someone, you still feel alone."

"You never loved her?"

"Never. We used t' talk about it, wish we felt more for each other. But we just never did."

Inside her opened garment he ran his hand down her cool back, down her cold buttocks. She pressed closer and found herself amazed at how little guilt she felt at letting him fondle her so intimately.

"Scott?"

"Shh!" He kissed her and swept a hand around her hip, to the front, down her stomach.

She drew back gently and halted it. "There's something I must say to you. Please . . . please stop and listen."

He obeyed, holding her by both hips, while she rested her hands on his chest.

"When I was leaving Proffitt, Violet said something to me that has been on my mind a lot since then. She confessed that when she was young she had a lover. She called it the most wonderful experience of her life, one that no woman should miss."

"Violet?"

She sensed his surprise, though she could see nothing of his face in the blackness. "Yes, Violet." With her fingertips she feathered the hair on his chest. "Then she said she hoped Mr. Gandy would see the light and take me for his lover, if not for his wife. I imagine that's where this is heading, and I want you to know, Scott, that if you want me for only a lover, I'll agree. I'll invite you into my room and . . . and . . . I would learn to . . . that is . . . I would do whatever . . ."

In the dark he tipped her chin up and kissed her, then folded both arms around her and clasped his hands at the base of her spine.

"How brazen of you, Miz Downin'."

She knew the dimples had appeared, though she couldn't see them. Flustered, she rushed on. "But if it's possible that you want me for something more than a lover, I'd like to request respectfully that we put this off so that it can happen in the master bedroom, in the bed where you were conceived and born, because I should not want to conceive any of your babies anyplace else in this house." She felt the chuckles building in his chest and her face became hotter and hotter, but she drew a shaky breath and forged on. "And if there is not even the remotest possibility, well, then I respectfully request that we delay this until I have the opportunity to ask some personal and highly feminine questions to Leatrice, because I'm quite sure she would know how I might prevent myself from getting with child."

Now she was certain she felt his chest shake with silent laughter.

"Why, Agatha, is this a proposal?"

She bridled slightly. "It most certainly is not. I'm simply stating my wishes before it's too late to do so."

"But you've even brought up conceivin' babies—it certainly sounds like a proposal t' me. Shouldn't we have the light on for this?"

"Don't you dare, Scott Gandy!"

She felt his hands enclose her upper arms and put her away from him. When he spoke again, all vestiges of teasing had left his voice. "Button up anything you want buttoned, and tie anything you want tied, because I'm goin' t' turn the lantern back on, Gussie."

"Please, don't, Scott." She would wither with self-consciousness when the lamp shone on her flushed face. But it flared to life and she had no choice but to cover herself hastily and confront the man who'd just caressed her wet, naked skin in the dark.

He held both her hands and looked her full in the face, utterly sober now.

"Agatha Downin', will you marry me?" he asked—just like that. Her mouth dropped open and not a word came out as he rushed on. "In the wedding alcove with everyone we know and love actin' as witnesses? Just the way my parents planned it, and with Willy there to put his stamp of approval on us, which is the way it oughta be since we're already a family, right?"

She covered her lips with three fingertips and her eyes flooded.

"Oh, Scott."

"Well, you didn't think I was goin' t' let you conceive my bastard babies in the downstairs bedroom just so Willy could have some playmates, did you? What kind of example would that be for the boy?"

"Oh, S . . . Scott," she blubbered again. But she was clinging to his neck and crying. "I love you so much." She kissed his neck, hard. "And I've wished for this, for Willy and you and me, for so long, but I never thought it would happen."

With his excitement growing, he held her far enough away to delve into her eyes with his own. "Say yes, Gussie.

Then we'll wake up Willy and tell him."

"Yes. Oh, yes."

She hugged him once more. Then they kissed, standing in their mutual puddle, with her bare toes on top of his and her hair plastered to her head and his drying in spikes.

When she backed away, she laughed and covered her hair with both hands. "Scott Gandy, you're awful, asking a woman such a thing when she's wet and bedraggled. If you knew how many times I'd imagined this scene, and how many times I fussed with my hair and primped with my dresses because I knew I was going to be with you. Then you pick a time like this to ask me. I look awful!"

He grinned. "I was just goin' t' mention that, Agatha." Then he handed her the lantern—"Here, hold this"—and plucked her up in both arms. "You look fine t' me," he told her as he headed for the grand staircase. "However, if you're goin' t' turn into a nag, I may decide t' change my mind."

She folded her free arm around his neck. "Just try it."

"Oh, and by the way, the weddin' night at Waverley is fine, but I intend for us t' honeymoon at White Springs, where we can have a little privacy."

"White Springs . . . mmm . . ." she murmured against his lips.

Climbing the stairs and kissing simultaneously made for uncertain progress. But they managed it beautifully.

Heedless of their damp clothes, they sat on the edge of Willy's bed and shook him awake.

"Hey, Willy, wake up."

Willy opened puffy eyes and screwed up his face. "Hmm?"

"We have somethin' t' tell you."

He sat up and rubbed both eyes with his knuckles. "What?" he demanded grumpily.

"Gussie and I are goin' t' get married."

Willy's eyes flew open. "You are?"

"How 'bout that?"

"Really married?"

Agatha beamed. "Really married."

"You mean so you could be my ma and pa then?"

"Exactly," she repeated, "so we could be your ma and pa then."

"Garsh!" he enthused. Full realization hit him and a crooked smile began to tilt his face. "Garsh . . . really?" He lit up like the Willy they'd expected, and he popped up on his knees to hug Agatha, the closest one.

"A real ma and pa!" He backed off suddenly. "Hey, you're wet!"

"We've been swimmin'."

"Oh." He considered a moment, then said, "In the middle of the night?"

"We were hot," Scott added.

"Oh." Without missing a beat, he inquired, "Could we have some babies then?"

Agatha colored, laughed, and flashed a brief glance at the man behind her. "It's all right with me if it's all right with Scott."

"Could we, Scotty? I want a brother."

"A brother, huh? What about a sister?"

"I don't want no sister. Girls are dumb."

Scott and Agatha laughed. Then he agreed. "All right, one brother. But will you give us a while t' work on that, or do we have t' have him as soon as the knot's tied?"

Willy grinned and suddenly decided to act silly. He braced his hands on the bed and kicked twice like a donkey. "Right away! Right away!"

Agatha recognized wildness when she saw it coming on. "All right, Willy, you can celebrate in the morning. Now it's time to tuck back in again."

When they'd kissed him and received giant hugs and Willy had exuberantly beaten his heels against the mattress, and they'd laughed and settled him down once more, they slipped from his room, leaving the door ajar.

Scott picked up Agatha in his arms and started down the stairs.

"You don't have to carry me, you know."

"I know." He nipped her lips with his own, then licked her ear. "I like to."

She laid her head against the arch of his neck and savored the ride. Reaching her room, he pushed her door wider with a bare foot, carried her through sideways and laid her on the bed, then braced a hand on either side of her head.

His voice became an intimate murmur in the dark. "I want t' start workin' on that baby brother right now, y' know."

"I know. So do I."

"Are you sure you want one?"

"Maybe more than one. How about you?"

"If they all turn out like Willy, how about seventeen?"

She laughed and pressed her stomach with both hands. "Oh, please, no."

Their playfulness ended and he kissed her lingeringly. "I love you, Gussie. And, God, it feels so good."

"I love you, too, Scott, and I'll make the best wife you could ever wish for—just wait and see."

He kissed her again until they both felt their resolve dangerously weakened.

"See you in the mornin'," he whispered.

She held him to her with sudden fierceness, marveling that he was he, and she, she, and that fairy-tale endings happened after all.

"And for all the mornings for the rest of our lives."

He kissed her forehead and slipped from the room.

When he was gone she crossed her arms over her breasts, fists tight, guarding it all fiercely so none of it could escape, not a nuance, not an iota.

Mrs. LeMaster Scott Gandy! she rejoiced disbelievingly.

CHAPTER
22

They would be married the afternoon of July 15, a day that began with heavy morning rains. When the sun came out it blanketed Waverley with sweltering heat. Inside, the mansion was bearable, however, with the veranda doors and jib windows thrown open downstairs, the rotunda windows opened high above.

One of the wedding guests would be Violet Parsons. She'd come a week earlier to help Agatha make her wedding gown, and now, as Agatha donned it, the blue-haired woman tittered and beamed.

"I think it's the prettiest one we ever made. *Tt-tt.*" She held the gown while Agatha slipped it on, then secured the twenty-two covered buttons up the back. It was made of rich sleek silk the exact hue of a waxy magnolia flower, with high neck, form-fitting torso, and caterpillar sleeves ruched from shoulder to wrist. Its skirt was sleek at the front, flowing at the rear, with deep trailing scallops.

Violet joined her hands and sucked in a breath, pleased. "My, don't you look lovely."

They stood in the master bedroom before the cheval glass that had been brought up from downstairs. It reflected a bride with thick burnished hair twined high on her head, narrow shoulders, trim waist, and pale, dark-lashed eyes. Her air of total happiness gave her an almost ethereal glow.

"I *feel* lovely," Agatha admitted.

"Absolutely perfect, if I do say so myself."

Agatha turned to press her cheek to Violet's. "I'm so glad you're here."

"I am, too, though I must admit, I'm a tad jealous. Still, if I can't be the one marrying that handsome Mr. Gandy, I'm glad it's you. But I've told him . . ."—she shook her finger at the bride—" . . . if it doesn't work out he only has to crook his little finger and I'll come running. *Tt-tt.*"

Agatha held Violet's cheeks and laughed. "Oh, Violet, you're priceless."

"I know. Now I must go pick the magnolias. I'll send Willy up with them."

When she was gone Agatha moved to the front window. The lane was lined with carriages, and blue awnings ornamented the great lawns. Below, the guests were entering, the food was being prepared, the minister had arrived, and the wedding alcove was flanked with bouquets of yellow day lilies and English ivy.

Agatha pressed a hand to her fast-tripping heart. It was still difficult for her to believe it was all happening, that she was standing in Waverley's master bedroom, where tonight she would share the high rosewood bed with the man she loved; that her clothing lay beside his in the bureau and hung beside his in the closet, where the scent of his tobacco mingled with that of her sachet; that it would be so for the rest of their lives. And there, outside, the carriages continued to roll in, bringing guests to honor the occasion.

It was as she looked down at them that she heard the sound behind her—the soft plaintive weeping of a child.

She turned. No one was there but the sound continued. Agatha remained remarkably calm, almost as if she'd been expecting the visitor on this auspicious day.

"Justine, is it you?" she asked.

Immediately, the weeping ceased.

"Justine?" She looked in a full circle but found herself alone in the room.

It began again, softer this time, but unmistakably real and distressed. Agatha reached out a hand.

"I'm here, Justine, and I'll help you if I can." The sound softened but continued. "Please don't cry. It's much too happy a day for tears."

The room grew silent, but as Agatha proffered her hand she felt a presence as clearly as if it were visible.

"Is it because I'm going to marry your father? Is that it?" She paused, looked around. "But you must believe that I'm not trying to take your mother's place in his heart. What she was to him will remain precious forever. You must believe that, Justine."

Agatha hushed, and all remained silent.

"I know you've met Willy already, and you've accepted him. I hope you'll accept me in the same way."

The change could not have been more evident had thunder suddenly ceased. The tension eased; peace settled over the room. Nothing touched Agatha's hand except a soft sighing wind, tinged with the scent of flowers. But as she dropped that hand to her side, she experienced a great sense of tranquillity.

Then Willy burst in with two magnolias.

"Here, Gussie, Vy-let and me picked the best ones we could find."

She leaned down to kiss him. "Thank you, Willy." When she straightened, she glanced around the room, but the manifestation had vanished completely.

"Hey, you smell good!"

"Do I?" She laughed and accepted the flower.

"And you look so pretty! Wait'll Scotty sees you!"

Agatha cupped his cheeks and kissed his nose. "Have I told you lately that I love you?"

He giggled and scampered to the window. "Did you see all the carriages?"

"I did." As her thoughts turned back to the wedding, her exhilaration mounted. "Where did they all come from?"

"Columbus. Scotty knows everybody there."

Agatha turned to the mirror and secured one of the magnolia blossoms in the back of her hair.

"Vy-let says to tell you it's time now."

Agatha stepped back and pressed a hand to her heart. *It's time now. Time to step out and meet your groom and walk with him to the wedding alcove and join your life with his and never be alone again.* The realization put a serene radiance on Agatha's face. Willy came to stand beside her, looking up, his hair combed and oiled with Macassar into the familiar peak over his brow, undoubtedly done by Scott. She remembered clearly the first time Scott had combed it that way, after the two of them had taken baths, when Scott brought Willy back to her millinery shop wearing the new clothes she'd made for him. Looking at the boy both she and her future husband loved immensely, she felt infinitely blessed, certain that the fates had brought the three of them together with this in mind. Carrying a single magnolia—her bridal bouquet—she extended her free hand.

"Let's go."

He smiled and they walked to the door. Just before he opened it she smoothed his collar and asked, "Now, you remember what to do, don't you?"

"Yes, ma'am." He opened the door a crack and peeked out. "Come on. He's waitin'."

Agatha caught and held a deep, steadying breath, closed her eyes a moment, and listened to Ivory's piano music drifting up from below. But neither deep breaths nor music did anything to calm the nerves trembling within her stomach.

She stepped to the doorway and her eyes met those of her espoused.

He was indeed waiting, standing diagonally across the balcony, just outside the children's room door, dressed in unbroken ivory, waiting for the first glimpse of his bride. Their gazes locked across thirty feet of open space surrounded by nothing but spooled railings and a sense of heart-lifting anticipation. Below them their guests lifted anxious eyes, but in that first moment, bride and groom were conscious of nothing but each other.

She was radiant, in waxy white, with her dress trailing and the simple flower in her hair.

He was breathtaking, in a swallowtail jacket and tapered trousers that dramatically set off his black hair and moustache.

They stared at each other with hastened pulses and fluttering stomachs, compressing this moment to carry within their hearts always, until at last the murmur of voices from below intruded upon their absorption and

Agatha smiled. Gandy's smile answered. Then it flashed to Willy, who cupped his fingers and gave a tiny, secret wave. Scotty answered with a broad wink. Then Willy gave his elbow to Gussie and escorted her to the head of the west stairway, while Scotty stepped to the head of the east.

Their descent would be talked about for years—bride and groom, resplendent in matching ivory, watching each other with dazzling smiles as the twin stairways led them down, down to where the stairwells curved toward each other like the interrupted arches of a heart; how they reached the bottom and met in the center of the rotunda floor, as if completing the heart's pattern; how the black minister, Reverend Oliver, from the tiny Baptist church up the road, was waiting there with the question, "Who gives this woman," and how Willy answered, "I do," then, with all due gravity, gave his future mother over to his future father, receiving a kiss from each of them; how the groom took the bride's hand and tucked it into the crook of his elbow, and escorted her across the grand rotunda to the wide parlor doors and a wedding alcove adorned with baskets of fragrant yellow day lilies and English ivy.

The room was crowded with guests but Agatha scarcely realized it as she dropped Scott's arm and stood formally beside him.

"Dearly beloved . . ."

Reverend Oliver offered a meaningful discourse on what it took to make a marriage thrive, on the importance of giving of oneself; the value of forgiving, the rewards of constancy, the virtue and scope of love. He spoke of the children with which this union might be blessed and Agatha felt Scott's elbow press firmly against hers. She glanced up from the corner of her eye to find his gaze fixed steadily on her face and thought about having his children and knew a burst of hope so profound it rocked her. His crossed hands parted, and in the folds of ivory satin at Agatha's hip he found her hand and squeezed it hard, doubling her joy.

Jube sang "Wondrous Love" in her faultless, crystal voice and the words filled Agatha's heart as richly as the scent of lilies filled her nostrils. And all the while Scott secretly held her hand, rubbing his thumb firmly along hers.

Then she was facing him and they were holding hands for all to see, and his cheeks were flushed, his palms damp, and she realized that she wasn't the only one shaken.

"I, LeMaster Scott Gandy, take thee, Agatha Downin' . . ." His voice, deeper than usual and carrying a slight tremor, betrayed a depth of emotion. But his dark, intense eyes never wavered from hers as he spoke his vows gravely.

Her heart swelled with love so intense it created a sweet hurt in her breast. *Scott, before you there was nothing, and now I have everything . . . everything. A lifetime hasn't enough days in which to lavish you with the love I feel.*

" . . . till death do us part."

And then it was her turn.

"I, Agatha Noreen Downing, take thee, LeMaster Scott Gandy . . ." As Scott held Agatha's hand and listened to her soft, quavering voice, he realized she was very close to tears. He saw them glimmer on her eyelids and was touched in the secretmost corner of his heart. He squeezed her delicate fingers, thinking it a miracle that a woman like her had come into his listless life just when he needed her to make it whole and give it meaning again.

Gussie, he thought, *I intend t' keep these vows, t' spend the rest of my life thankin' you for what you've made of me.*

" . . . till death do us part."

"The ring," said the minister in an undertone. Scott removed the glittering diamond from his little finger and slipped it onto Gussie's hand.

She watched it sliding over her knuckle with a sense of wonder, realizing it truly bound them forever. Then their gazes locked over their joined hands, and within their hearts the vow was sealed.

"I now pronounce you man and wife."

Scott's dark head bent over Gussie's burnished one, and their lips touched fleetingly. The kiss ended and he lifted only enough to look into her luminous green eyes while their breath mingled and the import of the moment settled within their souls. Husband and wife. Evermore.

He straightened, then squeezed her knuckles tightly, and his face broke into a flashing smile accompanied by deep dimples. Her glad smile blossomed in response, releasing the guests from the thrall in which they'd been held, many of the females misty-eyed.

The groom tucked the bride's hand into the crook of his arm and the two of them moved to a polished table where the family Bible lay open. There on a page already bearing many entries, Scott wrote:

July 15, 1881,
LeMaster Scott Gandy
married to
Agatha Noreen Downing

Then he kissed her again, this time hard, abrupt and exuberant, then wrapped his arms around her and dropped his lips to her ear.

"I love y'," he whispered.

"I love you, too!" She had to shout, for the piano had burst forth with a spate of exultant music and the murmur of their guests' voices rose to a considerable volume. Then Willy was there, demanding kisses again, as happy as the bride and groom.

In minutes they were separated by the congratulatory crowd and, strangely enough, saw each other only fleetingly during the remainder of the day. There were so many guests for Agatha to meet for the first time, so many old acquaintances for Scott to renew. A wedding feast was served buffet style and people scattered onto the lawns, wandered the gardens, or visited in the house. Some sat upon the rotunda steps, others on the bois d'arc benches. The heat was oppressive and champagne punch was served as a cooler. Children chased the peacocks and fed iced cakes to the horses. Dancing began in the rotunda and Scott captured Agatha briefly, beside one of the curving stairways, looped her arms around his neck, and lifted her free of the floor, then took her softly turning in his arms with their bodies pressed intimately close, their lips brushing. But they were discovered and separated by guests and the realization that they had more host and hostess duties to perform.

An hour later they bumped into each other in the doorway of the front parlor and scarcely had time to exchange a fond glance before they were interrupted by Mae Ellen Bayles and her daughter, Leta, and A.J., who by now had become Willy's fast friend. Mae Ellen commanded Agatha's attention and when next she saw Scott he was standing under one of the blue awnings, smoking a cheroot, visiting with a thin man in a striped suit and another with great hairy ears. But a pair of young ladies of marriageable age came to *ooh!* and *ah!* over Agatha's diamond and ask questions about her wedding gown and she had to do the polite thing.

The day moved on toward evening and the heat intensified, the breeze stilled. Agatha grew hot and weary. Scott grew impatient. Violet drank too much champagne punch and flirted outrageously with a portly merchant named Monroe Hixby. Willy came tattling that he'd found the pair kissing in the grape arbor. Agatha wished she, too, could escape to the grape arbor for some stolen kisses and time alone with her groom. While visiting with one of Waverley's current paying guests, a Mr. Northgood from Boston, she restrained a sigh and searched furtively for Scott. She saw him across the lawn, tipping his head toward Mrs. Northgood. As if he felt Agatha's gaze, he looked up and this time when their eyes met they exchanged no smiles.

I want to be alone with you, his long-suffering look said.

And I with you, hers replied.

Mrs. Northgood rambled on about the cost of heating homes in Boston in the winter, but Scott heard little of her prattle. He watched Gussie straightening her spine and pressing her left hip as she turned to attend to something Northgood was saying. Scott frowned and touched his guest's elbow, interrupting her filibuster as she drew a breath. "Would you excuse me, Mrs. Northgood?" he asked, his concerned eyes fixed on his bride. Then he skirted the surprised woman and headed across the grass to give Gussie some needed relief.

Reaching her, he took her elbow proprietarily.

"I believe your wife is lookin' for you, Mr. Northgood."

Without apology, he led Gussie up the marble steps, across the crowded rotunda, and into his office, where a group of three men sat smoking cigars and talking commodities.

"Gentlemen, would you excuse us, please? We're expectin' Reverend Oliver with the marriage certificate for us t' sign."

The three moved off apologetically into the rotunda and he closed the door behind them.

"But we've already signed the marriage certificate," Gussie reminded him.

"I know." He turned to find her standing in the middle of the office floor wearing a weary grin, her weight on one foot—a sure sign that she was tiring. "I wish they'd all leave," he said baldly.

"How unkind of us to say so."

"You're tired."

"A little." He came toward her slowly, arms at his sides.

"I saw you rubbin' your hip, and now you're keepin' your weight off it."

"It's nothing. It always aches at the end of the day."

Without warning, he swept her up in his arms and dropped to a deep leather wing chair, draping her feet over its arm. Smiling, she looped her arms around his neck, while he settled them comfortably, slumping back, dropping an ankle over a knee. A teasing grin climbed his cheek, bringing one dimple into play.

"So. Agatha *Noreen*, is it?" He lazily pulled the bow from his tie.

"It is."

"Now why didn't I know that before?"

She playfully coiled a lock of his hair around her finger. "A woman without secrets is like an answered riddle. There's nothing to guess about."

"Oh, so I married a woman who'll keep secrets from me."

"Now and then, maybe."

"So tell me, Agatha Noreen Gandy, what else don't I know about you?"

"Mmm . . ." She tilted her head back and appeared thoughtful, threading her fingers together at the back of his neck. "Justine visited me today."

"Really?"

"Just before the wedding, in our room. I made my peace with her, I think."

"And so you believe me now."

"I always did, didn't I? I believe she was right there in the parlor, witnessing our exchange of vows. And I think she approved."

His absolute love for her became reflected in his eyes as they roved over her face. He ran a single fingertip from her hairline down her nose to her mouth, where it gently misshaped her lower lip while his dark eyes followed the movement.

When he spoke, he wore no smile. His voice was low. "Mrs. Gandy, I've been dyin' t' kiss you all day."

Her heart fluttered as he satisfied his urge, joining his mouth to hers while she tightened her arms around his neck. His shoulders came away from the back of the chair and pressed her across his lap. Their tongues joined in lush complement. Their blood and skin and muscle hearkened. Their hearts took up an impatient beat as his hand came from beneath her knees to caress her breast within its tight confines of ivory silk.

Her breathing hastened, rushed out against his cheek. Her flesh changed shape and he fondled it with his thumb, feeling its hard core pressing up to meet his touch.

"Shall I send them all away?" he whispered against her mouth, his hand still at her breast, shaping and reshaping her as this day had reshaped her life.

"I wish you could," she murmured.

He kissed her once more, wetting her lips, feeling his own washed by her tongue, letting his hand play down her ribs, along her hip, to her stomach, flat and hard and withheld from him by her tight, satin skirt. Down farther, to the suggestion of femininity between her legs where he was again thwarted by the stovepipe shape of the garment, which allowed no room for exploration.

She rolled close, freeing the rear of her dress in invitation. He slipped his hand between it and the free-hanging rear drapery, found a tape tie, and tugged, then slid his hand inside against her warm curves, down the back of one thigh.

Their kiss grew insatiable, brought the thump of impatience resounding through their bodies.

Someone knocked on the door. "Mr. and Mrs. Gandy?" Reverend Oliver opened it and stuck his head inside. "Somebody said you wanted me in here?"

Agatha and Scott started guiltily to their feet, their faces aflame.

"Oh . . . uh . . . yes!" Scott groped for a plausible explanation and suddenly remembered the gratuity. He leaned over the desk, opening its center drawer from the opposite side. "I wanted t' give you this." He withdrew an envelope. "It's not much, but we want you t' know we appreciate your performin' the service in our house, especially on a hot day like this." He shook Reverend Oliver's hand. "Thank you again."

"My pleasure." The minister pocketed the envelope. "It isn't often I get to perform the wedding service in a setting like this. Definitely my pleasure." He smiled benignly, adding, "And of course I wish you a lifetime of happiness. Looks to me like you're well on your way to that already."

"We are, sir," Scott agreed, then reached for Agatha's hand and drew her against his side, interweaving their fingers.

"Well . . ." The minister ran a finger around the inside of his clerical collar. "It is a hot one, isn't it? Believe the wife and I will bid our good-byes and head for home."

Scott left Agatha to see him out and she lost her husband once more to their guests, ending their brief escape and interlude.

It was well after eleven o'clock before they saw the last of the carriage lanterns flicker off down the road. Everyone was gone at last and the houseguests had disappeared to their rooms. Willy had finally collapsed and Scott had carried him upstairs. In the dining room the punch bowl was empty. The remnants of the celebration lay scattered in the front parlor and on the lowest steps of the double stairways, waiting for morning to be cleared away.

"Y'all wants I should put out d' gas jets in heah?" asked Leatrice, entering the rotunda, where Scott and Gussie sat on the bottom step.

"No, I'll do it. You go on t' bed, Leatrice."

"Reckon I will. Mah bunions is killin' me." But she waddled over and stood before them. "It wunt mah place t' say it befo', but now dat y'all took a missus agin . . . well, it's 'bout time ya come t' your senses. And ya sho' picked a good one, Master. Yo' mama an' daddy be pleased. Maybe now Waverley have some pickaninnies, like it ought to. Been too many yeahs since any babies born in dese walls. Yessuh, too many yeahs. Now come here and let Leatrice give y'all a hug 'fore she starts runnin' salt all ovuh de floors."

He rose and hugged her. Tall as he was, his arms wouldn't reach around her, but he rocked her lovingly and kissed her wiry hair.

"Thank y', sweetheart."

Immediately, she pushed him away and smacked him with mock severity. "Watch who you callin' sweethot, ya young pup." Next she swung to Agatha, motioning. "You next, girl. Come heah so I can git dis bawlin' ovuh wid an' res' mah bunions."

Then Agatha took her turn at being enfolded against Leatrice's spongy bulk.

"Ah loves dat boy," came her scraping voice at the bride's ear. "Y'all be good t' him, heah?"

"I will. That's a promise."

"An' have lots o' pickaninnies. He be good at daddyin'."

With that final word of advice, she set Agatha from her and waddled out the back door, grumbling once more about her bunions.

When she was gone, Scott and Agatha looked at each other and laughed. Then the laugh faded and they stood in silence, alone, with Leatrice's parting injunction and its underlying message drawing their thoughts to the big rosewood bed above.

"Wait here," Scott whispered, and left her standing while he extinguished the jets. In total darkness he found her once more, kissed her with a deep mingling of tongues, and lifted her into his arms to carry her upstairs. In their room the overhead flames flickered softly and the jets gave off a faint hiss. He took her inside and closed the door with a heel and still they kissed, savoring the realization that they were free to express their love in whatever way they desired. At last.

They lingered for long savory minutes of fully clothed delight, letting the wondrous sexual suppression build. He lifted his head and they gazed into each other's eyes. The flames from the overhead chandelier seemed to catch and flare within his dark irises and her pale ones. Their breathing had grown erratic and their pulses drummed in strange places within their bodies. He let her feet slip to the floor and still they stared, while his hands rested at the sides of her breasts . . . close, but still delaying.

"Mrs. Gandy," he said rejoicingly. "God, I can't believe it."

"Neither can I. Tell me I'm not dreaming."

"You're not dreamin'. You're mine."

"No, Mr. Gandy, I believe it's you who are mine."

He took both her hands and held them loosely. "And happy t' be."

"Can wives really kiss their husbands any time they choose?"

"Any time they choose."

She kissed him, simply to exercise her right—a chaste, light kiss on the mouth, but a miracle nonetheless to one who'd for so long had nobody. He let himself be kissed, standing docilely, and when it was over he smiled warmly into her uptilted face. "I used t' like the involved kisses, but the simple ones have their own sort of appeal, don't they?"

In answer she gave him a far wetter one, ending with a surprising amount of suction. "I like them all."

He laughed and slipped an arm around her shoulders, turning her toward the room. "Someone has been here and prepared a few surprises, it looks like."

"Violet," Agatha whispered fondly, her eyes sweeping the room.

Who but dear Violet? She had turned down the bed and freed the netting from the corner posts, sending crosschecked shadows over the crisp white sheets. She had brought up one of the baskets of sweet, sweet lilies from the front parlor and set it on the commode beside the bed, from where their heady perfume filled the entire room. And, irrepressible romantic that she was, she had carefully laid out Agatha's newly made white nightgown with its lovingly crafted open work across the bodice and its narrow blue ribbon waiting to be tied in a bow beneath a bride's virginal breasts.

The room glowed softly in the light of the gas lamps, the flowers bade a welcome, as did the soft shadows within the netting. The window sashes were lifted to the night air and into one a white moth flitted, moving to explore a woman's brush and hair receiver upon the bureau, then on toward the flowers and finally to the white net, where it beat its wings to no avail. Not even a moth would be allowed to disturb the two who'd lie there. All this from Violet.

"She insisted on making the nightgown herself," Agatha told Scott, "wishing all the time she could be here instead of me." He might have denied her claim, but her respect for him grew because he didn't. Because he understood love in its many guises more than any human being she had ever known.

"Would you like t' put it on now?" he asked simply.

Her cheeks flared but she lifted her face. "It's been so hot today. Could we ... I mean ..." She glanced at the pitcher and basin. "I thought I might like to wash up first."

"Would y' like t' take a swim?"

"A swim?" Her eyes flew to his.

"It wouldn't take long. We can be in and out like a flash."

She thought longingly of the cool, cleansing water and welcomed the temporary reprieve.

"Together?"

"Of course." He took her by both arms and turned her around, began freeing the buttons that held her rear draperies on. "We'll be settin' habits tonight, habits we'll probably keep for the rest of our life. A swim before bedtime might be one we'd never be sorry we started."

But she knew the habit he was concerned with was not the one of which he spoke, but the one he was initiating behind her at this very moment. Nonchalantly, he stepped around her and laid her outer skirt across one of the matched blue chairs. She watched with her heart hammering in her throat, thinking of the padding on her hip. As if it were most natural, he returned and set about freeing the buttons down the back of her dress. When it was open he kissed her shoulder, then circled her and skimmed the dress down her arms and held her hand as she stepped out of it. When it, too, lay on the chair, he removed his jacket and tossed it atop the dress, then returned to stand close before her. She was fully aware that her cotton combination revealed the vague image of nipples underneath. He let his eyes drift down to them briefly, then back up.

"Is there anything you'd like t' do?" he asked quietly, waiting. "There's no need t' ask, y' know."

She glanced up, then quickly down, and her fingers trembled as she reached for his vest buttons.

"I'm afraid I won't be very good at this." She laughed nervously.

He tipped up her chin. "You must promise never t' apologize at these times. And you must certainly know that nothin' pleases a man more than a blushin' woman."

His words only added rose to the pink already in her cheeks. When the vest was free she stood behind him and removed it—too formally, she realized too late, though he didn't seem to mind. He loosened his cuff buttons while she applied herself to those on his chest. When all were open to his waistband, she looked up and laughed nervously again, unconsciously gripping one hand with the other.

"Pull it out," he ordered softly. "Then the next move is mine."

His trousers were tight. When she tugged at his shirttails, his hips swayed toward her, but he only grinned and let her struggle. The tails were warm from his body, pressed into a network of wrinkles. Looking at them seemed as intimate as studying the flesh that had warmed them and made her heart canter. To show she had some spirit, she sailed the shirt across the room and let it fall near the chair. But when he reached for the button on the waist of her petticoat, she grabbed his hand.

"Scott . . . I . . ."

His hands stilled but remained at the button. "Are you shy? Don't be shy, sweets," he said, touching her cheek.

"Be warned . . . I'm . . . I'm crooked."

His brows lowered. "You're what?"

"I'm crooked. My deformity . . . my hips . . . one is lower than the other and I . . . I pad one . . . and . . . and . . ." She had stammered only once in her life, after she had been attacked in Proffitt. How disconcerting, how embarrassing to be doing so again, half-undressed before her bridegroom.

But he attacked the problem directly. He put both hands on her hips and squeezed. "Is that what this is about? This puny wad of battin' I feel here? Let's see." In an instant her petticoat lay at her feet and her secret was exposed. He held her by the hips, dipped his knees and bent back, inspecting her. "I knew a woman once who put these in her bodice. Stuck my hand in there and came up with a bale o' cotton instead of a breast, and you can imagine what I . . . oh, damn my hide, I don't think I was supposed t' say that on my weddin' night, was I?"

Long before he finished she was laughing. She flung her arms about his neck. "Scott Gandy, I love you. I was so worried about it. So terribly worried."

"Well, worry no more, my lady. The point is, nobody's perfect, includin' me."

"Yes, you are."

"No, I'm not. Come here and sit down." He hauled her toward the portable steps beside the high bed. "You're not shy about your feet, are y'?"

"My feet?"

"Because I'm goin' t' take your shoes off."

He nabbed a buttonhook from the bureau and squatted before her wearing nothing but his wrinkled ivory trousers. Taking her heel in hand, he placed her foot flush against his crotch, and she couldn't help staring at the unexpected sight. Each time he wielded the hook, her foot bobbed against him. Heat rose in her body and her imagination ran wild. The shoe came off and he set it aside carefully, taking her silk-clad foot firmly in both hands, massaging it. She lifted her eyes to find his rising from the dark patches at her breasts to her own eyes.

"Anybody ever taken your shoes off before?"

"N . . . no." Her eyes skittered down again, drawn against her will to the seam of his trousers, then up his corded arms to the scar on the left one.

He kissed her instep. She felt her face grow hot, her insides liquefy, as he regarded her with apparent calm. When he spoke, his voice was unnaturally silky.

"You have very pretty feet. Did y' know that?"

She stared at her white-stockinged foot in his dark, kneading fingers and couldn't think of a word to say. Feet? All this could happen inside a woman while a man fondled her *feet?* When her eyes flashed back up to his, he was grinning. Then he dropped his attention to her second foot, removed the shoe, and rested his elbows on his knees . . . still squatting as before.

"Take off your stockin's. Y' won't want t' get them wet."

He made no pretense about doing anything but enjoying the sight of her rolling the silk down her legs and plucking it off. But he waited until she had finished the task before rising and reaching for the button at his waist. "I like watchin' you do that," he mused, while she wondered what protocol demanded at a moment like this. Before she could decide if a woman watched or turned away, he shucked off his trousers and stood before her in thigh-length cotton-knit drawers. He reached for her hand, abruptly changing moods. "Come on. Let's go swimmin'."

They made the journey in haste beneath the black shadow of the magnolia, along the white ribbon of driveway, across the road, along the dew-laden grass to the swimming house.

"Scott, we forgot the lantern."

"Should I go back for it?"

Foolish question, after what he'd been doing to her in the bedroom. As if she wanted to waste time any more than he.

They swam in the dark, plunging in with scarcely a thought about the icy water or any dangers it might hide. They cleaned themselves secretly, thinking of the soft glow of the gaslights in the bedroom, the thick, high mattress, the filmy white netting, the rich scent of lemon lilies. She heard him go under and come up with a toss of the head that sent splatters across the water. He heard her strike out for the far end and followed. Then they turned together and swam a lap back to the marble steps, with him pulling ahead all the way. He was waiting when she got there, and caught one wet, slippery arm and hauled her against him, stealing a hot, wild, impatient kiss while pressing his turgid body full against hers.

She broke away, breathless, holding him by two handfuls of hair. "What were you doing back there in the bedroom, Scott Gandy?"

"You know. Don't tell me you don't know." She heard the seduction in his voice. "Tell me what it did t' y'."

She could no more have voiced it than she could have kept the color from leaping to her cheeks while he placed her hand on his intimate parts.

"Scott, you're wicked."

"Not wicked . . . in love . . . in rut . . . doin' matin' dances with my wife, who loves them but is too shy t' admit it. I'll show you every step before I'm done."

He kissed her. Their lips were cold, their tongues hot. Her sleek arms caught him about the neck and their wet skins glided sinuously. And there, in blackness as absolute as space, he caressed her cold, shivering body through the wet cotton—breasts, hips, and, for the first time, the intimate spot between her legs. Water streamed down their noses, cheeks, through his moustache, into their mouths, along her back, and over his arm. Silken water that bonded them together like a liquid coil. His left arm caught her just below the shoulder blades, and she flattened her hands on his sleek back, while his free hand roved where it would.

"Gussie . . . Gussie . . . I want you. I'm goin' t' be so damned good for you."

It was good already, having his hands on her. Even through cold, wet cotton he made her gasp, and he covered the sound with his own mouth, then uttered, "Say it, Gussie . . . say what you're feelin'."

"I love your hands . . . on me . . . I feel . . . beautiful . . . whole."

It struck her how coupling need not be reserved for rosewood beds with their counterpanes turned down and their meticulously laundered linens—how a body, when incited, might settle for a sleek, wet marble slab, if only this agony of waiting could be brought to an end.

Without a word, he led her from the pool. A cursory toweling, an impatient kiss, and they were hurrying through the ebony night to the great white house that took them in once again.

Their gaslights waited, casting a thin band of yellow across the balcony spindles as he carried her again up the curving staircase. When their bedroom door closed he stood her on her feet and caught her close in a single movement, their lips and arms clinging. The long, plodding hours of the day had served their purpose. Two aroused bodies, denied too long, strained together.

She had no time for shyness; he would allow none. When he stepped back it was without compunction, to free the buttons at her shoulders and roll her wet undergarment down to her hips, where it angled and clung. Cupping her breasts, he lifted them, looked down, adored.

"Look at you . . . ah, Gussie." He dropped to one knee, took a cold puckered nipple into his mouth, and warmed it with his tongue, plucked it with his lips, caught it lightly between his teeth. Her eyes closed. Her breath caught. Tendrils of feeling coiled downward and a gamut of incredible sensations became hers. He warmed her other breast as he had the first, his moustache prickling faintly as he played the same arousing game with it—teeth and tongue, ebb and rush.

Her head fell back, her eyelids closed. The awkwardness she'd expected was nowhere to be found. To be a woman so loved took away all but the rightness of standing before a man while his lips ran over you.

He kissed the hollow between her ribs, caught the recalcitrant cotton undergarment, and rolled it past her hips until it dropped to the floor.

She lifted her head and her eyes came open. In them he saw that she was stunned by her own arousal, by each touch, each new plateau of passion he awakened in her. He touched her again, deliberately, while she looked down, a passing brush of his fingertips up her hair, stomach, breast. Then he stood and rolled his own wet drawers down and kicked them aside.

Her eyes locked on his face.

"Are you afraid?" he asked.

"No."

He waited, watching her pale eyes flicker with hesitation. "Would you tell me, if you were?"

"There's no reason to be. I love you." But her voice shook and her eyes refused to lower.

He lifted her hand and pressed his lips to her wedding ring. "Perhaps we shouldn't disappoint Violet. Would you like your new nightgown on? I'll only take it back off again, but that can be fun."

Without awaiting her answer, he crossed to the bed, brushed the netting aside, and picked up the nightgown. She watched him—naked and lean and unashamed—and thought, *I am twice blessed. Not only a beautiful man, but a gentle one. Gentle and patient with his ignorant virgin bride.*

He returned and she watched him, understanding that he was giving her time to acclimate, to study, to learn.

"Lift your arms," he ordered, and slid the nightgown down to cover her, then gathered the blue ribbon beneath her breasts and painstakingly tied it in a bow.

She touched his hands as they finished the task. "You're a very beautiful man, I think."

He took a long moment to study her face, slowly scanning the green eyes, the broad forehead, the mouth and jawline he'd first admired. "And you're a very beautiful woman, I think. We should do well together, shouldn't we?"

He picked her up and carried her to the bed, placed her on the high mattress, and joined her. Beneath the tester it was shadowed and private and the scent of the lilies drifted about their heads. Beyond the netting the moths continued their dance, while within it bright dark eyes held pale green ones.

He had a way about him—oh, indeed, a way. Easy and natural, taking her in his arms and lying full-length against her, kissing her languorously, while his hands began once more the magic they'd worked in the pool. She had expected moments of awkwardness, but how could one feel awkward with such a man? Ah, such a man.

He gave each part of her body its due—hair first— plucking the magnolia from it, laying it on her breast, while discarding hairpins until her tresses lay like a pool of copper beneath her. Lips next—warm, lush kisses in which his tongue invited hers to dance. Ears, neck, and breasts, brushing them first with the magnolia petals, then bestowing textured kisses through Violet's white cotton handiwork, biting her gently, wetting the cloth, and her, and bringing a murmur to her throat. He freed the blue ribbon he'd so recently tied and explored her flesh beneath the gown. Just the surface, skimming flat hands lightly over thighs, stomach, breasts, collarbone, as if memorizing the exterior before delving deeper.

"Mmm . . ."

"You like that?"

"Oh, yes . . . your hands. I know them so well. Behind my eyelids I'm seeing them while they touch me."

"Describe them for me."

"Beautiful hands with perfect long fingers, black hair— enough to make them incredibly masculine—reaching down from a narrow wrist, a wrist with a white cuff showing beneath your black jacket. That's how I pictured them while we were apart."

"You pictured my hands while we were apart?"

"Always. Lighting a cheroot, holding a poker hand, tousling Willy's hair. I used to go to bed at night in my apartment and think about your hands and wonder what it would be like if they did this."

"And this?" She held her breath and shifted in accommodation as he touched her intimately again.

"Ohhh, Scott . . ."

She felt the gown being jerked over her head with much greater impatience than it had been donned. They lay with nothing between them but time to explore.

"Touch me," he told her, "don't be afraid."

He was a revelation—firm, hot, and resilient. And when she reached he fell still. Still as the hand of a sundial while the world swirled on. He took her in hand to tutor her, and at her first stroke his breath grew labored in the quietness of the room. He rolled against her, and away, touching her with promise soon turned to fulfillment. Within her, spring arrived—a bud swelled, burgeoned, blossomed, and made her call out mindlessly as she reached the peak she'd been too ignorant to expect.

"Scott . . . oh, Scott . . ." she appealed afterward, wondering at the tears in her eyes and the slackening shudders that had claimed her.

"That's what it's all about, Gussie. It's wonderful, isn't it?"

She had no form of expression to convey all she felt—the wonder, the discovery, the newness. So she threw her arms about him and kissed him, squeezing her eyes shut. And before the kiss ended the miracle happened—she was at last filled, virgin no more. His body joined hers with the same ease and grace of all that had come before. He rested within her, unmoving, letting her adjust.

She felt his presence and spoke a single word, whispering it at his temple while he poised within her.

"Welcome."

"Gussie . . . my love . . ." he replied.

And all that followed was beautiful. His agile movements, his tensed muscles, the murmurs, the approval, the shift of position, the pause to appreciate and study each other at close range . . . then the beat again carrying them both on strokes of silk, restoring in her once more the wondrous charm of desire that burst its bounds a second time moments before he shuddered . . . and lunged . . . with teeth bared.

In the after minutes they fell to their sides, replete, touching each other's faces as if for the first time. They lay still as the shadows of the netting that textured their skin, giving the moment its due.

"Are you all right?" he whispered at length.

"Yes."

"Your hip?"

"Yes." She had forgotten all about her hip.

He took her to his breast, looped his leg over hers, and molded their bodies together like the wilted petals of the magnolia that lay crushed beneath them. He sighed, long and satisfied, and toyed with the fine mahogany hair at her nape, and she brushed her fingertips over his back. The moths beat against the netting, their shadows dancing over the entwined limbs of bride and groom.

"No one ever told me before," she said to him, awed.

"Told you what?"

She wasn't certain how to express all she felt—the wonder, the incredulity. "I thought it was ordained for procreation only."

He laughed—thunder beneath her ear. "Violet told you."

"Mmm . . . but not eloquently enough." She drew back to look into his face. "Scott . . ." she whispered, touching his eyebrow, his cheekbone, needing so badly to articulate her feelings. But words would sound paltry in the face of such immense emotions.

"Yes, I know."

"I don't think you do. Not about the years I lived alone and longed for the simplest things, like someone to share a table with at suppertime, and a clothesline where I could hang baby clothes, and something besides a ticking clock to listen to—another human voice, a kind word. But this . . ." She touched the wedge-shaped scar on his arm, recalling the night she'd seen the knife lodged there, thinking how close she'd come to losing him. "You've given me so much. Gifts that can't be bought and—"

"I haven't—"

"No." She touched his lips. "Let me finish. I want to say it." As she went on, her fingertips outlined his lips, then rested beside his mouth. "To swim, to ride, to dance—those are things I never thought I'd experience. They freed me, don't you see? I was earthbound until you gave them to me and made me feel no different from anyone else. But they were as nothing compared to Willy. I can't ever thank you enough for Willy, and at times when I realize he'll be ours forever, it still brings tears to my eyes."

"Gussie, you were—"

But her heart needed spilling, for it could not contain all it had been given. "And as if Willy weren't enough, you gave me a family, something I never had in my entire life. All these gifts you've given me . . . and now . . . to-night . . . this. Something more than I had ever imagined. Myself. Scott, you gave me myself." As she kissed his lips lightly, her own trembled. "I want to show my gratitude, to repay you, but there's nothing I can give. I feel . . . I . . . oh, Scott . . ."

Tears came to her eyes and she choked on the words.

He covered her lips with one forefinger. "And what about me? What do I get out of this marriage? Let me tell you somethin'. When I saw you step out of the bedroom door with Willy, it was like . . ." He rested his chin on her head, searching for the end of his thought.

"Like what?" she prompted.

"I don't know." He captured her eyes again, cradled her cheek in one palm. "It was too great t' describe. You, lookin' pretty as a magnolia blossom, dressed in that white dress. And Willy there with you, and everybody I love waitin' downstairs, and the house full o' people again. I felt like I'd been reborn. Gussie, I've been at loose ends for so long. Wanderin', lookin' for my place in the world. All those years I gambled on the riverboats, then the saloons, one after the other. You can't know how empty I felt. I think, if I hadn't met you, I'd have kept right on wanderin', searchin', not knowin' for what. You're the one who made me see that I had t' come back here before I'd be happy again. You're the one who made Willy possible in my life and who made me take a second look at what I had with Jube, which was only an imitation of what you and I have. You talk about gifts—do you think you haven't given me any of your own?"

She burrowed against him again, pressing her cheek to his hard chest, closing her eyes, feeling as if another word would burst her full, full heart.

"I love you," one of them said.

"I love you," the other replied. It mattered not who spoke first, for the truth of it was absolute.

He kissed her, and when their lips parted, he looked solemnly into her eyes. "For always."

"For always," she repeated.

He rose to extinguish the lights. She watched the trellised shadows from the netting whisper across his skin and disappear as blackness stole him from her sight, but returned him to her in the flesh—firm, warm, and reaching.

In the dark his lips found hers. The yearning returned, and they welcomed it, nurtured it, and made love once more in the soft secret folds of night. And while about them Waverley spread its protective wings, and while the ghosts of its past mingled with the promises of its future, and while across the hall Willy slept, and outside the deer fed secretly on the boxwoods . . . L. Scott Gandy planted within his wife the greatest gift of all.